Also by Kathryne Kennedy

Everlasting Enchantment

The Relics of Merlin

KATHRYNE KENNEDY

sourcebooks
casablanca

Published by Sourcebooks Casablanca, an imprint of Sourcebooks,
Inc.
P. O. Box 4410, Naperville, Illinois 60567-4410
(630) 961-3900
Fax: (630) 961-2168
www.sourcebooks.com

Printed and bound in the United States of America.
VP 10 9 8 7 6 5 4 3 2 1

Prologue

Long ago a great wizard was born with magic in his very blood. He lived for thousands of years and went by many names, but the one we know best is Merlin.

Merlin passed his magic down through his offspring, and the power made his children rulers. Some inherited more magic than others, and eventually titles reflected their gifts. In Britain, kings and queens held the strongest power. After the royals, dukes had the greatest magical abilities in that they could change matter. Marquesses could cast spells and illusions and transfer objects but not change them. Earls mastered illusions, while viscounts dabbled in charms and potions. Barons had a magical gift, which could be as simple as making flowers grow or as complicated as seeing into the future.

And then there were the baronets. Part man, part animal, the shape-shifters were Merlin's greatest enchantment… and eventually his greatest bane. For out of all mankind, they were immune to his magic.

Merlin created thirteen magical relics from the gems of the earth, a focus for some of his greatest spells. After Merlin's disappearance, his children tried to find the relics, since these items held the only magic stronger than their own. The relics *proved to be elusive until his children discovered that the shape-shifters they so despised could sniff out the power of a relic.*

Over the centuries the relics faded to legend. But the most powerful of Merlin's descendants did not forget, and shape-shifters became the secret spies of many rulers.

One

London, 1839

Where magic has never died…

THE DUKE OF GHOULSTON'S COACH ROCKED TO A STOP in front of Buckingham Palace and Millicent Pantere growled low in her throat. A throng of finely dressed lords and ladies made their way beneath magical shimmering arches of color into the massive double doors of the palace to young Queen Victoria's ball.

"I don't belong here," murmured Millicent as anger curled through her belly. Why couldn't the duke have ordered her to fight a legion of ogres armed to the teeth? Now *that* she could have managed with relish. But no, he had to send her up against the cold eyes and knowing whispers of the nobility. As if she had any hope of fooling them into thinking she was a lady.

The door of the coach flew open and the duke's footman leered in at her. "Time for the ball, Cinderella."

Millicent's low growl turned into a snarl. She had the satisfaction of seeing the footman blink with fear before the duke spoke from the seat across from her.

"You'd best behave yourself," he remarked, those black eyes glittering even in the shadows. "We've doused you with perfume but we can't be sure it will entirely hide your scent from the other shape-shifters. You animals have such gifted noses."

Millicent tried to take a deep breath but her new corset stopped her halfway. The blasted thing crackled whenever she moved, the fabric stiff against her back and belly, the whalebone inserts lacking the suppleness of age and wear. When she gathered her brocade skirts together and exited the carriage, they felt just the same—stiff and unnatural. She suppressed the urge to kick at the horsehair petticoats when they threatened to trip her up as she stepped onto the glittering walkway. Instead she swept her gloved hands gently over the swell of fabric below her waist, adjusted the heavy satin cloak about her shoulders, and waited with feigned patience for the duke to join her.

The coach bounced upward as the duke stepped out. Time and rich food had robbed him of the handsomeness he must have possessed as a youth, but the powerful confidence he radiated almost made up for it. His sharp black eyes swept over her as he held out his arm. "You look lovely, my dear. See to it that all the months of preparation are not wasted tonight."

"It won't work," snapped Millicent as she took his arm with a forced smile, revealing the slightly long canines at the corners of her mouth. "You can't turn an animal into a lady in just a few months."

"You'd best *make* it work," murmured the Duke of Ghoulston as he squeezed her arm. "You have more to lose than I."

He swept her into the crowd on the walkway, his height a match to hers, only his top hat making him appear taller. Arches of brilliant, magical color towered over their heads, the flagstones glittered at their feet, and the walls of the palace reflected the enchanted light within their diamond-studded walls. Although she could look through the illusion if she tried, Millicent did not bother using her immunity to magical spells to do so. She might as well derive what enjoyment she could from her task.

She squinted against the glare. Even after months of living aboveground, she still couldn't get used to the abundance of light. The people up here appeared to be spoiled by sunshine, for even at night they had to light their streets and rooms too brightly with fire and magic.

They entered the doorway, gave up their coats to a footman, and made their way to the ballroom, lining up with the other guests as they waited for the young queen to appear. Millicent tried not to crane her neck upward and stare. The colored arcs continued into the ballroom and swept across the enormous ceiling, cascading down the walls in sapphire, crimson, and yellow. It reminded her of something she'd seen once, but she couldn't quite recall it.

"Rainbows," whispered the duke as he followed her gaze. "Surely you've seen a rainbow before?"

"Of course," she replied. Although sunshine didn't often penetrate to the depths of the Underground, she'd found an old complex of tunnels where shafts of sunlight filtered down the slimy brick walls, making a splay of color shimmer in the air. The magical rainbows that decorated the ballroom outrivaled those, however, even if they appeared to her only as a transparent illusion. "Do not think I'm impressed by your kind's magic. I'm immune to your tricks."

"Ah, but that's what makes you so useful, my dear." He bestowed a fleshy-lipped smile on her. "That, and your animal senses."

Millicent scowled. "It might not even be a relic," she whispered. "Merlin's relics are only a myth, after all."

"Are they?" replied the duke. "Take a look around. A good look."

Millicent blinked against the glare, but studied the room. They stood at the beginning of the line, among the upper nobility who possessed the highest titles and therefore, the most magic. At the end of the line stood the shape-shifters who were immune to magic. Most of them rivaled the other nobility with their physical beauty, but that wasn't what held her attention. The duke had told her that aboveground, the Master of the Hall of Mages—uncle to the queen—championed the baronets. If the Duke of Ghoulston thought Millicent could steal this relic he suspected was hidden here, it made sense that other baronets could sniff out a relic as well. Perhaps that explained their value to the Crown.

"Are there usually this many baronets at a ball?"

"Good girl. No, they detest society as much as we detest them."

Millicent's nostrils flared. Now that she knew their nature, she could catch the scent of the other weres, despite the smells of perfume and melted candle wax and fairylight dust. "Predators. All of them."

"They hunt, my dear."

She nodded. The Underground harbored many shape-shifters. But besides Bran, who could shape-shift to bear, they mostly consisted of jackals and hyenas and the like. Scavengers. She'd never seen so many akin to her. She smelled lions and tigers and leopards. Oh my.

Millicent frowned. "And you expect me to find this relic before they do?"

"You have an advantage, my dear. Me."

If he called her *my dear* one more time… Her anger stirred the beast inside her and Millicent counted beneath her breath to ten. By the last count the red haze had cleared, and she could think rationally again. She huffed out a breath. She should be grateful for the duke's arrogance, if it meant that she would succeed in her task.

The duke's gaze followed hers, and his bushy brows lowered as he stared at the group of shape-shifters. "If anything goes wrong, meet me back at my underground castle. Use the graveyard entrance I showed you."

"So you're not as confident as you pretend to be," scoffed Millicent.

The duke squeezed her arm painfully. "Do not, by any means, return to my mansion in Gargoyle Square. Do you understand?"

It took all of her willpower not to fling him across the room. "Don't worry. The beast of darkness will return to her lair."

He nodded in satisfaction, completely missing the sarcasm in her voice.

A hush descended over the guests and a diminutive woman entered the room. Millicent would never have guessed her to be the queen if her ladies and advisors hadn't surrounded her. Queen Victoria slowly went down the line of nobility, stopping occasionally to speak to an honored few. By the time she reached the Duke of Ghoulston, Millicent's muscles had tightened like a bowstring within her costume. She would never be able to fool the Queen of England into thinking she was a lady.

"Ah, Lord Ghoulston," said the queen, holding out her hand. "Did you ride today?" Her blue eyes looked at him owlishly. The queen had an innocent gaiety that made Millicent feel much older than her one-and-twenty years. And tarnished by comparison.

The duke swept his fleshy lips just above the surface of her lace glove and straightened. "Yes, Your Majesty."

"How did you find the weather?"

"Er, quite fine."

"That's good. I also went riding… and who is this lovely lady?"

Millicent kept the bland smile on her face by sheer force of will.

"The cousin of a cousin," replied the duke. "Up from the country to experience the delights of London."

Millicent remembered to curtsy. She managed it without falling over and with only a slight pinch from her corset, rising with a grin of relief.

"I see." The queen leaned toward her conspiratorially. Millicent bent down, embarrassed by her height for the first time in her life. "The gigot sleeves are quite out, you know."

Millicent had no idea what the queen meant. She

glanced at her puffy sleeves, seeing little difference in the queen's own, except for a narrowing at the shoulders. She struggled for a response. "Thank you for the advice, Your Majesty."

The queen smiled beatifically and moved down the line. Before Millicent had the chance to comprehend that the queen had actually thought she was a lady, and had spoken to her as one, a real lady stepped in front of them. "Willie. What a pleasure to see you."

Millicent smothered her smile at the lady's use of the duke's first name. She wondered how many people managed to get away with the impertinence, and took an instant liking to the other woman.

"Lady Yardley," crowed the duke. "You look as elegant as ever. May I introduce you to Lady Millicent?" He lowered his voice. "She's just up from the country and this is her first soiree."

The woman turned and gave Millicent the full force of her smile. Despite the past several months of training to transform her into a true lady, Millicent now could see the real definition of one. Lady Yardley's auburn hair had been curled at the sides of her head and formed into an elegant knot at the top— with not a single strand loose about her face, unlike Millicent's own straggling coiffure of inky black hair. The woman's soft hazel eyes spoke of sophistication, while Millicent's own amber gaze glittered with the hardness of surviving in a cruel world. The lady's calm demeanor commanded respect, something Millicent could never hope to imitate.

The duke scowled at Millicent and she remembered to curtsy again. He gave Lady Yardley a look that apologized for the ill grace of a country bumpkin. "Millicent, my dear. May I introduce Lady Yardley, Lady of the Bedchamber to the queen, and daughter to the Earl of Sothby?"

"How do you do?" mumbled Millicent.

The duke's ploy of passing Millicent off as a country lass appeared to work. Lady Yardley's eyes softened with sympathy and she held out her arm. "This must all appear very grand to you, I'm sure. Just remember that half is magic and the other half self-delusion."

Millicent smiled uncertainly and stared in alarm at the lady's silk-gloved hand. What under-the-earth was she supposed to do with it?

Lady Yardley solved the dilemma by curling her arm under Millicent's. "Allow me to introduce you, dear girl. Your striking looks are sure to cause a stir and I shall be ever so grateful to be in the thick of it. You don't mind, do you, Willie?"

"As you wish, Lady Yardley," mumbled the duke as he gave Millicent a triumphant wink.

Millicent allowed the lady to escort her through the press of people. She feared that the duke might be a tad too confident. Just because he'd managed to pair her with the cream of society didn't mean the lady had fallen for their ruse. She expected her companion to halt at any moment and denounce her for an imposter.

Instead she found herself introduced to one gentleman after another, until they had a trail of handsome young men following in their wake. Not only did they accept her as a lady but not one of them suspected her were-nature. And fortunately Lady

Yardley didn't introduce her to any baronets, who would surely be able to sniff out her secrets.

Millicent began to relax. To her surprise, she began to enjoy herself.

When the orchestra struck up a tune, Millicent declined one dance invitation after another, even though she gave the rainbow-draped floor more than one wistful glance. She'd just been taught the steps to waltz a few weeks ago and didn't trust herself not to stomp upon her partner's feet. Besides, she didn't want to draw any further attention to herself. Lady Yardley appeared to be doing a bloody good job of that already.

"You are breaking hearts right and left," laughed the lady. "Don't you wish to dance, Lady Millicent?"

"Please, call me Millicent," she replied. She'd always hated the title of lady, since it lacked an estate to make it meaningful. And in general, people had no use for titles in the Underground.

"Then you must call me Claire."

"Well, Claire, I'm afraid I'm only used to country tunes."

"Of course, I should have realized. Still, it's been such fun being the center of attention. But you don't appear to enjoy that either, do you? As your new friend in London, I'm determined to make your first ball memorable. You'll have to give me a clue as to how I might manage to accomplish that."

Millicent felt dismayed by Claire's declaration of friendship. And then she reminded herself that Lady Yardley's friendship could only be as real as Millicent's own charade. She had best concentrate on her task so she could go back to where she belonged.

She glanced around and noticed that two baronets had their gazes locked on her from across the room. A solid chap with a mane of golden hair and a scarred face studied her with a confused frown. The other shape-shifter tossed a thatch of orange-streaked hair off his forehead and stared at her with an angry, almost hungry gaze. They started to move in her direction.

"I should very much like to meet Lady Chatterly," blurted Millicent. The duke had told her that rumors had the relic in the possession of Lady Chatterly, and although Millicent had hoped to eventually meet her, she feared that she now didn't have the time for a chance encounter.

Lady Yardley's elegantly arched brows rose in surprise, and then she giggled. "Oh, my. I should have known. She is rumored to be rather fast, isn't she? I imagine her reputation would shock… and fascinate you, yes?"

Millicent lowered her lashes. "You won't tell His Grace about my request, will you? I'm afraid he wouldn't understand."

"Why, Willie has—" The woman gave a delicate cough. "No, of course not. I shan't breathe a word of it to him."

"Oh, thank you." Millicent looked over her shoulder. Two pairs of predatory eyes blinked back at her. She suppressed the growl that threatened to shoot up her throat and turned back to her companion. "I'm most eager to meet the, er, famous lady. Shall we?"

Instead of taking offense at Millicent's tug on her arm, Claire laughed and pulled in the opposite direction. "She's this way. And don't think I didn't catch that little stumble. I think *notorious* would be a more likely description than *famous*." She breezed right past the two baronets, who glared at Millicent and spun to follow them.

The crowd parted easily for Lady Yardley. Not so for the baronets, and they soon lost the men in the press of people. Millicent breathed a sigh of relief. And then she realized the direction Claire had taken.

Millicent ducked her head as they pressed through a group of baronets. She hardly dared to breathe. She had intended to escape only two, and now Lady Yardley had dragged her into a pack of them.

"That's a charming dress," said Claire, eyeing Millicent's brocade gown, chatting gaily away, as if being surrounded by predators didn't matter to her one whit. "Where in London did you find a seamstress who can craft such skillful rosettes?"

Surely her companion knew that baronets had the strength to rip them to shreds? Millicent could barely focus on a reply, while every hair on the back of her neck stood upright with alarm. She had no idea where the dress had come from. But she'd learned that when in doubt, a half-truth is better than an outright lie. "His Grace provided me with a wardrobe. He said my country clothing would put him to shame."

"Hmph. Well, he was probably right. Willie has always had impeccable good taste. I think that's why I admire him so—you certainly aren't blocking my way, are you, sir?"

A large man with a hawkish nose stood in front of Lady Yardley, his enormous liquid eyes fixed on Millicent. He bowed aside at her companion's words but not before he shot Millicent a look of raptorial hunger. Ordinarily a bird of prey wouldn't frighten her. But a shifter's were-form could be larger than their human form. Did Claire truly not know what type of creature she brushed aside? Or did her status as a lady provide her with such confident security?

Millicent didn't have such protection.

Her companion finally tugged her into the space between the shape-shifters and another cluster of aristocratic gentlemen. Millicent took a deep breath and refused to turn around and look into the eyes of all the weres that burned holes in the back of her neck. She'd noticed several female baronets among them, but apparently the aristocracy knew of their natures and they also weren't allowed to penetrate their group.

But the gentlemen parted for Lady Yardley and her companion. The Duke of Ghoulston had been right. Millicent's anonymity provided her access.

The heightened senses of her were-nature allowed her to overhear the comments of the aristocrats as she passed.

"Here come two more ladies."

"Hush. I'm trying to hear what they're saying."

"Well, I'd jolly well give my best horse to know what they're *hiding*," said his fellow loudly.

Lady Yardley's mouth curled into a secretive smile.

"Haven't you heard? Lord Dunwist told me that his wife has been acting strange lately. Ever since she made friends with Lady Chatterly, she's been as demanding as his mistress."

"Good gawd, man, that's preposterous! Ladies should behave according to their station."

"I hear there's some sort of powerful magic involved."

"Damn it, man. I say we should do something about this."

But they didn't appear to know precisely what that might be, because as Millicent passed through their group to where a circle of ladies stood, not a one of the top hats made a move to follow them. A tall woman with iridescent strix feathers in her hair glanced up and smiled. The circle of women opened to let them in, their wide skirts smashing back together as they closed the gap behind them.

"Lady Chatterly," said Claire. "How good to see you again."

The feathers trembled. "We were just about to retire to the salon. It seems that we have attracted some attention." Her clear gray eyes focused on Millicent. "And who have we here?"

"Allow me to introduce you to Lady Millicent. She's from the country."

Millicent blinked innocently at the notorious lady, who bestowed an anticipatory smile upon her. "She may join us, since you vouch for her, Lady Yardley. It should be… amusing to have her amongst us."

With a sweep of her skirts, Lady Chatterly made for a door set near a golden urn at the bottom of one of the rainbows. The other ladies followed, their gowns looking like so many silk flowers clustered in a bouquet. Millicent snuck a glance behind them as she passed through the door into the salon. The group of curious gentlemen followed, and the shape-shifters watched with angry, hooded eyes.

The last lady through the door firmly closed it behind her, drawing the bolt with a resounding snap.

The room had been decorated years ago, rather garishly, with portraits of the royal family in huge gilt frames, heavy furniture of mauve and crimson, and silver candelabra stands in every corner. A fireplace large enough for Millicent to stand nearly upright in crackled with a merry blaze against the autumn chill.

Lady Chatterly enthroned herself on a chair set before a highly polished table. "Ladies, please sit down. I have much to tell you and I fear we have little time."

Millicent sat near the closest window, the cold seeping in around the panes and cooling her hot cheeks. Sunshine spoiled the dwellers aboveground in other ways, for they kept their rooms too warm for someone who had lived her entire life in the cold dank of the Underground. She watched the eager faces of the other ladies, hoping that whatever Lady Chatterly had to say would involve the relic. Claire took a seat close to Millicent, as if to protect her, which she found endearing.

"First," said Lady Chatterly, "we must strengthen the wards to keep the prying magic of our men from the room."

Millicent's heart skipped as several of the women clasped hands to perform a warding spell. She blew out a sigh of relief when several of the ladies just folded their hands in their lap. They must not have the title or the power to perform such a spell, and wouldn't think it amiss that Millicent didn't join in either.

She could see the magic forming as a slight haze, feel

it prickle the skin on her arms, but otherwise the spell didn't affect her. It wouldn't affect the other weres in the ballroom either, so the doors and walls would have to suffice. Millicent hoped they were thick.

"Now then," said Lady Chatterly when they finished the spell. "There's a back exit across the room." She nodded toward the far wall. "And a carriage waiting for the one the relic will choose. As some of you already know, the only condition is that you tell no one the relic is in your possession, and you return it to me on the morrow. Are you newcomers clear on that?"

Several women nodded their heads, although a few looked frightened. Millicent mimicked the expression of fear while her mind calculated with truly frightening intensity. The duke had been right; the relic existed. These women had been harboring a dangerous secret. But why would Lady Chatterly allow other women to borrow such a powerful thing?

"You are so generous, my lady," breathed Millicent, trying to sound adoring instead of suspicious.

Lady Chatterly shrugged. "I made a promise." She didn't elaborate on her explanation and Millicent resisted the urge to press. Besides, what did it matter, when it only made it easier for her to get her hands on the relic?

Instead Millicent worried about what the woman meant when she said the relic would choose one of the ladies. She would have to follow the woman somehow, catch her alone or asleep in order to steal the thing. At least she had a significant advantage over the other shape-shifters still in the ballroom. She would know which of the women had the relic. She studied the ladies around her, some old, some just barely out of the schoolroom.

Lady Yardley leaned forward, her hazel eyes bright with reflected candlelight. "He's real then?"

"Of course." Lady Chatterly gave her a dreamy smile. Several other women nodded just as dreamily with her. "Quite real, I assure you."

"And how will the relic choose?" persisted Claire. "Really, darling, you must quit being so mysterious and give us more information. There are too many of us innocents here tonight."

The feathers in Lady Chatterly's hair swayed with her nod. She removed her gloves and then set her reticule on the shiny surface of the table. The fidgeting of the younger girls ceased as they all stared at the embroidered silk bag. An expectant silence fell, only the muffled strains of the music from the ballroom disturbing it.

Lady Chatterly loosened the drawstring and removed an exquisite ivory fan, a gold-embossed dancing card, and a silver filigree perfume box. Silk swished and corsets strained as the ladies leaned closer for a better look. With a dramatic flourish, the lady dug something out from the very bottom of the bag, set it on the table, and swept everything else aside.

Some of the ladies sighed with disappointment, but Millicent's heart skipped. It looked old. Old enough to be a true relic. A solid band of dull silver with a round stone set in the center. The blue-gray shimmer of the jewel hypnotized her for a moment; the wink of the fire reflected in the depths made her heart twist with something she couldn't define. "What is that gem?"

"A moonstone," murmured Lady Yardley. "A common enough jewel, although I've never seen one with quite so much translucence."

"Each of you will try it on. Like so." Lady Chatterly slipped the large band easily over her hand and up her arm. "I know it looks rather big, but if you're chosen, it will tighten to a snug fit." She stared at the relic for a moment, then sighed in disappointment as it fell off her wrist. "Well, one can still hope."

"What do you mean?" asked a rather matronly woman.

Lady Chatterly answered the question in a round-about way. "He will come to you at midnight and disappear with the dawn. He won't appear twice to the same woman, so there's no use in keeping the relic longer." Her gray eyes glittered as her voice lowered to a husky whisper. "He will make your every desire come true. And some that you didn't even know you had."

"Who?" demanded Lady Yardley.

"His name is Gareth Solimere and he wears the clothing of a knight of the Round Table… yes, as in King Arthur. He has been trapped in the relic for a long time."

Questions spun around inside Millicent's head. She could see her questions mirrored on the faces of the others, but Lady Chatterly held up her hand to forgo them. "Trust me, they are not important. Once you look into his brown eyes, run your fingers through his ebony hair, feel the touch of his lips upon yours…"

Giggles and gasps followed her words but Lady

Chatterly seemed lost in rapturous memory. Millicent rolled her eyes in disgust. So that's what all these women were in such a twitter about? A man? Her mother had taught her about men. Enough to know to stay away from them.

She fought the urge to stomp from the room.

One of the youngest girls—her cheeks a bright pink—had the temerity to say, "What did he do to you?"

"Aah. Shall I make my reputation even more notorious?" Lady Chatterly asked herself rather loudly.

"Is it possible?" countered Claire with a laugh.

"Certainly." Those pale gray eyes sparkled in challenge and her feathers danced a jig on her head. "I thought I knew myself. I have been married, after all."

The few women who had kept themselves apart from the circle around the table suddenly drew closer. The room had been fraught with tension since they entered. Now the walls fairly vibrated. Even Millicent couldn't resist the urge to lean forward expectantly.

Lady Chatterly's voice lowered to a mere whisper. "He knew exactly how to ignite my passion. He knew how naughty I've been…"

Her hand flew to her breast as her breath quickened. "He slowly removed my clothing piece by piece…"

A handful of the younger girls, and a few of the older, swooned.

"…and he spanked me soundly."

Skirts flew up right and left as several of the ladies fainted. Millicent reflexively rose to catch someone but couldn't decide whom and froze in indecision. Lady Yardley blinked at her in surprise. Millicent's were-nature allowed her to move faster than an ordinary human, so it was probably just as well she had frozen before fully betraying her true nature. She gave Claire a weak smile and slowly sat back down.

"I stand corrected," said Lady Yardley as she pulled smelling salts out of her reticule and handed them to another woman to administer to the fallen. "Your reputation is now even more notorious, Lady Chatterly."

The matron who had spoken earlier gave an elegant snort, then quickly slipped off her gloves, pushed back the voluminous sleeves of her black gown, and held out her arm. Lady Chatterly gave her a knowing grin and slipped the band of silver over the woman's knobby-knuckled hand up to her wrist. Then easily pulled it off again.

"Maybe next time," murmured Lady Chatterly in sympathy before trying it on another woman. And then another.

Millicent's heart started to pound and she felt a little faint while the lady drew closer as the relic failed to tighten around anyone's wrist. Bloody corset. It didn't allow one to breathe properly. Of course they would expect her to try it on.

Lady Chatterly suddenly stood next to her, tapped her slippered foot impatiently while Millicent carefully removed her gloves. The lady thrust the bracelet at her. The cold metal touched her fingers and Millicent suppressed a shudder. She had nothing to fear. It wouldn't choose her... she had no use for any man. Besides, her immunity to magic meant it couldn't cast a spell on her. Although hadn't Lady Chatterly assured them that the bracelet, and the man trapped within, were as real as the chair she sat upon?

Then she would be just as vulnerable as any of these other women.

But the last thing she would ever desire in her life would be a man. No, she was nothing like these other women.

When the metal warmed and tightened around her wrist, it took every ounce of willpower Millicent had to suppress a choking snarl. Magic might be making the bracelet shrink, but the metal felt wholly of this earth, and her immunity to magic would not help. She wanted the relic for the duke, but not this way! She tried to push the bracelet off, but it would no longer fit back over her hand.

"Ah, the country girl," crowed Lady Chatterly. "Don't look so alarmed, dear. You wanted to gain some sophistication from a trip to London, and now you shall have more than you could have ever dreamed."

Millicent dug her fingers under the silver, trying to rip the thing off using the full strength of her were-self. Several of the women patted her shoulder in congratulations and then headed toward the door to the ballroom. Millicent turned and stared at Claire in horror.

"I didn't think… truly, I'm so sorry, Millicent."

"Nonsense," snapped Lady Chatterly. "You did her an enormous favor. The girl just doesn't know it yet. Now, come along. The ladies are anxious to get back to the ball and we must get you out of here before they open the door."

Millicent could only nod and follow. Her plan had been to steal the relic so she could give it to the duke. She had no desire to possess it herself. And she certainly didn't care a whit about the man trapped inside, or his ability to pleasure a woman.

Lady Chatterly led her into a dark hallway and handed Millicent over to a young footman who took her out into the night and ushered her into a black carriage. The horses snorted and stomped their way into the foggy streets of London while Millicent tried to reassure herself.

Lady Chatterly said the bracelet would stay on her wrist for only one night. So Millicent figured all she had to do was let this Gareth person know it had been a mistake for the relic to choose her, and then give it to the duke the next morning.

Surely it would be as easy as that.

And then the gem on the bracelet began to glow, and a man appeared across from her, and Millicent's mouth dropped open.

Two

GARETH BLINKED FOR A MOMENT, ALLOWING THE FUZZ to clear from his head, which always happened whenever the relic spat him forth. He appeared to be in a coach, the roll of the wheels a gentle rumble beneath him.

"She said you had brown eyes and ebony hair," murmured a sultry voice.

"Who?" asked Gareth, staring at the shadowy outline of a woman seated across from him.

"Lady Chatterly."

Aah. He ran his fingers through his very blond hair. He remembered her, the woman who liked to be chastened. The woman who kept her promises. "And what do *you* see, my lady?"

He could feel her eyes upon him. From the top of his head to the pointed toes of his leather ankle boots. Her gaze lingered longest on the sword at his hip and the red dragon embroidered on his outer tunic. "You have wavy blond hair and light eyes… perhaps blue? And you look younger than I expected."

"Perhaps you like younger men."

"I beg your pardon?"

Gareth fell back against the cushions of the carriage with a tired sigh. He always awoke with new hope. But after centuries of disappointment, it had become difficult to keep faith. "My appearance changes to what the holder of the relic desires."

"But I'm immune to magic. Your spells have no effect on me."

She said it with pride and a touch of arrogance. Gareth's interest stirred and he straightened, trying to make out the woman's features. "A shape-shifter, are you? I've had a few over the years, my lady. Verily, they have always seen past the illusions cast on me. But they succumb to my charms just as easily as the others."

She snorted. "Well, I'm not bloody likely to. It's all a mistake, you see."

With a grace born of centuries of practice, Gareth transferred himself from his seat to hers. Better. He could see her features now, and smiled with genuine pleasure. Silky black curls had escaped her coiffure and danced across soft pale cheeks. Red lips formed a perfect crescent below a pert little nose. But he admired her eyes the most, a golden amber that appeared to glow in the darkness. She was probably the most striking woman he'd ever seen. And he'd seen a lot of them. "You're beautiful, my lady," he murmured.

She narrowed her eyes. "I imagine that most women melt from your flattering compliments and soulful gaze. But not I. I didn't want to wear your relic."

"No?" It didn't bother him when they protested. They always changed their minds. It just took hours instead of minutes to seduce them… and allowed him to hope for a little while longer.

"I only wanted to bring the relic to His Grace. It wrapped around my wrist by accident."

He couldn't help touching the softness of her cheek. But then again, he couldn't help touching beautiful women. It's what had landed him into this predicament in the first place. "Must we waste time talking?"

She wasn't even aware that she leaned into his touch. "Bloody hell, you're a slick one."

She looked like a lady but had lapsed into speech worthy of the East End. What a delightful puzzle. Well, he had until dawn to figure her out. His heart sickened at the thought but he tried to keep his hope alive by focusing on the delightful creature next to him. "Not many women see me as I truly am. Is it possible you're the one?"

"The one what?"

His fingers slipped down her cheek, traced a path across the side of her neck where he could feel the strong beat of her pulse. "The one who will free me from my curse." Gareth leaned in, breathing in the scent of her. Roses and musk. "You see, my lady, I am seeking my savior."

She blinked, and a slow rumble started in her throat. Aah, a were-cat of some sort, for she purred beneath the petting of his hand. "I don't know what she looks like, for in my imagination it is always dark. But I think I will know her by the touch of her naked body against mine. By the weight of her breast in my palm. By the feel of her as I bury myself deep inside."

Her purr skipped on a sharp intake of breath.

Women couldn't seem to resist the desire to find out if they were special. Special enough to save him. Gareth wished, by all that was holy, that one of them would finally be able to do so.

"So that's why you seduce women? To find this savior?"

He nodded, bringing his mouth slowly closer to hers. "Will you help me, my lady?"

She stared into his eyes and for a moment he thought he'd won her. But the coach hit a pothole and she blinked, then quickly pulled away from him with a frown. "So what will happen when you find her?"

Gareth studied her with a sad smile. What had made such a lovely creature so hard inside? He could feel her strong will like a tangible wall between them. "I hope her love will break the spell and set me free of the relic."

"Well, I can assure you, sir, I am not the one you seek. So you may as well save yourself the trouble of—"

The coach lurched to a stop, flinging the girl across the floor to the opposite seat. She tucked and landed on all fours within a froth of skirts and petticoats. Gareth had but a heartbeat to assure himself that she had come to no harm before the shouts of a man had him flinging open the door of the carriage. "Stay inside," he commanded as he leapt onto the street.

He drew his silver-coated blade the moment his feet touched the cobblestones. Nary a lantern lit the crumbling brick buildings that lined the fog-shrouded street, but enough moonlight shone from the heavens to outline the shaggy mane of the lion that crouched across from him. The beat of enormous wings ruffled his hair and he cast a glance at the coachman, who appeared to be losing his battle with the giant bird that harried him from above with beak and talons.

The lion shifted to man, a jagged scar from temple to jaw ruining his even features. "Give us the relic and you won't be harmed."

Gareth smiled sadly. "I'm afraid that's not possible."

Within a blink, the man shifted back to lion and pounced. Gareth stepped into the charge and crouched, his sword held two-handed above him, slicing the underbelly of the beast as it flew over his head. He heard a growl of surprise and then a thud as the lion slammed into the side of the coach. Gareth spun to his feet, head low, sword at the ready.

But the lion appeared to be stunned, lying unmoving on the cobbles. Then the carriage rocked, and more growls could be heard from within. The horses reared and strained at their traces and Gareth feared they would bolt.

"My lady," he shouted as he leapt forward. Concern for her safety caught him unawares. Fire raked his shoulder as the bird attacked from overhead with its talons. Gareth didn't even look up. Just thrust his sword as high above his head as he could. A satisfactory caw of pain followed his strike; a few black feathers rained down.

"My sword is edged with silver," warned Gareth. "And you fight with a knight of the Round Table. This will be your only chance to cry mercy."

The sound of a laughing caw from overhead made his heart twist with sadness. He had done so much killing over the centuries. He tired of it. But it seemed that neither beast nor man would ever change.

The bird dove. Gareth could hear the arrow-sharp swiftness of its flight as it cut the air. He had no time for finesse, for he feared for his lady. The snarls from within the coach had died. So as he spun aside from the bird's attack, he savagely struck with his sword, slicing off the beast's wing. It flew in one direction as the body rolled off into another.

It had taken but seconds.

Gareth sprinted for the carriage as the coachman toppled from his perch, the frightened horses finally reaching their breaking point. He managed to catch the brass handrail as the team lunged forward. His legs scrabbled beneath him and his muscles strained until he found purchase with his feet and swung himself into the driver's box. He cursed as he hauled on the reins, then lowered his voice to a reassuring tone as the horses slowed, sweating and shivering from their flight.

Gareth tied the reins securely to the bar and swung back down to the street. "My lady?"

The door had broken from its top hinges and swung drunkenly open before him. He could see nothing inside the pitch-black interior.

"He ruined my dress," snapped that sultry voice.

Gareth smiled with relief and held out his hand. The moonstone winked from the relic on her wrist as she grasped his fingers and ducked out the door. He froze for a moment, surprised by the shock that went through him from her touch. His body must still be stimulated from battle, as he'd never quite experienced any feeling like that before.

She twisted from his hold and he covered his disappointment with words. "Are you hurt?"

She shook her head, the rest of her carefully sculpted coiffure falling apart, allowing her black hair to tumble down her shoulders like a river of night. "It's his blood, not mine." She wiped ineffectually at several dark spots.

"Whose?"

"That shape-shifter from the ball. A tiger, I think, but it happened all too fast to tell for sure."

Gareth went down to one knee. "Forgive me, my lady, for failing to protect you."

"Very gallant of you, I'm sure, but I hardly needed your protection. I thought one of my own kind would be more of a challenge, but he fought like an overgrown hyena. And I've had plenty of experience with those."

She confused him. This was the part where she begged him to rise and fell into his arms. When it became apparent that she had no intention of doing so, Gareth stood. How did he seduce a woman tougher than the blade of his sword?

The lady tore off the voluminous sleeve of her gown, grimacing at the tattered cloth before tossing it to the ground. "He was heavy though. It took most of my strength to shove him out the door, and that's saying a bloody lot."

"What exactly are you, my lady?"

"I'm not your lady." She tore off the other sleeve of her gown. He caught it before it hit the ground and used it to wipe off his bloody sword.

"Although I suppose it's just a habit of yours to

address a woman that way." She eyed him with disbelief. "Lady Chatterly said you were a knight from the Middle Ages. Are you really that old?"

"Yes." He couldn't keep the weariness from that word. "Although my body appears not to age. I often wonder what will happen if the spell is ever broken. Will the years catch up to me and turn me to dust? Will the lady of my destiny bring about my salvation or my doom?"

"If you don't know, why do you keep looking for her?"

Gareth fisted his hands. How could he explain his loneliness to a woman who relied solely on herself? "I long for a mortal life."

She shrugged her shoulders. "I can't figure why. You're hurt, you know."

Gareth glanced at his shoulder. "A flesh wound. And I heal quickly. Another facet of the curse."

"Don't tell me. A big black hawk? And perhaps a lion, too?"

He raised a brow. "You know them?"

"No. But I had a feeling they wouldn't give up without a chase. I suppose I should thank you."

Gareth shoved his sword back into his scabbard. So much for tumbling into his arms. "You're welcome," he replied, sensing it would be the best he would get. "And you didn't answer my question."

"What question—oh, never mind. You really don't expect me to stand about talking when they might have friends following us?"

He shrugged. Hard as ice, and mysterious as well. The lady had probably spoken the truth earlier. He couldn't imagine her falling hard enough in love with anyone to break a spell. "As you wish. Do you ride?" Gareth walked over to the horses and began to release a gelding from its traces.

"Ordinary horses don't like shape-shifters. Especially my kind."

"We will need speed, if we are indeed being pursued by others. Do not worry about the horse. There's never been one born that I couldn't handle." Within minutes he had the gelding freed. Gareth swung up on its back and held out his hand to the lady. The horse nickered and shied away from the girl, but he quickly brought the beast under his control.

"I'm impressed," she said as she caught his hand and leapt up behind him. She'd barely needed his assistance and he marveled at the strength inherent to shape-shifters. She curled her arms around his waist, but kept her body rigidly away from his back.

Gareth sighed. "Which way, my lady?"

"Oh, do stop calling me that. My name is Millicent. Millicent Pantere. And continue down this street to the old graveyard at Thieves Chapel."

He smiled as he gently kicked the horse into a walk. He'd been right about her being a were-cat, if her last name was any indication. She couldn't even answer a personal question outright but had to reveal herself in an obscure manner. He wondered if she was suspicious of men in general, or just him in particular.

When he felt sure the lady would hold her seat, he urged the horse into a gallop. The wind felt good in his hair, the silence of the night a warm cloak around his shoulders. For a brief moment he felt joy in the freedom of their flight. But he remembered another mantle of warmth, from a time so long ago it seemed like one of his dreams. Had he truly once felt the heat of sunshine on his shoulders? Had he galloped through a sun-dappled meadow with a laughing woman's soft breasts pressed against his back?

He glanced down at his pale hands. Had they once been browned by the sun?

"Pull up," said Millicent. As soon as they came to a halt, she slid to the ground. "This is the place."

Gareth looked around at the tombstones wreathed in fog. "This is where you live?"

"Of course not." She studied him for a long moment, those golden eyes disconcerting in their intensity. "Your sadness is a weight I can almost feel. Perhaps that's part of what makes you so irresistible to women."

Gareth's brows rose in surprise. And pleasure. Perhaps the lady had decided to quit pretending to be unaffected by his charisma. But before he could form a reply, she hitched up her stained and ragged skirts and picked her way down an overgrown path. He removed the halter from the horse and let it free and then followed.

The path led to a crumbling church and Millicent's steps seemed to lighten as if she neared the safety of home, but Gareth couldn't imagine anyone living inside. The lack of a roof had allowed weeds and grass to flourish nearly waist high. Near the back of the chapel a portion of the roof still stood, and the lady stopped near a huge slab of stone.

"My eyesight is better in were-form. I shall have to shift to lead you below."

A hint of worry strained her voice and Gareth couldn't figure why. Then in a breath she shifted, her clothes transforming into a sleek, black coat of fur, the silver bracelet nothing more than a bump around her front paw. Her tail swished and she half crouched, staring at him with those same amber-gold eyes. He stepped forward as if in a trance, completely unmindful of the size of the cat, for Millicent appeared larger in were-form, her paws bigger now than his own hands.

Gareth slowly held out his fingers as he would have done with any animal, and she sniffed them, her whiskers a gentle tickle on his skin. She seemed to smile at his gesture, and if a panther could laugh, she surely would have. He admired the size of her fangs while he ran his fingers through the soft fur on the top of her head. She purred when he scratched behind her ears.

"You're magnificent," he murmured. That shadow of worry in her eyes disappeared to be replaced by arrogant pride.

She twitched her head from beneath his hand and turned, looking back at him from near a black hole at the corner of the slab of stone. Gareth stepped forward and peered inside. A black darker than any night. "We're going down here to hide?"

She crouched over the edge of the pit and slapped him with her tail. When he stared blankly at her, she snorted and swept the soft end into his hand.

"You don't mind?"

She rolled her eyes and Gareth shrugged and grasped the end of her tail. Millicent led him below with that guide, and he stumbled along behind her, through what felt like an ever-shrinking tunnel. When he felt as if the weight of the earth would surely crush them both, the passage widened, and shapes began to form to his sight. At first he thought he might be imagining it, but soon it brightened even more until he could see the faint outline of the craggy walls. Some type of glowing plant grew on them to relieve the complete darkness.

Gareth dropped Millicent's tail. She glanced back at him and then appeared to shrug, as if to say it was his folly. And he did have the devil of a time following her after that. Her black coat melded into the darkness as if a part of it.

But she never allowed more than a few inches between the two of them, leading him around footfalls and sudden chasms. They walked long enough for Gareth to realize that she hadn't taken him to hide. They appeared to have a destination beyond these tunnels and he felt a bit of excitement stir in his chest. In all his years of living, he'd never been to the Underground, although he'd heard of it, the stories seeming as mythical as others thought the relics to be.

Gareth tried to memorize the direction their path took, but Millicent took so many turns into branching tunnels that he finally gave up. It really didn't matter if he got lost. He'd wind up back in the relic at dawn.

The outline of her were-form began to glow and he realized that an opening ahead caused that brightening. She stopped at the end of the tunnel and sat back on her haunches, looking over her shoulder at him. He stepped forward and stared.

Fairylights glowed above a cavern so vast he couldn't see the other side. He'd heard tales of a group of wizards practicing black magic beneath the streets of London, but what spread out before him looked like an entire city. A river branched out into streams, separating the cavern floor into streets, the water looking like a large glistening spiderweb.

"*This* is where I live," said Millicent, having shifted back to her human form, her fur transforming back into her tattered dress. Gareth nodded. She looked more comfortable and relaxed. As if she'd come home, to a place she knew as well as the back of her hand. It made him wonder anew about her life.

She headed to her left, staying near the walls of the cavern, purposely skirting the dwellings below. Openings peppered the walls and his mind whirled at the thought of how many tunnels branched from the city. Millicent suddenly stopped in front of one of those openings, took a deep breath, and stepped inside. He followed, his hand on his sword, feeling her anxiety and prepared to do battle for her again.

Gareth's hair crackled and shivers went up his spine. He recognized the magic of a warding spell as Millicent blithely walked through it with the relic on her wrist. Of course, she was immune, and Merlin's power surpassed that of any human's. And since he was tied to the relic, the spell did not harm him either.

Two guards stood within the entry and Gareth had his sword free from its scabbard before the men could blink. But Millicent shook her head at him and he lowered his weapon.

"We been waitin' fer ye," said one of the guards, a man with a scar from eye to jaw. He gave Millicent a leering grin. "Wot's this, ye got yerself a friend? And here I'd been hopin' to be the first to warm those icy lips."

"Close your mouth, Jok," snapped Millicent, "or I'll—"

Gareth didn't give her a chance to finish her sentence. The edge of his blade met the ruddy skin of the guard's throat and he stared into the man's bloodshot eyes. "Apologize to my lady, sir, or I shall be forced to demand a duel for her honor." His voice lowered to weariness. "And you shall lose."

The guard sputtered. His companion slowly reached for the pistol tucked into his belt.

"Don't," Gareth advised the other guard with deadly calm. "I'll have both your heads before you cock your weapon."

Jok's lips curled despite the sword at his throat. Then his grin slowly faded as he returned Gareth's steady gaze. "Do as he says." He finally said to the other guard. "The man ain't boastin'."

Millicent made an impatient noise of disgust. "Apologize, Jok, so we can be on our way."

"Aye, that I will. I meant no disrespect to the lady, sir." Gareth increased the pressure on the man's throat. "Oh, aye. Me apologies, Millicent. Ye know I was only jestin'."

"I know. But my friend here has an overblown sense of chivalry, I'm afraid. Not that I'd be too upset if he skewered you right now, mind you, but His Grace might not understand." She blew out a breath. "My honor is satisfied, Sir Gareth. Please remove your weapon from the wretch's throat."

"As you wish, my lady. But first, Jok, you will hand

me your weapon." The man pulled it from his belt and Gareth took the pistol and tucked it into his own. He'd been dismayed when guns had been invented, making his sword skills almost obsolete, but soon had gotten familiar with them. He would have liked to own one, but it didn't matter what he took with him when he went back into the relic. When he next appeared, he always had on what he'd been wearing when Merlin had first spelled him into the moonstone.

Gareth took a step back from Jok but did not lower his sword. "I'll take yours as well," he instructed the other guard, who managed to hand over his weapon without arguing.

Jok rubbed his throat while he let them pass. Gareth did not turn his back on them until the tunnel rounded and cut them off from his view.

"Worthless guards," muttered Gareth, although he had his senses trained behind them, just in case. "They let me pass with my weapon and gave up their own."

"My claws are just as dangerous, sir. But Ghoulston knows I'm in no position to make use of them." Before he had a chance to ask her what she meant, she continued speaking. "Which begs me to point out your foolishness. I am in no way in need of your championing. Nor am I your lady."

"You are as long as you wear the relic," snapped Gareth, surprised at the possessiveness in his voice. Of all the women he'd seduced, he'd had no desire to keep any of them. Only one woman had ever made him feel that emotion, and because of her he'd lost his honor and his freedom. It worried him that he felt that way for this fierce woman when he'd yet to even bed her. And made him wonder anew if—despite her cold manner—she could be the one.

"Well, that will be remedied soon. I'm sure Ghoulston will find a way to remove this dratted bracelet."

Gareth watched the sway of her hips. Removing the bracelet would be entirely up to her.

"I've never seen anyone move as fast as you," she continued as they journeyed ever deeper into the tunnel. "Except maybe another shape-shifter. And I've never seen a man use a sword with such impressive skill."

"I have been a warrior for centuries, my lady."

"I thought you were a lover?"

He smiled at her quick wit. This one would make his time of freedom interesting. "I am both, it would seem. But not by choice."

Again she met his eyes with that direct gaze of hers. She couldn't be more than one-and-twenty, and yet her golden eyes bespoke of too much knowledge of the world and its people. Much in the same way that he often felt.

"You're quick with that charming smile," she whispered, "but it never quite reaches your eyes."

Gareth sheathed his sword and closed the distance between them. Of all the thousands of women he'd taken to his bed, not a one of them had ever noticed such a thing about him. And he had thought her cold-hearted. He took her hands and felt her tremble, an answering echo throughout his own body. "It's a habit I've developed. I smile to seduce, not to reveal." He lowered his head slightly, bringing his mouth closer to hers, surprised to discover that she stood only inches in height below him. "Have I succeeded in interesting you, my lady?"

"Millicent."

"Ah yes, Millicent." He stroked her name with his tongue, liking the way it sounded on his lips.

She shivered and his smile broadened.

"Bloody hell," she said. "Sensuality flows from your very pores. It will be a miracle if I can keep you at arm's length until dawn."

He swept his mouth over her soft cheek. "Perhaps since the sun never rises here in your Underground, I will not fade back into my prison."

"Perish the thought."

Gareth told himself she had no idea what she meant. That she couldn't conceive of the hell imprisonment had become for him. But when she twisted her hands out of his, he quickly released his hold.

Millicent began to walk down the passage at a rapid pace. "You have a remarkable gift of taking the most outlandish liberties and making them seem quite natural," she tossed over her shoulder.

He caught up with her in a few strides. "I have a lot of practice."

"I wager you do."

She sounded angry. Good. Perhaps he'd finally managed to crack a bit of her hard interior… as she had managed to relieve some of his infinite boredom.

The tunnel finally widened and Gareth stared at the hulking black castle seemingly carved out of the stone wall opposite them. It lacked the defenses of a typical castle, boasting only crenellated walls and a portcullis. More palace than castle. "This is your home?"

"No," she replied. "I can't go home yet. This monstrous pile of stone belongs to His Grace, the Duke of Ghoulston."

He frowned. "Why can't you go home?"

For a moment he thought he saw a shadow of her were-beast, a vague outline of fang and whisker. "Because the duke has something precious of mine. And he won't return it until I give him something in exchange."

She strode up to the portcullis and spoke to the guards on the other side of the iron grating. "The duke is waiting for me."

"That we know, Millicent," answered a giant of a man with red hair. "He is pacing the study as we speak."

"Then you'd best let me in," she replied. The giant eyed Gareth. "He's with me. His Grace will want to see him."

"Perhaps. But he'll not enter until he gives up his weapons."

Gareth folded his arms across his chest and shook his head. He'd had the pleasure of a pistol only for a few moments and felt loathe to give it up. But his lady touched his arm and beseeched him with her eyes. So, to win her favor, he would be required to enter the monster's lair unarmed. He huffed a breath and handed his weapons to the guard.

The portcullis rattled up with a shriek of grating steel. The giant followed close behind them as they passed into a courtyard strewn with some type of colorless trees that apparently didn't need the sun for nourishment. He took Millicent's elbow as they ascended steps of some blackish stone to a wooden door carved with ancient runes. Powerful wards shivered his skin as they passed into the hall.

Gareth stared at the lewd images carved into statues and sewn into tapestries. "You did not say, lady, what you are giving the duke in exchange for your precious thing. Although I can guess."

She turned that amber-gold gaze upon him again. "And you would be right. I must give him you, Sir Gareth Solimere."

Three

MILLICENT EXPECTED MORE OF A REACTION FROM THE knight, yet he appeared unruffled by her words. He just nodded his head and continued to stare at the duke's wicked artwork with a knowing smile.

She'd never met a man who smiled so much. It made her uncomfortable. Possibly because every time he did so, she felt his charisma like a tangible thing and had to stop her body from swaying into his arms. He was simply the most gorgeous man she'd ever seen in her life, and despite the warnings in her head, she wanted to touch him.

She could kick herself.

A door opened down the long hallway and slammed shut, the sound echoing along the cold stone floor and up to the high ceiling. A woman glided toward them, her footsteps soundless, her arms slightly spread beneath a sheer black pelerine. She wore a black silk dress covered in glittering black beads, the neckline so low Millicent marveled that her flesh didn't pop out of the top. More black beads dotted the elegant coiffure of her brown hair, the entire effect of her costume making her look like glittering midnight.

"Hello, Selena," sighed Millicent.

"Ah, the she-cat returns. With the prize, I assume?"

Millicent felt too tired to play any of Selena's games. "Just take me to Ghoulston."

"Not so fast," she replied, her lips barely moving with her words. "Who have we here?"

Millicent felt the exact moment Selena's eyes met Sir Gareth's. A crackle of heat flared from Selena to the knight, a physical awareness that annoyed Millicent to no end. With Gareth's sensuality and Selena's lust for anything with blood flowing through its veins, she should have expected it. Still, she had to resist the urge to step between the two of them.

He bowed, his wavy blond hair tumbling over his forehead, making him appear even more rakish. "Sir Gareth Solimere. I'm honored, my lady."

"How delightful," crowed Selena. "Please rise, brave knight."

Millicent rolled her eyes. Selena ignored her, gliding over to Gareth with a closed-mouth smile. She placed her hand on his shoulder, where the blood had dried on the torn cloth of his tunic. He didn't flinch and Millicent marveled at how quickly his injury had healed.

"And what are you doing with *her*, Sir Gareth? A man of your nature requires a more… inspired companion," Selena said.

He smiled and a red glow shimmered in the depths of Selena's glossy black eyes. Millicent knew Gareth could take care of himself, even without the benefit of his sword. He'd proven his prowess when he'd fought two were-beasts and managed to survive the encounter relatively unscathed. She might even owe him her life. She should also expect that any woman he encountered would respond to his obvious charms.

And that Selena would lust after fresh blood.

But for some reason, Millicent couldn't bear to watch the two of them trade knowing looks. Couldn't stomach Selena's possessive smile. Her annoyance turned to severe irritation. "I shall be happy to inform His Grace that you kept him waiting."

Selena turned and hissed at her, finally forgetting to keep her lips over her teeth, revealing two sharp front teeth and even pointier fangs at the corners of her mouth. "You are never any fun, Millicent. One day I'll find out if the blood in your veins truly does run so cold." She spun, a glitter of black silk, and headed back down the hall.

Gareth and Millicent followed, the red-haired giant still at their backs.

"You're jealous," whispered Gareth, a note of triumph in his voice.

Drat, the man was persistent. He would soon realize he was only a bargaining piece for the one person she had ever allowed herself to truly care about. Just because she found it difficult to resist his charisma didn't mean she cared enough for him to *be* jealous. "Don't be ridiculous. I just thought I should warn you about her first. I owe you that much."

"Warn me?"

Millicent nodded at Selena's back. "She lusts after any man."

"So?"

"She wants more than to share a man's bed. She wants his blood—which is why the duke did not trust her to steal the relic for him. She's a shape-shifter, Sir Gareth, and cannot control some of her particular tendencies."

"A were-vampire bat," he said. "I know. Verily, it amazes me that you think I didn't. Perhaps it's diffi-cult for you to understand how truly long I've lived. Besides this underground world of yours, there's very little I haven't seen, my lady."

Millicent didn't quite know what to say. She'd never met a man like him before. So young looking, and yet so very old inside. "Oh, quit calling me that," she finally managed.

Selena stopped in front of a paneled door and threw it open with a flourish of fluttering silk.

The room looked remarkably similar to the duke's study in his mansion aboveground, except it lacked sunshine streaming through the paned windows and the fresh flowers his housekeeper managed to fit into every nook and cranny. Millicent doubted anyone above even knew about his residence in the Underground.

The Duke of Ghoulston had been pacing in front of the roaring fireplace and turned eagerly as they entered the room. His beady eyes studied their group for a moment, lingering on Sir Gareth with a frown. Then he quickly focused on Millicent. "Did you get it?"

She held up her arm, the moonstone reflecting the fire's flames within its depths.

He rubbed his hands together, the dry, raspy sound enough to make her shiver. "Jolly good. I won't ask if you had any trouble. I can see you did by the condition of the very expensive dress I loaned you."

Millicent could give a bloody farthing about his expenses. "I want to see Nell."

Selena hissed a laugh and glided across the room to an ornate cabinet, pouring herself a decanter of red wine and sipping it while she undressed Sir Gareth with her eyes.

The duke flopped into a padded wing chair, his belly vibrating with the aftershock. "Not quite yet. First you give me the relic… and explain why the hell you brought this man to my home."

Millicent glanced at Gareth. He looked entirely unconcerned by the duke's sinister tone, examining him as if the other man were an insect he seriously considered squashing.

"Don't do anything foolish," she told him. Sir Gareth raised those blond brows, a slight quirk to his lips. His hair glowed a shade of gold in the firelight and he looked so boyishly handsome she wanted to scream at him. Instead, she lowered her voice. "Please. For my sake."

He gave her a slight bow, with barely a nod of his head.

Selena choked on her wine, as if stunned that the knight followed Millicent's bidding.

The duke narrowed his eyes and leaned forward. "Explain him, Millicent. Now." She'd forgotten the giant had followed them into the room until the duke looked pointedly over her shoulder at the guard, who took a warning step closer to her.

"He's part of what you wanted. He's—"

The knight stepped forward. "Sir Gareth Solimere, a knight of the Round Table and, at this moment, my lady's protector."

The duke ignored Gareth and kept his steely gaze fastened on Millicent.

"He belongs to the relic," she explained. "Well, he came out of it anyway. It's what all the society ladies have been gossiping about. Not the relic itself, but the man who has been trapped inside."

This time the duke gave Gareth his full attention. "So, you're not a madman. By your clothing, I assume you've been trapped inside the relic since the Middle Ages?"

Gareth planted his legs and crossed his arms over the red dragon emblazoned on his tunic. "As you see."

Millicent winced at his aggressive posture and hurriedly spoke. "He can come out only from midnight to dawn. He'll be gone again in"—she glanced over at the gilded French clock on the mantel—"a few hours."

The duke leaned back, steepling his fingers beneath his nose. "Interesting. What else have you managed to find out about the relic? What magic does it possess?"

"That's not our deal," said Millicent. "I bring you the relic and you hand over Nell. As simple as that."

"Life is never simple, my dear. But never mind. I won't let it be said that the Duke of Ghoulston does not honor his bargains. Otherwise my minions won't think I mean what I say." He glanced briefly at Selena, who slammed her glass of port down on the table, sloshing red over her fingers. The duke grinned. "Hand over the relic, and you can have your Nell and go."

Millicent took a deep breath. "Um, there's just a little problem."

The duke's relaxed manner vanished and he stared at the silver band on her wrist like a hound dog would stare at his favorite bone. "I don't like problems."

"It's only a temporary one," Millicent hastened to assure him, hating the sound of her conciliatory tone. If she hadn't been so unwise as to care for another, she wouldn't be in the position of having to bargain with a slug like Ghoulston. She would gladly shift to cat and kill him on the spot. "I can't remove the relic until dawn."

"Why not?"

Despite her earlier words, Millicent decided it would be wise to give the duke enough information to pacify him. "It tightens around the wrist of whomever it chooses."

The duke narrowed his eyes suspiciously. "But you're immune to magic, my dear."

"The spell inside the metal doesn't affect me directly. And the silver is as real as you or I. Believe me, it won't come loose until Sir Gareth is swallowed back inside. Lady Chatterly said he won't appear to the same woman twice, and that's why it's been passed along to other ladies."

The duke rose and faced Gareth. "I've heard rumors that our properly raised women have been introduced to, shall we say, the pleasures of the flesh. I assume we have you to thank for their ruination?"

Gareth bowed with a flourish of his arm. "Guilty, as charged."

Millicent could see the anger simmering in the

duke's eyes and stepped closer to the knight, speaking rapidly. "It's not entirely his fault. You see, he was foretold of a woman who can free him of his curse. And he knows only what she feels like, so he—"

"Gets them naked, yes, I follow." The duke side-stepped Millicent and began to walk a circle around Sir Gareth. "Tell me, Sir Knight, does your skill at seduction come naturally, or is it enhanced by the power of the relic?" Gareth looked down his nose at the duke and tightened his lips. "Ah, well. Perhaps you will tell me why you were trapped in the relic in the first place?"

Only the harsh breathing of the two men disturbed the silence that fell over the room.

"I see," said Ghoulston, dispersing his anger with a sigh. "I think when the relic is in my possession you will be more amenable to answering my questions. You see, I desire your friendship, Sir Knight. Surely that's not too much to ask?"

Gareth raised a skeptical brow and the duke let out a hearty laugh, slapping him on the shoulder. "Hmph. You feel real enough. Not an illusion then. Come now, man. We have a lot in common, you and I." He chuckled all the way back to his wing chair, sitting down with a sigh of self-satisfaction. "I have been imprisoned as well, don't you know? In a prison of obscurity and disrespect. I mean to change all of that with my scientific studies of magic."

Millicent had cringed when the duke slapped Gareth, but the knight stood frozen. She wondered where he had learned such iron self-control and admired him for it. And felt a kernel of guilt. She knew the duke's methods. First he would offer friend-ship, and when that didn't work, he'd try blackmail. If he couldn't find that leverage... well, she'd heard rumors of what the black wizard could do.

And then she shook herself. Hadn't she vowed never to allow herself to be vulnerable again by caring for another? And besides feeling a bit of gratitude for Gareth's skills in beating the other weres who'd sought to take the relic from her, she didn't care for him a whit. She really didn't even know him.

"Well, my dear Millicent," said the duke, "it seems that you will be my guest until the morrow. Perhaps you can show her to the red room, Selena?"

"But this is nonsense," replied Selena. She stepped forward, purposely brushing Gareth's shoulder as she glided past him. "You don't believe any of this, do you, my lord?"

She pointed at Millicent with a sweeping gesture that caused her pelerine to flutter like wings. "Just look at her! Do you really think the relic would choose Millicent Pantere? That this passionate knight would bind himself to such an unwilling creature?"

The duke settled deeper into his chair. "Ah, my sweet Selena. You are an endless source of entertainment."

She gave him a wide smile, her needle-sharp fangs glinting in the firelight. Then spun her silks again, grabbed Millicent's arm, and caressed the silver bracelet. "It's wasted on her."

Sir Gareth, who had stood as still as a stone, twitched when the were-bat touched Millicent.

Selena looked up at him and Millicent could smell the musky scent of the woman's lust for the knight.

"Why must we wait another minute?" she continued, twisting the metal and Millicent's skin along with it. "Look, it's loose enough to remove. It requires only a bit of pressure."

"Unhand her," said Gareth, his voice deep and low.

Selena dug her fingers beneath the silver band, gouging Millicent's skin with her sharp nails, and yanked as hard as she could.

Millicent fought to keep the growl from her voice, and kept her tone even. "I've already tried to get it off, Selena. It won't go past the bones of my hand."

The other shape-shifter continued to tug and Millicent had to resist the impulse to yank back and send the smaller woman flying across the room.

"Then try," panted Selena, "to squeeze the bones of your hand together. Or perhaps we should just cut off your wrist."

The duke slapped his knee and howled with laughter.

Gareth spun and slammed the heel of his palm up into the guard's chin. The red-haired giant managed a grunt of pain before his eyes rolled back in his head. The knight removed the two pistols from the other man's belt as the guard fell, spun again, and leveled them at the duke's laughing face.

"Unhand her," he said again.

Selena froze, her mouth dropping open in surprise.

The Duke of Ghoulston wiped the tears from his eyes. "Good gawd, man, Selena was but jesting. Why make a mess when I can have the relic in a few hours? Then I can discover its secrets."

Gareth cocked both barrels.

The duke started to raise his hands and Gareth shook

his head. "Your spells may stop the bullets, but they won't harm me. I'm surrounded by the power of the relic, which no other magic can touch. I'm not a wizard to be able to use the power, but I don't need it to kill you with a pistol."

"Don't hurt him, Gareth," said Millicent.

"I will not allow anyone to harm you."

Selena dropped Millicent's arm and stepped away from her.

Millicent prayed for patience. "If you hurt His Grace, I will never find Nell."

"Who is Nell?"

"She's my friend. My only friend. And the duke has her locked away somewhere to ensure my cooperation."

"This Nell is the precious thing you would trade me for?"

Millicent didn't like the way he'd said that. He almost sounded as if his feelings had been hurt. As if she'd betrayed him. "I told you. The relic chose me by mistake. I wanted it only for His Grace."

"Yes." Gareth's brilliant blue eyes clouded and he lowered the pistols. "We came together only by mistake, but that's not how we will part, my lady."

"What do you mean?"

"Lady Chatterly's assumptions about the relic are not accurate. It will only loosen from your wrist... after."

Damn it. Millicent should have known it wouldn't be simple. "After what?"

"After you make love to me."

Millicent took a step backward, staring at him in shock. "But I already told you, it was a mistake that the relic chose me."

"Was it?" mused Gareth. "Or has fate played her fickle hand again?" He spoke wearily, as if he'd encountered fate so often it couldn't surprise him anymore. Never had his youthful face stood in such strong contrast to his ageless eyes as it did now.

Despite the ring of truth in his words, Millicent didn't want to believe him. It was simply too preposterous. "But that means Lady Chatterly… and all those other women… They wore it only for a night!"

Gareth's lip twitched. "It's rare a woman refuses me for longer than that." He gently uncocked each pistol and set them down on a delicate tea tray.

The duke finally set loose his spell with a negligent toss of his fingers, which Millicent could vaguely see as a dark black cloud. It curved around the knight, dissipating into the paneled wall behind him. "Forgive me, Sir Gareth," said the duke, looking not a whit sorry. "But I had to try. I find all of this quite fascinating."

And Millicent realized the clever duke had found out more about the relic and its powers by his pretense of friendship than if he'd threatened or tortured them. She glanced over at the were-vampire bat, who had returned to the wine cabinet and refreshed her glass. Selena held her drink up in a mocking salute before tossing it down her throat.

"I won't do it," said Millicent. "There must be another way to get this cursed thing off my wrist."

"Wasted," muttered Selena. "The relic is totally wasted on her."

The duke ignored the vamp, his intense gaze fixed on Millicent. "I suggest you find a way then. That is,

if you ever want to see your Nell. Although person-
ally, I'd recommend you just sleep with the lad and
get it over with. The old lady doesn't seem to do well
in captivity."

Millicent growled loud enough to make Selena let
out a reflexive whimper.

"Enough," snapped Gareth. "I'll not have her forced."

The duke chuckled. "Oh, Sir Knight, I don't
think that will be necessary. Despite her protests, the
girl wants you. A few hours alone with you and she
doesn't stand a chance."

Millicent flushed. Of course she found Sir Gareth
tempting. Any woman would. But she hadn't realized she'd allowed her attraction to show. She must
dissuade the duke of the notion that the knight meant
anything to her at all. Otherwise, Ghoulston would
use that to his advantage. Bad enough that she'd
allowed her concern for Nell to show.

"Do you really think I'd give myself to any man?"
she said. "After what my mother—I'd rather you went
ahead and cut the relic off my wrist, than allow Sir
Gareth to touch me."

Selena took a step toward Millicent, her eagerness
to suit Millicent's words to action obvious in the red
glow of her eyes.

But the duke only chuckled, rubbing his hands
together again. "This is rich. Ice-cold Millicent Pantere
must surrender her virginity for her only friend." He
stilled and glanced at the mantel clock. "Frankly, my
dear, I don't give a farthing how you manage to get
that relic off your wrist. But you had best do it. And
you have only a few hours. It would be unwise of you

to make me wait until tomorrow night. Selena, my pet, show them to the red suite."

Selena pinched her lips but sailed to the door, stepping on the fallen guard with vindictive pleasure. Gareth waited for Millicent, who saw no other option than to follow the other shape-shifter. Perhaps when she was alone with the knight he would tell her more about the relic. Something that would allow her to give it to the duke without giving up the one thing she owned of value. At least to her.

She felt Gareth's warm presence at her back as she followed Selena through the cold stone hallways to the upper level of the castle. They climbed innumerable curving stairways until they reached a landing surrounded by doorless stone walls. Selena headed across the space, stopped before a niche, and pulled the carved statue inside. Stone shuddered, and when a square opening appeared, she waved them past her with a glitter of black beads.

Millicent ignored the smirk the girl gave her and entered a room unlike anything she'd ever seen before. The walls had been painted a deep red, and paintings even more graphic than the ones in the castle hall littered the room. It looked like a parlor, although it lacked the normal tables and chairs that made visiting possible. Instead, it boasted a thick rug surrounded by pillows in front of the hearth, and a multitude of armless sofas and fainting couches.

"Bloody hell," said Millicent.

Selena grimaced. "Too bad all this splendor will go to waste. Tug the bellpull if you manage to remove the bracelet. I want first dibs on his knightliness, here."

She gave Gareth one last lingering look before she left, the stone door grinding to a close behind her.

Millicent crossed the room, stepping over plush carpets and enormous Indian pillows, and looked out the narrow window. This side of the castle faced a craggy ravine, small waterfalls erupting out of the stone to plunge into the depths below. The fairylights on the cavern ceiling hardly penetrated this shadowy side of the fortress and she couldn't tell if the walls provided any handholds.

She spun. Gareth studied a painting, nearly cocking his head upside down to make out some detail in it. Millicent inspected their prison. She found a door that led into a windowless washroom, and another leading into a bedroom—which didn't have any way of escape either. She stood at the threshold and crossed her arms over her chest, scowling at the enormous canopy bed with its blood-red satin coverlet, the mirror-paneled walls and ceiling.

There had to be another way to remove the relic. She turned and faced Gareth. "Surely you couldn't have seduced *every* woman who wore the bracelet."

"True," he replied, still intent on those scandalous paintings. "A few times the relic chose grandmotherly ladies who viewed me as a son. I stayed with them for years, until the relic loosened when they died." He straightened, smoothing back the blond curls from his face. Again he wore that veil of sadness that somehow twisted her heart. "There were several women who didn't prefer men in their beds. I changed their minds or stayed with them until they died. Is that why you don't wish to bed me?"

Millicent's arms fell to her sides. "Certainly not. Of course I want—that is, I like men. I just don't prefer to take one to my bed." She kicked a pillow that sat near the door, the small bells around its seam jangling with the movement.

Gareth smiled at her words. It lit up his face and made her knees go weak. His blue eyes met her own amber gaze and for a moment she couldn't breathe. "So you finally admit you want me. Why, then, do you fight it so?"

Drat, the man could drag the secrets out of a mountebank. He spoke as smoothly as he moved. "That's none of your concern. Now, are you telling me there are only two ways the relic will come off? Sex or death?"

"If I knew of any other, I would tell you."

She believed him. He was a true knight of the Round Table, full of honor and chivalry and truth. It wasn't just his sensual handsomeness that attracted her. Millicent yearned for that goodness within him. She wanted to surround herself with that light that shone like a beacon in her dark world. She wanted to take it inside her and somehow make it a part of her too.

She swayed toward him.

He reached out, started to close the distance between them.

Millicent held up her arm. "Don't. Don't come any closer." She wanted an impossible dream and she'd best snap out of it, so she could deal with the reality of her life. Her dark soul would probably snuff out that goodness within him as easily as she put out a candle.

"Millicent." His voice caressed her name.

Her traitorous human body swayed toward him again. Millicent quickly shifted to panther. The hair on her back stood up in a line of warning. She snarled and bared her teeth, swishing her tail in fury. Any other man would have trembled with fear, but Sir Gareth just looked puzzled. He watched her pace the room, a caged animal with no place to go, no room to run.

Millicent didn't *want* to want him, damn it.

She should never have put that bracelet around her wrist. She should have just snatched it and run. Then Selena could have put on the relic and satisfied her obvious lust for Sir Gareth. It would now be around the wrist of a woman who would relish a night of pleasure in the arms of this sensual man...

Millicent paused on top of a thick carpet. She flexed her claws repeatedly into the deep pile while she thought, a slow purr beginning to rumble in the back of her throat. She shifted back to human, ignoring the fuzzy shreds of yarn now piled at her feet.

"How bound are you to the wearer of the relic?"

"I like your were-beast," he commented absently, stretching out on one of the couches, his tunic pulling up with the movement, revealing muscular thighs through that thick woolen hose he wore. "You move with sensual grace."

"Predators usually do. It's how we manage to catch our prey." She smiled without humor, revealing the unusually long human canines that mimicked her beast. "Now would you please answer the question?"

"I'm not forced to make love with the wearer, if that's what you mean. Although it would be foolish of me, since she may just be the one who could break my curse." He locked his arms behind his head, making his chest appear even broader. Pulling up his tunic even higher. "I do not have to stay by her side, either. But no matter how far away from the bracelet I roam, it always manages to swallow me when the sun rises."

Millicent averted her eyes from his recumbent body, wondering if he wore some sort of drawers beneath that tunic, or only the hose… which didn't seem quite so thick now. "No, I mean, can you make love to someone else? Even while another woman wears the relic?"

"It would have been some long years with the grandmothers if I couldn't." He frowned at her, a hint of anger in those pale blue eyes. "Verily, I don't need the relic to seduce a woman."

"That's bloody obvious."

He raised himself up on his arms, lowering his head and gazing at her through hooded eyes. Every movement he made seemed designed to inflame a woman's desire. "I will not force you."

"So you've said. But how willing are you to help me?"

Gareth shrugged. "I'm not bound by the relic to do so. But honor demands it of me. My sword is at your service, my lady." He looked down at his empty scabbard in chagrin. "Forsooth, it would be if I had it."

Millicent smiled. "Ah, but that's not the weapon we'll be needing, Sir Gareth Solimere."

Four

GARETH SHOULDN'T HAVE BEEN ANNOYED BY Millicent's plan, yet he found himself tugging the bellpull with enough force to tear the embroidered fabric from its rope. He stared at the cloth in his hand with chagrin. Why was he reacting this way? Millicent's idea actually had merit, and he had no doubt he could seduce the were-vampire bat into revealing where the duke had imprisoned this Nell woman.

He admired the skillfully sewn visions of nude women feeding grapes to recumbent men onto a velvet settee, before he tossed down the bellpull, and turned to frown at the closed bedroom door where Millicent had taken refuge. He shrugged his shoulders, trying to dismiss his irritation. It's just that he wasn't accustomed to a woman throwing him at another. Indeed, he'd often had to prevent the relic-holder from physically harming another woman who dared to even look at him. He hadn't realized until this moment that a woman's possessiveness had fed his vanity… or that he'd become a vain man. Gareth had always taken for granted his extraordinary charisma as just a part of who he was.

He smiled when he realized Millicent had made him look at himself anew. Something he hadn't done in over a hundred years.

The door to their prison slid open into the thick wall beside it and Selena stepped into the room, a guard behind her. She arched a brow at the smile on Gareth's face, and obviously assumed she knew the reason for it. She shivered inside her black costume, making the beads glitter in the candlelight. "That didn't take long... I knew she couldn't resist you."

Gareth shrugged.

Selena licked her red lips and took a step toward him. "Where's the relic?"

His gaze slowly traveled the length of her. "You have no need of it, my lady."

She caught her breath and then smoothed her hands down her bodice. "Perhaps not, but His Grace..."

Gareth abruptly strode forward and tore the sheer black fabric off her shoulders, crushing her waist against him as he buried his face in her neck. "Must we wait?"

She chuckled and he felt the vibration against his lips. "You know how I like it, don't you?" Her hands stole beneath his hair and her nails skittered across his neck. "Ah, yes, but of course you do." Still, her lust hadn't clouded her senses yet, because she quickly asked, "Where's the relic?"

Gareth ran his tongue across her skin. "It's still in the bedroom with the were-cat. Shall we say she is a bit... tied up, at the moment?"

"Isn't little Millicent full of surprises," murmured Selena. She glanced back over her shoulder at the guard hulking in the doorway. "If I don't ring within an hour, return with your men."

Gareth glanced up to meet the envious eyes of the guard before the door shuddered closed. Selena tore at his surcoat, returning the favor of her ruined pelerine, and he heard the much-sturdier fabric rip as he struggled out of his sword belt. Gareth released her and quickly removed his tunic and the thinner one under it. She stepped back and her black eyes grew even larger as she studied him. "Sweet Hades, what a deadly combination. That youthful face and body with those wickedly knowing eyes." Her fingers flew to her back and soon her silk gown lay at her feet, only a few buttons rolling across the room in the process.

"Tell me, Sir Knight. Will you abandon your code of chivalry for me?" She dragged off her petticoats.

Gareth swallowed. She wore no chemise, just a corset that lifted her breasts in offering, and stockings tied with black lace around her naked thighs. His body quivered at the lascivious woman and yet his mind recoiled. For a moment, he froze with the shock.

"Have you ever made love to a were-bat before?" she asked as she stepped forward, her hand eagerly finding the hard ridge of him beneath his braies.

"The relic has never chosen one," gasped Gareth. His thoughts strayed to the closed bedroom door and the listening woman behind it. Why was he thinking of Millicent while a beautiful woman teased his body? Some of the women he'd slept with liked to perform in front of others and he'd overcome shyness hundreds of years ago. So he couldn't be concerned that she'd overhear them. And the were-cat had asked him to bed Selena, so it couldn't be his honor that bothered him.

Why, then, didn't he want Selena?

"You will remember me," promised the were-bat as she leaned forward and licked his neck. Gareth's hands caressed her shoulders and expertly started to untie the laces at the back of her corset without any conscious thought from his addled head. His body knew the steps of the dance and could manage without him.

The bedroom door flew open and he turned his head in time to see Millicent shift into her were-form. But Selena ignored the interruption, her mouth sucking at the skin of his throat, and when his gaze turned back to her, he noticed she'd sprouted black leathery wings. The pressure of her mouth on his neck increased and she uttered tiny mewling sounds. And then she bit him. Hard enough to draw blood. Gareth reflexively tried to push her away but the pain from the bite quickly eased and a shudder went through his groin. A distant part of him realized she'd released some drug when she'd pierced his skin, but his body sang with lustful fire and didn't seem to care. He could hear the lapping of Selena's tongue as she fed on his blood, and it excited and repulsed him all at the same time.

Millicent's roar shook the walls and broke through the haze that befuddled Gareth's mind. He grasped Selena's shoulders and tried to gently pull her away from him but the woman fought, beating her wings and digging her nails into his back. He'd forgotten how strong a shape-shifter could be. With an oath,

Gareth shoved her hard. At the same time he saw a flash of black fur slam between them, knocking him backward and sending Selena head over heels to land on a velvet settee, the color of the fabric nearly a match for the blood that smeared her hairy snout. Most weres quickly took either human or animal form, but Selena appeared to manage a half-shifted state, with only her bat wings and snout marring her human features. She hissed at Millicent, who now stood between them, tail swishing in fury.

Gareth pressed his hand against the wound in his neck to stop the flow of blood. "Do you think that was wise, my lady? You will never find out where your Nell is now."

Selena shifted fully to human, licking the blood from her lips, a dreamy smile lighting her face. Millicent snorted at the other woman and turned to him, shifting to human as well. "I couldn't let her... I didn't think..."

Gareth smiled. Perhaps she didn't want him yet, but she didn't like seeing him in the arms of another woman. His hopes soared anew.

Seemingly at a loss, Millicent settled on glaring at him. "That vamp would have sucked you dry."

Selena rose, her glossy black eyes fixed intently on him, a strange new softness in their depths. "No, Sir Knight, I would never do that." Then she blushed and ducked her head. "I could never harm the man I love."

"What's wrong with you?" Millicent snapped at her, exchanging a startled glance with Gareth.

He had to admit Selena's change in demeanor

surprised him as well. Many women had professed their love for him, but it was usually *after* he'd seduced them.

Selena threw the were-cat a venomous look before stepping around Millicent to clasp his hand and bring it to her lips. "You believe me, my darling, don't you? I admit it's hard to control my nature, but once I tasted you, I knew. You are my one true love. Don't you see? I am the one who will break your curse."

Gareth flinched and Millicent growled.

Selena pressed her body against his. "Please make her go away so we can finish what we started."

She had gone mad. That was the only thing Gareth could fathom. "Nay, Selena. Perhaps later." He gently patted her arm. "Why don't you get dressed, now?"

She stuck out her lower lip. It might have looked coy if it hadn't still been stained with his blood. "Only if you promise we'll be together later."

Gareth frowned. He could not in good faith make a promise he had no intention of keeping.

"Blast your damn honor," muttered Millicent under her breath as she stepped past him. She raised her voice to Selena. "He might be yours once you have this." She thrust her arm forward, the moonstone in the relic glowing like a beacon. "You know His Grace won't let you have him all to yourself when he finds out you have it. He'll be too busy trying to figure out a way to use the relic to his advantage."

Selena eyed the bracelet with fevered intensity, reached out a shaking hand to touch it. "Give it to me now."

Gareth blocked Selena's hand with his own before

she could touch Millicent. He could not allow the
woman to hurt the relic-holder again by trying to
wrestle off the bracelet.

The were-vampire bat stared back and forth at the
two of them, her lips tightening with jealousy.

"I'll give it to you," assured Millicent. "But first
you have to take me to Nell. Then we'll leave the
castle, and you can have Gareth all to yourself. You
want to get rid of me, don't you?"

"Nothing would give me greater pleasure." Selena
turned toward her jumble of clothes.

Gareth went into the washroom, poured water
from a cobalt-blue pitcher into a matching porcelain
bowl, and washed the blood from his chest and
throat. He had only a small hole in his neck from
Selena's bite.

"She's gone completely barmy over you," whispered Millicent from the doorway, apparently having
followed him.

Gareth shrugged. He would not admit that Selena's
lovesick behavior startled him as much as it did
Millicent. He reached for a dry cloth and turned
toward the girl, drying his skin with slow, rhythmic
movements. Her amber eyes roamed the contours of
his chest as if hypnotized.

"I suppose you're used to it. Women throwing
themselves at you."

He took a step toward her and felt the air crackle
between them. "There's only one woman I need. I'm
hoping I've finally found her."

She narrowed her eyes and he felt her body snap
rigid with icy cold. "Fortunately, I don't need anyone.

Except that bloodsucker, at the moment. And I don't trust her."

Gareth tossed the cloth over a brass bar. "Have you ever trusted anyone?"

"No. It's how I've managed to survive."

"Well, my lady, it appears you have no other choice but to trust Selena, if you wish to free your Nell. But what will you do when she demands the relic in payment and you cannot remove it from your wrist?"

Millicent smoothed back her shiny black hair and purred. "I'll think of something."

She turned and joined Selena in the parlor and Gareth followed, glancing around with regret. A room worthy of the finest brothel in London, with myriad soft surfaces to cushion the backsides of the most passionate of lovers. He had so hoped to seduce the relic-holder here.

He pulled on his surcoat and tunic while both women watched him in silence. He shook the hair out of his face and buckled on his sword belt, his hand automatically patting his empty scabbard. He felt more naked without his sword than he had without his tunics. When he looked up at the women, they both released a sigh, although with entirely different inflections. Gareth smiled.

Apparently, Selena had already rung for the guard, for the stone door began to groan. She didn't remove her eyes from Gareth as she said, "There should be only one guard, since it's been less than an hour."

Millicent shifted to panther and before Gareth could move, she lunged through the opening in the door. A loud thud followed a muffled oath of surprise.

Gareth entered the landing and took the sword of the unconscious guard, hefting the blade to get a feel for its balance, checking to make sure some silver laced the blade.

Selena joined them and shot Millicent a look of amusement. "You lack finesse, my dear."

She answered with a twitch of her whiskers and an angry flick of her tail.

Gareth dragged the guard into the room and pulled the statue on the outside wall, watching the door grind to a close with satisfaction. Then he crossed the landing and peered down the stairway, seeking hidden guards within the shadows. Selena brushed her body against his as she took the lead, the black beads of her dress winking at him from the glow of the fairylights that lined the walls. She'd left her torn pelerine in the room and her white shoulders gleamed. Gareth had to admit she was truly a lovely woman. His neck ached with the thought.

Millicent brushed by him, almost making him stumble, putting her furry self between him and the other woman.

Selena's course took them down stairways again, but this time they appeared little used, and Gareth sheathed his sword and took a fairylight from one of the sconces to light his way when he realized they'd become scarce. His night vision wasn't as strong as the shape-shifters'.

His sense of direction told him they'd turned a circle, and as the walls grew slimy and then dripped with moisture, he realized they'd entered passageways carved into the stone mountain that backed the castle.

The air grew close and thick, until it seemed as if he could feel the weight of the stone surrounding them.

Selena appeared to revel in the space, but Millicent began a soft whine in the depths of her throat. Gareth wondered if she even realized how contrary to her nature her life had been, that panthers belonged under the open sky, flourishing in the freedom of plain and meadow.

He tucked the small globe of the fairylight into his belt, pushed beside her, and draped his arm over her neck, absently caressing the longer fur at her throat. Her whine grew into a purr and they traveled that way for a time, until Selena led them into narrower, roughly hewn tunnels, and they were forced to walk single file.

Gareth bumped into Millicent's furry backside when she came to a sudden halt.

"Stay here," whispered Selena as she entered a slightly wider opening. Millicent ignored her and started to follow. "You owe me a dinner," continued the were-bat.

Millicent snorted and sat on her haunches.

Selena disappeared and Gareth soon heard a man's startled oath.

"Selena, what are you... no, damn it. The last time you barely left me enough—" A gasp followed and then the guard sighed with rapture. "Gawd, woman, just leave me enough to walk afterward."

The sound of slurping made Gareth shudder with the memory and he took a step forward. But he couldn't get around Millicent without hurting her and she refused to budge. She glanced behind her at him, those golden eyes glowing with annoyance.

Gareth sighed. "We should stop her now," he whispered.

Millicent shifted to human, making him blink at how quickly she transformed. "It's better this way. Do you think he'd prefer that I tear out his throat, or that you run him through with your sword?"

He longed to know what had been done to her to make her into such a hard woman. And knew he'd have to discover it before she would allow him to possess her. "He doesn't need to die."

"He has kept Nell imprisoned in that filthy cell. Do you think I care?"

The sadness that sometimes gripped him nearly choked the breath from him. Gareth picked her up, swung her behind him, and drew his sword. He crossed into the open chamber, wondering if he'd have to use his weapon as a lever to pry Selena off the man.

But she appeared to be sated, her hand covering her mouth as she leaned drunkenly against the wall, the guard crumpled at her feet. Gareth sheathed his sword and knelt down to feel for a pulse.

"I left him enough," mumbled Selena. He glanced up at her as her black, leathery wings shifted back into her body. "The duke doesn't like it when I drain his men dry."

"I imagine not." Gareth stood and scanned the chamber—a scarred wooden table with a single lantern, a few chairs, a keg of ale, and a stone slab that could be a door, although it lacked a statue to open it. Millicent already stood near it, her hands running over several holes in the wall.

"It doesn't bother you, does it?" asked Selena as she drew next to him. "My nature, that is?"

Gareth could smell the coppery scent of blood and the musky odor of lust.

"Because if it does, I'll stop." She hiccupped. "I swear I'll never touch another drop."

"Where is the key to the prison door, Selena?"

Her glossy black eyes widened and then she grinned. "Oh, there isn't one. The duke likes these clever doors, you see. You put your finger in the proper holes and push the release knob inside. This one just needs—"

Stone ground against stone and they both turned toward the sound.

"Hasty, hasty," sang Selena. "If she'd stuck her finger in the wrong hole, she would have lost it."

Gareth glanced back down at the guard. He lacked two fingers on his left hand. His stomach twisted at the thought of Millicent being hurt and he cursed at her rashness while he strode toward her. She disappeared into the black void where the door had stood.

Gareth followed, his nose stinging from the sharp odor of stale urine. He pulled the fairylight from his belt and held it aloft to relieve the absolute darkness. Red fire flashed in the corner of the dirt room, and it took him a moment to realize it was but the glow of the reddest hair he'd ever seen. Millicent crouched just above that head of extraordinary hair, and Gareth slowly approached.

"If they've harmed you, I'll kill them," muttered the were-cat as she gently touched the small woman's shoulders. "I don't care if the duke has a legion of men and monsters. I'll swear vengeance and track him down like the dog he is and then—"

"Crikey, Millie, stow it," rasped the woman.

"Can you stand, my lady?" interjected Gareth.

The redhead's eyes widened as she looked up at him. Gareth studied her in turn. Even standing, the woman would barely reach his waist and he wondered if she had dwarven blood in her veins. But she lacked the sturdy look of those folk. Instead, she had the build of a sprite, with thin, delicate limbs. Her small, pinched face made her beaked nose look even larger. This close he could see the gray that streaked her hair and the knobbiness in the bones of her hands. Wrinkles seamed her face and her violet eyes measured him with experienced wisdom. "And who the hell are ye?"

Gareth bowed and Millicent sighed. "Nell Feenix, this is Sir Gareth Solimere, a knight of King Arthur's Round Table…" She held up her hand to stop the old woman's questions. "I know, but it's a long story, Nell. I'll explain it all when I get you out of here."

"Hmph. Well, it'll take the both of ye to straighten out these hollow old bones."

He took the hint and gently grasped her one arm while Millicent held the other. They both slowly pulled her up, amid crackles and pops that made him wince. They led her from the room and Nell's face lit when she spied the keg. Gareth made sure her legs would hold and then strode over to the table, wiping down the guard's tankard before filling it with fresh ale. The man himself still lay in a stupor.

The old woman studied him when he walked back

to her but didn't say a word until after she'd drained the cup. "Yer eyes tell me ye're older than me, yet ye move like a dancer I once knew. He was the best lover I'd ever had." She laughed at whatever expression had bloomed on his face. "Can't wait to hear this one's story, Millie."

Millicent frowned. "You won't believe it even after I explain. It's the worst thing that ever could have happened to me."

Gareth experienced the oddest pain in his chest. This woman had the uncanny knack of wounding him in ways he'd never felt before.

The old woman squinted up at Millicent. "Why ye talkin' so peculiar?"

"The duke trained me to be a lady."

Those purple-blue eyes widened. "Whatever for? No, wait, never ye mind. I want to be out of this here place even more than I want to know what the duke's been up to. Let's go home."

"I don't think that would be wise," said Selena, who'd been watching them from across the stone chamber. Whatever giddiness she'd experienced from her feast had faded, to be replaced with a restless energy. "His Grace is going to be very annoyed that you left without his permission. He'll forgive *me* once I show him the relic, but I wouldn't be surprised if he set a few of his nastier minions after you to make a point."

"Relic?" whispered Nell. "This is soundin' worse 'n' worse."

"Never mind," hushed Millicent. "Selena, is there a way out of the castle from here?"

"Mmm. Several. But they all lead back to the cavern. And you'll probably manage to get lost." Her red lips widened as she appeared to relish the thought of Millicent and Nell wandering until they starved to death.

"I will see them safely from the duke's demesne," said Gareth, striding forward and taking up her pale hand in his. "Surely you will show us the way, Selena?"

She blinked. Her fingers trembled, and she swayed toward him. "Of course, love. Anything for you."

He smiled and gave her his deepest bow. Millicent snarled and Nell snorted. Gareth ignored them both as he followed Selena out of the prison chamber. He would save them despite their hostility toward the were-vampire bat. He hadn't quite figured out what he'd do when Selena demanded the relic in payment, and discovered he hadn't seduced the holder when it wouldn't come off of Millicent's wrist. Despite the habits of Selena's nature, he rather liked her. And he could never physically harm a woman, especially one so obviously infatuated with him.

Gareth offered to carry Nell, for he didn't think she had the stamina to walk very far. But Millicent shifted to panther and the old woman climbed on her back as if she'd done it hundreds of times before. Again Selena led them through twisting tunnels until the walls began to drip with moisture, and a huge, thundering noise made speaking impossible. Not that he had any inclination to do so, for his mind spun in hopeless circles.

How would he manage to seduce a woman who thought he was the worst thing that could have happened to her?

Light shone ahead of them, and the walls dropped away until they were surrounded in a rush of falling water. The spray stung his face and wind from the fall twisted his hair about his head. Despite the chill that crept into him, he couldn't help but admire the beauty of the shimmering blue-white curtain. It took a glorious half hour before they finally reached the end of the water tunnel and stepped into the comparative brightness of the enormous cavern that sheltered the duke's castle.

When the sound of the waterfall finally faded to a soft roar behind them, Selena turned and pointed to another path that branched off from the one they'd taken. "Keep to this trail and it will take you back to the city. If I were you, I'd get as far away from His Grace as I could, were-cat."

Millicent ignored her and batted a paw at a tiny winged shape that flitted down in front of her. Another one swept across Gareth's shoulder and another appeared before Selena's startled face. The small beings looked like messenger sprites, but not the sort that the aristocracy conjured. They sported black, jagged wings and spindly limbs. Their large, round eyes appeared almost colorless against their dirty blue skin, and when they laughed, they exposed too many pointed teeth for their small mouths.

"The little spies," hissed Selena as the sprites flew away as quickly as they'd come.

Gareth spun. They stood on an incline at the wall of the cavern, the portcullis of the keep to their left. The iron grating had been raised and guards swarmed from beneath it. He turned back to Millicent. "Run."

She snarled, the skin behind her velvet nose wrinkling, exposing the length of her fangs and the points of her own sharp teeth.

"Not before she gives me the relic," said Selena. She grabbed Nell's arm and yanked her off the panther's back. Nell fell to the ground hard enough to make her cry out. "Shift, were-cat, and give it to me, or I swear I'll drain the old woman dry."

Gareth took a step toward them when he heard the muffled sound of a shot, and then the dirt at his feet kicked up a small plume. Selena dropped Nell's arm and turned to gaze from his boots to his face, a smolder of red appearing in the depths of her glossy black eyes. "The fools," she hissed. "They could have hit you."

She shifted fully to her were-bat. Gareth blinked. Selena's eyes stared back at him from a face that sprouted sharp, ridged ears and a snout he now thought resembled a swine's. Two sharp, pointed teeth hung from the top of her mouth, and the charming cleft in her human lip had spread into a wide V. Her brown fur looked coarse compared to Millicent's silky black coat. Her wings had grown larger than when she'd taken a half-shifted state, fully encasing her arms and legs as she spread them wide and took to the air.

Millicent nosed Nell, and Gareth quickly went to the old woman and helped her to her feet. "Are you well?"

"Hmph. That old bat didn't hurt me none."

He smiled and her violet eyes widened and she trembled when he picked her up and set her carefully on Millicent's back. The panther met his gaze.

"Get your Nell out of here," he commanded as

he turned around. The guards had made it halfway to where he stood when Selena attacked them, harassing them from above with clawed feet. Gareth drew his sword and felt Millicent nudge him from behind.

"Ain't you comin' with us?" asked Nell.

The group of fighters had recovered from the surprise attack from above, and snatched at Selena's legs, while their comrades took some wild shots. Pistols rarely shot straight in the best of circumstances, so Selena hadn't been hit yet, but Gareth feared one of the balls might find their target.

"She fights on my behalf," he answered. "I cannot allow her to come to harm."

Millicent snorted and he shot her a glare as he said, "You have your precious thing, now save her. And allow me to fight for what *I* value."

He'd meant his honor but Millicent's golden-brown gaze flew to the were-vampire, who now struggled against the hold of several of the men. Did he imagine a brief flash of jealousy in those amber eyes before she turned away? By all that was holy, she was the most vexing creature he'd ever met.

Nell lowered herself flat on the panther's back as the beast lunged down the path. Gareth gave a sigh of relief that the relic-holder would be safe and then charged down the slope, weaving as he ran, not knowing if that would save him from the pistols now shooting in his direction, or plunge him directly into a ball's path.

His pace didn't slow until he met the crush of bodies and began to swing his weapon in the age-old dance of war. He had despised the duke before, but as he took down one monstrosity after another, he began to hate the man. For the group of guards held within their ranks caricatures of men, seemingly taken apart and pieced together with parts from animal, plants, and other men. They lacked the intelligence of true men and fell easily beneath his sword: a giant with two heads, a man with arms of green vine, another with the hindquarters of a bull.

"Sir Knight," screamed Selena. Too many hands now held her and the beat of her wings could no longer keep her aloft. "Help me!" They pulled her down until she disappeared beneath a wave of beating fists.

Gareth fought harder. His sword dripped red and green and began to grow heavy. He realized some of his opponents were nothing more than illusion, unable to hurt him as the greater power of Merlin's curse protected him, but since he could not tell what he faced, he must waste his strength on them.

Selena continued to scream and he continued to fight things with long tentacles and rotting flesh, men with four legs and some with two. He'd seen much in his long years, but the duke surely held the most varied selection of nightmares in one small place.

He'd finally cleared a path to the were-vamp when he felt it. Gareth hadn't truly believed his curse wouldn't hold just because the sun never rose in the Underground.

His body began to feel disconnected from the earth and he felt himself scatter, as if a wind pulled the pieces of his being apart. He screamed in rage while he swung his sword at the last guard that had the folly to still hold Selena within his hands. When he fell, the rest of the men surrounding her backed away, and she shifted to human. Gareth's vision began to splinter, and the last thing he saw was the sly grin of satisfaction on Selena's face as she looked at the carnage he'd left in his wake.

Five

MILLICENT RAN FOR HOURS WITHOUT STOPPING. AT first she followed the path Selena had shown them, but as soon as she found a tunnel familiar to her, she took it. She didn't trust the were-vamp not to send them flying off a ledge into a gorge.

She barely felt the weight of Nell on her back. The old woman's vibrant personality always made Millicent forget her diminutive stature.

A large cavern opened before them and Millicent circled the milky pool in the center, avoiding dripping stalactites as she searched for the opening between three tall stalagmites. It would take her deeper into the earth, farther from the Underground city and the duke's lair. Not many humans traveled this far into the wilds, but Millicent decided she'd take her chances with the denizens of the deep rather than the wrath of the duke.

She slid between the three white cones and entered another tunnel, hoping Nell remembered to keep her head down. For a moment, a thrill of satisfaction flowed through Millicent as she realized she had indeed saved her friend. Even though she told herself the Duke of Ghoulston would release Nell once she'd done his bidding, she'd feared the old woman wouldn't survive her captivity. That she'd never again see the shape-shifter that had become family to her.

Then why didn't she feel completely satisfied? Why did she keep thinking of soft blue eyes and wavy blond hair? Of his blood spilling on the ground as the swarm of guards overwhelmed him?

Of the way he'd left her to save another woman. And Selena, at that.

Millicent huffed. The man meant nothing to her but trouble. She'd best concentrate on how to get the relic off her wrist without giving up a part of herself to him.

The tunnel began to warm and the walls to glow, relieving some of the blackness. She'd had to rely on her cat senses to get them this far. Millicent picked up her pace without jogging Nell any more than necessary. The old woman's grip had become tenuous and she knew she had to find a place for them to rest soon.

The tunnel abruptly ended and Millicent narrowed her eyes at the brightness. A large cavern opened before them and she struggled to breathe, adjusting to the thick humidity of the chamber. She slowly sat and Nell slid off her back. When Millicent shifted to human, she blinked at the sudden wealth of color.

A glowing forest of emerald, sapphire, and scarlet spread out before them. Spindly-limbed trees, much taller than those aboveground, swayed in a warm breeze Millicent thought might be created by the heat of the hot pools mixing with the cold air of the tunnels that vented the chamber. Another sort of growth hung suspended from the roof high above them, but she could not decide if they were flat vines or roots, since they looked more like glowing lace fans than anything else. They swayed more wildly than the trees below them.

"What is this place?" croaked Nell.

Millicent turned and studied her with a frown. Nell's time in that prison had weakened her, dulling the bright sheen of her red hair, adding even more gray to it. And she was too thin. "I've been here only once before, when I first discovered this place. It's beautiful, but something about it…"

"It's alive," said Nell.

"That's just a wind making everything move. We're not used to that in the Underground."

"It's more than that. Can't ye hear it?"

Of course she could. The trees swayed against each other, their rubbery texture creating an eerie sigh, the fans above a gentle whispering. The undergrowth on the sandy floor moved as well. Tubular plants seeking flying insects of glowing blues and oranges brushed against pitted stones of opalescent white.

Millicent rose. "Don't get spooked by a bit of wind, Nell."

"It ain't that, I tell ye. The forest knows we're here, and hasn't decided whether to welcome us or not."

"Well, then," said Millicent, smiling at her friend's vivid imagination. "Let's hope it decides to like us, 'cause we're staying for a few days. You need food and rest, Nell. And this is the only place I could think to get it that the duke doesn't know about."

Nell was weaker than Millicent thought, because she gave up the argument too easily, closing her eyes with a tired sigh. Millicent shifted to cat, the transformation taking a bit longer than usual, testament to her own fatigue. She'd carried her friend many miles through the Underground, and despite her were-strength, she did have her limits. She couldn't remember the last time she'd slept.

Nell felt as if she collapsed on top of her, more than climbed on, and Millicent slowly padded her way through the forest, the temperature climbing with each step she took. Despite her bravado, she avoided the touch of the glowing limbs as best she could, and tried not to step on any living growth. She went deep into the forest, careful to cover her tracks, hoping to make it difficult for the duke's men if they'd managed to follow her through the twists of tunnels.

Tiny clicks sounded in the undergrowth and Millicent fought the urge to hunt. The round, hard-scaled creatures made an excellent dinner, and her mouth watered at the thought. But she needed to find them a safe place to sleep first.

She didn't quite manage it. When Millicent stumbled across a soft patch of sand, carpeted with the deadfall of the fans above, her limbs gave way, and she sank with a tired sigh. The heat and humidity had drained her of what little strength she had left. She noticed the trees created a thick circle around them, and as her eyes began to droop, it seemed that they swayed with the wind, growing denser, creating a barrier of protection to hide them.

Maybe Nell was right. Maybe the forest had some sort

of intelligence, and had decided it liked them after all.
Millicent fell asleep with that oddly comforting thought.

And awoke to the sensation of being watched.

She felt Nell's slight form curled up behind her, the
old woman's snores the only discordant sound in the
rhythmic whisper of the forest. Millicent cracked her
lids, her were-vision especially attuned to the slightest
movements around her.

Sir Gareth sat across from her, his back against a
tree, his pale blue eyes fixed on her own. He wore
only a short pair of drawers and his belt, the scabbard
of his sword digging in the sand. His hair curled with
dampness and the smooth skin of his chest shone with
a light sheen of moisture. Millicent's stomach did a
little flip at the sight of him and she covered her reaction by yawning widely, revealing her impressive set
of fangs and teeth. She rose with a stretch, careful not
to disturb Nell. When she shifted to human, her vision
bombarded her again with the color of the forest.

She blinked. "How long have you been here?"

She noticed he had his own sword back in his
scabbard again, and she couldn't even see a red mark
where Selena had bitten his neck.

He glanced at Nell and replied just as softly. "Not
long. Where are we?"

Of course. He'd probably still been with Selena
when the relic sucked him back in. "Far away from
the duke's underground mansion. Did you save her?"

His brow wrinkled. The tree he sat against glowed
an emerald green, making his hair appear tinted with
the same color. Blast, no man looks good with green
hair. But he did.

"Oh," he replied. "You mean Selena. I managed to clear a path around her just before I disappeared. She was still alive."

Millicent shrugged. "A blooming shame."

He smiled that devastating smile of his and stood, one smooth motion of rippling muscle beneath gleaming skin.

"You're half-naked," she blurted.

He shrugged. Blast, he shrugged. It did things to his shoulders and chest that made her want to explore those muscled contours with her fingertips. She'd seen many a man half-clothed and she'd never had this kind of reaction. Millicent averted her gaze, focusing on the changing colors reflected in the sand at his bare feet.

"It's hot as Hades in this chamber," he replied.

Of course it was. Millicent's petticoats stuck to her legs and stopped the breeze from reaching her skin to cool it. But she hadn't taken half her clothes off just because of a little discomfort.

He crossed the distance between them and touched her hand. "I'm glad to see that you and Nell are unharmed. Is this place an illusion?"

His touch tingled. The shock made her look back up at him and she pulled away. "No. Nell and I would've seen through it."

His smile turned sad when she pulled away from him, but his eyes quickly sparked with curiosity at her words. "Then... Nell is a shape-shifter as well? What is her nature?"

Millicent noticed he hadn't said "beast." It made her feel—oh, she didn't know. Oddly warm inside. And she found herself telling him more than she would have otherwise. "Nell is a firebird. But she rarely shifts anymore. It takes energy to change to were-form, and she's old and tired."

His gaze traveled to the loudly snoring woman. "In all the years I've lived, I've never seen a firebird. They are very rare." He sounded almost reverent. "What does she look like?"

Millicent closed her eyes, picturing her. "She's beautiful. Brilliant red plumage and a tail so long it trails like an elegant skirt behind her. She can breathe fire, and her feathers get hot enough to burn with orange flame. But fire doesn't bother her. Even in her human form, I've seen her caress it as if it were an old lover."

"I hope I can see her were-form, sometime."

She felt his breath on her face. When had he gotten so close to her? Millicent's eyes flew open and she took a step back. "I hope you don't. She shifts now only when she's threatened or furious."

"Verily?" He looked into her eyes. He had very large, very blue eyes, his lashes several shades darker than his hair, outlining them so they appeared even larger. "It bothers you, doesn't it? The thought that age might rob you of the ability to shift."

"Of course. How would I protect myself without my were-form?"

"Perhaps you will have someone to protect you."

"Not bloody likely."

Gareth curled his hand into hers and tugged. "Come, I want to show you something."

Millicent allowed him to lead her through the multicolored glow of the forest, his touch no longer a threat to her senses, but somehow comforting. As if she didn't feel so quite alone. Although Nell sometimes acted like a grandmother, they rarely touched each other. And no man would dare attempt to. But Sir Gareth seemed so casual about reaching out and making a physical connection, as if he couldn't help himself. She supposed that after centuries of seducing women, it came as natural to him as breathing.

That thought bothered her and she twisted her hand out of his grasp. "I can't leave Nell for too long. She might wake or—"

"Don't worry, my lady. It's not far."

The willowy trees opened onto a small clearing of sand that butted up against the wall of the cavern. A small hump of pitted rock sat on the left, steam billowing from the center. The temperature of the pools varied, and this one must be boiling. The vapor swirled about them, picking up the glow from the trees and creating ribbons of emerald, turquoise, and violet. A small path led up the side of the wall onto an opening.

Millicent followed Gareth into the tiny cave and stopped and stared. It felt cooler and dryer than the forest below. Three beds had been made with layers of foliage, separated by walls of branches for privacy. A flat stone near the front of the cave made a table of sorts, with three low stools clustered around it, made from branches tied with stiff plant fiber.

The middle of the stone table held a cluster of opalescent flowers in a hollowed-out gourd. Millicent didn't know where he got them, but the flowers gave off a more intense glow than that of the trees, lighting the cave with soft, pearly splendor.

"You did all of this?" she whispered.

Gareth bowed. "Your new abode, my lady. Do you like it?"

Millicent didn't answer his question. She couldn't. No one had ever done anything like this for her before. It felt like a home. Could he even guess that she'd never had one? She stroked the petals of the flowers. "You'll have to show me where you picked these. Although this place is no illusion, magic surely went into the making of it."

The knight sighed, as if he hadn't truly expected her to thank him, and took a step toward her. "The wizard who made it must have missed the ocean."

She looked at him blankly.

"You've never seen the ocean, have you? It's a large body of salty water, where enormous fish and plants live. There are even shape-shifters within its depths, men and women who can transform to fish."

Millicent bristled. In the few months she'd spent with the duke above, she'd seen only a bit of London and most of it looked little different than her twilight city. Abovegrounders always thought their world was so superior. "We have lakes down here. Black lakes with creatures living in them."

"Ah, but you've never seen sunlight sparkling on waves of water, foam crashing against the beach." His eyes shimmered with sadness and his voice lowered to a husky murmur. "I barely remember it, myself."

Then his eyes cleared as he studied her face. "You've lived in the darkness as much as I have, haven't you, my lady?" Again he reached out and touched her, his fingertips as soft on her face as the touch of a fairy's wing. "I wish I could take you there."

Millicent suppressed a derisive laugh. "Wishes are for fools and dreamers, and I am neither." She turned and scurried back down the path. If he kept it up, the man would have her mooning after dreams herself. But he still had hope that his curse would be broken. She'd lost her hope of a happy ending to her life many years ago.

Sir Gareth called out to her and she shifted to panther so she couldn't answer him. For a moment there, he'd almost had her convinced that he cared about her. She'd never heard of a man seducing a woman by making her a home from a cave, but if he'd thought to soften her heart, he'd managed to come close to figuring out how.

She reached the patch of sand where she'd left Nell and shifted back to human. "No thanks," she muttered.

Nell rolled over and blinked up at her sleepily. "No thanks to wot?"

Sir Gareth strode into the clearing, one of those hard-shelled creatures in his hands. "It appears that my lady is not satisfied with my attempts to see to her comfort."

Nell sat with a wince, her knobby hand rubbing the small of her back. "Crikey, did ye say comfort? I'd give a sweet shilling to get off this hard sand and away from the little gnats that live in it. And what's that ye got in yer hands?" The nostrils of her beaked nose flared.

Gareth set his offering before her and cracked open the round top, exposing fleshy meat. "I don't know what it's called, Lady Nell, but when cooked it tastes like lobster."

Nell smiled at his use of the honorific, and without

further ado, dug into the food, pulling out strings of moist meat and popping them into her mouth.

Millicent's own mouth watered. While her were-cat preferred raw meat, the food smelled heavenly to her human nose. "How did you manage a fire?"

When he took a step toward her and she quickly backed up, he stopped and frowned. "I didn't need one. That small pool cooks these to perfection."

"Of course. Well, it's nice of you to bring Nell some food, but I can take care of her myself."

"I never said you couldn't, my lady. I just thought you'd be too tired to hunt this morning, and sought to make things easier for you."

Nell's sharp eyes flew back and forth between the two of them while she continued to munch.

"I don't need anyone to make my life easy. I don't need to get soft." Millicent spoke her next words slowly, as if to a simpleton. "I don't need you."

"Nay, I fear you don't. But I can't say the same."

"Dammit, I'm not the one, I tell you. Can't you get that through that thick skull of yours?"

They stared at each other, the very air seeming to crackle between them. Millicent felt peculiar, though. Oh, she was mad at his stubbornness, right enough, but her anger made the beast within her shiver with sultry heat. What madness had overcome her cat?

Nell set down her shell of food, gave a satisfied burp, and leaned back. "Millicent, if this here lad can follow us, the duke's men can as well."

"He didn't follow us." She held out her arm and pointed at the band of silver circling it. "He comes out of here. No matter how far I go, I can't get away from him."

Nell rose unsteadily to her feet, a few bones creaking with the effort, and took her arm, studying the jeweled bracelet. "This is the relic ye spoke of before. And it's tied to this lad? I think it's past time ye told me what the duke had ye up to, my gel."

Millicent took a deep breath and told the entire story, while the trees continued their gentle sighing and the fans above pretended to cool the air. By the time she'd finished, sweat trickled down her legs and within the valley of her breasts.

Gareth watched her with a half smile, looking cool and comfortable in nothing but his linen drawers.

Nell turned to study him and suddenly he didn't look as composed. "Well, lad, I must say the relic picked the wrong gel. Me Millicent won't have nuthin' to do with ye, despite that sinful smile of yers and that sleek, muscled body. Now me, on the other hand…" She cackled at his blush.

"It isn't funny, Nell," snapped Millicent.

Her eyes narrowed as she nodded. "No, my gel, it ain't. And I'll spend some thought on how to help ye out of this, to be sure. Seein' as it's my fault and all."

"It's not your fault."

"Ye wouldn't have done it if Ghoulston hadn't used me against ye."

Millicent shook her head, damp strands of hair brushing her shoulders. "It doesn't matter, now. What's done is done."

Nell nodded and straightened her shoulders. "Well, at least ye look and talk like a lady now." She turned to

Gareth. "Now then, lad. While we consider a way out of this mess, I'm not opposed to a bit of comfort meself, and I seem to remember ye mentionin' that word. Do what ye will, Millicent, but I don't like livin' rough."

The knight gave her an elegant bow. "It's humble, Lady Nell, but I will be happy to take you there." He strode forward and swept her up in his arms as if she weighed nothing more than a stone. The old woman wrapped her arms securely about his neck and gave Millicent a wink over his shoulder as he carried her away.

"Drat it, Nell," Millicent muttered as she followed them. Her sweaty skirts tripped her up and she cursed the duke and his fancy clothing and shifted to panther, her fur not much cooler, but at least she could move with ease.

When they reached the cave, Nell crowed over her soft bed, which looked to be made of shredded plant fibers, and settled back with a sigh. She looked so much more at ease in the cooler, dryer air that Millicent didn't have the heart to protest about their new lodgings. But she didn't have to eat the food he provided.

She spun and slunk back into the forest, looking for the hard-shelled creatures he'd cooked for Nell. Millicent caught several of them, breaking them open with her strong jaws, worrying out the meat inside. But her prey had arms that ended in strong, jagged claws, and after being pinched on the lip more than once, she decided her belly was full enough.

And she didn't trust the knight to protect Nell as well as she could.

So she returned to the cave and ducked inside to

check on her friend. Gareth sat on one of his stools, twisting together tough strands of thin, long leaves to form a sort of net. Several empty shells sat on the table in front of him, and Nell snored loud enough to make them tremble.

"There's spears, of a sort, back in the corner," he said with a glance up at her. "Jab the creatures in the soft part between the shell to capture them. I haven't seen any cool springs to net fish, but when I return, I shall look. In the meantime, you can use this to bag your prey." He held up the sturdy-looking net.

Millicent flicked her tail and gave him a look.

"Your lip is bleeding," he said. "And so are several other places on your paws. I just thought it might be easier to hunt in human form. With a spear, you don't get close enough for them to pinch you with their claws."

He made a good point. She turned in a circle until she found a comfortable position and sat, licking the wound on her right paw. Those claws bit deep.

When she looked up again, he had disappeared.

Millicent should have realized that the relic would take him soon. The work he'd done to make the cave a home must have taken many hours.

"So the magic man is gone, eh?"

Millicent shifted to human and turned. "Magic man?"

Nell sat up and nodded her head. "In more ways 'n one, I suspect." She sniffed and then grimaced. "I stink."

Millicent's lip quirked. Leave it to Nell to get to the important things first. "There's a pool not too far from here where the water is but warm."

"As opposed to boiling our skin off, I suppose." Nell rose and hobbled over to the entrance of the cave. "Although that might not be so bad. Ye know, the bastard never gave me enough water to bathe. That was worse'n the food he gave me."

A haze of red covered Millicent's eyes and she tamped down the fury of her cat. It took her a few moments to speak again. "Can you walk, Nell? It isn't far."

"Course I can. Blast, I ain't no hothouse flower. Whichaway?"

Millicent led her down the path and through the trees to the spot she'd found when hunting. A large pool spread out and disappeared beneath an overhang of rock, only a few lazy wisps of vapor rising from the surface of the water. She helped Nell up the pitted rock sides that surrounded it, and they both slid in with all their clothes on.

They soaked for a time, just enjoying the feel of the warm water. The flowers Gareth had picked for their table grew around the pool, their pearly light dampening some of the colorful emerald glow of the surrounding forest. Unlike Gareth, Nell didn't look one whit attractive with green-hued skin, and that red hair had combined with the emerald to make a muddy shade of yellow.

They helped each other undress and then washed their clothes as best they could, pounding and ringing the dirt from the fabric. Millicent slammed the creaky corset the duke had given her especially hard against the rocks, unconcerned about the silken sheen, only determined to make it a bit more flexible.

She envied Nell's timeworn corset. There was an advantage to wearing cast-off clothing.

"How long we got until they find us?" asked Nell as they spread their clothing along the rock to dry as best as it could in the humid air.

"Maybe never. We're deep into the wilds of the Underground."

"Ach, my gel. Ghoulston won't stop looking as long as ye wear that."

Millicent scowled at the bracelet on her wrist. The moonstone imbedded in it winked mockingly back at her. "I should have at least a few days to figure a way to get it off."

Nell shrugged, a myriad of wrinkles appearing with the movement. "The knight ain't so bad, though. I could think of worse fates than bedding such a looker."

"Not me."

Those violet eyes studied her with unblinking intensity. "Ye won't wind up like yer mum, Millie."

"Hmph. You can't know that. Once I've crossed that line, there's no going back."

"Giving up yer virginity don't make ye a whore."

"Are you suggesting—"

"I ain't doing no such thing. I jest see the way ye look at him, and I don't want ye blaming yerself if ye can't resist him."

Millicent climbed out of the pool. "Which would make me no better than my mother." She swished the water off her skin with the palms of her hands. The forest didn't seem as hot now, after her soak, but she eyed her clothes with a frown. She couldn't put all that back on, especially if she wanted to hunt in human form.

Nell struggled into her corset, turning her back so Millicent could help her tighten the laces.

"I knew ye wouldn't listen," she grunted as Millicent yanked the ties. "But I think he's a nice lad, cursed or not. Ye could do worse in a mate."

Millicent stifled her frustration. "So let's say I can't resist his charms. Poof! He goes back into the relic and I never see him again. Enough, Nell. I'll handle it my way."

While her friend put on a thin, worn petticoat and her loose cotton dress, Millicent eyed her clothing with a scowl. She picked up a petticoat that could have served as a skirt with the quality of the fabric and began to tear out the horsehair lining that stiffened the hem. With just her chemise, corset, the petticoat, and corset cover, she'd be garbed well enough, by Underground standards.

They made their way back to the cave through glowing colors. After being in this place, the Underground would appear even more dank and gray.

"Nell?"

"Yes, luv."

"Do you think I won't be able to shift when I get as old as you?"

Nell looked up at her with a grimace. "Despite the red still in my hair, I'm very, *very* old, Mill." The trees swayed and the fans swished above them. She sighed. "I'm not sure."

Millicent nodded. "But it's possible."

"Oh, my gel, in my experience, anything is possible."

Six

SHE WAS WAITING FOR HIM WHEN THE RELIC SPAT HIM forth again. Gareth studied her with appreciation while he collected his wits, which always seemed a bit scattered when he materialized from a smoky haze to solid form. She'd discarded half her clothing and looked the cooler for it. Fashions had changed over the centuries, and although he admired the gowns that made women look like delicate flowers, they had to be uncomfortable to wear. And deuced difficult to get them out of.

"I want you to teach me how to fight."

She shouldn't be able to surprise him. He'd known thousands of women. But this one always managed to do so. "I am at your service, my lady. But it seems that your cat knows how to use her claws."

She shook her head, tangles of midnight hair sweeping her shoulders. "No. I want you to teach my human form how to fight."

Gareth started to shed his clothes. This place might be beautiful, but the heat and humidity reminded him of the jungles of Mogow. He remembered their conversation about Nell being unable to shift to fire-bird at will, and thought he knew why Millicent had made the request. His lady did not want to have to rely upon anyone's protection.

Now, or in the future.

He allowed his admiration for her to show in his eyes as he removed the last of his upper clothing.

"We'll start with staffs, then I might let you work with my sword."

She nodded as if she understood the importance he placed on his weapon.

A cackle of laughter from the depths of the cave made him realize Nell had taken a double meaning from his words. He turned and bowed to the old woman, strode over to the pallet of brush she lay upon, and took her hand. "How do you fare, my ladybird?"

"Ladybird—eh, ye're a smooth one," murmured Nell. "My poor gel has no chance against ye at all, does she?"

"It is my fervent desire that she does not."

"Hmph." She raised her voice. "Off with the two of ye, then. It's not my idea of fun to watch two grown people whack each other senseless."

The old woman confused him. She seemed to be sure of his failure, while at the same time aiding his cause. As if she could no more make up her mind to it than Millicent. He still felt in awe of the small woman, and the firebird she could become. He would have honored her wishes to stay away from Millicent if she had insisted.

But she did not.

Gareth bowed to her and took his leave, following

the relic-holder from the cave, watching the sway of her hips with appreciation. Perhaps he might not have been able to stay away from his lady even if the firebird had insisted.

Millicent stopped at a smooth clearing of sand. He saw the strokes of a branch across the grains and realized she'd prepared this place in advance. Perhaps she was *too* keenly aware that he could deny her nothing.

She picked up two sturdy branches, and he recognized the spears he had made. Millicent tossed him one and held her own upright in front of her. Gareth shook his head.

"Hold it horizontal across your body, like so." He stepped forward and took her hands, positioning the weapon correctly. It always shocked him when he touched her. A sort of shiver through his blood. "Staff work is different than real swordplay, but you must learn this first."

She allowed him to touch her without pulling away. So, there would be an advantage to this after all. He'd never met a woman so unused to being touched, and his hopes soared that sparring with him would enable her to become accustomed to it.

If he managed to survive the day, that is. More concerned about harming her than protecting himself, she managed to bruise him more than once.

"You retain the speed and strength of your were-cat," he panted after several hours of tutelage. "This gives you the advantage over me."

"But not much," said Millicent, scowling. "Not enough to beat you." The thin skirt she wore stuck to her body with the sweat from their exertions, outlining the long length of her legs. When she turned to set down her spear, he swallowed at the sight she afforded him.

"You can't expect to learn so much in a day, my lady. Remember, I've had centuries of experience."

Millicent turned and collapsed on the sand, still breathing hard from their bout. She sat with her arms around her knees, staring off into the forest, her eyes following the movements of the multicolored mist that danced and wove through the trees.

Gareth sat beside her, shoulder to shoulder, pleased when she didn't immediately pull away from him. The lady made such small allowances seem like a great gift. He flexed his arms, enjoying the loose feel of his muscles. It had been too long since he'd had a challenging fight. True battle left him angry and sad, but a session of strength and skill always relaxed his mind and body.

Millicent appeared to be feeling the same quiet contentment, for they sat a time in silence, listening to the soughing of the branches in the wind.

"How long do you plan on staying here?" asked Gareth, his voice low, hesitant to destroy the peaceful feeling between them.

She closed her eyes, tilting her head back to catch an errant breeze. "Long enough for Nell to recover her strength. Shape-shifters don't take well to confinement."

He admired the smooth curve of her throat, the outline of her full lips. "And then?"

"And then we travel deeper into the Underground until I find a way to get this relic off my wrist."

Stubborn wench. He'd already told her there was only one way to remove it.

"There *must* be another way," she continued as if she'd read his mind. "Tell me exactly how you got trapped in the stone."

Gareth sighed. He would do anything to convince her he spoke the truth. "I seduced Merlin's lover."

Millicent huffed. "Why am I not surprised?"

"I was young and foolish," replied Gareth defensively. "And I thought I was in love. Those are the only excuses I can offer, lady." The colorful glow of the forest faded as his vision turned inward. He still remembered every detail of that day. The feel of triumph when Vivian surrendered to him. The look of betrayal on Merlin's face when he'd found them together. "Merlin wove a spell that shivered the stones of Camelot. I could almost see the magic he called, forming in his palms, twining about my body. I remember struggling into my clothes, telling him I loved her, worried I'd have to draw my sword against the king's advisor. "'Twas bad enough I had broken faith with Merlin, but I didn't want to be forced to do so with my king."

She stared at him with ever-widening eyes, as if she couldn't quite believe his world had once existed. But when she spoke, her voice sounded no louder than the sigh of the wind, tinged with awe and sympathy. "What did Merlin say to you?"

"He said, 'Only true love will break this spell, boy, and I curse you to search until you find it.' And then I fractured into a thousand pieces, and knew despair when I later materialized to Vivian from out of the relic, and she could not break the spell."

"Merlin said nothing more specific?"

"No. Why should he? He intended for me to suffer for my betrayal. He did not want to make breaking the curse easy."

Millicent frowned. "So. You began to search for your true love."

"Yes. I had to learn to become intimate with a woman quickly, to sense her desires and longings, to discover if she could truly love me. If she might be the woman who could break the spell, for I long for nothing more than to be free."

"I understand. My were-cat values freedom more than life itself."

Gareth brushed her shoulder. He believed her. It felt good to be understood, if only a little. And it felt good just to be with this woman, to talk and share their minds if not their bodies. The thought startled him, for he had never experienced such a feeling before.

He changed the subject, suddenly eager to know more about Millicent's own life. He wished to understand what might have shaped this fascinating woman at his side. "If you do not return home soon, won't your family and friends wonder what's become of you?"

A lizard-like creature scurried across the sand toward Millicent, and Gareth redirected its path with a nudge of his boot, not knowing if it might be poisonous or not. He'd yet to find anything in the forest that would harm his lady, but he would take no chances.

The corner of her mouth twitched. "I have no family, and Nell is my only friend. I suppose Bran might wonder what happened to me. He won't easily find a replacement."

Gareth felt a prick of jealousy. Alas, it had been long and long since he'd felt that particular emotion. "Who is this Bran?"

She lowered her head and looked at him. "He's the tavern owner of the Swill and Seelie. Where I work."

"And what do you do in this place?"

Her golden eyes danced. "I wipe tables, serve ale, and between Bran and me, keep the patrons from dismembering one another."

She laughed at the look on his face.

"It's the favorite pub for my kind, and our animal-natures don't always mix well. Fortunately, I'm one of only a few predators in the Underground, and most don't want to tangle with me. It's why Bran hired me. A were-bear likes it peaceful."

Gareth found himself smiling with her. "Bran shape-shifts to bear?"

"Mmm. He likes honey and scratches his back on door frames and speaks slowly." Her smile faded. "Yes, I suppose he just might wonder what happened to me."

Gareth noticed she didn't say this Bran might care about her. His tone became low and coaxing, unsure of how far to push her confidences. "What became of your family?"

For a moment he feared she wouldn't answer. Her expression became guarded and wary. But she deigned to reply, and in that moment, he knew she'd decided to finally trust him.

"I don't know who my father is. And my mother died when I was little." She took a deep breath, as if afraid that her voice would falter on her next words. "My mother had been used poorly, by one man after another. Men like to torment a beast, you see. Or enrage it."

Gareth had met many men with twisted desires. He had yet to understand it. "I'm sorry, my lady."

She looked genuinely confused. "For what?"

"That your life has taught you to care for so few."

Millicent smiled widely at him, exposing the long canines at the corners of her mouth. "Ah, but Sir Gareth. Don't you see there's freedom in that?"

His name on her lips sounded as sweet as wine, and for the first time, he understood her nature. She seemed to read that understanding in his eyes and accept it.

He had wanted this woman before. Now it became a burning desire. "There's freedom in loving too, my lady. Won't you allow me to show you?"

She froze and the air became charged between them. Gareth leaned forward to face her, moving slowly, not wanting to frighten either the lady or her beast. But there was no fear in her eyes when he locked gazes with her, just confusion and doubt.

"It's true," he assured her, leaning closer, his lips but a breath away from her own. "Freedom… and joy." He tilted his head and pressed his mouth against hers. She tasted salty sweet and unlike any other woman he had known before. Her lips felt warm and soft—but completely still, as if she feared to move.

Gareth pulled slightly away from her, studying the sweep of her brow, the cat-shape of her eyes, the golden depths within. "Breathe, my lady."

She let loose her breath with a gasp, and he tilted his head farther and leaned in, taking advantage of her parted lips. This time her lips stirred beneath his, mimicking his own moves with shy hesitancy. When he opened his mouth farther, she did as well. When he dipped his tongue inside, she touched her own to his, a slow dance of wet heat that grew to feverish intensity. He felt a vibration and realized she'd started to purr, a low sound in the back of her throat.

Gareth's body responded with a rush of blood to his groin. But he reined in his desire, grateful that centuries of experience granted him such control. An ordinary man would never have managed it. He allowed her to leisurely explore his mouth, guiding her with a gentle touch whenever she faltered, letting her discover the exquisite joy within a kiss.

Every nerve of his felt afire, and he dug his fingers into the sand to prevent them from touching her. He longed to feel her body against his, to touch every curve he'd admired from a distance. But he couldn't push. Gareth must give her time to adjust—

Her arms wrapped around his shoulders, her strength still astonishing him, and she crushed his body against hers, her purr interrupted by a growl as she flipped him over onto his back and lay half atop him, continuing to ravish his mouth. Gareth sighed with relief, brushing the sand off his palms before wrapping them around her hips and positioning her fully atop his body. He explored the curves of her back while she tangled her fingers in his hair. He covered her buttocks with his hands while she sucked on his lower lip.

She wiggled atop him, unaware of the torture she caused. Or so he thought. For suddenly she jerked her head back, blinking down at him with passion-glazed eyes, a shock of realization blooming within their depths.

Gareth brushed a tendril of hair away from her cheek. He knew she'd felt his need for her. "Don't let it frighten you."

Millicent spun away from him, coming to a crouch on all fours.

He slowly rose to a sitting position, ruffling the sand from his hair. He pretended that naught of significance had passed between them, seeking to maintain that air of camaraderie they'd shared earlier, hoping to assuage her fears. But her kiss had shaken him to the core. What had started out as only a means to seduce her had turned into something… larger. Something he did not understand. How had her kiss managed to make him feel… somehow… complete? How could it make the world spin, when he had gone through the same motions with thousands of other women with nary a twist of his senses? "I'm going to bathe. Do you wish to join me?"

She leaned toward him as if to comply, passion still shimmering in her eyes. One hand lifted to touch her swollen lips. "How can you—aah, you're a slick one. If I didn't know you had another reason for seducing me, I might even be able to believe in the tenderness you've shown me."

Gareth gazed at her solemnly. "I would never lie to you, lady. In word, or deed."

She shook her head in frustration, jet-black locks flying around her face. "That's the worst part," she said. "I think I believe you." And then she shifted to panther and disappeared into the trees before Gareth could form another thought.

But as he stared at the emerald glow that shimmered in the mist from her hasty flight, a slow smile spread across his face. Gareth rose and sought the pool not far from the cave. It had never taken him this long to seduce a woman before, and it had frustrated him. And yet today he found himself enjoying the chase.

He realized he liked Millicent. Liked her independence and strength and stubbornness.

Gareth stripped off his hose, braies, and boots when he reached the pool and lowered himself into the water. It took away some of the aches of his bruises, but not the pounding in his loins. He'd never taught a woman to fight before, and it had been a surprisingly arousing experience. Images of her flashed through his mind. The blaze of those golden eyes when she launched an attack at him. The twist of her body while muscles rippled beneath that smooth form.

His desire had already been complete before he'd kissed her. Holding back while she explored his mouth had nearly driven him mad. But the contrast from the warrior-woman he'd fought to the innocent who kissed him so passionately aroused him as no other woman had ever done before.

And the glimpse into her soul she'd allowed him when she'd spoken of her life, engaged his heart like none other.

When he rose out of the water, the fullness of his member didn't surprise him. But it seemed to shock Millicent as she emerged from the tubular bushes, taking the path back to the cave, a load of netted clawed-creatures slung over her back.

Of course. Despite his insistence that he would

provide their dinner, she continued to hunt for her own meals.

Several pools lay hidden within the forest. Gareth could have chosen any one of them. But he'd purposely chosen the one closest to the cave, on the path she would have to take when she returned.

She stopped dead in her tracks and stared her fill of him. He froze likewise, unembarrassed by his nude state. He had no shyness whatsoever when it came to his body. He'd lost that centuries ago.

He felt her eyes like a tangible thing as they swept over his face and chest, as if she left a burning trail on his skin. When her eyes lowered, his member rose even higher, as if it had a mind of its own.

She licked her lips and shivered in the wet heat.

Gareth knew he could've taken her right then. She wouldn't run away this time, for her body wanted him too badly. He'd driven her to this need with his kiss and his words. It would take but little more to push past her final defenses to make her his. And he yearned for her to be the one who would break his curse.

He took one step toward her when a sudden thought occurred to him. What if... what if she wasn't the one? Then the relic would loosen from her wrist and she'd give it to the duke and he'd never see her again. And he realized he didn't want that to happen. Not yet. For the first time in his memory, he cared more about a woman than gaining his own freedom. A confusing, frightening realization... but one he wanted to explore further.

So instead of reaching out to her, instead of striding

forward and wrapping her in his arms and kissing her senseless, he raised a mocking brow.

Millicent bristled, then shot him a look that should have dropped him dead where he stood. And he let her walk away.

Gareth pulled on braies, hose, and boots, and wondered if he should curse himself for a fool as he strapped on his sword belt. What if she *could* have broken the enchantment? He was not used to these conflicting emotions. The pattern of his life had been quite simple. He slept until the relic tightened around a woman's wrist. Then he seduced her. Then he slept again until the relic chose another.

He made no decisions. He followed the pattern Merlin had laid out for him. Why had it not bothered him until now?

When he returned to the cave, the melancholy that often cloaked him became overwhelming and he couldn't overcome it. Neither could he take his eyes off Millicent. He sat down on one of the low stools next to Nell and watched the girl crack open a shell of boiled food with a rock, then give it to the old woman. His gaze followed her as she replaced the flowers on the table with fresh ones, their glow brightening the gloom of their small cave. Every blink of her lash, each flutter of her hand, now seemed a small torture to him.

He could not control his lust for the shape-shifter. Yet now he hesitated to act on it, for he did not want this time with her to end so quickly. It made his desire multiply tenfold, and he couldn't help but devour her with his gaze.

And he longed to kiss her again. To see if he had not just imagined the feelings it had evoked in him.

Eventually she turned to him with a glare. "Stop it."

He shrugged helplessly. She watched the muscles of his bare chest rise and fall, and swallowed.

"I'm going to bathe," she told Nell over her shoulder, and then shifted to panther and practically flew into the forest.

Nell tsked at him from across the makeshift table. "Crikey, lad, what 'ave ye done to me Millie?"

Gareth dropped his head in his hands. "I did what I always do, my lady. I tried to seduce the relic-holder."

She snorted. "That bracelet still looks tight to me."

"It's complicated," he mumbled.

"How so?"

Gareth rose and walked to the opening of the cave, his back to the ladybird. He owed such a one an answer, and yet he'd already delved into so many confusing thoughts today that he could not make sense of them. Ah, well. Perhaps it might help if he voiced them aloud while he searched for some truths in those knowing violet eyes.

So he combed his hair back with his fingers, and stared at the glowing forest. "It has occurred to me that I have been dancing to Merlin's tune for centuries. The relic chooses a woman while I sleep in the stone, I seduce her… and she is never the one to break the spell. I suffer disappointment again and again, and I am tired, my lady. So very tired of it." His voice now sounded almost as low as the swaying fans above the cavern. "I do not even truly know how the enchantment will be broken. And now there's Millicent…"

Nell allowed his silence for a time. It seemed to Gareth that the fans overhead swished more quickly than they had but a moment ago. As if they echoed the confusion in his soul. Even the trees swayed their long branches a bit more briskly.

"So," she finally prompted, "wot's this about me Millicent?"

He turned, and Nell blanched at whatever look he wore on his face. "Don't you see? For the first time I am questioning my role. For the first time, I am afraid to take a woman to my bed, for then I may never see her again." He curled his fingers into fists. "By all that is holy. I think I don't care whether she can break the curse or not. And what madness is that?"

Nell studied him a long time, those violet eyes intent, as if she tried to see into his very soul. Then she grunted. "Eh, boy. Per'aps it ain't madness. Per'aps it's time ye took yer destiny into yer own hands."

"And how am I supposed to do that?"

"Try following yer own heart fer a change—" Nell's red eyebrows rose as she glanced behind Gareth.

He spun. Millicent stood in human form just below the cave entrance, her mouth open in shock. Gareth cursed her were-cat nature, which allowed her to move just as stealthily on two feet.

She stared at his face for a timeless moment, as if judging the truth of what she'd just overheard. Then her gaze snapped to Nell. "They're here," she blurted.

Gareth looked out upon the forest. The movement of the trees hadn't been his imagination. Their branches whipped back and forth now. The fanlike growth above waved so violently that it broke apart some of the delicate-looking foliage and tumbled it down to the ground.

"Where?" he demanded.

Millicent pointed in the direction she'd come. "I heard them shouting. And then the forest started to do this"—she waved at the frothing color—"and I couldn't hear them anymore. But they didn't sound too far behind me." She shifted to panther, and Nell did not hesitate to swing onto the beast's back, clutching black shiny fur in her bony fists.

Gareth tried to follow, but the beast quickly disappeared into the foliage, her pelt blending with the shadows beneath the glowing trees. He should have known she would leave him behind. The only person she cared for was her precious Nell, and without the speed of a shape-shifter, he would only slow them down. He should admire Millicent's intelligence. He would stay behind and engage her enemies, thereby giving the women more time to escape, and perhaps—

The burgundy leaves in front of him rustled, and a set of amber eyes peered out between them, a black paw reaching out and scratching impatiently at the sand. Nell's voice crackled from behind the bushes. "Wot the hell are ye waitin' fer?"

Gareth smiled, and followed the panther and ladybird into the multicolored forest.

Seven

MILLICENT SLOWED ONCE AGAIN, WAITING FOR THE knight to catch up. At least he moved quietly, barely rustling the leaves and vines. Her nostrils flared as she scented the air once again. The duke's men had found their cave, and had quickly turned tail in pursuit, making enough noise to tell her she would reach the bridge long before they did, even if her nose hadn't been able to track them by their stench. But her beast scented something else, a familiar smell she couldn't quite remember…

He said he didn't care whether she broke his curse or not.

Millicent snorted and ducked beneath a low-hanging branch, weaving through the fall of moss draped over it. Nell muttered something, and blew out her breath as if she'd received a face full of the stuff despite Millicent's maneuvering.

Millicent stole a glance behind her. Nell carried bits and pieces of the jungle with her, moss and twigs and leaves. But the knight moved like a dancer, barely touching the forest, as if he had become one with it.

Or as if it cleared a path for him. His golden-blond hair curled in the humidity, across his forehead, down his smooth shoulders. His naked chest gleamed with perspiration; his hose stuck to his legs, outlining the muscles in his thighs with every step he took. It hurt to look at him.

Those brilliant blue eyes caught her gaze for a moment, and Millicent quickly turned back around. Back by the pool he had made her want him, his face tender and his body aching for her. How had she allowed this to happen? Didn't her mother teach her that men used soft words and gentle touches at first, but soon grew bored and either left, or lusted for the fury of the beast?

No. She had to be stronger than her mother. For what would happen if she allowed herself to succumb to this man? Even if he seemed different than the men her mother had known, he would still disappear back into the relic, and would stay within until the relic chose another. She could not even consider that she would be the one to break his curse, for she did not have enough love in her heart to manage something so significant. She was a dark beast of the Underground, and he, a golden man of light from above. She would not allow what she had overheard to sway—

Millicent came to an abrupt halt, Nell sliding a bit forward on her back. The tree line ended, nothing but a smooth expanse of crystal rock stretching out in front of her, a jagged chasm separating the forest from the next tunnel. Millicent tensed, and Nell plastered herself even closer to her back, burying her face in the thick ruff on her neck. Her were-beast could cross the distance in a blink, long before the duke's men caught up with them, but the knight would be too slow. By the time he reached the chasm, he would be dodging bullets, and the only way across was a bridge of crystal, an odd tubular growth that had fallen across the gap and would be slick as ice.

The trees rustled, and Millicent turned and pinned Gareth with her gaze, hoping he could read the warning in the eyes of her beast. He understood, but did not appear concerned with the threat of peril. She kept forgetting his long years, and imagined he must have faced worse odds than this. He nodded, glanced up at the open ground before them, then quickly back into the forest, where the loud progress of the duke's men could now easily be heard.

"Don't wait for me," he commanded.

Millicent's beast gave him a short, low moan, then she turned and leaped out of the forest, her paws sliding across the smooth surface until she gained the trick of maneuvering across it, using her claws for some sort of purchase. She used all of the speed and strength of her were-self to reach the bridge, but stopped and turned before crossing it, for the sound of Gareth's strides had faded too quickly behind her.

He had managed to make it only a few yards past the tree line. The duke's men stood beneath a scarlet-leafed tree, the reflection of the glowing color making them look like so many devils. The men who held pistols leveled them at Gareth. The motley assortment of twisted creatures and scavenger shape-shifters accompanying them hesitated, waiting with eager anticipation for the volley of gunfire.

Millicent growled.

The sound of the discharge shook the walls of the cavern. The flare of light made her blink. The smoke from the weapons exploded in a cloud and drifted upward, and even from this distance, the sharp odor made her snort. Gareth stumbled, regained his footing, and continued to run toward her, until she could clearly see the grim determination on his face. And the blood running down his chest.

Their eyes met for a timeless moment—his so round and as blue as the sky—and then his steps slowed, and he looked down, clutching at the gaping hole in his chest. He looked back up at her, his handsome face twisted with some emotion... perhaps resignation, or sadness.

He fell face forward, his hair a tumble of gold around his head and shoulders.

Millicent screamed, a caterwaul of sound that rivaled the puny noise the pistols had made. She leaped toward Gareth, but Nell yanked on her fur, hard enough to bring tears to the beast's eyes.

"Don't be a fool, gel. Look to yer left."

Within a cluster of spindly fanlike trees stood a circle of predators, their sharp eyes taking in the duke's men, Millicent and Nell standing near the bridge, the fallen knight. That familiar smell she had scented earlier... now she could place it. The baronets from the ball still followed her. The Master of the Hall of Mages had not given up his own search for the relic.

Lions, tigers, wolves, jaguars—some as black as Millicent herself, leaped in her direction on stealthy paws, their silence more foreboding than if they had growled and screamed their bloodlust. But they had to cross the line of sight of the Duke of Ghoulston's men, and although the hyenas and jackals headed toward the knight's fallen body, the monsters eagerly pursued the baronet shape-shifters.

"Ach, let them fight it out, gel, while we make our escape."

Millicent could not leave Gareth to the scavengers. She must save him. Her muscles tensed to spring, and Nell yanked on her fur again.

"Don't be foolish. Do ye think in all his centuries, this is the first time the knight has died? He is immortal, gel, but we are not."

Nell. She must protect the old grandmother. But a few days ago, she had been willing to give up Gareth to the duke's twisted evil. Bloody hell, when had he become so important to her that she would risk Nell's life over his?

Nell was right. Gareth was immortal. He would end up back in the relic, in the same clothing, the same healthy body. She had witnessed his power of healing.

And yet, Millicent still hesitated.

The lion in the lead of the pack of baronets snarled, his black lips twisted in a smile as his prey stood there and waited for him to reach her.

Millicent closed her eyes as a shudder wracked through her from head to tail, then turned and carefully put a paw to the makeshift bridge. The crystal looked like nothing more than a felled tree lying across the chasm, round and smoother than bark. One slip, and they would fall to their deaths, with plenty of time to consider her clumsiness, given the unknown distance to the bottom.

Millicent snuck a glance behind her. The lion had lost his smile; his lips now curved in a grimace of fury as one of the duke's monsters caught up to him and reached out to snag his golden tail. She turned back around and concentrated on her footing. She had come this way only once before, when exploring the tunnels leading out of the city. The black wizards had excavated beyond the city, using their magic to dig deeper into the earth, to create odd caverns of mystery, like the glowing forest. Millicent had taken to exploring the Underground at a young age, an escape from her life of misery and poverty.

Her knowledge had proven useful over the years, but never more so than now.

Millicent blessed her cat's balance and agility, for they reached the other side of the chasm with nary a slip to frighten Nell. She studied the crystal bridge, gave it an exploratory shove with her furry shoulder. No, it had lain too long in its place, becoming a part of the crystal floor. She did not have a chance of moving it, of plunging it into the chasm, despite her formidable were-strength.

"They'll probably kill each other off, anyway," said Nell, guessing her intent. "Nobody will be left to follow us—and good riddance to 'em."

Millicent huffed and entered the third tunnel on her right. For her part, she did not think the duke's men stood a chance against the baronets, monsters or no. She knew the Master's spies would follow her, and she could think of only one place where they would not be welcome. Where she might stand a chance of evading them.

The underground city.

The denizens of the deep did not like intruders. Most of the wizards who controlled the city lived above, and used their underground homes only to practice the dark arts—and their even darker inclinations—in secret. They cloaked the entrances and shrouded the existence of the Underground in myth and mystery. They would not care about the purpose of a group of intruders. They would kill them before words could be spoken.

Millicent twitched her whiskers in a grim smile and entered the tunnel, her sight quickly adjusting to the darkness. This tunnel was the shortest path to the city, but she would have to be careful when they reached the larger cavern. The heat and treacherous footing would make it difficult, but she knew the way, and any shape-shifters who followed her did not. Nell rocked on her back, a small snap accompanying the movement, and suddenly a gentle light lit their way. The old woman had taken some branches from the glowing forest.

Millicent padded into the crystal cavern, taking shallow breaths of the hot air. The reflected glow of Nell's meager light bounced off the thousands of crystals and dazzled Millicent's sight for a moment. She slowly wound her way around blocks of crystal, crystal shaped into round spheres, crystal dripping from the walls like a frozen waterfall. Enormous beams of the stuff crisscrossed her path, stood like soaring columns in a palace, formed shapes of stars and pointy flowers.

Nell muttered something, but Millicent ignored her, concentrating on the path, for shards of the crystal layered the smooth walkway, waiting to cut the pads of her paws with one unwary step. She did not look up until they reached the second chamber, and this time she shared Nell's huff of wonder.

Some wizard must have been as enchanted with the crystal formations as Millicent, and had used his magic to shape it into soaring statues that defied the size of the chamber. The white crystal formed the layers of a lady's gown, the wings of a dragon, the curly beard of a gnome... even the crystal armor of a valiant knight. Millicent's beast gave a low mew of anguish, and she fought the urge to turn back around. Nell was right. Gareth was immortal, and would surely appear from the relic once again whole and unharmed. But she found it difficult to banish the doubt and worry, and the thought that he might actually be dead made her feel as if a heavy weight pressed on her chest, making it even more difficult to breathe.

As they walked farther, the fanciful shapes began to change to something darker, as if matching her mood. Color had been added to the stone. Red demons loomed over the path, their forked tongues dripping stalactites overhead. A green ogre battled a black Cyclops with claws of silver and fangs of livid yellow.

"Do ye think one wizard made all of these, Millie?"

Millicent grunted. If that was the case, it was a sad reflection on the wizard's growth to manhood, as the statues slowly became ugly and depicted ever more violent scenes.

They passed a deformed unicorn impaling a fang-toothed harpy.

Nell swayed. "It's hot, gel. It's hard to catch me breath."

Millicent turned and glanced at her friend, nodding her head to show she understood, trying to show encouragement in her eyes. Her beast lacked the vocal chords of human speech, which oddly enough, frustrated her only occasionally.

Far down the cavern, a stalactite fell, a ringing note accompanying the shattering of crystal. Millicent glanced upward at the thousands of sharp cones dangling right above their heads, and picked up her pace. Were some of the crystals so delicate that the vibrations of Nell's voice made them shatter?

A growl of fury echoed through the cavern from behind them.

Perhaps not only just Nell's voice had caused the crystals to shatter.

"They've found us, Millie."

Another ringing note sounded in the distance.

"I think... I think the ruckus they's making are causing the cones to fall..."

They reached the exit of the cave just as the growls grew into howls of triumph. The predators had found Millicent's scent. More crystals fell from the ceiling, this time closer to the trail.

"Idiots," snapped Nell.

Millicent curled her lips, opened her great maw, and screamed in defiance as loudly as she could. The answering howls made the very walls of the cave shiver, and started an avalanche of falling crystal. She spun and left the cave entrance, taking the smallest tunnel to her left, Nell chortling softly above her. Millicent soon smelled the rank odor of the city, and used her nose to guide her the rest of the way home.

The radiance of the fairylights illuminating the cavern did not soften the makeshift buildings, or hide the muddy streets and filthy rivulets of water that swept away the worst of the refuse. Millicent took the back alleys, which somehow managed to number more than the actual streets would account for. Most of the buildings were made of stone mined from the tunnels, a mossy slime growing rampant on the lower portion. Roofs were often added only to discourage theft, since they were not subject to the weather.

Millicent had spent several months aboveground learning to be a lady. It'd rained once while she had been walking the avenue, and she'd stood stock still in amazement and wonder, her tutor scolding her for standing like a dolt and getting her borrowed clothing soaking wet. But she had ignored the tirade, for, oh, it had been such a glorious sensation. Almost as marvelous as the feel of full sunshine on her cheeks.

When they reached the tavern, Nell slid off her back, and Millicent shifted to human. She saw two of the duke's men lurking in the shadows, and knew they would bring reinforcements soon. She would have to manage a fast explanation to Bran. Millicent shoved open the door to the pub, the smell of ale and unwashed bodies hitting her like a wet blanket.

Nell hurriedly spoke from behind her. "The duke's minions were watchin' the pub."

"I know." Millicent smoothed her petticoat and corset cover. She might have passed for a streetwalker above, but down here she looked positively elegant. "Those baronets—the lions and tigers and wolves that are following us—are spies for the Master of the Hall of Mages. And they want the relic just as much as the duke."

"Ahh. And they are from above. They wouldn't dare enter the city."

Millicent raised her voice as she stepped into the crowded room, skirting tables and wandering hands. "If they make it through the crystal cavern... Yes, I rather imagine they *will* follow us to the city, Nell. A predator doesn't give up his prey so easily."

The smart old woman answered with a cackle. "And ye're hopin' the Undergrounders will finish 'em off fer us?"

"Aye."

"Finish who off?" growled Bran, his finger in a tankard of honey, his long brown hair flowing over his broad shoulders onto the bar. He took in her borrowed clothing, Nell's rattier-than-ordinary appearance, with only a raised brow. A large man, with a tendency to think before speaking, and speak his words slowly when he did, he was one of the few predators in the Underground who managed to run a profitable pub.

Millicent stepped up to the bar. "I'm in a bit of trouble, Bran."

"When aren't ye?"

"That's unfair," piped up Nell, her red head barely managing to clear the stained counter. "She's a good gel, is our Millie."

Bran ignored her and kept his gaze fixed on

Millicent. "Ye took off with nary a word. I've had thirteen fights I've had to break up meself since ye been gone. Annoying, that."

Millicent nodded. She didn't have time to argue. "The Duke of Ghoulston took Nell, and I had to… acquire something to get her back. And now I… I can't get rid of it, and I've got half the world chasing after me. From below and… above."

Bran slowly licked a sugary finger. "Half the world, eh? That's a fair amount of enemies fer a gel who usually minds her own business."

Millicent breathed a sigh of relief. He didn't appear too angry. He seemed to understand that none of this was her fault.

"Abovegrounders, ye say? And I suppose ye led 'em right here?"

She grimaced and shrugged.

"Well now, at least it's a fight I won't be minding havin'. Be good to have some competition fer a change. I suppose it's best if ye two take the back way out."

Before Millicent could utter her thanks, the door to the pub flew open. She felt surprised to see the baronets in the doorway, for she had counted on the duke's minions to make it here first. At least the predators looked decidedly worse for their adventures, their fur scraggly with blood and more than a few sporting splinters of crystal.

Bran raised his bushy brows as he stared at the intruders. "Lions and tigers! Crikey, ye're full of surprises, gel." And before his patrons could notice the threat at the door, he turned to a narrow-faced man and said, "Hey, Joseph. Thomas Weezel called yer mother a whore."

Millicent grinned. Thomas sat slumped over the back of a chair, so deep in his cups she doubted he felt the fist that knocked him out of it. But he managed to shift quickly enough, his face elongating into a weasel, his retaliating strike so fast that Joseph barely managed his shift to jackal before Thomas struck. Both shape-shifters crashed into the table next to them, and the chaps sitting there erupted from their chairs, indiscriminately swinging their fists.

"Too easy," muttered Bran as he launched his bulk over the bar into what now looked like the usual Saturday evening brawl. The baronets pushed their way into the midst.

"Idiots," muttered Nell for the second time that day.

"Just out of their element," replied Millicent. "Let's go."

As they made their way out the back door, she watched Bran direct the fight at the abovegrounders like a man orchestrating a symphony. The small tavern soon became a seething mass of fur, teeth, and fang. Nell cackled a laugh, took a step out the back door, and a creature of green slime and knobby limbs caught her up in its vine-like arms.

Millicent glanced back. A lion swatted a weasel aside, his golden eyes intent on her and Nell. The beast took a step toward her, hampered again by the weasel, who had wrapped his sharp little teeth around the lion's leg. She turned and faced the duke's men, far less appealing to the eyes, but if she had to choose between two evils, she preferred to choose the one she knew.

"Don't hurt her," she ground out between clenched teeth. It frustrated her to give up so quickly. But Nell already looked blue in the face from the monster's tight grip. "I'll come along without a fight."

They dragged her and Nell back to the duke's lair. Oddly enough, Ghoulston barely gave them a glance as he ordered Selena to take them back to the burgundy prison. The duke appeared preoccupied, which bothered Millicent more than if he had been furious by their attempted escape. He also allowed Nell to stay with her, and as Millicent fell asleep on the perfumed bed, she wondered if that might portend something even worse for her dear friend. And to her chagrin, found herself worrying about Gareth, as well.

He came to her at night, while sleep still shadowed her thoughts. Millicent could hear Nell's snoring from the other room, even through the closed door. The perpetual twilight that lit the Underground filtered through the open window of the duke's castle, outlining Gareth's golden hair with a halo of half-light. He wore the clothing she'd first seen him in, his sword at his side, his body healthy and whole.

"You are alive," she breathed, relief making her voice tremble.

He sat on the bed, rustling the burgundy-silk covers. He smelled of fresh linen and moonlit nights. "Did you doubt the strength of the curse?"

"No."

He lowered his face to hers, waves of gold strands

falling down his forehead, across his cheeks. "Alas. Could it be possible that you worried for me?"

"Yes—no. Nell said you would be fine."

"The ladybird is more than she appears, I think."

She could feel his breath on her lips, the warmth of his body through the thin silk sheet.

Millicent trembled.

He frowned, shadows playing across his straight nose, his full lips, the angles of his cheeks. "I would never harm you."

"I—I'm not afraid of you."

"Then you will not fear if I do this." And he pressed his mouth against hers, gently, hesitantly, as if he touched some delicate object that would shatter with the slightest pressure. Millicent's eyes drifted shut as all of her senses focused on that caress. On the warmth of his mouth and the sweet slide of his tongue across her lips. She knew the moment she saw him standing nude in the pond that she wanted him, no matter what arguments her mind managed to conjure. Because of her mother's habits, Millicent had seen many a naked man, and not a one had caused such a response within her body.

Gareth groaned and pressed closer to her. She could feel his muscles tremble as he fought to keep his touch gentle.

Millicent buried her fingers in his hair and showed him she would not break. Perhaps… perhaps the moment she had truly known she would make love to him was when she had thought he'd died. When she had felt such an overwhelming grief that she would have blindly rushed forward to save him if it hadn't been for Nell reminding her that he was immortal.

Or was he?

Millicent easily pulled his face away from hers, heard him catch a breath at the reminder of her were-strength. "I cannot break your curse. I do not have enough love in my heart to do such a powerful thing."

"I do not care."

"So you said. But what if... what if it were possible? Will time catch up with you and turn you to dust?" Her voice cracked, betraying her emotions, her fear of making the wrong choice.

His eyes looked like twin pools of midnight, the light blue barely discernible. "I do not care."

"I will lose you either way."

"Are you sure you want to keep me?"

"I—" Millicent frowned. She did not know what she wanted beyond this moment.

He slid his finger across her cheek. "Merlin's spell be damned. I will make love to you for no other reason than because I want to... because I have to... because I need to make you a part of me, if only for one night."

And Millicent's heart, who had lain strangely quiet within her, sensed her weakness and suddenly rose up, demanding this man for her mate. She could not stop the low growl that sounded in the back of her throat. Could not help but pull his face to hers once again, kissing him with a fierceness she feared would startle him.

But Gareth only moaned, met her fierceness with his own, pushing her back against the bedding, his tongue tasting the inside of her mouth, his hands roaming over the silk, exploring, kneading, demanding.

Millicent did not know how he managed to keep her senses overwhelmed and remove his clothing at the same time, but within moments she felt his naked body slide next to hers, his skin warm and smoother than the silk. He felt perfect, his muscles molding against hers, as if they somehow fit like a puzzle into one form. And yet... a flutter of anxiety twisted through her, and she fought the urge to push him away. She wanted him, yes, but feared him all at the same time.

Her beast growled, chiding her for being a coward. But the animal lacked the vulnerabilities of a human heart, acting on instinct and need alone. Her beast had always been a part of her, even in human form, and she had used that side of her nature to save her life and sanity more than once. But she had always controlled the inclinations of the were-cat.

Until now.

Millicent twisted her body on top of Gareth's, almost tumbling both of them off the bed. The silk sheet flowed off her as if made of water, revealing her nude body to the twilight.

The knight sucked in a breath, staring up at her as if he'd never seen a naked woman before. *Ha.* Surely he had seen hundreds, perhaps thousands. Millicent growled, confused that the thought made her furious. She shook her head, black strands of hair flying about her face, across her shoulders. Nothing mattered but this moment. She would not think beyond that.

"You are beautiful," he murmured, gliding his fingers up her hips, to her waist. "Did you know your eyes glow like your cat's?"

Millicent blinked. She knew her human eyesight held some of her beast's strength, but no one had ever mentioned that they glowed. The thought made her smile.

Gareth gripped her waist, as if he suddenly feared she would flee. Or as if he sought to hold on to her forever. "I want you, Millicent Pantere. Let me show you how much."

She would not allow him control. This was her decision, her choice... not his. She would never fall prey to the thought that he had used her. "No."

And she clasped his hands, brought them up over his head, beside his golden hair. Sadness glittered in his eyes for a moment. But only a moment. For Millicent knew what went where and how—she had not lived with her mother without learning such things. She adjusted her hips, felt the hard length of him slide between her legs, and leaned forward, catching the tip, encasing him with her warmth, impaling herself quickly, with a half growl from her beast.

He murmured her name.

Millicent froze for a moment. It hurt. She had forgotten it was supposed to hurt the first time. But her beast did not care. It urged her to move, to find a rhythm. And before she knew it, the pain had faded to be replaced with... ecstasy. Shivers of pleasure that flowed from her inner core to the very tips of her fingers. Gareth moved beneath her, somehow finding new areas of pleasure inside her.

She let go of his arms to sit up, to arch her back. Yes, it drove him deeper inside her, to a new wealth of feeling. He filled her completely, became a part of her. She had not expected that. Had not expected warmth to flow from him to her heart. Her eyes burned, and it took her a moment to realize that tears caused the sensation.

Tears of happiness.

With his hands free, Gareth sought to touch her everywhere. His callused fingertips felt like hot brands of fire, but like a flame they only licked her body, gently, softly. He created new sensations to add to the heady mix. She arched her breasts into his hands, tingles of heat spreading outward from his touch. He made her throb even harder, until she leaned forward again and tried to press her nub against his skin, hoping to slake that need along with the one already raging inside her womb.

He knew what she needed. Of course he knew. His hand delved between them, those fingers of fire finding the exact place where she needed to be caressed. Millicent fought a scream, her were-beast settling for a gasping mew as her rhythm atop him turned into a mindless frenzy. She did not know what she wanted; she only knew it was just beyond her grasp, just over the yawning precipice before her...

And she fell.

Spinning and twisting, pleasure wracking through her entire being. An overwhelming explosion of sensations that Millicent had never experienced before, had not even known existed. She heard Gareth cry out, felt his body tense and release in time with hers. The beast inside her growled with satisfaction, as if it had instinctively known exactly what would happen.

But she had not known it would be this... rare and wonderful thing.

She collapsed on top of him. Spent. Elated. Confused. And Gareth wrapped his arms around her, easily accommodating her weight, just as he had managed her were-strength.

Such a remarkable man.

Such a pity she would never see him again after tonight.

Eight

GARETH AWOKE A FEW HOURS LATER, A SMILE CURLING his mouth as he glanced down at Millicent's tousled head, her body wrapped around his as if she would never let him go. She had been more magnificent than he had ever dreamed, more beautiful and fierce than he could have ever hoped for. By all that was holy, he thought... he thought he might be falling in love with her. He loved her rough exterior that hid a vulnerable heart, and her devotion to Nell despite her need to protect herself. He even loved her other half. The beast that skulked inside her, acting on instinct, offering a dangerous side to her that no other woman could match.

He could not fathom why this woman seemed so different than all of the others he'd met over the centuries. Gareth only knew he had never felt this way before.

His heart skipped a beat.

Could it be possible?

Was this what Merlin had foretold?

His feelings for Millicent felt much different than

what he had thought he'd once felt for Vivian. The decades trapped inside the relic had given him some wisdom, at least. Merlin's lover had been forbidden fruit, a conquest his youthful arrogance had felt compelled to pursue. He had fooled himself into thinking he was in love with Vivian, had twisted lust into love until he was blinded to the truth.

But Merlin had known. And had cursed Gareth to find his true love, a thing more rare than one of Merlin's relics.

Millicent sighed and rolled over. He allowed her to unwrap herself from around him, and sat up, blinking in the dim light. He had spoken the truth to her. He had not thought of the curse when he'd asked to make love to her. But he could not help thinking of it now… could not help hoping…

Would these feelings for her break the spell? He knew his heart to be true, for this tenderness that swelled within him could not be denied or mistaken. Surely…

He rose, lit a candle, the light seemingly brilliant for a moment, the burgundy walls and furnishings and bed coverings making the very air appear tinged with red. Millicent had thrown out one arm, the other curled next to her cheek, the bed covering twisted about her, revealing tantalizing glimpses of bare skin. Gareth ignored the impulse to reach out and touch her, and instead forced his attention on looking for the band of silver about her wrist.

He could not see it.

But he did not know what might happen to the relic when the curse was broken. Would it stay firmly on her wrist, proof that Millicent would be his one true love? Or would it dissolve into a thousand bits?

Gareth strode around the bed, his eyes searching, his breath shallow and erratic. He pulled back a corner of the silk sheet, exposing Millicent's bare arm, the relic lying a few inches away from her bent elbow. The gleam of milky opalescence winked at him, the moonstone gem mocking all of his hopes. The bracelet had loosened from her wrist. He could still feel his soul bound to it. His feelings for Millicent had not broken the spell.

Fury welled up inside of him. He had been fooling himself. Whatever feelings he thought he had for Millicent weren't strong enough. He thought he might have been falling in love with her... but after all these centuries, did he even know what true love was? Aah, the relic twisted his thoughts, made him doubt himself.

And it still bound him; he could almost hear it now, calling to him. Wanting to choose another woman, to tighten the metal about her wrist and shackle her to him. But Gareth wanted to explore these feelings he had for Millicent. He did not want to leave her yet.

His anger faded as quickly as it had come, settling within him to be replaced by grief. He should not have hoped. It always failed him. Perhaps it had all been a lie. The spell would never be broken. He would be trapped inside the relic forever, doomed to watch Millicent grow old and die, and forced to live on without her.

Gareth collapsed on the bed, holding his head within his hands, fighting the despair. He could not give up. He must believe that Merlin would not be this cruel. Perhaps… perhaps only a woman's love would break the curse. Perhaps *she* must love him. His shoulders slumped. Verily, that would be harder than anything he had ever thought possible. For Millicent feared love too much to fully embrace it.

"I told you I wasn't the one."

He glanced up. She looked lovely, with her midnight hair spilling about her creamy shoulders, her amber eyes glowing like beacons of golden-etched flame.

His heart lifted at the sight of her, and he straightened. "I thought my love for you would be enough."

Her eyes widened. "Love? You think you're in love with me?"

Gareth frowned. "I thought so… I think so. The relic has me all confused. But… I do know that I don't want to leave you. That I'd like to explore these feelings I have for you."

"And give up your quest for freedom?"

Gareth hesitated to tell her about his theory that perhaps it would take her love to free him. Millicent already felt unequal to the task. "I am tired unto death of dancing attendance on Merlin's curse. And I think your firebird gave me good advice."

"Nell? What did she say?"

"That I should follow my own heart. Make my own path."

She picked up the bracelet, weighing it in her hand. "So what do you want me to do with this?"

Gareth stretched toward her, laid his head in her lap. She started, but a throaty purr sounded in the back of her throat. "What do *you* wish, my lady?"

He would not force himself on Millicent. The relic had forced him on so many women, that he could not stomach the thought of doing the same. He felt her eyes on the length of his body, and he instantly hardened, bringing a flush to those pale cheeks.

She hid behind a scowl. "Well, I certainly will not turn the relic over to Selena. Despite her sudden overwhelming devotion to you, she'll still go along with whatever evil plans the duke manages to come up with."

Gareth had a lovely view of the underside of her breasts. "Then shall you turn it over to another? Whom will you choose to bed me next?"

Her purr turned into a low growl. "I will not... I cannot... What have I gotten myself into?"

He smiled. He had so hoped she would object to relinquishing him to another, but with Millicent, he could never be sure. "Perhaps you might keep it."

She gripped the relic in one strong hand, but reached down with the other to gently smooth the hair away from his face, to run her fingers through the tangle. His eyes half-closed from the pleasure of her touch.

"How is that possible?" she breathed. "Lady Chatterly said it will remain on a woman's wrist for only one night, and then choose another after... you know."

Gareth found her hesitancy to say the words rather charming. Such contradictions, his Millicent. He sat up, took the bracelet from her. "Does it matter whether it fits your wrist or not? Why should the enchantment always choose whom I should be with?" He shook his head. "Nay, it is time for me to choose. And I choose for you to keep it if… if you will have it."

She looked uncertain, and hesitated to do his bidding, the circle of silver held poised over her hand. "If I continue to wear it, you will not be able to find the woman who can release you. I cannot condemn you to your prison, even if the thought of another woman touching you makes me want to tear her apart with my claws."

Gareth smiled at the possessiveness in her voice, the weight of eternal sadness he always seemed to carry inside of him suddenly easing its grip. "This is my choice, my lady. And I choose to stay with you."

She sat silent for a time, and finally murmured, "I will keep it on just until we are away from this evil place. Then I will let you go."

"Will you?" Gareth reached up, stroked the underside of her breast, and felt her shiver.

"I have to. You deserve to find your true love."

He did not argue with her. He had lived too long, had too much experience with women, to succumb to the temptation. She loved him a little, or at least thought she did. If he had learned one true thing about women, it was that they would not take someone to their bed unless they thought they were in love.

She would realize soon enough that she would never let him go.

He would not allow it.

She slipped the bracelet over her wrist, and the band of silver tightened. He felt her recoil, as hesitant at being trapped as he. "What just happened?"

Gareth stared at the bracelet. "I… I am not sure.

I did not know it would tighten about your wrist...
I have never asked a woman to keep it before." His
heart soared. Could it mean he had a chance? That
Millicent had the *potential* to be his true love? Damn
Merlin and his enigmatic curse!

"It cannot possibly mean—"

"I do not know what it means, my lady. I seem to
always have more questions than answers."

"Well... just don't get your hopes up. I am not
some heroine from a fairy tale, whose sweet nature
and kind heart can break a curse. I am sure it will fall
off once we make love again."

Gareth's heart skipped a beat. Aah, she was already
thinking about making love to him again. He leaned
forward and buried his face in her sweet-smelling hair.
"We should not wait a moment longer to find out—"

"Shh. Did you hear—?"

Her gaze snapped towards the door, and Gareth
turned toward it, but he did not have her animal-
senses, and could hear nothing but silence. Silence?
Nell had been snoring but a moment ago, the sound
loud enough to penetrate the thick plank of the
bedroom door.

Millicent shifted so quickly that Gareth flipped
over at the sudden increase of mass. He expected
her panther to leap for the door, to attack whatever
intruder her keener senses had detected. But instead,
she opened her massive jaw and went for his throat.
Thank the Lord for centuries of experience, for his
body reacted without thinking, twisting to avoid her
attack, then leaping for his sword that he'd left lying
next to the bed.

When he rose to his feet, he stared at the weapon in his hand. At the bristling fury of the black panther now facing him amid the rumpled silk sheets. He could never harm Millicent—or her beast. His hand loosened on his sword, and he was about to drop it when the door burst open.

Selena strode into the room, the long sleeves of her black gown flapping behind her like the wings of her were-bat. Her black eyes went from his sword to Millicent's furry hide, and she smiled, exposing her dagger-sharp teeth. "So, you have still been unsuccessful in seducing her, Sir Knight? I am sorely disappointed in you."

She tossed a bundle of clothing at the foot of the bed, ignoring Millicent's growls. "Put these on, she-cat. His Grace wants you to join him, and he will not tolerate anything less than a lady at his table."

Gareth breathed a sigh, giving Millicent a long look of admiration. She had orchestrated this little tableau so Selena would draw the proper conclusion. The duke would still think the bracelet could not be removed. But didn't the little minx realize he could have hurt her? His reflexes had been honed—

Millicent shifted to human, pulling the sheet up over her breasts, making the other woman smirk. "What does he want?"

Selena shrugged her shoulders, taffeta rustling with the movement. "How should I know? And I wouldn't tell you if I did."

Millicent glanced from the other woman to Gareth, her forehead creased with puzzlement. "My, my, how you have changed, vamp. What happened to your devoted love for Sir Gareth? You are as fickle as the wind."

Selena frowned for a moment, turning to stare at him. He realized the glazed look of love in her eyes had faded, and she seemed as bewildered by her change of heart as Gareth had been when she'd professed her love for him.

"I still want him," snapped the were-bat, a bit sullenly. "I can remember how it felt, but not... never you mind. Just hurry up and get dressed, or I'll send in the guard to carry you down wearing what you've got on." She gave Millicent one last malicious grin before she spun and left the room.

Gareth pulled on his clothes while Millicent dug through the garments the other woman had left. He dressed as quickly as he managed to disrobe, so he took up the laces of a linen corset and began to tighten them for her.

"What do you make of it?" he murmured.

She let out a breath as he tugged. "I swear she was madly in love with you a few days ago. She still wants you, of course, but how could her feelings have changed so dramatically?"

"I do not know. I've had many women fall in love with me, but not so mercurially as all that."

Millicent put on the ruffled petticoats, and Gareth picked up the gown: a golden velvet trimmed with black lace. He buttoned up the back, and when she turned around, he decided the duke had exquisite taste. The gold fabric brought out the color in her eyes, and the black trim matched her jet hair. She slipped into gold brocade slippers while he searched a mahogany vanity laden with enough bottles of perfume for a thousand overnight guests.

"The duke treats his prisoners quite well."

"I shudder to think whom he has kept in these rooms—and why. What are you doing?"

Gareth ran his fingers through her hair, separating the strands. "I'm going to fix your hair. Now hold still." He didn't need to repeat the command as he started brushing, for her shoulders relaxed and she started to purr.

"I imagine you have quite a bit of experience at this."

She sounded annoyed.

Gareth smiled. "There are many ways to seduce a woman, my lady."

"Hmph."

"However"—he expertly twisted her hair up into a knot, securing it with the hairpins he'd found next to the brush—"you are the first woman I ever seduced by teaching her how to fight."

"Is that supposed to make me feel special?"

He stuck one final pin in the coiffure to secure it and spun her around. "No, this is." And Gareth kissed her breath away, until he felt her melt in his arms, until the impulse to drag her back to the bed and ravish her actually made him ache. Verily, he had never wanted a woman as much as he wanted Millicent.

Nell's strident voice penetrated through the door, and Millicent stiffened, pushed him away. "You make me forget the rest of the world exists. I find it extremely annoying, Sir Gareth." And she spun her golden skirts and left the room.

Gareth raked his hand through his hair and followed.

The ladybird sat on a velvet couch, her brilliant hair a vibrant clash against the burgundy upholstery. Selena stood over her, the black sleeves of her gown seeming as if they would surround the smaller woman and swoop her up at any moment, bringing the thin, wrinkled neck up to those pointed teeth to be feasted upon. Millicent made a low sound in her throat, but this time Gareth moved faster, brushing the were-vamp aside.

He went down to his knee. "Are you well, my lady?"

Nell honored him with a gap-toothed smile. "I ain't got enough blood in these old veins to slake *her* thirst. She don't scare me none."

The two guards who accompanied Selena had moved forward, but she waved them back. "I wouldn't be too sure of that, old woman. I imagine the blood of a firebird would be hot enough to make it worth the effort."

Millicent's were-form shadowed her for a moment, elongated teeth and sharp claws. "It would be the last thing you ever did, bloodsucker."

Those glossy black eyes narrowed. "If my master did not forbid it, I would enjoy pitting my beast against yours, alley cat. It is my fondest desire to watch the life fade from your yellow eyes as I slowly suck you dry."

"Aw, gawd, stow it," snapped Nell, as if chastening squabbling children, rather than two dread beasts. "I'm hungry."

Gareth smiled and held out his arm, and the old woman took it, rising to her feet with a grunt and a few groans. She turned to Selena. "Didn't ye say we was invited to dinner?"

"Not you. Just the two of them."

Millicent shook her head, tendrils of black falling from her coiffure. "I don't go anywhere without Nell. I don't trust that she'll be here when I return."

Selena shrugged. "Suit yourself. If you want to annoy His Grace, that's fine with me. Do it often enough, and perhaps he'll give me leave to drain you."

Before they could start a renewed bout of threats, Gareth stepped forward and held out his other arm to Millicent, but before she could react, Selena insinuated herself beneath it. "Don't look so surprised, Sir Knight. I know you would never hurt me... unless I wanted it that way, of course. Millicent may not know what she's missing, but I do."

And the vamp had the temerity to bat her eyelashes at him.

So they walked through the twisted passageways of the back of the castle, until they entered the more sculpted ones of the front, Nell and Selena at his side, Millicent slinking behind them. The guards kept their eyes on her. Gareth hid a grin, glad that they underestimated him. His code of chivalry did not extend to armed men. And Selena made him wish it did not extend to deadly women.

They entered a dining room so lavishly appointed it looked ridiculous. Macabre paintings of ogres feasting on human remains decorated the walls, ornate gilt frames encasing each portrait. Gold etched the walls and ceiling trim, which had been so heavily applied one could barely see the black silk behind it. An enormous fireplace skulked at the end of the room, the mantel and sides sculpted as an open mouth, with twin mirrors mimicking eyes above it. Heavy crystal and candelabra ornamented the table, winking bloody red in the firelight, completely overshadowing the warm light of the candles.

A feast had already been laid out on the black lace linen. An entire pig, with some sort of vegetable in its mouth carved to look like a heart. A steaming peacock with feathers still displayed in an open fan around it. A haunch of beef dripping red juices, bowls of grapes and apples and pears, towers of pasties and sweetmeats, decanters of sparkling wine and brown ale.

Despite the vulgar display, the aroma made Gareth's mouth water.

Nell's stomach growled.

"You have joined me at last!" The duke sat at the head of the table, his white gloves cast aside near his plate, his fingers and fleshy lips greasy from the leg of some fowl. He waved the meaty bone at Millicent. "Sit down next to me, my dear. I'm anxious to hear of your adventures over the last few days. Yes, Sir Gareth, please seat yourself at her side. No, dear Nell, sit here on my right, next to Selena. There, now. We are all gathered quite cozily, are we not?" And he dipped his meat into a silver bowl of gravy and continued his gluttony.

Gareth shared a glance with Millicent, shrugged, and began to help himself to the platters of food. He supposed the duke would reveal his purpose for this meeting in due time, and he knew Millicent had to be as hungry as Nell. He indulged for her sake, for she seemed as determined to ignore the food as Selena did.

The were-vamp condescended to sip at her wine

when Millicent started to eat, and so for a time, nothing could be heard but the crackle of the fire, the duke's rather loud eating habits, and the clatter of silver and crystal.

Ghoulston finally sat back and belched. He eyed Millicent's plate. "Was the meat bloody enough for you, my dear?"

Millicent raised a raven brow at him.

"And the wine? How did you enjoy the vintage? It's made from a special blend of grapes magically enhanced by a group of nuns who believe their God gave them the power to make it taste like a bit of heaven."

She set down her silver fork. "What do you want?"

His dark eyes sparkled merrily, and Gareth fought down a trickle of sadness. Evil men, evil doings. He had seen too much of it.

"Why, my dear, I want nothing more than for you to sleep with the good knight and give me my relic. Have you managed to spread your legs for him?"

Millicent flushed, and Gareth gritted his teeth, his hand inching toward his sword. It bothered him that the guards had not taken it from him. Several of the men stood at both entrances of the room, and they did not even flicker a lash at him. Did they truly underestimate him, or did they think his sword such a paltry threat to the duke's magic?

What sort of instructions had the duke given his minions for this eve?

Gareth placed both his hands back on the table. It would be better for Millicent if she just gave the relic to the duke. Then she and Nell would be free…

Millicent turned her head—ostensibly to take a sip of

her wine, but threw Gareth a warning look before turning back to the duke. "If I thought it might make a difference, it might be worth giving up my virginity to give you the relic. But I rather doubt it will. Come, Your Grace, admit the true reason for this meeting. I suspect something rather significant has occurred during our absence."

"Perceptive girl," said the duke, leaning back in his chair. A footman hurried forward with a finger bowl and towel, and Gareth studied the servant's face. As with most of the humans in the duke's employ, the man did not look quite right, somehow. The nose appeared broken, or disjointed, the eyes slightly skewed, the mouth twisted at an unnatural angle.

The Duke of Ghoulston experimented with magic in dangerous ways.

"I have a favor to ask of Sir Knight."

Gareth turned his attention back to the duke and tried to look mildly interested.

Millicent frowned. "Gareth? But he has already told you he has no magic. And little control over the relic."

Gareth narrowed his eyes at the duke. "*I* find it puzzling as to why you think I might do you a favor... other than cutting your throat, that is."

Nell hooted, sloshing the wine in her cup. Selena gave the firebird a disdainful look.

The congenial smile that the Duke of Ghoulston had adopted all evening suddenly faded. "I rather thought you wouldn't. Not until I hold the relic and exercise some power over you."

Gareth shrugged. The man had it all wrong. Possession of the relic would not change anything. For all of his arrogance about his scientific studies, the man appeared to know little about powerful magic. "Then why mention it?"

"Because I believe you will be begging to grant me this favor once you know…"

The absurd man let his words trail off into silence. Selena leaned forward in her chair, her mahogany hair gleaming in the lamplight, her delicate features taut with anticipation. Nell's hand shook, and she sloshed more wine onto the tablecloth, a red glow appearing in the depths of her violet eyes. Gareth could feel Millicent tense, could sense her were-cat coiled like a spring within her, ready to erupt.

The guards at the door blinked, glancing around the room at the sudden change in the atmosphere.

Gareth sighed. "All right. I'll bite. Once I know what?"

But the duke turned his attention away from him and directed it at Millicent. "Did you enjoy the wine, my dear? You never did say."

Millicent stared at the goblet in her hand, and carefully set it back on the table. "What's in it?"

"Ah, did I not just mention how perceptive you are?" He laughed, his jowls bouncing. "The nuns say it will bring you closer to heaven—if you're deserving, that is. Somehow, I doubt you will wind up in the clouds, my dear. But do not worry. I hear hell is much more interesting, anyway."

A cold feeling rose in Gareth's chest, and it took him a moment to recognize it. He had learned to control fear long ago. But the threat was to Millicent, whom he loved more than freedom, more than life itself. "If she dies, so do you."

The duke fingered his cravat. "Perhaps. It is a risk I am willing to take, for the hour of your departure draws near, Sir Knight. Or have you not noticed the time?"

All eyes turned to the ornate clock on the mantel, but Gareth could not tell the position of the hands from this distance.

"With the antidote, Millicent will experience the joy of heaven, but without it, she will suffer a truly agonizing death. In a few minutes you will fade back into the relic, while Millicent's muscles twist and tighten until she screams for mercy. By the time you appear again, it will be over. Does your consciousness stay aware while you are trapped in the relic, Sir Gareth? How many hours will you spend thinking of her pain? Thinking of her slow death?"

Selena grinned. "Oh, how delicious."

"I thought you might appreciate it, my dear."

Gareth felt the blood drain from his face, and for a moment, he could not breathe.

Millicent shook her head. "I'm afraid you have miscalculated, Your Grace."

"I think not. If you die, I get the relic off your wrist. If you don't, it will be because Sir Gareth granted my favor."

She pushed her chair away from the table, arranged the folds of her skirt. "You are trying to blackmail Sir Gareth by using me as leverage, in the same way you used Nell to manipulate me. But I am afraid that in order for your plan to work, the knight must care for me. And he does not. He will no more grant your boon than I will bed him, and when he emerges from the relic once again, he will kill you. Your magic is no match for the power of a relic."

The duke no longer looked so self-assured. He now tore at his cravat. He could not be sure if Millicent was bluffing or not.

Gareth admired her tenacity, but the stakes were too high. He stood, ignoring her hand on his arm, her hiss of warning. There was no way on God's good earth he would allow Millicent to die. "What is this favor you would ask?"

The heavy man looked up at him with something akin to relief. "It is nothing as bad as all that. I only need..." He glanced at Selena. "A cup of your blood."

Gareth's brow rose in surprise. "An odd request, sir. Why not just have your men hold me down and take it from me?"

"Let's just say, I feared it might get tainted. And I need it pure."

"Indeed? And why—"

Millicent lurched forward, and Gareth bent down and caught her in his arms. A light sheen of sweat covered her brow, and a low moan escaped from her clenched teeth. "Don't give him what he wants," she gasped. "No good will come of it."

"Do you truly think I would allow you to die?"

She groaned, hunching so far over that he guided her to the floor, kneeling next to her puddle of golden skirts, his hands on her shoulders the only thing holding her upright.

"It's better than what the duke has planned, I'm sure." Millicent sucked in a breath. "Don't let him manipulate you, Gar—" The rest of her words turned into a scream as her body twisted, flinging her backward against the marble floor, only Gareth's hands cushioning her head from the stone.

"Nell!"

But the old woman already knelt at his side, her red hair appearing to ripple like fire. He nodded, and she cradled Millicent's head to her thin chest, stroking the rest of the twists out of the coiffure Gareth had so artfully arranged, while Millicent continued to scream. And scream.

The duke raised his voice. "It seems I did not misjudge the knight's honor, were-cat. Of course he must rescue a damsel in distress, whether he cares for her or not. Perhaps you cannot understand it, but a gentleman such as myself recognizes the sentiment... although I've never had much call for it myself."

Gareth rose to his feet.

Selena stood at the duke's side, watching Millicent's contortions with a grin of satisfaction. "I don't think she can hear you, Your Grace."

Rage swelled within Gareth, and he did not know where he found the strength to pull his sword without running both of them through. But instead, he swept the blade across his wrist and held out his bloody arm.

Selena licked her lips and darted forward. The duke reached out and grabbed her skirts, hauling her backward.

"Damn were-bats can never control their instincts. Guards, hold her." He rose, shoving the girl at his men. "I will have to do this myself." He picked up a golden goblet off the table and held it out, staring at the blood dripping from Gareth's wrist as if it were gold.

Gareth dropped his arm. "Give my lady the anti-dote first."

The Duke of Ghoulston did not argue. He strode to the sideboard and opened a small drawer, held forth a vial of black liquid. Gareth snatched it and brought it over to Millicent, his blood staining the golden velvet of her gown while he forced it past her taut lips. She swallowed once, twice, and then her body stilled.

He rose and faced the other man. He had no choice but to trust him, and it rankled. "She will recover?"

The duke nodded. "Hurry up. If I have calculated the sunrise aboveground correctly, we have only a few minutes left."

Gareth held his arm over the goblet and watched it fill with his blood. Then he felt the tug at his soul, the call to return to the relic. His sight began to fade as he turned and glanced back at Millicent. She lay so very still now, her chest hardly rising and falling. If the duke had lied... if she died while he was trapped within the relic...

He could not leave her like this. He would not! The relic could not take him...

Nine

MILLICENT WOKE IN THE RED BEDROOM ONCE AGAIN, every muscle in her body aching. She opened her eyes. Bloody hell. They ached too. She sat up with a groan, glanced around the room, the fuzzy memory of her dinner with the duke slowly coming back to her. Someone had stripped off her golden gown, and it sat on a velvet wing chair, crimson blood still staining the skirts.

Gareth. Nell.

She crawled out of the bed, stood on shaky legs, and forced them to take her across the room. By the time she opened the door and walked into the parlor, her muscles had loosened enough to almost make her drop with relief at the sight that awaited her.

Gareth lounged on a low armless sofa, his wavy blond hair falling across his sculpted cheekbones, his sexy mouth curled in a smile as he played some sort of card game with Nell. The old woman had a pile of buttons in front of her, apparently gathered from several of the cushions in the room, and cackled as she hauled another pile of them toward her.

"Ye've got no luck with the cards," chided Nell with barely stifled glee. "Let's have another round, shall we?"

But Gareth turned his head, his brilliant blue eyes suddenly fixing on Millicent, and he did not answer. His gaze held her transfixed, for she saw so much in his eyes that she wanted to weep, or scream, or fall into his arms. No one had ever looked at her like that before. As if she were the most precious thing on earth.

Then his lids lowered, and those blue eyes darkened as his gaze roamed her body. Millicent realized she wore nothing but chemise, petticoat, and a rather loose corset. But she could not imagine donning the gold gown with his blood staining it. Besides, he had already seen her without a stitch on. She should not feel this self-conscious.

"Ach," said Nell, turning to follow his gaze, oblivious to the tension in the room, "ye are awake. How do ye feel? Are ye hungry?"

Millicent could only nod weakly.

Nell muttered while she slowly rose and hobbled over to the sideboard, and slapped cold meat and cheese onto a silver plate. "Bloody duke and his evil schemes. If I were only a few years younger, I could have flamed the hair right off his bushy brows, I could. But the shape-shifting don't come as easily to me anymore, ye know. My bird likes to surprise me…"

While the old woman rattled on and arranged a setting near their cards on the table, Gareth continued to watch Millicent in silence. She felt his affection and desire curl around her like a warm blanket. He had tempted her before, with his blatant sexuality and compelling charisma. But now that it had been combined with the reality of their lovemaking, Millicent did not know how she would manage to stay in such close quarters with him and keep her composure.

The beast lurking inside her made it even more difficult. The urge to claim him as her mate again made shivers run through her.

She gritted her teeth and sat on a pile of cushions in front of the low table. Her stomach growled, and she began to eat the feast Nell had prepared. Thankfully, the food managed to soothe her cat.

"You are well, my lady?" murmured Gareth.

He had abandoned Nell on the sofa, and settled himself on a cushion next to her. She had been acutely aware of his every move, while trying to pretend otherwise. Again, she could only nod.

"It's cold," said Nell, lowering her old bones onto the sofa with a pop and crackle. "The dinner, that is. The vamp brought it just before Gareth came forth from the relic. She brought some more gowns, as well, but nothing that would fit me. She seemed in an awful hurry to avoid ye, Sir Knight. Per'aps she's afraid she won't be able to resist ye?"

Millicent *felt* Gareth shrug. Bloody hell, she could feel his *body heat* next to her, smell the clean scent of his skin. She could not blame Selena. The man was simply irresistible.

"See what we found, Millie? A faro box! How abouts another game while she eats, Gareth?" Nell rubbed her hands together in anticipation.

"Of course, my lady. Whatever you wish."

Millicent kept her head lowered, her eyes on her plate, trying to hide another surge of emotion that went through her. Gareth treated Nell so gently. So kindly. As if she were a queen, and not an old woman dressed in rags who had spent most of her existence being disdained by those around her. He made Millicent feel... unworthy, somehow, all that goodness and honor such a contrast to her own inner darkness. No wonder she could not release him from the spell. A love like hers held little consequence in the grand scheme of his world.

Bloody hell. Did she truly love him? She cared for him as much as she cared for Nell, although in an entirely different way. Was that love? She had no experience with this new feeling, and abruptly decided it would not matter anyhow. He would not remain in her life for much longer.

Millicent wiped her mouth on an embroidered napkin and watched as Nell took the next card out of the faro box.

"Right again," she crowed.

Gareth smiled, looking not the least bit perturbed by his shrinking pile of buttons. "I shall have to tear apart a few more cushions, methinks."

Millicent blinked. Every now and then, he would use an antiquated word that reminded her of his true heritage. She must seem like a child to him at times. She stood, suddenly anxious to go through the pile of clothing that lay draped across one of the numerous couches. The duke had provided them with several gowns of sturdy cotton, none as fine as the golden velvet, but all of them quite serviceable.

Such generosity. How long was the duke planning to keep them imprisoned?

Millicent picked up two gowns and held them over her chest like a shield. "We must escape soon. If he finds out the truth, he will only think of new ways to coerce you to do his bidding."

Nell seemed entirely intent on her card play—the inveterate gambler—but Gareth had not stopped watching Millicent. She felt his gaze upon her as a constant caress. And he knew exactly whom she referred to. "The duke has tripled the guards around the castle perimeter. And I imagine Selena has orders not to open that door during the time I am released from the relic."

Millicent tried to keep the jealousy out of her voice. "Because she cannot resist you?"

He shrugged. "That may be a part of it. The duke may fear she will succumb to her madness for me once again. But I also believe he fears my sword as well. Nell said the were-bat had over a dozen guards at her back."

"He's not taking any chances that we shall escape again."

"Indeed. But what worries me the most is the blood he took from me. I have thought long on it, and cannot fathom a reason for it."

"No doubt he is performing evil experiments with it," interjected Nell, not as unconcerned with their conversation as Millicent had thought. "Ye know we can't leave until we find out what he intends to do with it."

Millicent exchanged a look of surprise with Gareth.

"She's right," he said. "Besides, in order to escape

we need a diversion, and I imagine we will have it in due time."

Millicent frowned. "What do you mean?"

Nell turned her attention to dealing the cards, while Millicent began to pace. Unlike Gareth, she had not been trapped in a relic for centuries, and was not used to imprisonment. The thought of being trapped in this room for an indeterminate amount of time made her skittish.

Gareth watched her, which made her even more... *skittish*. "The lion that pursued your coach and found us in the underground forest is a spy for the Master of the Hall of Mages, is he not?"

"Yes—how did you know?"

"The royals have been tracking my relic for years, and their baronets do not give up so easily. They will find the duke's underground lair, and when they do, we shall take advantage of the diversion they offer. I have made good use of them often enough in the past."

He seemed to take for granted that he could outwit the spies, who were certainly a fearsome group of predators. His blue eyes turned to flinty ice, and Millicent suppressed a shudder. She had never feared the knight, despite his obvious prowess with a blade, but now she wondered if she should.

"Nay, Millicent," he soothed, "you need never fear me."

She tossed her chin, ready to deny that quick flash of fear, but Nell quickly spoke up. "So we may as well get used to our prison fer a time. Wot say we switch to a game of Commerce, Sir Knight?"

"Whatever you desire, my lady." But he had not removed his gaze from Millicent, and his voice lowered, as if he spoke the words to her but with an entirely different meaning.

Millicent sucked in a breath, fighting the tingle of excitement that suddenly raced through her chest, and fled into the bedroom, putting on a gown as if she donned a suit of armor. She sat on the bed a moment, considered hiding in the bedroom. But the satin sheets kept reminding her… and she could hear his laughter just beyond the door… and her beast kept whining to be near him…

Millicent searched the wardrobe, and with a sigh of relief, found a sewing basket and returned to the main room with it, along with a second gown she had chosen. If she could not keep away from him, or keep her cat's thoughts off him, at least she might manage to keep her hands occupied.

She sewed badly, but had learned it out of necessity. It would be a perfect distraction.

Millicent held out the gown to Nell. "I… I thought this might do for you. With a little adjustment, that is."

The old woman glanced up, and those violet eyes grew suspiciously shiny. Nell knew how much Millicent hated to sew.

"Ach! That's too fine fer the likes of me."

"I disagree," said Gareth. "The gown is not fine enough for *you*, but I suppose we shall have to make do."

Nell cleared her throat. "Ye are a smooth one, aren't ye?"

"I speak the truth."

Millicent had thought only to keep busy, but the

look on Nell's face made her anxious to start the task. "Come, Nell, let's put it on, and I shall see how much I need to alter it."

Nell would be able to do without a corset, but Millicent decided to alter a chemise for her as well as a petticoat. The old woman had never complained about clothing. But Nell never complained about anything Millicent provided for her. She should have known that, as a woman, Nell would enjoy a new wardrobe, and the duke owed them that much, at least.

They returned to the withdrawing room, Nell's face wrinkled in smiles. Millicent settled herself in an odd chair with a cup-shaped round cushion, and found it surprisingly comfortable. For the next few hours, Gareth and Nell played cards while Millicent sewed and pretended not to notice the knight's every move. Every glance. Every consideration.

He found several lanterns and lit them next to her, so she would have more light to sew by. He won enough hands of cards so Nell felt she had earned her winnings when he lost to her the majority of the time. He told stories of a long-ago time of chivalry and jousting, of secret loves and strange magics.

He rarely took his eyes off Millicent, and found excuses to touch her for no reason. He brought her wine and sweetmeats from the sideboard—and insisted on tasting the wine first, although Millicent did not think the duke had plans of poisoning her again. Gareth exuded enough sensuality with his every action that she had a difficult time keeping her eyes off him.

She noticed his strong hands moved with gentle

grace, his blond hair held shades of red, gold, and white, and his pale eyes darkened to a smoky blue in the lamplight. The muscles in his thighs and shoulders rippled exquisitely every time he moved. And when he smiled at her or Nell, it now reached his eyes.

Millicent's beast had retreated into a small corner of her being. This growing desire for Gareth was entirely from the human side of her nature.

"Blast," Millicent muttered for the fifth time. She stuck her finger in her mouth and sucked off the drop of blood.

"Yer finger's not a pincushion," said Nell.

The room grew very quiet until Millicent could hear the soft ticking of the coal burning in the fireplace, the far-off sound of falling water outside the window, an occasional shout from one of the guards far below. She felt both of them study her intently. She refused to look up, for she might meet his gaze, and he would surely know her thoughts.

"Ye ain't got much time before ye're sucked back in the relic again," said Nell to Gareth. She yawned rather dramatically, and quite loudly. "This old woman needs her rest, and I sure can't get it with the two of ye in the room."

Millicent flushed. Apparently Nell wasn't as oblivious to the tension in the room as she pretended.

Gareth rose so quickly he scattered buttons on the floor. He held his strong hand out to her, and Millicent found her fingers gently encased in his before she could even think of the embarrassment she felt, or the utter relief of finally having the opportunity to be alone with him.

She threw Nell a look, and the cheeky old woman winked at her.

Gareth led Millicent into the bedroom, closed the door firmly behind her, and trapped her against the back, his hands placed flat on the oak, his forearms just above her shoulders. His mouth swooped down on hers, and she absorbed the shock, the welcome, heady relief of his lips against hers, his taste filling her mouth.

Her beast stirred, threatened to wake.

Millicent surprised herself by pushing her cat into the very recesses of her being. For the first time that she could remember, she wanted none of her animal instincts to overwhelm her. She wanted Gareth to make love to her without interference from the dominant nature of her beast.

Her knight pulled his lips from hers and stared into her eyes. "You will allow me to make love to you?"

She blinked in surprise at his shrewdness. "Yes."

He spun her around, nimbly unbuttoning her bodice while he kissed the back of her neck, sending shivers through her. Millicent turned her head and pressed her cheek against the cool surface of the door while he removed her gown, unlaced her corset strings, untied her petticoats. As he removed the rest of her clothing, he kissed the skin it revealed, the contrast of his warm mouth against the chill air heightening her senses until her concentration narrowed to one extraordinary thing.

Gareth.

He pulled her slightly away from the door so he could work his hands between her body and the polished oak. One hand cupped her breast while the other pressed between her legs. Millicent moaned, leaned back against him, surprised to feel the warmth of his naked skin. The man could shed his clothes faster than humanly possible.

His scent surrounded her, earthy and male and uniquely delicious. He nipped the back of her neck, gently twisted her nipple, and stroked her nub until she trembled for want of him. She pushed backward against his legs, silky skin sheathing hard muscle. She rose up to her tiptoes, wanting to feel the part of him that could bring her such pleasure, demanding he enter her.

He chuckled, low and a bit arrogantly. "Nay, my sweeting. It is my turn to love you, and I will not be rushed."

Millicent's heart turned in her chest. She couldn't fathom why his words affected her so strongly, but she felt her eyes burn and blinked away the ridiculous tears.

His lips wandered to her shoulders, to the middle of her back. His hands continued to stroke, to fondle, to caress, until she felt that singular sensation build inside her again. The one she knew would shatter her into a thousand bits when it exploded.

Anticipation made her pant, made her whisper his name between breaths.

Suddenly his mouth was at the back of her ear, whispering his love for her, his breath hot and making the side of her face tingle. He dropped his hands, and she had to bite her lip to silence a protest. He swept his palms down her arms, captured her hands within his, and pulled them up, placing them on the door in front of her. Then he gently pressed down on her back, maneuvering her hips toward him, until she bent forward, supporting the weight of her upper body on the door.

Bloody hell.

He bent his body over hers, his long blond hair tickling the sides of her face, his hands roaming, cupping her breasts, finding sensitive areas on her skin she hadn't known existed. Then his fingertips found her nipple again, and his other hand pressed between her inner thighs, gently coaxing her legs open.

Millicent eagerly complied.

He kissed her ear, then her cheek, while his fingertips found her nub again. She rewarded him with a sigh, turned her head sideways, and he captured her mouth with his, a rather fascinating angle that made kissing a different experience. But he was building that pleasure to a peak again, and Millicent started to tremble, found it difficult to catch her breath.

He broke the kiss, pulled his upper body slightly away from hers.

"No…"

But he would not listen. And he silenced her in a way she never could have imagined. He plunged his finger inside her.

"Yes…"

The arrogant man chuckled again. Did things with the rest of his fingers that made her tremble.

"Ah, my love," he murmured, dropping his hands and standing up behind her. He caressed her bottom, murmuring something about perfection, but Millicent could focus only on his touch, on this aching need he had built inside her. And when she felt the hot, silky length of him finally touch her, spread her apart and plunge inside, she thought she might scream.

She no longer wondered at this new position. She felt only the absolute delight of it. He held her hips, thrusting inside her, taking long, smooth strokes, touching her differently with each one, until he found…

Millicent gasped. A surge of pleasure went through her, the deeper one, the one inside her womb. He stilled, allowed the feeling to wash through her, before starting his rhythm once more, this time bending forward and stroking her nub again, building that pleasure to a new peak. And this time he allowed her to reach it, to tumble over the edge, her body rippling with ecstasy, like a flurry of waves washing through her. And that deeper pleasure joined it, until Millicent lost herself to mindless rapture.

He bent his upper body over hers once again, and whispered, "I love you. I love bringing you pleasure." And then he straightened, and started to gently move once more, to build her up to the heights of passion again.

And yet again.

Millicent came to earth the third time blessing her were-strength, for surely she would have collapsed. "Gareth," she pleaded.

"I want to hear you say it."

"Say what?"

"That you love me."

Millicent froze, a tangle of emotions welling up inside her. How to speak the truth, when she wasn't sure of it herself? She closed her eyes. "I love being with you. I love the way you make me feel. I love becoming a part of you like this, even if it's only for a short time. Please, Gareth."

He plunged inside her, taking her breath away, her thoughts away. He built her to that peak again, but this time allowed himself to join her, to take his own release the moment she found hers. And Millicent discovered a new joy. That bringing him pleasure increased her own tenfold.

When the world settled around her once again, she realized her arms and legs shook so badly she couldn't unlock them for fear of tumbling to the floor. But as usual, her knight came to her rescue, scooping her up in his arms and carrying her to the bed, lowering them both to the mattress without ever letting her go. He tucked her head into the hollow of his shoulder, pressed her close to him, allowing her leg and arm to flop over his lean torso.

Millicent could barely move…

Could barely keep her eyes open…

And woke to find him gone.

She sat up, aching in places she didn't know she could ache in, and pressed her hand against the indentation of his head in the pillow next to hers. She ran her palms across the sheet, imagining she could still feel his warmth in the rumpled bedding.

"I do love you, Gareth," she muttered to herself, "but don't you see it doesn't matter? I cannot keep you trapped within the relic and deprive you of a chance for freedom, and my love isn't strong enough to break the spell. We are doomed, you and I, and it's better not to forget that."

As if to prove the truth of her words, the relic had fallen off her arm. She frantically searched the bedding for the band of silver. It had fallen off the bed onto a thick red carpet, and the moonstone within it winked mockingly at her as she picked it up and slid it over her wrist.

Would it tighten around her arm again?

Conflicting emotions rose inside her as the bracelet shrank to fit securely on her arm. Fear, wonder, and a trace of anger at feeling trapped. She wished she knew what it meant... and realized it might mean nothing at all.

But still, she felt the smile on her face as she rose and began to dress.

She had managed to fasten only a few buttons of her gown when Nell screamed, with more terror in her voice than Millicent had ever heard before. She tore open the door and shifted to panther midleap into the withdrawing room, using her stronger vision to search for the danger. But Nell sat on a velvet settee, apparently unharmed, and Millicent could not see anyone else in the room. But she and Nell had been through some tight scrapes, and the old woman wouldn't have screamed like that unless she had a reason.

She shifted to human. "What is it?"

Nell pointed to a pile of cushions. "It flew in the window."

Millicent lit a lamp and approached cautiously, remembering the pointy teeth of the sprites the duke had set upon them before. Their bites might be as drug-inducing as Selena's. But the small creature sprawled across a beaded pillow did not resemble those nasty little creatures. Indeed, this one was quite... handsome, in a pointy sort of way. His brown hair stuck up in all directions, as if he had purposely used pomade to shape it that way, and his pointy nose and chin looked somehow appropriate for his narrow face. He wore a rather smart set of miniature clothing, with a waistcoat of gold brocade, and lace at sleeves and neck. His wings splayed out around him, a lovely display of gossamer iridescence.

He looked like the sort of sprite the gentry above-ground used to carry messages to one another, usually flowery love notes or secret assignations. What on earth was the little thing doing in the Underground?

When she got closer, she noticed the grime covering the lace, the ragged tears at the elbows of his coat, the worn cloth at the knees. Millicent sniffed. He smelled like rotten apples... and gin. Lots of gin.

"You're not hurt, you little scamp. You're drunk!" Millicent nudged him with her finger.

One eye opened. A very large brown eye, rather like a puppy's. "Never drunk, dear lady. Slightly foxed, perhaps. I'm sorry to say that I haven't been completely drunk since... hmmm, the year eighteen hundred and thirty. Or was it thirty-one...?"

Millicent folded her arms across her chest, catching her sagging bodice in the crooks of them. "What are you doing here?"

Nell walked over and began to button up the back of Millicent's gown, peeking around her arm to glare at the sprite.

The little man sat up, rubbed a hand across a face that hadn't seen a razor for a few days, and frowned.

"Well, a few years ago I woke up in an empty barrel of ale after getting a *wee* bit too foxed. The smuggler did not appear to appreciate my fine compliment to his beverage, and sold me to a young warlock, along with the rest of his supply. Imagine my surprise at discovering that the Underground was no mere myth, but a real city of dark mages and pubs. Many, many pubs. Since my previous, err, employer, had dismissed my services, I thought to myself: Ambrose, this is a serendipitous opportunity! You shall finally be appreciated by the young, uh, nobles, living down here, and as soon as you pay off your debt to the young warlock, you can be a free agent and—"

"Not in the Underground," snapped Millicent, flinging out her arms. Good grief, she had not expected his life story. She then pointed to the floor. "But in this *palace*."

The sprite—Ambrose—rose to his several-inch height and glanced about the room. "Where, exactly, am I?"

Nell had finished buttoning Millicent's dress and bent down to inspect the little man. "Ye are in the Duke of Ghoulston's castle, and it's a bad place ye've taken a wrong turn to."

"My dear woman, I have never taken a wrong turn in my life. Each of my adventures has led me to even greater heights—Ghoulston, you say? Oh, yes, I remember now. I have a message for Lady Millicent." His pointy gaze swept to Millicent. "A shape-shifter with black hair and cat-eyes. I presume I flew through the correct window, madam?"

Millicent could only nod, afraid if she argued

about the honorific in front of her name it would set
Ambrose off on another tale. And she was too curious
about who could have possibly sent her a message, and
why. "Yes. I am Millicent."

"I don't suppose you would happen to have a
drop of—"

She growled.

"No, I rather thought not." He let out a dramatic
sigh. "The sender of my message is none other than
Lord Bran of... err, of the fine establishment of
the Swill and Seelie." He bent over in a bow, and
promptly landed flat on his pointy wee face.

Ten

MILLICENT WHINED IN FRUSTRATION.

Nell glanced up at her. "There's a liquor cabinet near the sideboard. Shall I fetch a glass? Per'aps if I wave it beneath his nose it'll bring him to."

"Good idea."

Nell hobbled over to a carved mahogany cabinet tucked in the corner of the room, opened the doors to reveal a sparkling display of bottles filled with rich brown and red liquids. She chose one at random, uncorked it, and brought it to the sprite, waving it over his prone form.

The fumes of the brandy had a startling restorative effect on the sprite. His pointed nose twitched, his eyes flew open, and he scrambled to his feet with a bounce. "Jolly good. I knew you had to have some about." His wings fluttered as his gaze flicked to the cabinet. "An abundant stash, I see."

Millicent lowered her face to mere inches away from his. "What is the message?"

"Err, my memory is still rather fuzzy. I have found

that a few swallows of excellent—brandy, is it not? Yes, brandy—will often sharpen my faculties."

"Give me the message now, and you can have all the brandy you want. Continue to be a nuisance, and I shall pluck off your wings. Slowly."

Nell cackled, and Ambrose gave her an injured look, but quickly spit out his message.

"Bran is aware of your forced confinement, and feels that as your employer, he *bears* a certain responsibility for you." The little man grinned at his play on words.

Millicent blinked. How astonishing. She had never suspected that Bran felt anything other than a mild interest in her beyond the bounds of her ability to do her job.

"And he will send a force to rescue you. He has offered free drink for a fortnight to any volunteers, and has enough men to show the duke that he is a man—shape-shifter—not to be trifled with. He hoped I would find you so you would be prepared for his attack this evening."

Millicent glanced at Nell, who appeared to be just as surprised by the message.

"Per'aps it's a matter of pride," said the old woman. "Fer it's a foolish thing for Bran to go up against a sorcerer, even if he's immune to the duke's magic. Silver blades will cut him just as easily."

"Whatever the reason," replied Millicent, "we cannot accept his offer of rescue until we find out the duke's plans for Gareth. But you, Nell. We should get you away from here."

"And miss all the excitement? Ach, no, me gel, I'm staying right here with you and the knight."

Millicent huffed. It did no good to argue with Nell if she had her mind made up. She glanced back at Ambrose, who kept gazing at the large bottle of brandy with lovesick eyes.

"Ambrose."

He ignored her.

"Nell, fetch a thimble for him, will you? He's liable to swoon again."

Iridescent wings twitched. "I never swoon, madam. Lose my equilibrium, perhaps. But never swoon."

Nell fetched a thimble from Millicent's sewing supplies and carefully poured a drop into the make-shift tankard, and handed it to the little man. He downed the contents faster than any of the patrons of the Swill and Seelie, causing her and Nell to gape at him in admiration.

"Quality brew," he said, wiping his mouth on a well-stained sleeve, and looked up at Millicent with a renewed sparkle in his large brown eyes. "Now then, where were we?"

"I want you to return with a message to Bran. Tell him I have… unfinished business with the duke. Tell him to wait for a message from me to move. Then you come back here, so I can send him to you when it's time."

Those pointy brows furrowed. "There appears to be more afoot here than just a simple kidnapping. My services do not come cheap, my dear, and I would rather not involve myself in anything… too dangerous."

"You may avail yourself of the entire cabinet."

His gaze riveted on the sparkling bottles and their contents. "I daresay, that is rather generous—"

"As long as you can manage to fly with my message when the time comes," added Millicent.

"Madam. I assure you, I have never been unable to fly. I may wobble a bit—"

"But ye always manage to fly," finished Nell. "We gets it. Now off with ye, before…"

Millicent cocked her head at the door. "I hear it too. Someone's coming. Go on, Ambrose, and return soon." She watched the sprite test his wings, spin upward into the air, and out the window. She hoped he would come back.

The door to their prison finished opening and Selena stepped inside, clasping her hands in front of her with a flourish of rippling sleeves. She wore a black gown of such fine silk that it fluttered with every move she made.

"Don't you wear anything but black?" muttered Millicent.

She flashed her pointed teeth. "It suits my mood most of the time. And right now, I'm annoyed with having to fetch you for the duke."

Millicent lowered her lashes, hiding the spark of interest in her eyes, and spoke as surly as she could. "What does he want now?"

"Just put these on," snapped the were-bat, tossing a mound of golden silk at her. "And make it quick. It's past my feeding time."

Nell followed Millicent into the bedroom and helped her put on the clothing, a voluminous gown with long, puffed sleeves and multiple petticoats.

"Did ye notice they come for ye when our knight ain't around?"

Millicent wondered when Gareth had become "their" knight. "I rather think he scared the duke at his last appearance."

Nell snorted. "Per'aps. Or per'aps the duke has a plan that he don't want Sir Gareth buggering up. Or per'aps—"

"Hush, Nell. We all agreed that we must find out what the duke is up to. I'm counting on his ego to brag about it over tea."

"Still, I'm coming with ye."

"Not unless the duke demands it. I need you here in case Ambrose returns."

The old lady glanced at the bracelet on Millicent's wrist. "Our knight won't be out for hours."

"I know, and it hardly matters. Since when do I need a man to protect me?"

Nell raised one red brow, but did not say another word as she followed Millicent out of the bedroom.

Selena narrowed her eyes. "You look suitably ridiculous. Like a rat with a silk bow around its neck. Come on." She spun in a swell of black silk, toward a group of guards waiting just outside the door, then glanced over her shoulder at Nell. "The old woman stays here, of course, to insure your cooperation."

"With what?" asked Millicent.

"Apparently you have received an invitation to take tea with Lady Yardley."

❦

Millicent sat across from the Duke of Ghoulston in his private coach once more, but this time they left London until the windows afforded a view of the

English countryside. The light hurt her eyes, but she continued to squint at the vista of green spread over hill and meadow, the quaint cottages covered in roses, the grazing cows and rippling ponds. And an occasional touch of shimmering magic. Unicorns leaping over hedgerows, waterfalls that flowed upward into fountains of sparkling light, trees of rich purple shaped into umbrellas of shade. England was beautiful aboveground.

The duke sniffed and wriggled his bulk on the seat, rocking the coach even more than the pitted roads already managed to. He glanced at her with that secretive smile still plastered to his fleshy face.

Millicent scowled. "For the hundredth time, where are we going?"

He glanced out the window. "To Lady Yardley's country estate. I suppose we shall be there soon enough. Here." He handed her a gold box carved with delicate oriental flowers, their petals studded with precious gems that winked in the late-afternoon sunshine.

The box felt cool and heavy in her hands. It looked valuable enough to feed her and Nell for years. "What is this for?"

"You shall give it to Lady Yardley. It is a gift for the queen."

"What's in it?"

"Some tea. A rather unique blend of my own. You shall not mention that, of course."

"Of course." Millicent hid her smile of triumph. The man had been singularly reluctant to reveal anything about their outing up to this moment, and any information she could glean from him might help her understand his purposes. His nervousness made the hairs on the back of her neck tingle in alarm, telling her he had some serious evil in mind. "Why don't you just give it to her yourself?"

"Ah." Again he wriggled, the magically enhanced fabric of his coat changing color with his movements. "I have my reasons." He kept wiping sweat off his upper lip, and his black eyes glittered with some inner excitement.

"So, you don't want anyone to know the tea is a gift from you. Surely you could have used someone else for the ruse. Why me?"

His bushy brows rose in a mockery of innocence. "For some confounded reason, Lady Yardley has taken a liking to you. But more importantly, she trusts your naive facade. She will not think twice about your desire to give the queen a gift. It is something most new arrivals at court feel compelled to do. But this one will manage to reach her, since it will be delivered by her own Lady of the Bedchamber."

Millicent looked down at the box in her hands, quickly threw back the lid, and inspected the contents. Black tea leaves. "What did you put in your special blend? I will not harm the queen for any reason."

He sputtered. "Harm? The queen? Are you mad? Do you know what the penalty is for treason?"

His horror seemed genuine.

"I know you have some evil plan, Your Grace. I do not believe for a moment that you took me all the way from London just so I may deliver a harmless gift."

He shrugged. "Either you give my box to Lady

Yardley, or I finally indulge myself with an experiment on that were-firebird. I have an idea that her feathers may be used as the firing mechanism for an explosive device I'm working on. It's a pity I must pluck them out, one by one."

Millicent growled softy. There must be something in the tea, but she could not see nor smell anything abnormal about it. Not a whiff of magic. And the queen would have safeguards about her, preventing harm of any foreign magic to her person. Surely the queen had someone to taste her meals as well, so it would be foolish of the duke to put anything in it that might poison her.

"Oh, my dear Millicent. I see how your weak mind struggles to find answers to machinations beyond your scope of comprehension. Leave the thinking to me, were-cat. And just do your best to enjoy the outing."

The road suddenly became smoother and Millicent glanced out the window, then tried not to gape. Lady Yardley's country residence loomed into view down a long, tree-lined lane, and it looked more beautiful and elegant than Buckingham Palace. It did not need magic to enhance its magnificence, although Millicent did detect warding spells shimmering about the towers and parapets, giving it a rather dreamlike quality.

Her hand shook, shuffling the tea leaves in the box. What had the duke gotten her into? "I hope I do not manage to spill your gift onto the lawn. I can be rather clumsy in human form."

She glanced up when he did not answer. The Duke of Ghoulston no longer sat across from her. Instead, some demon from one of her worst nightmares lounged against the upholstery. Pointed horns, gaping mouth revealing pointed fangs, red skin shimmering with oily moisture. It took all of her self-possession not to shift to panther.

But her immunity to magic allowed her to see past the illusion, to the duke's rather smug face. She would not allow him to intimidate her.

"You forget your place, my dear." He spoke with a voice that seemed to resonate from the depths of hell. Crimson saliva dripped from the corners of his black lips. "I have been a gentleman with you, but do not allow yourself to forget your predicament. Or Nell's."

His illusion wore no clothing, and when the duke wriggled again, he exposed the demon's…

Bloody hell. It was as sharp and pointed as a dagger.

"You will care for that tea as if your life depended upon it."

Millicent quickly slammed the lid closed.

The coach rocked to a stop, and although she knew he could not harm her with the illusion, and her immunity to magic allowed her to see the demon as only a hazy form surrounding the duke, she still breathed a sigh of relief when it vanished.

The coachman opened the door and lowered the steps, and the duke scrambled out, turning to extend a gentlemanly hand to Millicent. She ignored it, managed to gather her golden skirts about her without falling from the carriage. She recoiled in disgust when Ghoulston wrapped a shawl about her shoulders with familiar intimacy.

"Easy, were-cat. Lady Yardley believes you adore me—your dearest cousin."

A liveried footman met them at the door, and Millicent stifled her growl and allowed herself to be led through the entryway of the castle, down a long hallway lined with ancient portraits. The pictures within the frames kept changing, as if the decorator had decided that too many frames would clutter the walls, but needed to display all of the castle's inhabitants. She squinted to see past the illusion, strengthening her natural gift of immunity to magic to see her real surroundings. Millicent feared she would need all the advantage she could get.

She handled the golden box with extreme care.

They walked down another hallway, this one lined with busts resting on carved pillars. The statues would open their eyes as they passed, curiosity within the white orbs of their sockets, and some would smile. Others would wink. And still others would move their mouths as if they carried on a conversation.

Millicent shivered.

"Lady Yardley finds them amusing," offered the footman, his steps slowing as they neared an open doorway. Millicent could hear subdued laughter and light chatter emanating from the room. She glanced at the duke's expectant face, took a deep breath, and stepped past the threshold.

At first the withdrawing room appeared as a mass of golden color, with gilt on the paneled walls, the enormous fireplace, the backs of chairs, and bric-a-brac on the tables. Millicent blinked and managed to see the true nature of the room, although still magnificent even with its loss of gilding. Tables covered in white linen had been arranged about the room, with silver tea services on each one, and enough food for a feast. Sweetmeats and lobster and tiny little cakes covered in sparkling sugar, little sandwiches cut into stars and hearts, biscuits lathered in cream, scones of chocolate…

Her stomach growled.

If Lady Yardley considered this tea, Millicent wondered what a full meal might be like.

The duke clasped her arm, gave it a painful squeeze, and led her over to a group of women.

Millicent lifted her chin as all eyes turned to study her from head to toe. Selena had managed to twist Millicent's hair into the semblance of a chignon, yanking as hard as the vamp could, of course, but it lacked the pearls and feathers and diamonds sprinkled into the other ladies' coiffures. Well, she might not be up to their standards, but she rather thought not a one of them could break up a bar fight, scare off a were-lion, or satisfy the magic man the way she could.

How odd. The thought actually brought her comfort.

"It's the country girl, is it not?" asked one of the ladies.

"Lady Millicent," greeted Claire, her hazel eyes sparkling with delight. "I'm so glad you could join us!"

"Lady Yardley," began Millicent.

"I'm sure it's her," interrupted a woman standing nearby. "Those eyes are most unusual."

"You are being quite rude, Lady Chatterly," said Claire.

"And since when do I care about social niceties?" Lady Chatterly bore down on Millicent, iridescent blue peacock feathers in her hair this time, the colorful eyes of the pattern seeming to stare intently at her. "I fear you possess something of mine that you forgot to return to me."

Millicent threw Ghoulston a disgruntled look. He had thrust her into this predicament.

"Perhaps you should discuss this in private," suggested Claire, tilting her head at the duke, who wore an expression of polite inquiry, as if he hadn't the slightest idea what they were talking about.

Lady Chatterly ignored her, stepping forward in her boldly striped gown and clasping Millicent's arm. "I demand to know who you have given it to."

Millicent growled softly. Who had made Lady Chatterly the keeper of the relic? What right had she to think she held any demands upon Gareth? Millicent struggled to retain her human shape as her cat tried to surface, for she did not suffer anyone to hold her against her will.

Then Lady Chatterly's face went through an abrupt change of emotion as she felt at Millicent's arm. She pushed up the billowy sleeves of Millicent's gown and gaped at the bracelet still tightly fitted around her wrist. "It's not possible… you could not have resisted him… what is *wrong* with you?"

"I… nothing, I assure you. He is not as irresistible as you seem to think."

"Nonsense!"

"Am I missing something?" inquired His Grace with just the right touch of boredom to his voice.

Claire patted Lady Chatterly on the shoulder. "My dear, you really must contain yourself. Come now, a nice hot cup of tea should do the trick."

"But… but… how is it possible? I've never known a woman to wear it for more than one single evening…"

"Astonishing, I agree. But remember, Lady Millicent is from the country, and they are rather… conservative in her area. I'm sure she will succumb soon, and then promptly return the, err, item to you. Isn't that right, Millicent dear?"

Millicent obligingly nodded.

Claire led Lady Chatterly to a back table, consoling the woman as she went.

Normal conversation resumed around the room.

"See what you've done?" hissed Millicent. "She'll come to you for the relic, now."

Lord Ghoulston shrugged, rather elegantly, drat the man. "I don't know a thing about it now, do I? And I hazard to guess she will be reluctant to discuss the matter. Besides, it shall be a wicked pleasure to send her on a wild-goose chase into the backwaters of the North. She's a bit of a harpy, that one."

He stepped over to the nearest chair and pulled it out for her. "My dear cousin, please take a seat."

Millicent frowned but sat, arranging her skirts with unnecessary fuss. What was so important that he had risked exposing the relic this way? She should warn Claire about this supposed gift for the queen, but she had no idea what to warn her *of*. She set the tea box on the linen tablecloth in front of her and glared at it.

"Tea, my dear?" inquired His Grace, filling her cup before she could respond. Then he turned to address the woman on his other side, whose gown revealed more of her charms than necessary as she leaned forward to smile at him.

Millicent sighed and took a sip. Perhaps it would calm her as easily as it had appeared to calm Lady Chatterly. Claire gave the woman one last pat on the shoulder, and hurried back to Millicent's table.

"Now, my dear," she whispered as she sat next to her. "You must tell me all about it."

"I assure you, there's not much to tell."

"But he did… come to you, didn't he?"

Millicent glanced at the duke, but he looked entirely engrossed in his conversation with the other woman.

"Yes. But you spoke truly, Claire. I come from a very conservative family."

"Then you must tell me all about them, for I cannot imagine…" She shook her auburn curls, as if chastising herself for bad manners, and then held out a silver platter to her. "Scone, my dear? Or perhaps a cucumber sandwich?"

Millicent nodded. She couldn't talk much with her mouth full, and she hated to lie to Lady Yardley any more than she had to. She truly liked the woman.

Another lady with blonde hair and a demure gown sat down on the other side of Claire, and began to speak to the table in general. "Did you know that Prince Albert is arriving to visit the queen today? The *ton* is atwitter with gossip. Various factions are pushing them to marry. This will be his second visit, and if rumors are to be believed, he has matured into a fine-looking young man."

All eyes went to the speaker, and that's when Millicent realized what tea parties were really for. Gossip.

"It is my understanding," said His Grace, "that she

was not so pleased with him on his first visit. I believe she referred to him as rather pudgy. And he could not dance worth a farthing."

"Perhaps," said Claire. "But since then I hear he not only learned to dance, but has also shed the baby fat of his youth."

Lord Ghoulston scowled. "Still, I do not think it a suitable match. The queen should marry someone from her own realm… not some foreigner."

"Ah, well," said the blonde lady, "there is no accounting for the vagaries of love, is there?"

The duke bestowed her with a brilliant smile. "Very true, very true. It is as unpredictable as the weather, is it not? And given the queen's impulsive nature, she may surprise everyone with a man of her own choice."

Millicent sipped her tea, washing down the bite of moist bread that stuck in her throat. The duke appeared more interested in this idle gossip than a man should be… or perhaps this was normal. How could she possibly know the inclinations of the gentry? But still, she detected something in the duke's tone that bothered her… or was she jumping at every little nuance, because she felt suspicious and bewildered by the duke's purpose in bringing her today?

"Why, Lady Millicent, what is this beautiful box sitting in front of you?" said Claire. "There are some unusual gemstones in it."

"Oh." Millicent set down her cup of tea. "It's, err, a present for the queen." She studiously avoided looking in Ghoulston's direction. "But if you think it gauche of me to offer a gift for the courtesy of inviting me to the ball…"

"Oh, quite the contrary. The queen loves unusual gifts. What's inside it?" And Lady Yardley lifted the lid and sniffed. "It smells rather odd."

"It's a special blend of tea leaves found only in the hills near my home. They say a great wizard once used magic to blend several leaves into one plant, and although he is long gone, his creation continues to flourish."

Ghoulston coughed into his embroidered napkin.

"Most unusual," said Claire.

"Indeed." Millicent curled her fingers into a fist. "Because of its unusual origin, I suggest the queen have it tested, or tasted, before she tries it. I wouldn't want to cause her any stomach upset."

Ghoulston kicked her beneath the table.

"Oh, do not worry," replied Claire. "The queen has many magic-users to ensure the safety of anything that nears her person. Just think, a new blend of tea. She will be most delighted by your thoughtful gift, Lady Millicent."

Millicent gave her a wobbly smile. She'd done the best she could to warn them. She just wished she knew more. She had a sudden image of Nell in were-form, tied up like a goose, the duke plucking out her brilliant feathers. One by one.

She should have followed her instincts, gotten Nell out of that prison of a palace, and left the duke to his own devious schemes. Now she felt a part of them, and responsibility for whatever happened would rest on her shoulders.

Lady Yardley laughed at something the duke said, calling him "Silly Willie."

She liked Claire. She had even liked the queen.

Getting involved emotionally with other people *never* turned out well for her.

Eleven

GARETH STOOD BY MILLICENT'S BEDSIDE AND WATCHED her sleep for a time, thinking he had Merlin to thank for one thing. Had Gareth not been trapped in the relic for centuries, he would never have met his one true love. For he no longer had any uncertainty about his feelings for Millicent. When the duke had poisoned her, and Gareth thought he'd lost her forever…

No, he did not doubt the strength of his feelings for her. Millicent's feelings, on the other hand, still remained a mystery to him.

The burgundy sheets twisted about her long legs, revealing tantalizing glimpses of pale flesh. He liked how she slept in the nude, unself-conscious in her bare skin, and wondered if her animal nature had anything to do with it. He had never known a woman like her… so passionate… able to take all he could give her. He did not want to live without her.

There must be some way to make her love him as much as he loved her! Surely that would release him from the enchantment. But with Millicent, it would take time to tear down all the walls around her heart, and he didn't know how much time they had left.

He glanced at the closed door, heard Nell's snoring from the other room, and quickly shed his clothing. Then he leaned down and kissed his sweeting, a featherlight touch intended to wake her gently. Her lips moved ever so slightly beneath his.

Gareth traced a path from lip to cheek, marveling at the smooth texture of her skin. He nuzzled her ear and softly whispered, "I love you."

Millicent sighed and her lashes fluttered.

He made love to her with only mouth and tongue, tracing a path down her neck, across the slope of her shoulder, to the lush curve of her breast. When he suckled a rosy peak, she stirred, a slow moan escaping from the back of her throat. He kissed his way down her smooth stomach, slid his tongue over the graceful contour of one hip, and then the other.

She smelled of wild roses and green meadows.

He kissed a path down her thigh, over her knee, along her muscled calf. She trembled slightly, her breath quickening, and Gareth knew she would be fully awake by the time he paid homage to her other leg.

When he reached her upper thigh, he angled his body half over hers, nuzzling the silky hair between her legs until she spread for him. And then he began his lovemaking in earnest. He knew exactly where to lick, precisely when to suck, until Millicent's breathing became ragged and hoarse. With a skill born of centuries of practice, he raised his body and slid effortlessly into her.

"Gareth," she breathed, those eyes now wide open,

shining golden in the twilight streaming in through the window.

"I love you," he whispered again, seeking to show her how very much. He sought the most sensitive area within her, keeping his lower body tightly pressed against hers, continuing the gentle pressure he'd used with mouth and tongue.

A slow, gentle friction.

Building to a gradual unfurling.

He reached his pinnacle when he felt hers begin, his body responding to the tightening of her muscles, his heart responding to the joy of her pleasure. Millicent continued to shake long after his own tremor of release had passed. He cradled her to him, feeling pleasure course through her again and again, like the ripple of waves across a calm lake.

She breathed his name again, this time with a bit of awe.

He would have smiled if he had not been so intent on the bracelet on Millicent's arm. Had he detected a slight loosening of the silver band? Alas, yes. It slid down another inch, falling off as it always did after he made love to the relic-holder. The stupid piece of metal did not recognize that Millicent was different... perhaps Gareth had given the enchantment too much credit. If it had been crafted to find his true love, it would not be falling off her wrist. Frustration flared inside of him. He needed more time with her. "Promise me you will never give the bracelet to another."

Millicent tugged the bracelet back up her arm, held it there until it tightened once again. "I cannot keep you forever, Gareth."

He twisted a lock of her silky hair around his finger. "Why not, my lady? Imagine a lifetime of the pleasure I just showed you. A lifetime within my arms."

"That's entirely unfair." She wiggled, putting a bit of distance between them. "You are too skilled between the sheets, Gareth, to allow a woman to think clearly afterwards."

This time he allowed himself a smile. "Promise me."

"I cannot keep you trapped within the relic for my entire life."

He leaned forward and kissed her. "Promise me."

She huffed. "Oh, bloody hell, all right. I promise. Why is it becoming so difficult to deny you anything?"

"Because you love me, my lady."

"But not enough." Her shoulders slumped. "Not enough to free you."

Gareth swept his blond hair away from his face. Damn Merlin. He could not bear to see Millicent unhappy. He reached for her again to comfort her, but she leaned away, stretching out her long limbs with the fluid grace of her were-cat.

As always, her inner strength rose to the surface once more, and she cocked him a saucy grin. "How I wish it were otherwise. I would not mind being woken up every morning in such a manner."

Gareth should have known she would not accept sympathy. He wondered if she had ever been offered it. He shrugged his shoulders, watching her gaze follow the movement with appreciation. He had never met a stronger woman, and wondered if that was the reason he had fallen in love with her. He needed her much more than she needed him.

"It would be my pleasure to wake up with you in the morning, my lady… but it is actually the dead of night." He reached out and curved his arm about her waist, pulling her into his lap. "The most difficult part of the curse right now is being taken from your side. I regret every moment I cannot be with you." He nuzzled her hair, breathing in the sweet scent. "Tell me what you did while I was gone."

She shivered, raised a hand to smooth it across the front of his chest, as if she tried to sculpt his muscles. "There is much I have to tell you. But I am afraid it's going to be difficult for me to concentrate if we continue to touch each other—"

A bolt of iridescent wings shot through the window into the room, plowing into a cluster of decorative perfume bottles on the vanity. Scent exploded into the air, an overwhelming mixture of lavender, rose, and vanilla. Gareth had his sword to hand before he knew what had invaded Millicent's bedroom, his blade and body protecting her as he sought out the source of the commotion.

"It's just Ambrose," she said, her voice laced with exasperation.

"What's an Ambrose?"

"Part of the news I had to share with you."

Gareth squinted. A little man staggered upright from behind a crystal bottle, his prismatic wings fanning the air to keep him steady… which served to scatter the scent even more strongly about the room. The sprite sneezed, wiping a pointy nose on an elegant but tattered sleeve.

"I beg your pardon," he said, "but the currents

from the waterfall beyond your window play havoc with my wings."

Gareth picked up his sword belt and slipped the blade back into its sheath, tossed it back on the table, and then turned a brow to Millicent. She shrugged, resulting in a tantalizing motion of her naked breasts.

"Bran sent him," she started, then noticed Ambrose's mouth drop open, and quickly tugged the sheet up over her chest. "He's a message sprite."

"And why did Bran send him?"

"On a most urgent matter," interrupted the sprite. "Of that I can assure you, good sir. I am employed only by the gentry—fallen as they are to reside in the Underground—but gentry no less!"

"What an annoying creature. Quit ogling my lady, little man, and get out."

"Ogling? Why sir, I may stare, but I never *ogle*." Ambrose raised his pointed brows and looked at Millicent. "But I swear, Miss Millicent, if you would but give me one more peek, I shall give up drink forever."

Gareth lowered his head. "Get. Out."

The little man huffed, but launched into the air, flying back out the window. Within a few moments they heard Nell screech from the other room, and Gareth assumed the creature had entered again through the withdrawing room window, and regretted that he had disturbed the ladybird. But Nell must deal with the little man for the moment. He needed answers to his questions without the sprite interrupting. He turned to Millicent.

"I am as astonished as you are," she said. "I did not

think Bran gave a farthing about what happened to me beyond my ability to keep order in his pub."

"Then he sent the sprite to help you?"

"Yes. Bran heard that Nell and I were taken prisoner, and he intends to help us escape."

Gareth's lip twitched. Ah, poor Millicent. She looked perplexed as to why another person would come to her aid.

She shrugged, smooth silk sliding over soft skin. "I did not ask for his help. I never have."

"Perhaps you've never really needed it before."

"Well, I sent the sprite back to Bran and told him to wait for a signal from us to move. I imagine he has every disreputable brawler in the Underground waiting to join a good fight. They fear the sorcerers, you know, but not as much as one would think—especially with enough gin in their bellies to give them courage."

"Good. Then we can escape as soon as we discover what the Duke of Ghoulston is up to."

"I doubt it shall be that easy, but…" She frowned. "Ghoulston took me for an outing yesterday. I'm sure it has something to do with his plans for world domination—or whatever his ridiculous goal is, but I cannot make sense of it."

"Where did he take you?"

"To a tea party at Lady Yardley's country estate. He gave me a gift to give to the queen, and he wanted to be very sure no one knew it came from him."

Excitement stirred inside Gareth. "What was this gift?"

"A golden tea box inlaid with gems. But I swear I could not smell any magic upon it. And His Grace would not dare to put any sort of poison in the tea leaves. It would be discovered quick enough. And despite his charade, the box could easily be traced back to him." She made a face. "He told Claire—Lady Yardley—that I am his cousin."

Gareth had seen many men conspire in many ways to gain wealth or power. He trusted Millicent's senses, for shape-shifters were known for their ability to sniff out magic, especially predators—the master of the Hall of Mages employed the baronets as spies exactly for that reason. So he believed the box and its contents carried no magic... and besides, he did not think Ghoulston would be so foolish as to try to put a spell upon the queen. He also doubted that the duke would poison the queen... it would gain him little. Unless he could manage to put a doppelgänger in her place... but it would be too difficult to keep up such a charade for very long. Doppelgängers were difficult to control, often prone to their own evil desires...

"But there has to be something unique about that box. And I believe we might be able to find out what it is." Gareth stood and pulled on his clothing.

Millicent watched him with an appreciative gaze. He liked the way she looked at him. Like a cat would look at a tasty mouse.

"How? Because I must get Nell out of here, Gareth. Ghoulston has threatened her one time too many. I cannot keep risking her, and she refuses to leave until we discover what the duke is up to. Although why Nell should care about what happens aboveground is beyond me."

He turned, studied her face until she blushed. "Do

you truly believe that? Do *you* hold such a disregard for the world above?"

"They have never cared about us, or what happens down here."

He leaned down and caressed her pink cheek with the back of his hand. "Because most of them think you are a myth, my dear. You know the sorcerers have gone to great lengths to keep this place a secret. And perhaps those aboveground do turn a blind eye onto what happens down here, but do you not realize that both places are intertwined? What happens above can affect the Underground."

She threw up her hands, displacing the sheet about her upper body, a puddle of satin forming around her hips. "I don't know what has happened to me! I have always minded my own business, and except for Nell, have made sure to keep independent of all others. I go my own way. I take care of myself. It has kept me from harm since I was a little girl. And now…"

"You have become involved in things larger than the shell you created around yourself," he finished for her. "Is it so very bad, my lady? Do you regret so strongly that I have entered your life?"

She sighed, the anger draining from her as quickly as it had come. His mercurial cat-lady.

"No, my dear knight. Despite all the complications… I have never felt so alive before. Loving you has been a gift I could never regret, no matter what happens."

Gareth understood her unspoken words. As far as Millicent was concerned, they had little hope of a happy future together. She feared he would resent her for keeping him trapped in the relic, or that he might be turned to dust if the curse were broken. No wonder she could not fully love him. She would be risking too much of her heart, and he could not blame her.

But he could not let her go, either.

He handed Millicent her chemise. "I have shown great restraint, my lady, but if you do not cover yourself now, I shall not be able to resist caressing those perfect breasts much longer, and then it shall be another hour until we have our answers."

She cocked her head, midnight hair spilling over pale shoulders, as if she seriously considered delaying. "Blasted cat," she finally muttered. "My penchant for curiosity is most inconvenient." And then she pulled the chemise over her head.

Gareth gently tugged the rope of the bellpull. The embroidered decoration he had ripped off when he had yanked it too hard before still lay on the table. It felt like such a long time ago, when he had first come to this room with Millicent, and Selena had helped them escape. He should have known they would wind up right back where they started, what with baronets and the duke's minions chasing after them.

He finger-combed his hair back from his face, took off his belt, and set it next to the embroidered scrap of fabric. He did not want Selena to feel threatened in any way. After further thought, he removed his surcoat and tunic, tossing them over a carved mahogany chair, his nipples tightening from the chill in the room. He would not bare his chest for most women, as it would decidedly put them off until they were abed. But Selena was not most women. Subtlety would get him nowhere.

A thump came from behind the closed bedroom door, a low growl following it. Gareth sighed, hoping Millicent would be able to keep Nell and Ambrose quiet while he spoke with Selena. He did not wish to explain the sprite's presence, nor did he want the were-bat reminded of the others in the next room. He wanted all of the woman's attention upon him.

The door to their luxurious prison ground opened and the vamp stood there gazing at him, armed guards shadowing her back. Selena's black eyes glittered in the candlelight. "So, you have finally managed to seduce the were-cat. I daresay it took you long enough."

Gareth lowered his voice suggestively. "I'm sorry to disappoint, lady, but that is not why I summoned you."

Her eyes widened, and she licked her lips, taking a step forward into the room. One of the guards who stood behind her grunted, and she halted just past the threshold. "Then why did you call me? His Grace is aboveground and—"

Gareth shook his head, his hair scraping his shoulders. "I do not wish to speak with Ghoulston. I want to see you."

Her gaze roamed his chest, and she licked her lips yet again.

Gareth strode forward. "You have been avoiding me. You come only when I am within the relic." The guards bristled, and Gareth stopped within touching distance of her. "What have I done to make you fear me?" he murmured.

Her spine snapped erect. "I do not fear you." She turned and waved dismissively at the guards. "Wait for me outside. I require some privacy."

The big red-haired guard glared warningly at Gareth from over Selena's head while he reached for the niche holding the statue. Gareth returned the man's look with a smile as the stone door closed.

Selena arranged her skirts on a settee upholstered in burgundy-striped satin and melted back against the cushions, her eyes hooded and lips parted.

Gareth kept his smile glued to his face and sat next to her. "How have you been, my lady?"

"Bored, bored, bored. His Grace will not allow me to accompany him aboveground, and without his... games, there is little to do."

Gareth reached out and curled a length of her hair about his finger. He could not help but compare it to the texture of Millicent's black silky locks, which were finer and smoother. "Why won't he allow you to go with him?"

She made a face. "I scare those above. Can you imagine?"

He shook his head. "Nay. Surely your beauty would make you the belle of any soiree."

She preened, then glanced suspiciously around the room. "Where's the cat and the bird?"

"Asleep." He traced a finger across her cheek. It lacked the rose-petal softness of Millicent's. "As you see, I am bored too."

"No doubt. Although I don't imagine a frigid cat and a crotchety bird are proper company when they are awake. I can only imagine how frustrated you must be." And she grinned, exposing all those pointy teeth.

Gareth suppressed a shiver, remembering how those teeth felt sinking into his skin. But he must go to great lengths to get Selena to tell him of Ghoulston's plans, for only then could he devise a way to untangle Millicent and Nell from the duke's schemes. Even if it meant giving up some of his life's blood.

He arched his neck in offering.

Selena shuddered and backed away from him.

Gareth frowned, different pieces of a puzzle twisting inside his head. He covered his blunder by tracing his hand down her neck to the mounds of flesh exposed by the bodice of her gown. She leaned into his hand and he spread his fingers, absently caressing her flesh.

"I am sure you can think of many ways to relieve our boredom," she breathed.

"Indeed." Gareth hid his revulsion. How odd, that he would be willing to give his blood, but cringed at the thought of bedding her. But the idea of someone other than Millicent in his arms made him feel... empty. He prayed words would suffice. "Perhaps you would like to hear of the many ways I can pleasure a woman."

Her black eyes sparkled. "Oh, yes."

He launched into a detailed description of a lover from decades ago who had a taste for the exotic, while his mind tried to fit the pieces of the puzzle together. Fear had passed across Selena's face when he had offered to feed her. Why? He remembered that she had acted strangely when she had fed from him before, her lust for him turning into a mindless infatuation.

The Duke of Ghoulston had taken a cup of his blood.

And then he had given Millicent a gift for the queen.

Ghoulston wanted power and position.

By the time he finished his tale, Selena's eyes had turned glassy, her pupils dilated and her breath coming hard and fast.

"I knew you would like that story," whispered Gareth, leaning closer to her.

"Such ingenuity," she murmured, stroking his bare chest. He remembered how Millicent had touched him, with tenderness and longing, as if the were-panther had tried to memorize the feel of him.

Selena scraped her nails across his skin possessively.

"Show me how you managed that position," she whispered.

"Shall I? I am not sure you have the courage for it, lady."

She blinked. "What do you mean?"

"You do not trust me enough to gain pleasure from it."

"I am not afraid."

He shrugged. "There is a part of you that fears me, and until I understand why, it is too risky. I would not harm you, lady."

"What are you talking about? I am not like stupid Millicent, frigid and fearful of being with a man."

"That's not what I meant."

"Then what is it?" She near shouted the words, her fingers curled into fists, and color rose in her pale cheeks.

Gareth judged her frustrated enough to speak carelessly. "When I offered to feed you, it made you nervous. Why?"

"Because it made me a mindless ninny before."

"How do you mean?"

"I did not know what happened to me at first. But His Grace deduced it soon enough. Your blood made me fall in love with you. A feeling I have never experienced before, and do not wish to repeat. It has nothing to do with bedding you."

Gareth started. "How is this possible?"

"I do not know. I'm just glad it wore off. Now, let us try..." She pulled at his waistband.

He grabbed her fingers. "Selena, this troubles me. I have never had anyone... drink my blood before. Is it part of Merlin's spell? How can it have affected you that way?"

"Oh, for the love of—" She twisted her hands out of his. "His Grace says it has nothing to do with magic. Or rather, it does, but it is natural. A result of the spell put upon you." She grinned rather maliciously. "He thinks that after all these centuries of seducing women, your blood has actually changed into some sort of love potion. Now, can we get on with it?"

Suddenly the pieces of the puzzle started to make sense. He needed to speak with Millicent. Gareth leaned forward and hugged Selena. "My dear lady, you have no idea—"

The bedroom door flew open and a snarling, spitting bundle of black fur leaped into the room. Selena grimaced and spun around, the shadow of her were-creature outlining her body. "Go away, Millicent."

The panther growled, soft and menacing.

"What is it? You don't want him, but no one else can have him either?"

The cat stalked closer.

Selena frowned, her gaze darting from Gareth to the were-panther. "I am not as stupid as you seem to think."

Millicent shifted to human, hands on hips, black hair tumbling over her shoulders. "I beg to differ."

Gareth sat back. What had Millicent done? If Selena suspected he had lured her here to find out information about the duke's plans...

"I do not know how you managed it," continued the vamp, "but you have bedded her, haven't you?"

Gareth tried to look innocent.

"The were-cat is too protective of you. Too jealous for me to believe she hasn't claimed you as mate. What I don't understand is how you kept the relic on her wrist."

Millicent stepped forward. "You are wrong."

"The hell I am. And I cannot wait for His Grace to get back so I can tell him." She stood, giving Gareth a glare that should have singed his eyebrows. "And you have been playing me for a fool. But do not mistake me, Sir Knight, for I shall have you in the end, only it will be with *your* hands tied above your head." She lunged for the bellpull.

Millicent leaped forward, shifting to panther in midair, slamming into Selena's back, and sending them both tumbling to the floor. She had her teeth around Selena's throat before the woman could shift to bat.

"Don't kill her," commanded Gareth.

The panther's eyes rolled to acknowledge him, but did not relax their hold around Selena's throat.

"We can use her," he continued, pulling his eating

dagger from his belt and slicing open his wrist. Red blood dripped down his hand. He strode over to the women and leaned down, holding his wrist over Selena's mouth. The vamp's nostrils flared and she swallowed several times, but clamped her lips tight.

"Drink it," he said. "Or I will let Millicent tear out your throat."

Whether she took his threat seriously, or the smell of his blood was just too much temptation for her to resist, he did not know. But her red lips opened and she sucked his hand when he placed it against her mouth. Gareth grimaced. He did not have the vamp's bite to inject him with whatever drug she released to dull the pain and bring euphoria to her victims. He could bear the pain, but the sensation of her lips moving across his skin, the suction of her mouth as his blood drained…

He watched the were-bat's eyes change as she stared up at him. Within moments they softened and she blinked at him in confusion.

Gareth straightened. "You can let her go now, Millicent."

She let out a mew of exasperation, stood, and shifted to human. "What is going on?"

"I appreciate your following my lead, my lady. Do you have aught I could use for a bandage?"

Her golden gaze darted from his bloody wrist to Selena's blood-smeared mouth. Nell chose that moment to peek around the doorway, the sprite perched on her shoulder.

"It is safe to come in, ladybird," said Gareth.

The old woman hobbled into the room, strips of

fabric within her gnarled hands, and began to wrap his wrist. Gareth pointed at the little man. "You. Ambrose. Return to Bran to summon his warriors."

He twisted his pointed face. "I would not call them *warriors*, Sir Knight. A *motley horde* perhaps, but not warriors."

Gareth picked up his tunic and pulled it on. "How long will it take them to assemble and get here?"

The sprite furrowed his brow. "Lord Bran said he stands at the ready... perhaps an hour or two."

"Make it one hour. Tell Bran it is now or never."

Twelve

AMBROSE BOWED AND LAUNCHED INTO THE AIR, HIS flight just slightly wobbly. "I shall return to save you, Lady Millicent. Have no fear!" He zipped out the window.

"Why does everyone think I need to be rescued?" muttered Millicent. "I have managed to take care of myself all of my life——" She spun on Gareth. "And you——you were supposed to just charm the vamp into talking. Not seduce her."

He shrugged. "Old habits are hard to break, my lady."

She snarled.

"But I promise you it shall not happen again."

Millicent nodded, then flicked a gaze at Selena, who rose to her feet and wiped the blood from her chin with the edge of her sleeve. The foolish chit gazed lovingly at Gareth… again. She could not be that fickle. "You made her drink your blood."

He winced. "We need her help."

"And you must have deduced the duke's schemes or you would not have sent for Bran. There is magic in your blood, then? This is why Ghoulston wanted it…"

Selena snickered. Gareth threw her a look and she hushed, clasped her hands to her bosom, and batted her eyes dolefully at him.

Millicent made a face. "How long do the effects last?"

Gareth shrugged. "I am not sure. And Selena says there is no magic in my blood. That over the centuries the magic has altered my blood into a natural sort of love potion."

"Ghoulston's gift for the queen! So that is what's in the tea leaves... a concoction of your blood. But what would the duke gain by making the queen fall in love with you?"

"If he controls the relic, he can control me. To an extent."

"You both have it wrong," interrupted Selena. "Shall I enlighten you, my love?"

Gareth started. "Aye, lady."

Selena threw Millicent a triumphant look as Gareth's attention settled solely on her. She patted her disheveled hair and adjusted the black lace pelerine at her shoulders. "The duke experimented with *my* knight's blood, and managed to find a way to add his own to it. The queen shall fall in love with His Grace, not Sir Gareth. But my master could not find a way to prolong the effects, so he added a bit of cocasha to it."

"Cocasha?" asked Millicent.

"An addictive narcotic created by a Viscount Casha over two centuries ago," replied Gareth. "Rumored to be made from the daydreams of pixies and the seeds of a bush germinated with the viscount's magic, it is mild and relatively harmless in small quantities."

"It tastes like chocolate," added Selena.

"Then even if it is detected in the tea, no one will think anything about it." Millicent began to pace the room, weaving between pillows and couches. "The queen will continue to drink the potion. My instincts were right. They gossiped about the arrival of Prince Albert at Lady Yardley's tea party, and Ghoulston reacted strangely. He must have been anxious for me to get the tea to the queen before she met with the prince again, for rumors had it that she might fall in love with her cousin. Ghoulston said the queen should marry a loyal subject... and spoke of the vagaries of love."

"Do you think your friend has already given the box to the queen?"

Millicent shook her head. "I have no idea. If she waited on the lady last night, it's possible."

"We must find a way to warn the queen."

Millicent came to an abrupt halt. "Who would believe such a story? Even now it is difficult to imagine the lovely young queen in love with that overbearing, evil... frog. Perhaps it won't work."

"Perhaps. But we must do something."

"We shall," answered Millicent. "We shall get Nell out of this place to somewhere safe, so the duke cannot use her against me anymore. You both agreed to that, remember?" And she glanced between Gareth and Nell. "*I* agreed to stay until we discovered the duke's plans. We can pass on this information to whoever might listen, but I will not get tangled up in affairs of the abovegrounders."

Gareth's blue eyes glittered, but he nodded his head. "As you wish, my lady."

Millicent fought an odd feeling inside her at the expression on his face. Didn't he understand that Nell must come first? That getting in the way of the duke's plans would endanger all of them? Why must he think they should come to the queen's rescue? Surely the lady had sorcerers and counselors who protected her. What could one were-cat, an old woman, and an enchanted knight do to change the fate of the world?

That he should make her feel guilty and selfish for protecting her own truly bothered her.

The door to their prison shuddered, and they all spun to face it.

"Lady Selena," called one of the guards through the widening crack in the door. "Ye have been in there a long time."

"Get rid of him," hissed Gareth.

Selena crossed to the door. "And you are interrupting! Go away."

But the crack widened farther. "The duke said to watch ye around the magic man," continued the guard, his face now wedged in the opening. "And ye have had long enough for a spot of fun."

"You're just jealous," snapped the vamp. "I told you, you don't own me, Jok."

Millicent rolled her eyes. "Jok? I thought you had better taste, Selena."

"Oh, do be quiet."

The door scraped the rest of the way open, and one of Ghoulston's most trusted guards stepped into the room.

"Too bad it's not the red-haired giant," muttered Gareth as he drew his sword.

Jok took one quick glance around the room and drew his own sword with a grin. "Eh, lookin' for a bit of sport, guvner? Most happy to oblige."

Millicent shifted to panther, putting her body between the men and Nell. She hoped Bran and his gang would get here fast, for it appeared they were escaping. Now.

Jok did not have a chance of beating Gareth in a sword fight, and knew it within the first few seconds. His cocky grin faded and he reached for his pistol. Gareth sliced his hand. When Jok bent over to cradle the wound, Gareth shoved him with a well-placed boot to the back. At least Jok was smart enough to stay down.

Gareth spun his sword in a dizzying display of naked steel and faced the other guards crowding the doorway. "Next?"

His voice sounded arrogant, but Millicent knew him well enough now to hear the weary sadness that lay underneath. She did not wait for the other guards to take up the challenge, or draw their pistols. They possessed none of the honor her knight did, and would not hesitate to shoot him. They did not fight fair in the Underground.

Millicent let loose her fiercest panther scream and leaped past Gareth into the mob of guards. She caught a glimpse of frightened eyes before she bowled over two of the men. Muffled grunts and confused shouts followed as they tumbled across the corridor. Millicent bit and clawed, felt the cold slice of a blade on her right shoulder. The steel must have been coated in silver, because it actually cut her. She screamed again, turned on the man who held the dagger, and clamped her jaws around his throat until he quit struggling. He stank of ale and sweat and fear.

Millicent snorted. Both of the men she had attacked no longer moved. She spun to face the rest of the guards.

Gareth stood like some warrior god, a bloody blade in his hand, fallen bodies surrounding him. His eyes blazed a fierce blue, and his handsome face held little emotion. Until he looked at her. "Are you all right?"

Millicent nodded. Swished her tail for emphasis.

"'Twas a foolish thing to do, my lady. You could have gotten hurt."

Millicent limped over an unconscious guard and nuzzled Gareth's hand. His lips tightened but he gently caressed her head.

"We have only just begun to fight, my love. Allow me to protect you a little." Then he released a sigh. "Let Nell bind your wound."

As soon as the old woman had tied a bandage around Millicent's shoulder, they joined Gareth and Selena in the corridor. The were-bat's nostrils flared from the apparently tantalizing smell of blood surrounding the fallen guards, but she kept her lust-glazed eyes fixed on Gareth's face.

"Can you lead us out of this labyrinth of passages again, Selena?" he asked her.

The were-bat fluttered her lashes at him. "Of course. But His Grace made sure to post extra guards along the exit we took before. It seems he did not trust me where you are concerned."

"Surely there are other exits we can take."

"Yes, but His Grace—"

"Posted extra guards there too," finished Gareth. "Perhaps we should just leave the same way we entered."

"By the front door? Hmm, yes, I don't think His Grace thought to post extra guards there. But the palace is surrounded by his minions. I do not think we will get far."

Gareth still held his sword in his hand, although he had cleaned off the blood. "We need only hold them off until the tavern keeper arrives."

"Are you sure you don't just want to stay here with me? Millicent could give me the relic…"

Millicent growled.

Gareth shook his head. "I am afraid that is not possible, Selena. And when the effects of your… last meal wear off, you will be grateful I am gone."

"Oh, but I could never be—"

Millicent growled. She would not watch Selena fawn all over Gareth another instant. Bad enough when the woman just lusted after him, but love made her a blithering idiot. Millicent stalked forward, nose high and tail rigid, Nell clutching her ruffled fur. Millicent could not hope to remember the path they had taken to the duke's main living quarters, but she could follow the scent of the kitchens, which lay just off the main hallway. Fowl roasted in the oven and something boiled on the stove. Potatoes, perhaps.

That faint smell grew stronger as they climbed down each circular stairway. Eventually Selena pushed past her and opened a door that led into the great hall of the castle. Only a few fairylights lit the space, casting dark shadows along the stone floor. Millicent could not see any guards, which raised her hackles even more.

"Trap?" whispered Gareth.

Selena frowned. "No, I swear. I would not put you in harm's way, my love. His Grace would just not expect you to use the front door." She gathered her black skirts and sailed down the vast hall.

Gareth still looked unsure, yet they had little choice but to follow. Their footsteps echoed hollowly through the high-ceilinged hall, even the faint swishing of her paws sounding as if a thousand cats stalked the passageway. Millicent could hear nothing but their own movements, and actually felt relieved when they were finally challenged near the doorway.

The red-haired giant of a guard stepped from behind a lewd painting of gargoyles sporting with a maiden, and raised his brows at Selena. "Look at ye! Ye couldna' resist feeding off the magic man again, eh? I told His Grace ye'd do it."

"Oh, shut up," she snapped, and shifted to were-bat, black wings stirring up the air, flapping enchanted tapestries against the walls, interrupting the moving scenes embroidered on them. She launched herself at him before the guard managed to draw his pistol from his holster.

She would have knocked down a smaller man, but the giant just let out a grunt and grabbed her wings and twisted.

Selena screamed.

The front door burst open, and several more guards ran inside, only to meet Gareth's drawn blade. Millicent positioned herself in front of Nell, growling and showing her teeth, claws extended at the ready.

But the men did not get past Selena and Gareth. Within moments, the guards lay bleeding on the floor.

Selena hovered over the giant's limp body, blood dripping from the corners of her hairy mouth. Then launched out the door.

Millicent had seen a ring of guards around Ghoulston's palace from her upstairs window, but the courtyard lay empty, and they passed through unchallenged. She could not see past the outer wall, but the portcullis had been raised.

"This is too bloomin' easy," muttered Nell.

Then the ground began to sink.

Millicent's paws sunk several inches before she realized the cobblestones had melted into some sort of sludge. She pulled out one paw, which made a sucking sound, and resulted only in forcing her back legs deeper into the ground. A low whine slipped from her throat.

Selena bobbed above them, the motion of her flight lacking any grace whatsoever. But at least she wasn't trapped. Millicent turned to look at Nell. With her slight weight, she had sunk only up to her ankles. Millicent growled, shook her head toward the portcullis.

Nell glared. "I ain't leavin' ye."

Something smacked Millicent's head. She turned. Gareth had chopped apart the odd colorless trees that lay potted about the courtyard, and held out a slender branch to her. Millicent grabbed it with her teeth as he tugged.

Gareth sank deeper into the sludge.

Selena let out a shriek and clutched the knight's shoulders with her small back legs, furiously beating her wings to keep him from sinking any farther. Gareth pulled both himself and Millicent toward the portcullis, Nell having a much easier time of it in following them.

It took forever to reach solid ground.

Gareth fell backward and yanked Millicent the last few inches out of the trap. Selena landed beside them, her wings quivering from exhaustion. Nell slowly made her way to join them. "If that's the best spell Ghoulston's got," she said, "then he ain't much of a wizard."

Millicent snorted. Drowning in that slime would be her worst nightmare. As far as she was concerned, Ghoulston had done a jolly good job of malicious spell-casting.

Gareth stood. "We're not out of here yet."

Nell shrugged.

Selena flew under the portcullis into the open. Shots rang out, and she spun and landed back next to them, shifting to human. "There's too many of them."

Millicent rose, looked past the thick stone wall, and blinked. Hundreds of men stood just beyond the castle, clustered on each side of the roadway that led out of the cavern. Although men might not be an accurate description for some of the beings. Ghoulston must have scoured the Underground for guards. Ogres and dwarves and golems usually kept to themselves, but they had joined the ranks. Other experiments of the sorcerers faced them as well, creatures made from spells which altered man into horrors that usually avoided any contact with others.

"Ghoulston must have paid them a lot," said Nell.

"But their hearts won't be in it," replied Gareth. "They'll run at the first sign of opposition. And I doubt if Ghoulston exhausted his magic or money by coating all their bullets and blades with silver."

Nell's mouth dropped open. "Ye can't be serious. I've never seen so many ogres in one place in me life. They won't run—ogres *like* a good fight."

Gareth narrowed his eyes, studying the far entrance that lay across the vast cavern. "What we need is a distraction."

"What we need is to turn around and go back," said Selena.

Gareth shook his head. "I've faced heavier odds than this."

Millicent did not doubt his words. But she could not lead Nell into such danger. She grabbed the old woman's skirt with her teeth and tugged.

"Ogres or no, we ain't goin' back," snapped Nell, yanking her skirt out of Millicent's teeth. "Ye may not care about Country and queen, Millie, but I do. We must get word to that sweet gel about Ghoulston's evil plan. Can ye imagine spending yer life in love with the likes of him?"

"The were-cat's right for a change," injected Selena, curling a hand around Gareth's muscled arm. "Stay here with me, love. I'll make sure you are happy."

Millicent scratched her front claws along the ground, rucking up grooves in the hard-packed earth. Sometimes she liked being unable to speak in were-form. It saved her from joining in frustrating conversations.

The small army that faced them suddenly began to

sway, a murmur of sound rising like a wave through the throng. They had been seen. Yet, the guards did not advance. Perhaps they had been ordered not to unless Millicent and her companions tried to escape.

Perhaps they had time to wait for Bran and his gang to show up.

Two ogres stepped forward onto the road and began to swing their battle-axes in showy maneuvers. The ogre with the green hair missed his last catch, and his ax dropped on the other ogre's head. A growling argument ensued, followed by swinging fists and then serious injuries. Small fights began to break out in the group of watching creatures.

Or perhaps not.

"Ogres are so stupid," grumbled Gareth.

"Ghoulston brought them here fer a fight and they been itchin' fer one," added Nell. "Dunno if Bran will manage to get here before they get too restless."

He nodded. "You're right, ladybird." He turned his fierce blue-eyed gaze on Millicent. "I will provide the distraction. Take your Nell and escape. I will join you as soon as I can." And he stepped beyond the protection of the portcullis.

"No," said Selena, grabbing his sleeve and trying to stop him. But Gareth shrugged her off as easily as he would a gnat and strode boldly out onto the road. Selena turned and glared at Millicent. "This is all your fault. If he wasn't so worried about protecting you, he wouldn't be taking such risks."

Millicent growled softly. Risks? The man was committing suicide. He knew he would die, but he counted on his reemergence within the relic. But she had seen the pain he went through when he had died before. Nothing could be worse than experiencing one's own death. And yet he offered himself for her yet again. She wished he would stop. She felt unworthy of his sacrifices.

She suspected he tried to change her by example. Tried to make her a better person… to make her a hero like him… to care for others. And she feared he might be accomplishing it. How could she cope with the responsibility of caring for so many?

Gareth strode boldly up to the ogres and they stopped fighting and bent down to listen to him. Whatever he said made them laugh, causing another ripple of sound and movement to flow through the crowd. Gareth stepped back a few paces, drew his sword, and balanced on the balls of his feet. The ogres began to circle him, making quick feints with their weapons to judge their opponent. Millicent could hear the crowd calling out wagers.

"I ain't watchin' that boy die again," muttered Nell.

Millicent whined, torn between protecting Nell, and joining Gareth in his battle. Oh, she had no doubt her knight could handle a few ogres. But he would continue to challenge any comers until he fell, trying to buy them time until Bran managed to get here. Gareth had taken the first opportunity for escape, knowing Millicent had already waited too long to free Nell, and now it might cost him great pain.

A sudden burst of light and heat made Millicent jump back, slam into the bumpy stone wall of the gateway. She blinked at the roiling ball of fire that had once been her Nell, and blinked again when the explosion settled into licks of flame surrounding a magnificent bird. Millicent had seen Nell take her were-shape only a few times, and the sight still awed her. Brilliant red feathers burned with orange flame, and an elegant tail draped behind her like the train of a ball gown. Nell's were-creature took on a bulk of four times her size, just as Millicent grew larger in her were-shape. The old woman's appearance now matched her personality.

That graceful yellow beak opened and spat a stream of liquid fire, which spread down the roadway like an uncurling carpet of blazing fury.

Gareth had the distraction they needed. As one, the crowd of guards turned to stare back at the castle and its now-blazing gateway. The ogres took advantage of the knight's inattention, and closed on Gareth. Millicent could swear she saw the knight's white teeth flash in a grin as he cut the knees out from under the two Goliaths in quick succession.

Selena's black eyes glittered with shock, and then fear, as she stared at what once had been a harmless old lady. Then she shifted to bat and took wing.

Millicent waited for the flames in the road to die before she leaped forward, confident Nell could now fend for herself. As she had feared, several more fighters attacked Gareth, stepping over the ogres' fallen bodies to get to him.

Her knight moved with such grace and beauty he appeared to be dancing. His sword emitted quick flashes of silver in the muted beams of the fairylights on the cavern ceiling. His hair flowed around his face like a swirling river of gold, and his feet moved so quickly he often appeared to be flying a few inches above the ground.

He was simply the most beautiful thing Millicent had ever seen. And she did not want to watch him die again. She did not want to see that lithe body broken and bleeding, his handsome face white with pain.

She screamed, her cry of challenge echoing off the cavern walls, and plunged into the crowd of fighters now challenging Gareth. Millicent guarded the knight's back, used her claws to slash at her assailants, only her long reach and speed saving her from getting sliced by a sword time and again. She heard an occasional shot ring out, but they fought too closely for the guards to avoid hitting their own people with a bullet, and few were foolish enough to try it.

A flash of red streaked from above, and a stream of Nell's fire sent more than one monster running for their lives. Nell appeared to be concentrating on the guards who stood outside their fighting circle, careful that her lethal flame would not accidentally fall on Millicent or Gareth.

Millicent's world narrowed down to the awareness of Gareth at her back, the next monstrous attacker to loom before her to be cut down, and the pile of fallen guards at her feet, which managed to at least slow down the next creature before it attacked.

Despite her were-strength, Millicent began to tire. She marveled at Gareth's endurance, for he had nothing but his human abilities to draw on.

"We cannot hold them off much longer," gasped Gareth from behind her. "Run, now, Millicent. Take ladybird out of here before—"

A creature with an enormous bald head, bulging eyes, and tentacles for hair tried to get past Gareth's guard. Her knight lunged forward, struck quickly, and danced back again. At the same time, a volley of shots rang out, and Millicent glanced up.

A ball of fire twirled to the ground, landing with a flurry of sparks.

Millicent screamed; leaped in the direction that fallen star had landed. Some of the creatures were smart, and got out of her way. Some, she tore through. Nell had been taken down by one of their bullets, despite the distance the firebird had maintained above them, nearly touching the cavern ceiling. Despite the horrible aim of pistols, and how few of them held silver bullets. She should have taken Nell out of here. She should not have allowed the old woman to fight. Of course they would use their guns on her—and it took only one lucky shot. How could she have been so stupid? So careless with her friend's life?

She could hear Gareth fighting behind her, trying to follow. But she had no thought but to reach Nell.

A black shape swooped above her. Selena. She had forgotten about the were-bat. Where had the sly girl been hiding? For despite the love potion, she had not gone to Gareth's rescue.

A large creature loomed in front of her. Some twisted combination of shape-shifter and human, with horns sprouting from a broad forehead, the blunt nose of a swine, the claws of… a cat. Claws as large as her own. Millicent launched into the air, aiming for the thing's throat. The creature went down beneath her, already dead before it hit the ground.

She looked up in surprise. An enormous bear stood beside her, his claws bloody and his mouth open in a grimace of teeth, the closest Bran could get to a smile in were-form.

The cavalry had arrived.

Millicent grunted her thanks and leaped forward again, leaving Bran to face another one of Ghoulston's minions. She must get to Nell. Surely, she had to be close. The ball of fire had fallen…

A ring of blackened bodies surrounded an open space, the earth scorched a dusty gray. At first, Millicent could not understand what she saw. A bundle of black wings covered the upper part of a small old woman lying on the ground. Nell had shifted back to her human form, a natural reaction to a loss of consciousness. Or a loss of life? Her legs lay twisted at an odd angle, her skirts charred about the edges.

Millicent screamed yet again, her throat aching with the sound.

The were-bat glanced up, wings pulling away from their shroud around Nell. Selena's pointed teeth dripped with red, red blood.

That red color grew in Millicent's gaze until it lay like a shadow over her eyes. She stalked forward, every muscle quivering, every inch of fur on her body bristling with fury.

Selena sat frozen, fear clouding her eyes.

Millicent glanced down. Perhaps a bullet had killed Nell before she hit the ground. Perhaps the fall had killed her. She would never know. Selena had finished whatever life Nell might have had left. The were-bat had always lusted after the firebird's blood, as if it held some special flavor that could not be found on any other human or shifter. Even with all the dead and dying bodies surrounding them that Selena could have drank from, she had gone after Nell.

Millicent had not realized until this moment how much the vamp truly hated her.

And had not realized she could ever be capable of returning such hatred.

Millicent leaped, landing on Selena's wings, which she had curled over her head for protection. But nothing could stop Millicent. Not Gareth's shout from behind her. Not her reluctance to kill if she didn't have to.

Selena had taken her Nell. The only person she had ever cared for. The nature of the beast always lurking within Millicent—even in human form—took over and she did not even try to control it. She struck blindly, mindlessly ripping and tearing with teeth and claw. Snarling and growling in unchecked fury. The were-bat tried to fight back. Then tried to run. She left half a wing behind to break free, but managed only two steps before Millicent fell upon her again.

Nothing but red. Nothing but the feel of skin and muscle shredding beneath her claws. Screams and then whimpers.

And then the hated thing beneath her lay still. And she heard the voice of her mate. Calling. Commanding.

Millicent spun. The cat recognized the scent of her mate. It soothed the beast until she could regain some control once more.

Millicent shifted to human and ignored the remains of her cat's fury, and focused her gaze on Gareth. The red haze slowly cleared.

He looked... stunned. "Millicent?"

She tried to wipe her hands on her bodice, but so much blood thickened the cloth she only spread the gore around. "This is what I am. A beast. A creature of the Underground, born in blackness with a soul to match. You! I am not like you, Gareth. I am not some valiant white knight full of honor and vows of chivalry—"

"Millicent." He took a step forward.

She growled. "Do not come any closer. You are responsible for all of this. I should have left you with Ghoulston and taken my Nell away from this place. But no, you influenced us all with your grand ideas of interfering in matters better left alone. What do I care of the world above? When has it cared for me?"

She tore her gaze from his and settled it on Nell. White, broken. Dead. "I have lost her because of you."

He made some strangled noise, had the audacity to take a step closer to her. But the small bundle of woman that had been Nell suddenly began to smoke, then to burn. Licks of orange fire cradled her face and body, as it did when she took her were-form. Those flames grew taller, until a column of orange-red fire grew upward, nearly touching the cavern ceiling. Silver tinged those flames. Silver and gold.

Millicent had not noticed the sounds of fighting until they suddenly stopped. Until she could hear the crackle of flames in the silence. The heat from that cyclone of fire made her step back again and again. She shielded her eyes with her arm, glanced away to see that Bran and his gang had managed to conquer the duke's army of guards. Most of the creatures left standing were shape-shifters.

With a roar of sound that rocked the cavern, the flame gave one last pulse, a flow of liquid fire curling and twisting up through that column, then quickly falling back to earth, winking out of existence as suddenly as Nell's life had been extinguished, leaving nothing of the old woman but a small pile of silver ashes.

Millicent shifted back to panther and lifted her head, hiding within her beast, allowing the cat to scream her anguish until her throat grew raw, until she could scream no more.

Gareth strode over to the small silver pile of Nell's ashes and collapsed to his knees, his head bowed, his shoulders hunched. He laid his hands around the ashes, as if he sought to cradle old Nell once more.

Millicent caught her breath on a sob, turned, and ran.

Thirteen

GARETH MATERIALIZED IN A DARK ROOM NO LARGER than a water closet, with a tarp for a ceiling and worn wooden planks for flooring. He could hear muted laughter coming from beyond the rickety door. The occasional clink of glasses and the sour smell of ale told him he stood within Bran's tavern, where Millicent worked. A dark shadow in the corner of the room stirred, and he turned toward the panther curled up on a pallet of old rags.

Millicent.

She had kept to her were-shape. He wondered if she always slept in her beast's form, and had stayed human when they slept together only because of him. With drunken louts only a few feet away, perhaps she felt safer with tooth and claw at the ready.

Or perhaps the events of last eve had allowed her beast to completely take over her humanity.

Gareth still felt a sharp sense of loss at the death of ladybird, so he could only imagine what Millicent might be feeling. She professed to be incapable of great love, yet if he could manage to make her love him half as much as she had loved her Nell, he would be a lucky man… which might now be an impossible task, since she blamed him for ladybird's death.

His eyes had adjusted to the gloom, and he could make out the glossy sheen of the panther's coat, the powerful grace of leg and shoulder, the beauty of those slanted eyes, long lashes closed in sleep. Ah, how he loved his Millicent and her beast. But would she ever be able to accept his love enough to return it? For he had thought he only had to capture her heart. He hadn't realized until yesterday that his obstacles might be insurmountable.

How could she love him, when she did not love herself? When she thought of herself as some kind of monster, a creature of darkness? He could see the goodness shining within her, the light in her soul that called so strongly to his own. So she had killed Selena… he would have done the same. That did not make her a beast; it made her human.

Gareth opened his mouth, then snapped it closed. Words. All he had to give her were words, and he had already given her many. They would never be enough.

With one last glance at the sleeping panther, he quietly slipped out the door into the hall. Although the exterior of the pub had been constructed with quarried stone like most of the buildings in the Underground, the interior walls had been made with wooden boards, with enough of a gap between for him to catch glimpses of the public room. A long, polished bar with rows of twinkling bottles behind, scattered tables with a ramshackle assortment of chairs surrounding them. More than half the chairs were still full, mostly with shape-shifters.

The tarp that made up the ceiling occasionally fluttered, and he imagined it had been put there for privacy, for the denizens of the Underground did not need to worry about snow or rain.

What an odd world to grow up in.

He entered the taproom and all eyes turned to him. Gareth sauntered over to the bar, faced the man who had helped rescue his beloved, and gave him a deep bow. "My lord, I thank you again for your aid—"

"Eh, none of that," interrupted Bran. "Shape-shifters may style themselves as lords up above, just because our nature honors us with a title. But we don't hold to none of that in the Underground. Just Bran will do."

"Very well. My thanks, Bran. And a word, if you please."

The tavern keeper raised his abundantly bushy brows, scanned the interested crowd in the room, and cocked his head toward a door behind the bar. "In here."

Gareth followed him into a room that apparently served the dual purpose of storage and living quarters. When Bran settled his bulk upon a crate of whiskey bottles, Gareth took a similar seat opposite, the slats creaking in protest.

"You found Millicent, then?" A rhetorical question, since she had obviously returned to the Swill and Seelie, but the relic had sucked Gareth back in before he had a chance to find her himself. And he didn't quite know where to start the conversation. He had

met men like Bran often over the years. No matter
the life fate chose for them—whether landed gentry or
peasant farmer—men of substance like the were-bear
commanded respect.

"Aye, and brought her home. She is taking the old
woman's death very hard."

Gareth nodded. "And the bag of ashes I gave you
to keep?"

Bran glanced over to a low shelf. "I'll mind it until
you can bury the old woman in a proper place."

"Thank you." Gareth did not know what impulse
had moved him to gather Nell's ashes, other than
a belief that his ladybird deserved a more respectful
resting place. Yet something more nagged at the back
of his mind... he rolled his shoulders to loosen the
muscles. With all the years he had lived, he often
forgot more than he knew. "Have you seen aught of
the Crown's spies?"

"Ah, the shape-shifters from above. They've been
sniffing around the pub. But they haven't dared
another attempt past my door since the last one." He
smiled, revealing an ominous set of white teeth.

"But they will continue to stalk her. And the
duke's minions will return to harass her as well, once
Ghoulston returns to the Underground."

"I can protect my own. I have proven that, last
night. These sorcerers will think twice before interfering with me again."

"Perhaps. But they won't leave her alone until she
gives up the relic."

"Then it seems a simple matter to me." Bran folded
his hands over his barrel of a chest and leaned back

against the wall. "Go find some other gel to play with, Sir Knight."

Gareth suddenly felt as if he faced Millicent's father, and the man was suspicious of her beau's intentions. He would respect the role Bran had chosen to assume. "I assure you, my feelings for Millicent are quite genuine, sir. I love her. I wish to marry her, if she'll have me."

Bran studied Gareth for a long moment, then threw up his hands. "Bloody hell. That makes things a wee bit more complicated."

"Indeed. And I fear there is more to this than just Millicent and myself."

"More to—aah, Ghoulston. What's the devious bugger up to anyway?"

Gareth suppressed a sigh of relief. The shape-shifter had not dismissed the duke's schemes as none of his business. He appeared genuinely concerned. "Ghoulston used Millicent to deliver a potion to our young queen. When she drinks it, she will fall in love with His Grace, and their marriage will provide him with the power and ambition he so desires. And I sincerely doubt his new position will benefit the English people."

Bran surged to his feet, glancing over at the far wall. Gareth followed his gaze, surprised to see a picture of Queen Victoria gracing the wall just as it did in most homes aboveground. Apparently, all those who lived below did not disregard the world above as much as Millicent did.

"We must stop him," snarled Bran. "We must protect the queen—wait. Surely the Master of the Hall of Mages will sense the magic within the potion. Queen Victoria is the most warded person in the country."

"If it held magic, yes. But it does not. And the ingredients are so… unusual, I doubt anyone will detect something wrong with it."

"But there is nothing on earth that will make someone fall in love if they don't want to—hmm, I sense ye have something to do with this, Sir Gareth. No, ye needn't explain. The important thing is to stop the queen from taking that potion. But I don't know that anyone above would listen to us—not that we can even get near the queen to warn her. Shape-shifters are not well thought of above. Even the Master's spies are known to be despised by the rest of the gentry."

Gareth nodded. "That is true. But there is one person who can take this message above and has a chance of being believed. The Duke of Ghoulston has already introduced her to society."

"Millicent."

"Indeed. And I need your help in convincing her to do it. I do not think she will listen to anything I have to say to her right now."

Bran shrugged. "She blames ye for the old woman's death, but she'll get over it. For a woman, and a shape-shifter, she can be pretty sensible. Hmm." He twisted his lips in thought and added, "Sometimes." Then he strode over to the door, opening it with a flourish. "The best way to deal with her is by not giving her a choice. Come along, man. If she's to mix with the gentry, we've got to get her a proper wardrobe. And arrange for a carriage. I don't have the resources of Ghoulston, but there is a particular lady friend of mine from above who may grant me a boon."

Gareth raised a brow, but returned Bran's earlier consideration and did not ask him any questions. Although few truly knew of their actual existence, he had no doubt many a bored aristocratic lady might find a dalliance with a man from the Underground titillating. If Bran had chosen to reveal himself to an abovegrounder, that was his business. Gareth had more important things to worry about, for he could only hope he was doing the right thing. Had he judged Millicent correctly? Or would she hate him even more for pushing her into this?

❦

"I won't do it." Millicent crossed her arms over her ragged bodice, glaring at Bran.

Gareth sighed. The tavern keeper had finally received a message back from his lady friend, who had obligingly granted him the use of her town house and staff for the morrow. Bran, Millicent, and Gareth now stood in an empty pub—except for one lone shape-shifter collapsed over a table, and one tired sprite snoring atop an empty saucer.

"Now see here, missy," retorted Bran. "Ye are my employee, and this is the job I've got for ye to do."

"Bloody hell, Bran, you know better than to get mixed up in the business of sorcerers. Since when do we pay mind to the world above?"

"Since when have we had a chance to make a difference?"

Millicent turned her blazing golden eyes on Gareth.

He had faced many a maddened warrior and had never been tempted to flinch. Until now. But he managed to calmly return her gaze, leaning back against the bar, crossing one leg over the other with bored nonchalance. Let Millicent roar. She looked lovely with her color up.

"You've been listening to *him*," she accused, still glaring at Gareth. "With all his talk of honor and chivalry. Well, I can do without it, thank you. It's what got Nell killed."

Gareth closed his eyes, allowing the pain of her words to pass through him. She spoke out of anger. She did not truly mean it. "And will you allow Nell's death to be for naught?"

He had spoken quietly, yet the room quivered with such stunned silence you would think he had shouted.

When Gareth opened his eyes, he saw such pain in Millicent's face he almost gave up his plan. But if he did, he would be giving up on Millicent, and he could not allow his love for her to turn him into a coward. "Ladybird wanted us to stop him," he continued. "She loved her queen and her country. And despite your denials, my lady, I believe you love them too."

They stared at each other, and he watched her strong will war with her heart, her stubbornness battle her anger. His Millicent was such a complicated creature, and he loved her for it... and allowed his love to show on his face.

Bran cleared his throat, turned his gaze away as if embarrassed by Gareth's naked display of emotion.

In Gareth's time, in the court of his king, such open displays of admiration were commonplace. Poems were recited to ladies, ballads sung in their honor. Swords were crossed for any slight to a maiden. Times had changed, and Gareth had adapted to them, but he still found himself falling back into old habits.

Perhaps it would be wise to remember them now.

"I would trade my life for Nell's to make you happy, Millicent." Gareth fell to one knee. "Indeed, my sorrow for the loss of ladybird, and your broken heart, are almost too much for me to bear. If you would blame me instead of Ghoulston, then so be it. I am at your service, my lady, to do as thou wilt." And he drew his sword and held it out to her.

Millicent snorted, made as if to turn away, and suddenly stilled, her lovely brow wrinkled in thought. Then her face cleared, and she glanced down at him. "Oh, for heaven's sake. Get up. I'll do it."

Gareth looked up at her in astonishment. "Am I forgiven?"

"There is nothing to forgive. I-I spoke from grief, and acted like a fool. But no more." Her eyes glittered. "This is all Ghoulston's fault. Every bit of it. And if I can foil his plans, it will be a handsome revenge. When do we leave?"

The were-bear raised his eyes, opened his mouth, then closed it, his face still an unusual shade of red.

Millicent curled her fingers into fists. "I'll make Ghoulston pay no matter what it takes."

Gareth shook the hair from his face and rose to his feet. Ah, well, not exactly the intention he had hoped for. He had wanted Millicent to help the queen, and by so doing, realize the goodness within herself. Instead, she now saw this as a way to destroy

Ghoulston and avenge Nell's death. He should have known this would not be so easy. How could he help Millicent see the beauty inside her, when she had no inclination to do so?

Well, at least she no longer blamed him for Nell's death. Her anger had weighed upon his heart, and the absence of it made Gareth suddenly feel lighter.

Bran stepped over to the bar and poked a finger at the small winged form lying facedown in an empty saucer of gin. "Ambrose. Wake up, ye sot. I have another errand for ye."

The sprite rolled over and cracked a lid, then struggled upright as he caught sight of Millicent. "My lady! How may I be of sher... servish... service?"

Bran rubbed a hand across his broad face. "Ye are to take her to the same place ye delivered my message to."

The pointed brow furrowed.

"Egads, man, ye were there less than an hour ago. Surely ye cannot have forgotten?"

The sprite waved a hand, the movement nearly upsetting his balance. "Course not. I know the aboveground like the back of my hand. I used to be a message sprite for the gentry above, don't you know?" And he leaned down toward the saucer, eyeing a small puddle of gin still wedged within the curve of the bottom.

"No more of that for ye until ye get back," said Bran, blocking the sprite with his hand.

"Jusht one for the flight..."

"No."

Ambrose sighed. "Let's be off then." And with an overly dramatic flourish of his arms he took wing, a dazzling swirl of iridescent color, which would have looked impressive if he hadn't been bobbing up and down like a jack-in-the-box. When he came to an abrupt halt by the simple expedient of smashing into the door, Gareth winced.

"Are you sure he can manage to find his way there again?"

Bran nodded. "Seen me a lot of drunks, and he manages his liquor better than most."

Gareth nodded, walked over, and gently picked up the sprite. "Are you all right?"

Ambrose rubbed his head, glanced at Millicent, and scowled. "Slightly wounded. Never incapash… incapacitated." And he took flight again, this time waiting for Gareth to open the door.

"Good luck," called Bran as they left the pub. "If ye're not back by tomorrow evening, Millie, I'm coming up myself to get ye."

She did not reply, just shifted to panther and kept her gaze resolutely focused on the message sprite. Those wings glowed somewhat, which made it easier for them to follow Ambrose through the twisted streets of the Underground. They crossed too many bridges for Gareth to count, the water smelling as bad as the Thames, carrying away the waste of the city. Two thugs challenged them once, a man with a deformed face and his dwarf partner, but at the sound of Gareth's sword sliding from its scabbard, they quickly disappeared.

They finally reached the outskirts of the city, where tunnels peppered the walls of the enormous cavern, and the sprite unerringly chose one, Millicent and

Gareth having to push to follow. Some sort of glowing fungus grew on the walls of the tunnel, so they had a greenish luminescence to light their way. Despite Gareth's excellent night vision, he still managed to stumble into Millicent. The first time she turned and looked at him, golden eyes glowing in the darkness, then continued up through the passage, ignoring him after that.

Gareth wondered if she had shifted on purpose to avoid conversation. Millicent still grieved for her friend, and he would comfort her if she would only let him. He had to remind himself that she was unused to comfort. Bran had mentioned as much, when they had been searching for her after she'd run away following Nell's death. The were-bear would have been more of a friend to Millicent, if she had but let him. But by the time Bran hired her, she had already been on her own for far too long.

Ambrose grunted as he slammed into another wall. He had managed to bounce off more than a few as he led the way.

The rocky ground slowly changed to more even footing, and soon they reached a rough-hewn set of stairs. Gareth could only imagine how many sorcerers had carved secret passages into the Underground to perform the darker arts, and began to wonder about this lady friend of Bran's. But the man would not send Millicent into danger. Perhaps the passage had already been there when the lady had moved into her residence and she had come upon it accidentally. And later discovered that the Underground was no myth. But how had the lady met Bran? Gareth now regretted his reluctance in asking Bran more questions. He had a feeling he had missed a rather interesting story.

The passage finally ended at a closed door. Ambrose lifted the knocker—his wings buzzing furiously—and let it fall with a muffled thump.

"There is a knocker?" said Gareth in disbelief.

"Of coursh," piped Ambrose. "How else would the lady know when Bran comes to call? You certainly aren't shug… suggesting he barges in unannounced, are you?"

"This is just a bit too civilized for an entrance from the Underground."

"Perhapsh. I must say it's shmuch… much better than how I first arrived here. Through a crypt, no less."

The door suddenly swung open and a liveried footman bowed to them, showing no surprise at welcoming a panther, sprite, and sword-wielding knight. "Lady Millicent and company? We have been expecting you. Please follow me." And he turned smartly on his heel.

Gareth had not felt odd within the Underground, but as they passed through a cellar, up the stairs, and into an elegant hall, he imagined they made an unusual group within the fine trappings of this home. Magic permeated the walls, with enormous paintings of sparkling lakes that rippled beneath a golden sun, where birds flew in a cloudless sky and fish jumped above the waves. Chandeliers of crystal beads wrought in the shape of teardrops created a glittering rainfall above them, and the mosaic floors beneath their feet shimmered with designs of silver minnows racing like lightning.

The footman halted halfway down the hall, threw open a pair of gilt double doors, and bowed them through.

A lady stood within a parlor, which was covered in shelving from wall to ceiling. So many different objects sat upon each shelf that Gareth could not make sense of the vision they created as a whole. He would have happily studied each in turn, from odd-shaped seashells to clear paperweights with moving figures inside, if the lady herself had not commanded his attention.

She wore a loose evening gown of soft pinks, the material floating around her as if she stood in a mild breeze. With tousled black hair, thin red lips, and an extraordinarily long, hooked nose, the lady was more striking than beautiful. Gareth bowed, and she nodded at him.

"I apologize," she said, her voice so at odds with her serene appearance that Gareth started. She punctuated each word with a soft honking noise. "I just had to meet these friends of Bran's... you are quite lovely, my dear."

She spoke to Millicent, who responded by sitting on her haunches and licking one black paw. Gareth's hope that she would shift back to human out of politeness faded. He stepped forward. "Sir Gareth Solimere, at your service, my lady. My companions; Ambrose the sprite, and Lady Millicent."

"Lady Roseus, good sir," she replied. "I thank you for allowing me to satisfy my curiosity about my guests." She glanced at Millicent, who responded by switching to lick her other paw. "My man will see you to a guest room, where I have laid out several gowns for Lady Millicent to choose from. They are all visiting gowns, since I understand she is to venture out tomorrow to pay a call on a friend of hers…?"

Gareth nodded, unwilling to satisfy the lady's curiosity to the extent of telling her the name of Millicent's friend.

Lady Roseus honked a yawn and quickly covered her mouth. "Please excuse me. I am not used to such late-night visits. But know that you are welcome here, and should you have need of anything, my staff is at your disposal."

"You are most gracious, my lady."

Millicent spun and padded out the door, Gareth following a bit more slowly. He turned and looked up at Ambrose, who hovered near his shoulder. "You should return to Bran and let him know we arrived safely, and all is well."

Ambrose wobbled in the air. "But… but Lady Millicent might have need of me…"

"Go."

The sprite threw a glance at Millicent, who flicked her tail but otherwise ignored him, following the footman up the stairs. Ambrose grunted sadly and then whizzed away, heading back the way they'd come. With a gratified sigh that the little man had left without much of a fuss, Gareth hurried up the stairs to catch up to Millicent, his frown increasing with every step he took.

By the time they reached the guest bedroom, Gareth wore a scowl.

The room had been decorated like the rest of the home, the walls painted with magical lakes fading to clear shallows. But a starlit sky glittered above these waters, and the floors had been crafted with carpets in flecks of brown and cream, with tiny bits of sparkling stone spread throughout, so the entire room appeared to be a sandy shore. An occasional swell of water would flow from the walls to lap over the floors at the edges of the room. A low bed sat in the center of the space, a canopy of bushy silklike fronds covering the top, one small window beside it.

"Ring if you need anything, sir," said the footman before closing the door firmly behind him.

Millicent sniffed the room, then settled on the bed, her nose on her paws, her eyes closed.

"I know what you're doing," said Gareth, leaning against the closed door.

The panther sighed.

"You're staying in your were-shape to avoid speaking to me."

He thought he detected a twitch of Millicent's lip.

"You were incredibly rude to Lady Roseus." He stepped over to a wicker chair, several gowns laid over the top. "And look how generous she's been." Gareth suddenly had an alarming thought. Perhaps Millicent cared for Bran more than he had imagined… surely not. But he prodded anyway. "Don't tell me you're jealous of her?"

At least his question had the desired effect of shifting Millicent back to human. "Don't be ridiculous. She's a *flamingo*."

Ah. That explained a few things about Lady Roseus, including her unusual decor. "So?"

"I am a panther." She sniffed. "In the hierarchy of shape-shifters, we do not compare."

Gareth stepped over to the bed, sat down beside her on top of a coverlet embroidered with flowering rushes. "Why are you avoiding speaking to me? I know what you must be feeling... do you still blame me for Nell's death?"

"No. I... I am sorry for blaming you. It was unfair of me." Millicent rose and stood facing the wall, a long stretch of indigo water with a night sky above, the twinkling of the stars reflected in the gentle waves.

Gareth rose and stood behind her, breathing in the scent of her hair. How did she always manage to smell like a grassy meadow? "You were overwhelmed by grief. And I do not think you are done with it."

Millicent firmed her mouth. "I will be when I expose Ghoulston."

Gareth laid a gentle hand on her arm. "My lady, do you still mistrust me so?"

"What do you mean?"

"I can see the grief in your eyes, in your face. You do not have to keep up your guard with me. Allow me to help."

She took a deep breath. "This is why I did not want to speak with you. You will not let it be... I wish I was still angry at you. It would make things easier." She turned, staring up at his face, her own features lined with a deep sadness. "What do you want me to do? Cry and tear out my hair? That won't bring Nell back."

Gareth thought his imaginary knuckles would be bloody by the time he finished pounding at the wall around her heart. "No. But acknowledging your grief might make her loss easier to bear."

"I haven't cried since… since my mother died. And it did me little good then."

He understood. She had been broken too long. But it was time for her to heal. "I love you, Millicent. I vow I will never leave you. Ever."

Her eyes suddenly welled with tears. "Damn you, Gareth."

He folded his arms around her. Her forehead collapsed against his shoulder, and she began to shake.

"Bloody hell," she sobbed. And then she spoke no more for a very long time, until she had soaked his tunic, and quit trembling.

Gareth spoke to her the while, nonsense words of comfort and love. His lady cried so quietly that he would not have known it but for the wetness of his tunic.

She finally looked up at him, her eyes rimmed with red, irises glistening an amber color in the starlight. "I feel… drained, now. Empty. Make love to me, Gareth. Fill me with your goodness."

"I fear you give me more credit than I deserve, Millicent. I am no better than any other man, often filled with dark thoughts and temptations."

"But you fight them, Gareth. And your actions are always noble. Let me be a part of that, for a while."

He would have protested more, but she leaned up and covered his mouth with her sweet lips, and Gareth lost himself in the delicious feel of Millicent.

Fourteen

She had been a fool to fall in love with him.

Millicent knew that.

Even as she wrapped her arms around him, as he drew her down to the carpeted floor that looked like nothing more than a sandy lakeshore, she chided herself for loving him. If she lost him the way she'd lost Nell…

No. She couldn't bear it. The darkness of her beast would finally overcome her humanity. Oh, sometimes the panther felt like a separate being living inside her. A beast she could control. Could tame. But more often than not, she could not separate it from herself. The desire to hunt and kill, to allow mindless instinct to take over, became an everyday battle. And when Nell died, Millicent could not stop from shape-shifting. For the first time, the beast had ruled her, taken over the change, and dominated her will. She had not killed Selena in self-defense. Millicent wanted her dead, with a blind fury her beast relished and gloried in. If Millicent had not realized her dark nature before then, the pleasure she took in feeling Selena's torn flesh beneath her claws made it readily apparent.

Millicent did not know how she had managed to return to the tavern, could not remember shifting back to human.

She growled low in her throat.

She could not allow that to happen again.

Gareth broke the kiss, pulling his face back to stare deeply into her eyes, his blond hair falling across his forehead and cheeks. "What is it?"

Millicent shook her head, pulled him down to her using her were-strength, and rolled them both over until she lay atop him. She supposed they might be more comfortable in the bed, but they lay near the wall, and a shallow wave from the enchanted mural lapped over their bodies, curled about his broad shoulders. She felt the cool slide of the water against her legs, felt it gently tug at the hem of her skirts. Starlight reflected off the lake and into Gareth's crystal-blue eyes. A light breeze tugged at the few loose curls in her coiffure, and she could smell the sharp scent of pine from the forest off in the distance, the lush scent of meadowsweet blooming in a clearing between the trees. She could see through the magic, of course, if she wanted to.

She didn't want to.

Millicent sat up, straddling Gareth's hips, and unbuttoned her bodice, the worn fabric allowing her to shed it easily. She tossed the ragged cloth aside, one of the best she owned, but nothing to compare to the gowns the duke had provided her with. Then she half turned so Gareth could reach the ties of her corset, giving him an arch look over her shoulder.

He grinned, that delightful one where his full lips curved to create two little lines next to the corners of his mouth. The smile reached his eyes, changing the brilliant blue to a soft azure. His skilled fingers made quick work of her laces, and he tossed aside her corset as carelessly as she had her bodice, then untied her skirt and petticoat, until they fell down her hips, allowing her to slide her chemise over her head.

Millicent did not bother to take the time to discard her skirts. She slid down Gareth's lap, untied his drawers, and pulled them down his angular hips. He was already hard, rigid, and full. She had intended to pleasure him slowly, to savor what she feared might be the very last time she made love to him. But she had spoken truly to Gareth. She had never felt so empty before, so very much alone. Nell had been more of an anchor than Millicent had ever suspected. She needed to fill this emptiness inside her, to selfishly lose herself in his love. To remind her of the joys of being human.

Millicent leaned forward and took him inside her.

He sucked in a breath through clenched teeth.

"Did I hurt you?" she whispered.

Gareth strangled on a laugh, clutched her hips, and began to rock her. Millicent fell forward onto her arms, sunk her fingers into the thick carpet, and opened her body and soul to her white knight. She tried to emblazon the feel of him in her mind, for the memory would have to last her the rest of her life. His strong fingers dug into her bottom as he pressed her down to him. She felt her nub rub against the smooth skin of his pelvis, and the friction added to the fire already burning inside her womb.

She threw back her head and arched her back, pulling him deeper inside her.

Millicent exploded unexpectedly, her breath coming in harsh pants as ecstasy shook her. She felt Gareth throbbing inside her; as always, his release a match to hers. She absently wondered if all men could do that, or if this was yet another one of his special skills. For it increased her pleasure twofold, and it took her a very long time to come back down to earth again.

When she became aware of her surroundings once more, she realized her coiffure had come undone, and she sagged over Gareth's lean body, her face hidden within the dark strands. She also realized she felt infinitely better… and that she had rushed their encounter.

Millicent slowly rose, regretting the loss of him inside her as soon as she did so. He lay spent on the sandy carpet, his eyes closed, his breathing still ragged. She quickly stripped off her skirts, stood naked in the magical starlight. Shallow water swirled about her ankles, over his muscular legs. But the illusion did not quite reach reality, for the waves looked nearly transparent, and her skin felt dry.

She walked over to the washbasin, wet a cloth, and cleaned herself, then wet another and returned to his side.

"Take off your clothes," she instructed.

Gareth opened one eye, grinned at her, and then sat up and proceeded to follow her orders. Millicent knelt next to him, placed her hand against his smooth chest, and pushed him back down after he tore off his last garment. Starlight gleamed in his hair, burnishing it gold. Like his eyes, it changed color according to the light, and she thought she liked it best right now, the shade akin to a shiny gold sovereign. And she liked his eyes best now too: twinkling with starlight and darkened to a smoky blue.

Millicent took her clean, wet cloth and smoothed it over his brow, watching the strands of hair around his face curl from the damp. She traced his nose, the fine straight shape—except for the slight turn up at the end, which she realized added to his boyish handsomeness. She smoothed the cloth over his full lips, noting the wide shape of his mouth. Then across his cheeks, the bones slightly prominent, and then along his firm, slightly square chin.

She must memorize every inch of him. She could not allow her memory of him to fade over the years. It would be all she had left.

His neck, the skin ridiculously soft and vulnerable. His shoulders, incredibly broad and strong. His chest, the sculpted ridges and valleys and the slight puckering of his nipples.

Gareth watched her with a quizzical look, which abruptly faded when she reached his pelvis, ran the cloth over his shaft. Even after their lovemaking, it had remained half-erect, and she watched, slightly amazed, as it stirred to life once again.

Millicent dropped the cloth, remembering how Gareth had made love to her with his mouth. She would not only memorize the sight of every inch of him, but his taste, as well. She dipped her head.

Gareth groaned.

Her tongue tingled. Slightly salty. Rich and heady, like strong ale. She explored the length of him, until he started to tremble, and clenched his fists at his sides. And then she retraced the path her cloth had taken earlier, until she reached his mouth, and he grasped the back of her head, kissing her with an intensity that made *her* tremble.

And then the world spun, and Millicent found herself on her back, Gareth inside her, slowly, sweetly making love to her again.

If she died tonight, she would be content.

She blinked the burn of tears from her eyes. She had shed more today than she had in her entire life, and she would never cry again. She vowed she would not have a reason to.

Gareth whispered in her ear, nonsense words of passion and endearments. He made love to her this time as if he sought to comfort her as well: gentle, gliding motions that slowly built a delirious heat inside her once again. And Millicent responded by dancing to the loving tune with him, touching him wherever her hands could reach. Saying good-bye with tender caresses.

They reached that peak together, and tumbled over it slowly, clasped so tightly together Millicent thought, for just that one moment, they might have become one being.

"Gareth," she murmured, tasting his name on her lips, memorizing the feel of it in her mouth.

He lifted his head, his eyes so incredibly blue, so incredibly intense.

"Millicent," he breathed… and then disappeared.

She blinked for a moment, startled by the cold air replacing the warmth of his body, his sudden absence. Dawn had come too quickly.

Millicent sat up, held her head in her hands for a moment. *Gareth.*

She sighed, and stood. The painting on the wall had lightened, and the one lone window across the room now glowed with the pale coming of the sun. Something she had little experience with. But it occurred to her that she stood in a room aboveground… and she had a task to do.

Muck up the duke's grand schemes. Revenge for Nell.

Millicent went back to the washbasin and splashed her face, dispelling the dreamy aura Gareth had created. By the time she finished washing, a beam of sunlight slanted into the room, fell on a glint of moonstone.

The bracelet.

As usual, it had fallen off her arm when they had made love. It must have been after the first time, but she could not remember losing the bracelet. She bent down and picked it up, cradling it in her hand. She had promised him she would never give the relic to another, that she would always return it to her wrist, so he would come to her again.

But she knew she could no longer keep that promise. Too many reasons bade her otherwise, but the most compelling one was simple. She loved him.

Millicent set the bracelet on the mahogany wood top of the washstand and strode over to the chair that held what appeared to be over a dozen gowns. Heavens. She picked up a chemise edged with fine lace and pulled it over her head, when a knock at the door interrupted her.

"Yes?"

The door cracked open, the beaked-nosed face of her hostess peeking through the crack. "I thought I might come myself to help you dress, dear, instead of one of the maids. Bran led me to believe there is a bit of... secrecy regarding your errand."

"I can manage fine by myself. I am not used to maids and whatnot."

Undaunted, Lady Roseus slipped into the room, a smile on her face. Despite her rather large nose, or perhaps because of it, she was a strikingly lovely woman. She wore a pink morning gown, the shade matching the color of her cheeks. "Here, let me help you with those laces."

She punctuated her words with a decisive honk. Millicent sighed and turned around, holding up the linen corset to her front. She did need help, and if Bran liked the lady, she should make an effort to do so as well.

"Where is Sir Gareth?" asked Lady Roseus as she tugged on the corset strings.

"You just missed him," replied Millicent, the ghost of a smile on her face. Apparently, Bran did not trust the lady enough to reveal any of their secrets. She would take her cue from that, for she could feel the other woman fairly quivering with curiosity.

"Your human form is just as lovely as your were-panther, Lady Millicent. The color of your hair matches your coat... sleek, black, and shiny."

"Thank you." Millicent turned around and studied the gowns.

"And your eyes," continued Lady Roseus, "such a lovely shade of gold, and slanted just like your panther's."

Millicent flushed, ignoring the lady's further compliments. She supposed she would just choose the gown on top. She picked it up, and Lady Roseus honked.

"Oh, my dear, not that one. With your coloring, let's see…" She dug through the pile. "This bronze poplin, now, this will be quite complimentary on you. I must apologize for all the pink gowns. I did not know what you looked like, and I have so many of them…"

She looked so earnest, and concerned, that Millicent could not help but warm to her, and tried to hide the dismay on her face as she gazed at the dress. "I'm sure this will suit." The dress looked extremely… fussy. But she supposed Lady Yardley would be impressed by it. The hem and sleeves and an apron-like square down the front had all been edged with scallops. Lady Roseus handed her matching bronze shoes, a small black lace hat trimmed with bronze beads, and a pair of light green gloves.

The lady tamed Millicent's hair into a presentable chignon, pinned the silly hat on her head, and handed her a bronze-beaded reticule and black lace parasol. Millicent retrieved the bracelet from the washstand and stuffed it into the small bag, fighting the urge to return it to her wrist. She turned and faced Lady Roseus, lifting her chin to combat the sadness in her heart.

"You look smashing, my dear," said the smaller woman. "The carriage is waiting, but my man will need a destination."

"I shall give it to him," replied Millicent.

Her hostess's face fell.

"I thought curiosity was *my* animal's faulty nature."

Lady Roseus pinked at the subtle gibe. "I am really quite fond of Bran."

Millicent raised a brow.

"I am interested in anything concerning him… especially if it could be dangerous."

"Do not fear, Lady Roseus. My task will not endanger him, or any of your household." Millicent studied the other woman. "You must care for him a great deal to aid him with little knowledge of the reason."

Her pink complexion darkened to rose.

"I will make sure to mention that to him."

The lady's face lit. "Oh, would you? I would be ever so grateful… men can be rather obtuse, at times."

Millicent nodded in agreement, followed her hostess from the room, down the stairs, and through the hall to the front door. A carriage did indeed stand waiting for her, and the coachman pulled down the step for her, and she climbed inside. The man gave her an inquiring look.

Millicent realized she had no idea where Lady Yardley lived in London. Or whether she would even be at home, instead of ensconced at her country estate, where Millicent had last met her. "Lady Claire Yardley… daughter to the Earl of Sothby."

When the coachman nodded and closed the door, she slumped in relief. As she had hoped, she did not need an address for such lofty personages. Lady Roseus had an excellent coachman… who would no doubt inform his mistress of their destination as soon as they returned. Millicent looked out the window as the carriage jolted forward. Her hostess still stood on the steps of her elegant town home, waving frantically. Millicent sighed. The lady gathered her skirts, as if she would run the carriage down unless Millicent acknowledged her farewell. Millicent finally waved back. Heavens, she had never met a friendlier woman. No wonder Bran had been drawn to her. As she had recently discovered, her employer possessed a gentle heart beneath his overbearing exterior.

Millicent continued to gaze out the window. She loved the rain, such an odd occurrence aboveground, but today the skies lacked any gray clouds, and brilliant sunshine bathed London. Although it hurt her eyes, she loved days like this the best. To feel warmth from something other than a fire, a gentle warmth that bathed her cheeks and hands, was something she could get used to.

The houses became grander, and more peculiar, as they drove through the affluent areas of the city. The aristocracy flaunted their magical powers with their very own homes. Imposing marble edifices snuggled up to fanciful towers of gemstone and spun sugar. Stately parks held animated statues, and fountains sparkled with liquid diamonds. Odd-shaped trees mixed with enormous oaks, while flowers of luminous color swayed next to bushes of tamed roses.

So bright and strange and beautiful. Millicent felt the sudden urge to stay aboveground forever.

She sat back against the cushions of the seat. She would never get an opportunity to do so. She belonged in the Underground, in the darkness, with the rest of the creatures of the night. Even now, she felt her beast clawing to the surface, panicked at all of the open space around her, the tall buildings and crowded streets only adding to her tension.

The carriage entered a large square, stopped in front of a mansion decorated with thousands of white peacocks. They roosted on every windowsill, abnormally long tails of delicate feathers sweeping down to the next story. Two stood silent sentry next to the door, and one enormous bird spread his feathers in a white arc on top of the home, neatly shading the entire house.

Millicent focused her attention, and the illusions faded to reveal a grand mansion of white stone and soaring columns. She frowned and relaxed her vision so the illusion could return. The home was impressive enough without the addition of the birds, and she wondered about the vagaries of the aristocracy.

When Millicent met with Claire within the elegant withdrawing room of Sothby Manor, she had her answers. Rich oak paneled the walls of the room, and the furniture had been upholstered in shades of lavender and blue. Each piece had been carved with intricate designs of cherubs and fawns and centaurs. A harp stood in one corner, the strings shivering to some muted tune, and the heavy drapes swayed to a nonexistent breeze. Just a touch of magical illusion then, but enough to give the room charm without being alarming.

"My heavens," said Claire as she breezed into the room. "What a lovely surprise."

"I'm sorry to call on you uninvited," replied Millicent. "But I have come on an important errand."

Lady Yardley froze, studied Millicent for a long

moment. "What has happened? You are… changed since I last saw you."

For just an instant, Millicent wanted to confide in Claire. Wanted to tell her about her relationship with Gareth, and her love for the magic man, and perhaps between the two of them, they could think of another way… But no, she had come for a greater purpose. Her own problems were of little consequence in comparison.

"I have something to tell you that might be difficult for you to believe. It involves the Duke of Ghoulston."

"Willie? Why, whatever could that old goose have done to put such a look upon your face?" She held up a hand. "Wait, let me ring for tea first, and let us get comfortable. I cannot forget my duties as hostess, no matter how outrageously curious you have made me."

Claire tugged on a bellpull, and then sat on a velvet settee, arranging her skirts around her feet, before patting the space next to her. Her blue morning gown made her hazel eyes appear a deep aqua, and her auburn hair had been dressed with miniature white peacock feathers.

At the same moment as Millicent sat down, a maid appeared in the doorway and one of the birds curled about the newel post in the hall let out a tremendous cacophony of screeches.

"I sense a theme, here," murmured Millicent.

Claire smiled rather sheepishly. "They are beautiful creatures, but I had no idea when I created them that they would be so loud." She turned and instructed the maid to bring tea, then looked back at Millicent with a shrug. "Father insists I practice, you see, and although Mother tells me to find a husband instead, I am determined to work on my craft. Unfortunately, my spells have a tendency to… multiply… *spontaneously*. I created the illusion of one bird, and the next thing I knew, the mansion was covered with thousands of them." She rolled her eyes. "Father is regretting his insistence that I practice, and Mother tells him 'I told you so' several times a day."

The maid brought in a silver service of tea, spread it on the table in front of them, and Lady Yardley began to pour. "Close the door on the way out, Sarah. Sugar, Lady Millicent?"

"Please."

"Just be grateful you did not choose to visit last week," continued Claire. "I had a passion for hummingbirds. Such charming little birds. One would *not* think a horde of them would be so alarming." She gave a delicate shudder. "We are still removing their nests from Mother's wigs."

The door closed.

"But enough of my problems. What has brought you here, Millicent? The last time I saw you… oh, is that it? Have you finally succumbed to the charms of the magic man?"

Millicent nodded.

"You poor dear. I imagine it was rather… alarming." She lowered her voice. "To discover one's most secret desires at such a tender age… and from such a conservative background… But do not take it to heart, my dear. It is better to know oneself before marriage, at any rate. It will make the choosing of a husband much easier. Not that I know myself… err, it is what Lady Chatterly always says."

Millicent nodded again, feeling as if her neck were made of rubber. Thank goodness she had not given in to the urge to tell Claire about Gareth. The other woman had obviously never been in love before. She would not understand.

"Dearest Millicent. I don't mean to be insensitive to your plight, but honestly, you have me atwitter with curiosity about Willie. If you don't share your gossip this moment, I may burst."

"It is not merely gossip, Lady Yardley. I am afraid you must brace yourself for some unpleasant revelations."

Claire sipped her tea, and set it back on the porcelain saucer with a clatter. "You are frightening me."

"I mean to. What I am about to tell you will be difficult for you to believe. The Duke of Ghoulston is a man with two faces. And I don't think you've seen the one I am about to tell you of. And I… I am not the person you think I am."

A peacock screamed.

Claire jumped, skirts rustling, then gave a nervous laugh.

Millicent took a sip of her tea. Chamomile. Perfect. The mellow flavor soothed her and warmed her throat. "It all began in the Underground—"

"Oh, Millicent, please. Secret caverns created by dark sorcery beneath London are nothing but a myth used to scare naughty children."

"Then I have lived my entire life in a myth." Millicent set down her tea and stood, walked across the room to the window. She opened the glass-paned windows, ruffling the feathers of the peacock that perched on the ornate ledge. She caught a glimpse of tiny iridescent wings off to her left, and realized that a few of Claire's hummingbirds must still be about. She shifted, her panther sniffing with delight at the delicious smell of the fat peacock. She leaped, grasped the neck of the bird with her jaws, cracked it with a shake, and began to gorge. Her beast growled with disgust, for the bird was just an illusion, and did not fill her belly.

Millicent shifted back to human with blood still smeared around her mouth.

She hoped she had judged Claire correctly, and the woman would not faint.

Lady Yardley's face drained of all color as she stared at Millicent. She clasped a hand about her throat and swallowed. "Was that really necessary? I already guessed you were a shape-shifter. I even deduced you were some sort of cat."

"Yes. But I doubt any of the shifters of your acquaintance—and they must be few, since they are generally despised by your kind—would be so impolitic as to snack on one of your illusions."

"My kind? Why, Millicent, you wound me."

"Perhaps. Even guessing what I am, you still befriended me. But I rather imagine your parents would not approve of me."

"They are old-fashioned... yes, you are right. And you have made your point. I shall not interrupt you again, and I will keep my skepticism in check. Will that do?"

Millicent really liked this girl. How wonderful it

would be to have her as a true friend… But she rather doubted Claire would want to continue the association once she told her story. The girl's good character could tolerate only so much, after all. Millicent took a deep breath and rejoined Claire, but this time took a seat opposite in an ornate chair carved with gilded cherubs.

Lady Yardley did not protest. But she waved her hand at Millicent's face, then at the bloody carcass near the window. The bloody remains disappeared, and Millicent assumed her mouth had been cleaned as well, for Claire gave a nod of satisfaction.

Millicent told her story from the beginning: how she had grown up in the Underground; how the duke had used Nell to blackmail her to find the relic for him. She left out the parts about her and Gareth, only indicating that they had developed a sort of friendship. She did not leave out the part about Nell's death, despite how difficult she found the telling. She had to make Claire understand that the duke was a dangerous man, and had a ruthless side to him within the Underground.

By the time Millicent finished speaking, her voice had grown hoarse and she finally allowed herself a sip of tea. It had grown cold.

Claire continued to stare at her in the ensuing silence. A peacock screamed again. "Well," she finally said. "It is obvious you believe every word of this. I would think you under a spell, except for your immunity to magic. So I must conclude that you are mad."

Millicent blinked.

"Willie? Using black magic? Consorting with were-vampires in the Underground? I must admit, it is a little odd that the queen has suddenly developed a fondness for the Duke of Ghoulston, but as he says himself, there is no accounting for the vagaries of love."

"It has taken effect already?" murmured Millicent.

"Oh, come now! You know perfectly well the queen's food and drink are tested and tasted by the most gifted magicians—that the royal family themselves possess the strongest magic in all of England. Would you truly have me believe she would partake of a love potion and not know it?"

"Claire... Lady Yardley. I know how outlandish it sounds. But remember. There is no magic in the kingdom that can counter the power of Merlin himself. And that power is contained in the relic. And Gareth—the magic man, has been trapped inside of one for centuries. It is entirely feasible that his blood has become infused with the power of the relic."

"Yes, but... oh, Millicent. Even if I believe you, who would believe *me* if I told such a tale?"

"The Master of the Hall of Mages."

Claire rose, began to pace the floor, her slippers swishing softly against the parquet. "I have met the Duke of Sussex only briefly. He sees me as a young girl who is too flighty to even control her own magic. I'm not even sure he would grant me an audience... you cannot imagine how many difficulties of a magical nature occur in England on a daily basis. And I have no evidence of what you are saying."

Millicent suppressed a grin of triumph. Claire had quickly gone from concluding Millicent insane to considering the possibility of presenting the story to the master. "I can help on both accounts."

Lady Yardley paused, her gown twirling about her, a few auburn curls dangling from her coiffure tumbling about her aristocratic cheeks. Even in her agitation, she looked every inch the lady. She found Millicent's story difficult to believe, because the concept of such evil was foreign to her. The lady radiated a goodness Millicent could never hope to achieve.

Millicent opened her reticule and pulled out the relic. The smile faded from her face as the moonstone within the bracelet caught the sunlight streaming in through the windows and reflected it within the gem, making it swirl and glow and change color. Just as Gareth's eyes and hair had a tendency to change color in different light.

"If you bring the master this, I believe he will grant you an audience. For weeks, he has been pestering me with his spies to obtain it."

Claire covered her mouth with her slender hand. "Oh, no. I do not want it. Give it back to Lady Chatterly."

"It is not hers," snapped Millicent. "He—it belongs to no one. Not yet." She gulped a breath. She did not think this would be so difficult. But something inside her chest ached so hard she could barely think. "If anyone could break his curse, Lady Yardley, it would be you. You are goodness and light and elegance. And he must be given the chance to be free. You cannot imagine what it is like to be trapped in a cage not of your own making."

Claire slowly reached out a hand, as if she could not resist such temptation. "Is it true he makes your every fantasy come true?"

Millicent closed her eyes for a brief moment. "Yes.

That, and more. When he comes to you at midnight, he will confirm everything I have said to you. And then... after..." Her voice broke. She could not stop the low growl of her beast that followed. Panthers mated for life. She could not hand over their soul mate to another woman. She could not... "You and Gareth can go to the master, and then he will believe you. And then Ghoulston will get the punishment he deserves."

Claire stepped forward, her eyes on the bracelet as if entranced, and Millicent had to force herself to hold it out to her. The gem winked and swirled with milky color as Claire slid it on her arm. She held it there for a moment, but it did not tighten.

Millicent's heart soared, and she fought against the rush of feeling. She thought Claire would surely be the one to break the enchantment... and had hoped she wasn't. She must stop these conflicting thoughts. If the relic did not choose someone, Gareth would be trapped forever.

"It does not want me," said Claire.

Millicent tried to keep calm and self-assured. "Then you must give it to another woman after you have convinced Lord Sussex of Ghoulston's evil plan. When Sir Gareth appears, you can explain to him what I have done. You can tell him the relic must be given a chance to choose another..." But she could not manage it. Her voice broke and she could not utter another foul word.

"Millicent?"

Millicent stood, nearly knocking over the tea tray. "Tell him... tell him I am sorry." And she fled the room. Her eyes stayed dry—she had resolved never to cry again—but a sort of haze blinded her as she ran through the hall and out the door. The white peacocks that stood sentinel on the portico screeched out their staccato cries behind her as she ran for the carriage, and another flash of tiny wings blurred somewhere off to her left. Millicent did not wait for the coachman to lower the steps. She flung open the door and leaped into the shelter of the dim interior.

The carriage lurched forward; Millicent collapsed against the cushions. She stared blindly at a tear in the upholstery of the seat opposite her. She had done it. She had set Gareth free, or at least, on a path where he could seek his freedom again. She felt happy for him, somewhere deep inside, but her misery at never seeing him again overshadowed it for the moment.

But she had done the right thing. And the Duke of Ghoulston would pay for his crimes. And Millicent would return to the Underground, among the forgotten, where she belonged.

If she had not been so sunk in misery, she might have realized sooner that the path they took back to Lady Roseus's town home differed greatly from the one they had taken earlier, and perhaps the lady's frantic waving as she'd departed meant something more. She would have been alert when the coach slowed down in a deserted mew.

But the spies had learned from past experience. They did not give her time to react. The coach door flew open, the chap with the scar and mane of golden hair covered her mouth with a cloth… and Millicent took a breath before thinking to shift.

The world faded to a fuzzy black.

Fifteen

GARETH MATERIALIZED IN A ROOM LIT WITH CANDLE-light, and decorated with so many feathers he resisted the impulse to sneeze. He blinked, taking a moment to gather his wits about him, remembering his lady had just made passionate love to him before the relic had sucked him back in.

Why then, did he face a reddish-haired woman in a strange room?

"Who are you?"

She sat in a prim chair, in a prim gown buttoned up to her neck, and twisted her fingers in her lap. "Lady Claire Yardley."

The name sounded familiar... "Millicent's friend?"

"Yes."

Gareth spied the wink of moonstone and strode forward, grabbing the woman's upper arm. "Where did you get this?"

"I... unhand me, sir. I did not steal it, if that's what you are thinking. Millicent gave it to me."

"Gave it...?" He staggered back a step. No, she would not do such a thing. She had promised... "When? Why?"

"This afternoon. She told me an improbable tale about a dear friend of mine. She said you would confirm the story."

Gareth collapsed on the edge of a bed covered with a downy blanket, absently noting it puffed around him when he sat. Surely Millicent could have come up with another way to convince Lady Yardley? If she had wanted to… but perhaps she did not want to. Perhaps this gave her the excuse to rid herself of him.

She had promised to keep the relic forever.

To keep *him* forever.

The prim lady leaned forward, her expensive skirts rustling softly with the movement. "Millicent told me to bring the bracelet to the Master of the Hall of Mages, and that you would convince him of Ghoulston's wickedness. She also said she is sorry, but the relic must be given the chance to choose another woman…" She blushed. "She thought I would be perfect for you."

"Indeed?" He had not intended to growl the word.

"I told her you—*it* did not want me." She slid the bracelet down her arm, where it dangled on her wrist. "See, it is quite loose. I can give it to you, if you'd like."

Gareth shook his head. "I would just have to give it to another. If Millicent no longer wants…" Had his voice just cracked, like some broken-hearted schoolboy? Did his chest truly ache, as if Millicent had taken his own sword and stabbed him in the heart? He had thought… after everything they had been through together… after making love to him the way she had…

He had thought she loved him enough to be faithful

to him forever. That he had broken down that wall around her heart, at least enough for her to consider them as one, united in purpose and deed and love.

But her need for revenge had outweighed her need for him. He understood it, because he understood Millicent. But that did not erase the feeling of betrayal that shook him.

For a moment his vision wavered, the walls of the room expanding and contracting, and he could not breathe. He crushed the bed coverings as he curled his fingers into fists, trying to keep an anchor in a world gone suddenly insubstantial. Gareth felt scattered, as he sometimes did when he first appeared from the relic. He heard a loud crack, which pounded at his ears, as if he heard his own heart break. And then the world righted, he drew in a long breath, and he could think again.

Millicent had forsaken him.

Is this how Merlin had felt, when Vivian had broken trust with him? No wonder the great wizard had called his magic down upon Gareth. He would do the same... but he had no one to curse but himself. After centuries of searching for true love, he now regretted that he'd ever found it. He did not know it would hurt so much.

"Sir Gareth. Are you well? Can I get you a spot of tea?"

"Can tea fix a broken heart?" he muttered.

"I beg your pardon?"

"Nothing." Gareth looked up at the woman. She looked... like a well-bred lady. Her eyes shone with the innocence of a woman who had led a sheltered life, attending balls and fetes, surrounded by gentlemen of only the highest pedigree. He doubted if she had ever been treated with anything but absolute respect. She commanded it with every line in her correct posture. He understood why it would be difficult for Lady Yardley to believe Millicent's story about the machinations of the Duke of Ghoulston. Such evil would be inconceivable to her.

He understood why Millicent had chosen this lady for him, damn her. Lady Yardley was the opposite of the shape-shifter. Goodness oozed from her very pores.

And he had no desire for the woman whatsoever.

Gareth leaned forward, determined to focus his thoughts elsewhere. "Millicent's tale is true, I assure you. The tea you gave the queen is laden with my blood. The blood of a man who has spent centuries seducing women."

She gasped at his indelicate words. And yet her eyes sparkled with sudden interest, and she leaned toward him. Innocent, yes, but a curious minx.

Too bad Gareth had no desire for her. Odd. He had never felt this way before. He had never met a woman he did not find attractive in some way or another. Perhaps Millicent's betrayal would have a worse consequence than just breaking his heart. If she had ruined him for other women, he would indeed be trapped inside the relic forever.

Gareth straightened his spine. He must keep his focus. He had more important things to worry about. "I assure you that Ghoulston is every bit as evil as Millicent has told you. Giving the queen a potion to make her fall in love with him is paltry in comparison to what he is capable of. Millicent told me the queen had fallen in love with her cousin, Prince Albert. Do you not think it odd that the queen's feelings have changed so suddenly?"

She nodded, delicate curls of reddish-brown hair curling artfully about her cheeks. Not wildly, as Millicent's black strands had a habit of doing. "We do not need to waste any more time in conversation, Sir Gareth. The longer I thought of Millicent's story, the more I came to believe it. I already have a carriage waiting for us. Millicent said the relic would grant us a conversation with the Master of the Hall of Mages, His Grace, the Duke of Sussex."

Gareth blanched. Surely Millicent had not realized the fate that awaited him in the Master's hands. Like all of the relics, the bracelet would be consigned to a heavily warded vault beneath the Hall of Mages. He would no longer be able to search for a way to free himself of the curse.

No, Millicent could not have known. He would not believe that of her. She had given the bracelet to a woman she deemed a friend, one whom Millicent judged "good" enough to release him from the curse. Millicent understood the torture of being trapped; he had seen her own anguish too often. No, she had not realized the consequences of handing the bracelet over to the Master.

But Gareth did.

He had felt the weight of the years for some time now. Only Millicent had lightened that heavy load. And she had abandoned him. Given up.

Gareth glanced at the relic. For the first time, he

wished it would draw him back inside and let him sleep, for without Millicent, he only felt tired.

But first he had a task to perform for his lady, and then Lord Sussex could lock him away inside a vault forever. It mattered little to him anymore.

He stood, shaking back his hair, his sadness. "Let us be off then, Lady Yardley. We have the task of saving the country, do we not?"

The lady smiled. She was indeed lovely. Her fingers trembled when he strode over and took her hand.

"Tell me, lady," he murmured, "what do you see?"

She blinked up at him. "I do not understand."

"My features. What do you see?"

She frowned, but replied, "Oh. You have dark golden hair, and eyes a shade lighter."

Gareth nodded. She did not see him as his true self. But Millicent had…

He followed the lady from the room, through a grand mansion oddly decorated with living peacocks from doorway to newel post, and so he felt no surprise when he saw a carriage shaped like a water lily and pulled by two white peacocks. Gareth unfolded a petal and handed Lady Yardley into the carriage, then ducked inside, admiring the illusion of sitting in a flower as they jolted along the streets.

"You must be talented," he commented. "It even smells as if we are sitting within a lily."

She flushed in pleasure at his compliment, and did not deny her magic had created the illusion, and she relaxed a bit as they traveled. London glittered by lamp- and fairylight, the aristocracy out in their finest, the late hour just the beginning of their social gaiety.

Grand mansions, decorated with even more fanciful illusions than peacocks and water lilies, shone with light from window and doorway. Guests entered and left: ladies dressed in gowns of sparkling silver and gentlemen in coats of prismatic color. Carriages passed their own conveyance, drawn by flaming horses, white stags with majestic glowing antlers, and even several types of birds: gold swans and crimson pheasants and long-legged herons.

Lady Yardley's peacocks paled in comparison.

They neared Buckingham Palace, the diamond-studded walls twinkling in the light of the moon. Near it stood a smaller building, no less impressive for its size, for the walls roiled in a dizzying motion of color from the magical wards surrounding it. The Hall of Mages, where titles were made or broken. The headquarters of the Master, and the training ground for many sorcerers.

And far beneath it, a vault containing many of the relics of Merlin.

"I have been here only once," murmured Lady Yardley, "when they tested me for my magical abilities. I had thought never to enter those doors again... it is such an odd place."

"There is nothing to fear," assured Gareth.

She gave a nervous titter. "No, of course not. I have a knight to protect me, after all."

He gave her a smile, and although he knew it did not reach his eyes, the lady looked reassured by it. When he exited the coach and turned to assist her down the steps, she clasped his hand with a firm grip, and nodded briskly at him.

"Right, then. We shall have to get past the front desk, and if it's anything like the Houses of Parliament, I will need all of my self-confidence to parley with the officious steward." She squared her shoulders, stuck her chin in the air, and strode for the door.

Gareth opened it in time for her to sail through, and lazily followed a few steps behind, glancing around the massive entrance hall. It held a desk, a few pots of greenery, and a gilded staircase, nothing exceptionally impressive, except for the multitude of doors lining the hall. Magic seeped through the cracks of the frames—a miasma of sapphire, emerald, and crimson color—and curled upward to snake along the ceiling.

"I would like an audience with the Master," said Lady Yardley to the bespectacled man sitting behind the desk.

"Madame, do you have any idea how late it is?"

"Do not be impertinent, sir. I am in complete possession of all my faculties and am quite aware of the hour. I should be attending a ball at this very moment, and the fact that I am not should impress you with the urgency of my task."

The man did not raise his eyes from the stack of documents in front of him. "His Grace is out, attending that very thing. Unless this is a life or death magical emergency, he cannot be disturbed. Shall I leave him a message?"

Lady Yardley crossed her arms beneath her bosom. "No, you may not. This could very well be a life or death situation... if you consider that falling in love with the wrong man could ruin your life forever!"

The clerk let out an audible sigh. "What *exactly*, is the nature of your business?"

Gareth took a step forward. "Me."

The clerk looked up. His eyes widened as his gaze traveled over Gareth's clothing, settling on the sword at his hip.

"What ball is his lordship attending?" demanded Gareth.

"It is not a masquerade, sir, so your costume is—"

A roar shook the building, rattling the teacup on the clerk's desk. Lady Yardley gasped as a group of baronets suddenly surrounded them. Gareth recognized the man with the mane of thick golden hair and the scarred face. The spy had been pursuing Millicent for weeks.

Gareth bowed. "Well met, gentlemen."

"I told you I smelled the stink of relic magic," growled the man to his fellows before turning back to pierce Gareth with a golden gaze. "You finally decided to give yourself up, eh?"

"Only for good reason."

The shape-shifter laughed, his booming voice echoing down the hall. "I told you he'd come for the girl, men. You won't be giving us any trouble now, will you mate?"

Gareth froze. "What girl?"

The other man frowned. "The were-cat. We caught her this afternoon… you didn't know, did you? Then why are you here?"

Gareth took a step forward. Several growls and hisses from the baronets followed his action. He ignored them, his attention completely focused on the were-lion. "If you have harmed her in any way, I will kill you."

The other man blinked, then threw back his head and laughed again. "Damn, man, I believe you." He lowered his face and wiped a tear from his eye. "Come now, I know all about the curse. We don't have anything against you, old chap; it's the magic of the bracelet we want. You just happen to be attached to it. And we can't have anything lying about that may be stronger than the magic of the Crown, can we? So be a good lad and play nice, and your lady will remain unharmed."

"Take me to her. Now."

The were-lion cocked his head and considered. "Give me the bracelet. Millicent—yes, of course we know her name—didn't have it on her."

Lady Yardley swayed beneath his hand. Gareth gave her a reassuring squeeze, and a meaningful nod.

"Are you sure?" she whispered.

"Most assuredly."

She drew up the sleeve of her gown, the moon-stone twinkling in the light of the wild magic dancing on the ceiling. Odd, it looked as if the gem had a small crack in it. But Gareth did not have time to study it, for the baronet with the orange stripes in his black hair made a purring sound similar to Millicent's contented rumble, and Lady Yardley yanked off the bracelet and handed it to the were-lion with trembling fingers.

"Well done," murmured Gareth. "Go home now, Lady Yardley."

She raised her face to his. She had lovely hazel eyes, but they could not compare to ones of golden-brown.

"You will still need me," she replied. "Besides, if you think I shall not see this through to the end, you are sadly mistaken."

Ah, he could see why Millicent had chosen her for a friend. Beneath her air of cultured sensibilities, the lady possessed a will of steely resolve.

Gareth turned and raised his voice. "You've got what you want. Now take me to her."

The clerk went back to perusing his papers again.

The were-lion clutched the bracelet tightly and nodded. "Follow me."

They strode down the hall, the half-dozen shape-shifters following, some of them shifting to their animal forms as they went: the tiger, an enormous raven, a shaggy-haired wolf.

"You will release her," said Gareth.

The lion-man shrugged. "She is of no use to us now, but it is not my decision to make. You will have to consult the Master."

They turned a corner, went down another hall. The building had not looked this large from the outside. The golden-haired man kept glancing at Gareth, curiosity lining his scarred features. Gareth waited. Thanks to Millicent, he had experience with the curiosity of cats.

"You did not answer me," he finally blurted. "If you didn't know I had your girl, why did you bring the relic here?"

"To foil a plot to overthrow the Crown."

The man stopped dead in his tracks, turned to face Gareth while the other shape-shifters made a circle around them. Lady Yardley shivered. They stood on a balcony overlooking an indoor garden of sorts, the trees and plants cultivated within it almost unrecognizable as any species native to England.

Gareth knew damn well the building was not this large on the outside. Dread magic, indeed.

"Your fears that the relic might prove a danger to the Crown were not groundless," said Lady Yardley. "Although Sir Gareth is not to blame—"

Gareth laid a hand on her shoulder. "Not now. We gave them the bracelet—we tell them nothing more until they give us Millicent."

Lady Yardley snapped her mouth shut and nodded, giving the shifter a mutinous glare.

The baronet did not argue. He spun and led them down a set of spiral stairs, the stone treads worn smooth from centuries of use. The light grew dimmer the lower they went, as windows no longer illuminated each landing. Fairylights lit the way instead, the enchanted dust within the globes reflecting sparks of glitter in the shaggy manes of their escort.

As they reached the final landing, Gareth could hear moaning that set his teeth on edge. They entered another hall of doors, these locked from the outside, with but a small opening lined with bars to see inside. The moan rose to a scream, and he bolted down the hall toward the sound, leaving the shape-shifters open-mouthed behind him.

Gareth recognized that scream.

He stopped at a door fairly vibrating with the sound. "Millicent!"

The screams rose in volume.

Gareth looked through the bars of the small window.

A cage with another set of silver bars sat within the stone chamber, and within that cage prowled a black panther, eyes glittering with near madness.

The shape-shifters had already caught up to him, leaving Lady Yardley far down the corridor. They were all as fast as Millicent.

Gareth called to her again, but Millicent was lost in some sort of hysteria, screaming and screaming. She threw herself at the bars of the cage, rocking the prison against the stone walls.

"You caged her," roared Gareth. "Like an *animal*. You—*you* of all people," and he swept a scathing glance at the shape-shifters.

The were-lion flushed. "It was the safest way we could transport her. We know our kind's strength—and no wards could hold a shifter. She was still unconscious when I left her!"

"Open the damn door."

His shame appeared to prompt him to obey the command, and he withdrew a set of odd-looking keys from his waistcoat, turning one in the lock. "I wouldn't go in there if I were you," he warned. "Take a look at her eyes, man. The beast has fully claimed her. You'd best wait until some trace of her human side—"

Gareth flung open the door. He couldn't be sure if Millicent's human side would ever come back, not after this. Not without his help. And if he was wrong—if she did not love him enough—he did not want to continue his existence anyway. He stepped into the room.

The beast stopping screaming, but continued to

growl a warning as she backed to the far end of the cage, watching him with wary eyes.

The door of the cage had a bolt on the outside. Gareth shoved it open. "Millicent. It is all right. I'm going to let you out of here, see?"

The panther's tail swished, and those golden eyes narrowed.

"It was wrong of them to put you in a cage." Gareth opened the steel-barred door. "I shall never let anyone do this to you again—"

The panther leaped forward, those heavy paws slamming against Gareth's chest, pushing him backward and down.

A scream and a shouted oath from behind him, and the outside door of the prison slammed shut.

The panther looked down at Gareth, teeth displayed in a snarl. He could feel the heat of her breath, the sharp points of her claws as they dug into his shoulders. Millicent weighed much more when in were-form and Gareth struggled to breathe.

"I… love… you."

Those golden eyes blinked.

"You betrayed… me."

Whiskers twitched.

"But only so I… could be free. I… forgive you."

And suddenly the weight lessened, and Millicent's beautiful human features loomed above him. "Forgive me?" she snapped. "There is nothing for you to forgive. I loved you enough to give you up—you should be *thanking* me."

Gareth smiled. "You are back."

"Well, of course…" Millicent rolled off him and

sat up, raked her wild hair away from her face. "No. Wait... how could this happen? My beast should have torn you apart. I felt its rage... I did not think I would overcome it this time."

"Love can overcome all odds."

Her eyes widened. "You. *You* brought me back."

Gareth sat up, a bit shakily, but that had been a close one. "You do love me, Millicent. Enough to bring you back to me. I had truly thought that when you gave the bracelet to Lady Yardley—"

"And yet you opened the door to the cage anyway? Are you mad? My beast could have..." She shuddered.

"But it did not."

"No."

They stared at each other for a timeless moment.

"You broke my heart," Gareth murmured.

"I am sorry you felt that way. Where... where is the relic?"

Gareth rose, extended his hand to her. "I gave it to the Master's spies."

Sixteen

MILLICENT STARED UP AT GARETH IN HORROR. "You did what?"

He shrugged his broad shoulders. "It was necessary."

"But why? Surely they believed Lady Yardley about the Duke of Ghoulston's schemes. The relic was only supposed to grant her an audience."

"We haven't told them about him yet."

"Then why—"

The prison door burst open, and the were-lion who had taken Millicent appeared in the doorway. She spun and growled at him. He had been the one to take her... the one to put her in a cage. And now she realized why Gareth had handed over the relic. So he could free her.

"Don't shift," murmured Gareth, placing a warm hand on her shoulder.

Amazingly, he prevented her from doing so. Her beast now succumbed to Gareth's will. The realization should have shaken her. It did not.

"Madam," said the were-lion, "please accept my sincere apologies. I should have suspected your reaction to being... caged." He winced, then his rather handsome face hardened. "But you have given us a merry chase over the last few weeks. I did not want you slipping from my fingers yet again."

Millicent growled.

The shifter sighed, then shrugged his broad shoulders, transferring his gaze to Gareth. "Sir. I believe you mentioned something about a plot to overthrow the Crown? I would be most interested to hear of it. *Now.*"

Claire suddenly appeared in the doorway, her lovely face near purple with exertion, her hand to her chest as she gasped for breath. "Millicent? Good... good heavens! Are you well? If they have mistreated you... in any way... they shall hear from my father! He wields incredible influence with the House..."

"From which the Hall holds a certain amount of immunity," interjected the were-lion.

Claire narrowed her eyes and glared up at the man. "What is your name, sir? I wish to make sure I mention it when I recount this... debacle, to the queen. Or were you not aware that I am a Lady of the Bedchamber?"

If Millicent had not hated the shifter so very much, she might have felt sorry for him at the moment. The spies might hold a certain autonomy in dealing with magical troubles, but *everyone* answered to the queen. And someone who held her special confidence was not to be taken lightly.

The man collected himself and bowed. "Sir Harcourt, at your service, Lady Yardley—if I recall your name correctly? And may I say, this is a dangerous business for a *lady* such as yourself to get mixed up in."

"Such as myself? I do not like your tone of voice, sir." She turned away from him in dismissal and held out her hand to Millicent. "Come out of there, this instant. I cannot bear to see you in such a place."

Her concern soothed the trace of fury remaining within Millicent, and she stepped forward, clasping her friend's hand. The were-lion narrowed his eyes, glanced from Claire to Gareth, and wisely kept his mouth shut.

Millicent felt Gareth protecting her back as they made their way out of the dungeons beneath the Hall of Mages.

"We are taking you to the Master," said the were-lion, who had taken the lead in front of them as if he still had control of the situation.

Claire threw him a glare as he glanced at her over his shoulder.

Millicent could actually feel the hostility crackle between the two of them.

"Yes, yes you are," agreed Gareth. "I believe he is attending a ball with the Duke of Ghoulston and the queen."

"How did you know?"

"A good guess. I fear the Master will have to leave the ball early, Sir Harcourt."

He turned his head again, avoiding Claire's gaze. "What do you mean?"

"The Duke of Ghoulston has used the relic to seduce the queen."

A series of snarls and growls from the shifters behind them followed his words, and Millicent could only admire Claire's stoic bravery as she ignored them. They had reached a balcony overlooking a garden, and while Sir Gareth outlined the duke's evil scheme and how he had managed it, she studied the plants below them.

Millicent could not remember anything between the time she had left Lady Yardley's mansion until she woke up in that cage. She had never been in the Hall of Mages, had never thought to, and wondered at the contrast of the interior of the place. Some sort of spell had apparently expanded the inside of the building to a maze of passageways and rooms all seemingly for the experimentation of magic. But unlike the Underground, dark sorcery didn't appear to be practiced here. The garden contained mazes of bushes growing fruits and flowers she had never seen the likes of before. At least, she assumed the globes of emerald with purple liquid inside were a sort of fruit, for a swarm of tiny jeweled bees swarmed the ones that had fallen to the ground. Miniature birds with wings like scarves perched on the globes, pecking at the skin, then pushing their sharp beaks inside to reach the liquid. Tall stems lined with satiny petals reached to the ceiling of the room, the flowers swaying to some nonexistent breeze. Trees with leaves sporting tiny gems twinkled, the stones falling to the ground when they reached the size of her thumb.

Millicent narrowed her eyes and concentrated, using her immunity to magic to see past the illusion. But the garden did not waver. The wizards must have used the natural fauna of England and altered it with magic to create entirely new species, which were now as real as Millicent herself.

But the fountains that sprayed crystal water high into the air were conjured from illusion, as well as the statues shaped like mythical creatures, who gazed benevolently around the garden, an occasional smile flitting across the face of a fairy, a gnome, an elf.

No twisted branches or deformed stalks or creatures formed from nightmares.

But Millicent remembered her glowing forest, and thought her Underground could hold just as much wonder.

The were-lion interrupted her musing, and she focused back on the conversation.

"So, you are saying Ghoulston has not used magic, specifically, on this enchantment over the queen?"

"Correct," replied Gareth. "So Her Majesty cannot detect it. Nor the Master himself."

"If you hadn't given me the relic," said the shifter, "I might not have believed you."

Millicent narrowed her eyes. She had no intention of allowing the were-lion to keep the bracelet. She could not understand why it had not chosen her friend, for Millicent had thought Claire would surely be the one to break the spell. But she did not imagine that the Master would allow it to leave his sight once he had it, and then Gareth would never have a chance of becoming free of the cursed thing.

No. Millicent could not allow Sir Harcourt to keep it for long.

"You must take us to the queen at once," said Claire. "She will still be under the influence of the potion, but she will listen to me."

"Not without his knightness, over there," replied

Harcourt, cocking his shaggy head at Gareth. "For we must convince the Master of this first… not that I doubt your influence with the queen, Lady Yardley. But if Queen Victoria is still as much in love with Ghoulston as she appeared the last time I saw her, we will not be able to convince her until the potion wears off."

A door ahead of them opened; a purple-robed acolyte stepped into the hall. He took one look at the pack of shape-shifters and ducked back inside the room, slamming the door on a cloud of lavender magic.

"We will not interrupt the queen's ball," continued Harcourt. "I will send for the Master, and he will speak with you first, and then decide how to approach the situation."

Claire made a disgruntled noise, but they all continued on in silence through the maze of passageways, up circular staircases, until they reached an elaborately carved door and Sir Harcourt threw it open.

"You will wait in here," he began, when a crash from inside the room interrupted him.

Sir Harcourt shifted from human to lion to human again so quickly that Millicent barely blinked between the transitions.

"Lord Sussex—Master! You are back… what are you doing?"

Harcourt stepped into the room and Claire and Millicent followed. Gareth stayed near Millicent's elbow, a strong, quiet… disturbing presence. She had thought she would never see him again, nor had she fully realized how his feelings of betrayal would affect her. Her insides twisted when she thought of the look on his face when he'd told her she had broken his heart. She did not want to think of how he must be feeling. Fortunately, events conspired so she didn't have time to delve too deeply into them at the moment.

The Duke of Sussex, Prince Augustus Frederick, Master of the Hall of Mages and the queen's favorite uncle, looked to be having a fine temper tantrum. For a man of over sixty years, he had done a rousing good job of scattering a silver tea service, a dainty set of porcelain china, and papers and books across the oak-paneled study. His jowls shook with fury, and his face appeared beet red against the contrast of his neatly groomed white beard and hair.

"She is mad," snarled the Master, his hands beginning to glow with magic. Millicent could see it, could smell it, and although it couldn't harm a shifter, Claire and Gareth held no such defense against a magical backwash of power.

Sir Harcourt looked stunned by the scene before him. Apparently, the Master wasn't prone to such fits of temper.

"Who is?" asked Millicent, stepping in front of Claire.

"The queen—who else?" The glow within his hands grew brighter, until it illuminated the entire room. A duke had the ability to change matter, and as a direct descendant to the royal family, his spells held more power than anyone save the queen—or a relic. Millicent truly did not want to see what he might conjure with the spell he was building up.

"What did she do?" she continued, hoping to keep him talking, and perhaps distract him from his magic.

"She is acting like a besotted young girl—and she

has always shown such a level head for her age. She has always known she would be queen—she has always conducted herself accordingly. And now this!"

Gareth kept trying to position himself in front of her, and she held him back only by the grace of her were-strength. Millicent kept her voice low. "She is not herself, Lord Sussex."

"Damn right she isn't! A queen cannot hie off to Gretna Green and elope! The country would not stand for it."

"These are not her decisions. She is being coerced, and we must save her."

Her words finally seemed to penetrate the older man's fury. The glow within his hands faded somewhat. He narrowed his eyes and peered at her. "Who are you?"

Sir Harcourt appeared to have regained his senses, and cleared his throat. "This is Lady Millicent, Lady Yardley, and Sir Gareth, my lord. He is the magic man from the relic—and brought it to us in hopes of saving the queen from Ghoulston." The were-lion held up the bracelet like a ritual offering.

The Master's eyes widened. "He brought it—but what is this about Victoria being coerced to marry that swine, Ghoulston?"

Harcourt glanced at Sir Gareth. "Apparently the blood within the magic man's veins has been altered by the curse he has been under for centuries. The Duke of Ghoulston used it to drug the queen's tea."

With the prospect of his dear niece acting so uncharacteristically, the Duke of Sussex appeared all too eager to accept any explanation for her behavior, and needed little convincing to believe the dread plans of Lord Ghoulston. "Ha! A love spell, is it? I knew she couldn't have fallen for that sop so quickly. But I scanned the queen myself for any sign of enchantment, and could find nothing."

"Because it is not magical in nature," interjected Gareth. "Although magic surely created it."

The old man frowned. "But what of this tea? Nothing passes Victoria's lips without being tested first."

Claire flushed. "I gave the tea box to her myself, Lord Sussex. As Lady of the Bedchamber, I am trusted implicitly."

"Nonsense. No one is trusted, including myself. But the young woman who tests her food... ho! She has been making moon eyes at Ghoulston herself—I should have noticed this before! But there is no such thing as a drug that can create true love—our best sorcerers have been trying to craft such a potion for centuries."

"It took one of Merlin's relics to do so, your lordship," said Harcourt.

"Indeed. Indeed. But enough of this jabbering! Victoria may be halfway to Gretna Green by now, and we must stop that coach." The old man stepped over the broken crockery and swept past them, the shifters standing just outside the door parting before him like the Red Sea.

Harcourt followed him. "Master—it's not wise to leave behind loose magic."

Lord Sussex glanced behind him, sparkling magic trailing from his hands. He gathered it to him, creating a small sun within his hands. When they reached the drive out front, he dispersed it over their heads, lighting up the night. "There, now. It will follow us to light the way... no broken legs for my horses. Sir Timison, sound the alarm to gather any other shifters in residence, and then fetch my coach, quickly."

The man with the black-striped hair shifted to tiger and raced off into the mews, returning shortly in human form on top of the carriage, the horses racing toward them at amazing speed. Although Millicent had not seen them in the group of baronets, the horses must be shape-shifters themselves to cover ground at such a pace.

She blinked. The group of shifters surrounding them had more than doubled with the sound of the alarm. The speed of her own kind could still amaze her.

His lordship turned to his baronets. "I suppose you shall all move faster in your were-forms. When we catch up to the blackguard, keep to the shadows. I don't want to spook the man. Ghoulston had his own guards with him, along with Victoria's. If Ghoulston doesn't stop his coach when I hail him, take out the guards, as quietly as you can. And try not to kill any of Victoria's men; she is rather fond of them."

He turned his sharp gaze on Millicent, Claire, Gareth, and Sir Harcourt. "I want you in the coach with me, to convince Queen Victoria if possible, to restrain her if necessary. She will not marry this man."

"If Ghoulston sees us," said Gareth. "He will know the game is up."

"Hopefully, I will have my niece in my coach before the man is the wiser." The Master clambered into the carriage, the springs squeaking. The four of them quickly followed; Claire, Millicent, and Gareth squished together on one seat, Sir Harcourt taking his seat beside Lord Sussex.

"The fastest road to Gretna Green," shouted his lordship, and the coach lurched forward.

Millicent gazed out the window, trying to ignore the jolt of excitement that flew through her at the feel of Gareth's warm body pressed against hers. Beyond the circle of the Master's magical light, she could see the dark shape of lion, tiger, wolf, and jaguar keeping pace with the horses, and occasionally a flash of fur atop the roofs, a gleam of claw within a back street. They could easily pass them if they wished, since the were-horses were hampered with pulling the coach, but kept a protective circle around them. Millicent did not need to gaze upward to know that eagles and hawks and falcons flew above them.

An astonishing company. Ghoulston would be frightened out of his wits, for his magic could not defend against a one of them.

A smile crept across her face. For Nell. Ghoulston would pay for what he had done to Nell.

The coach swerved and smashed Gareth even closer against her, Claire uttering a squeal at the wild movement. Were-horses galloped at a clip that ordinary horses could not match, and Millicent could only be grateful that the Master's coach appeared to be built to handle such extraordinary speed.

Gareth muttered an apology, which she felt more than heard, for the wheels crunched and the wind wailed and the carriage groaned.

Millicent scooted as close to the wall as she could and closed her eyes. What had it cost her to avenge

Nell's death? She had broken her promise to Gareth. A good man. A man of such honor, that she knew if their positions had been reversed, he would never have broken a promise he had made to her. And then she had the gall to tell him he should thank her for it.

Right after Gareth had saved her from the madness of her beast.

He would never forgive her. Indeed, why would she want him to? She had spoken truly, after all. If she could not free him from the relic, she did not want him to sacrifice his freedom to be with her. He might come to resent her, and she could not bear it. But it hurt to be so close to him and have to pretend she didn't care.

But Millicent had not thought about what would happen when Claire brought the relic to the Hall of Mages. She had not thought beyond her need to avenge Nell. Of course the Master would keep the relic. He would not allow Claire to walk out of the Hall with it, to allow the ladies of Society to lead him a merry chase again. And what would the spymaster do with the bracelet? Perform magical experiments on Gareth, as Ghoulston had done? Keep the relic within a warded vault, never to be placed around another woman's wrist again... trapping Gareth inside it forever?

No. Gareth would never forgive her. She had no right to ask it of him. She ignored the weakness in her foolish heart that kept wanting her to do just that.

Millicent glanced up beneath her lashes at Sir Harcourt. He had not given the relic to Lord Sussex, had pushed it up his forearm to keep it secure. The relic would not tighten for a man, and certainly not for Harcourt—despite his handsome scarred face and mane of golden-blond hair.

No, she could not ask for Gareth's forgiveness. She could barely meet his gaze. But she could make it up to him by taking back the relic. She just had to wait for the right moment.

Harcourt must have felt her gaze, because he looked over at her, his amber eyes bright with interest. He glanced at the bracelet on his arm, and then back to her. So. He would not make it easy.

They flew over the road for an eternity, Gareth a volatile presence beside her. It felt so strange to be awkward with him, when it had become so easy to touch him, to be close to him. And all of it her fault. She resisted the urge time and again to rub against him, to smooth back the blond hair that escaped his leather tie.

Claire leaned forward, glanced between Gareth and Millicent, and gave her a puzzled look. Thank goodness the rattling and banging prevented any conversation. Millicent had no desire to explain her complicated relationship with the knight.

The small door that allowed the occupants to speak to the coachman suddenly flew open.

"What is it?" shouted Lord Sussex.

"We've got company behind us," replied Sir Timison.

"Who?" growled Harcourt.

"Not sure yet," he shouted back. Then raised his voice even louder. "Magic ahead!"

The carriage swerved once again, bounced several times, and then steadied. Sir Harcourt stuck his head out the window, scanning the road ahead, the darkness behind. They had left London a long time ago; only shadows of hedgerows and trees flashed past them now. The shape-shifters hid more easily in the countryside. When Millicent looked out the window, she could no longer see a hint of claw or fang.

"Slow down," commanded Harcourt.

Millicent's ears rang with the comparative silence as the coach settled to a normal pace.

"Those are Queen Victoria's guards," said the Master, his balding head now stuck out his own window.

Harcourt pulled his head back inside. "Nay, my lord. It is only illusion."

Lord Sussex collapsed back into his seat. "Ghoulston's magic is stronger than I thought. But, by Jove, I have spies who are immune to it! What is really ahead, Sir Harcourt?"

"A motley assortment of creatures escort Queen Victoria's coach, my lord. It seems Ghoulston has brought up his army from the Underground."

"That many?"

"They are more than six times our number." Harcourt smiled, revealing his wicked canines. "I'd say the odds are about even."

But Lord Sussex did not look reassured. "I cannot believe the silly chit went off without her own men. She is the queen—Ghoulston's magic cannot be stronger than hers."

"She sees what she wants to see," said Gareth, "with the clouded gaze of a woman in love."

Millicent stiffened, unsure if she should take some hidden meaning from his words.

"They have seen us," called Timison's voice from the driver's seat.

"Stop the coach," ordered the Master. "And open the door for me." His intelligent gaze settled on Sir Harcourt. "We cannot risk any conflict with the queen inside that carriage. Lady Yardley will accompany me to speak with Ghoulston. He will not be suspicious of her. You three stay here. If I manage to get the queen back into my coach, you will have to find some way to convince her that Ghoulston is a blackguard."

Sir Harcourt growled. "I do not like this. On what pretense will you trade yourself for the queen?"

"I need to have a man-to-man discussion with the duke on the responsibilities of marriage. I am the closest thing she has to a father, after all. And I was remiss in my duties. But now that I have accepted the marriage, I must honor them."

Harcourt shook his blond mane. "I do not think he will fall for it."

"You underestimate my powers of persuasion." Lord Sussex turned to Timison as the were-tiger opened the door of the coach. "Tell Charles and Grayson to turn this carriage around and race back to London as soon as the queen is inside."

Millicent raised a brow at Harcourt.

"They are the were-horses," he whispered.

"Then why a coachman?"

"Lookout," he idly answered, his concentration focused on his master.

"But what of your lordship?" asked Sir Timison.

Lord Sussex raised his bushy white brows. "Join your fellows and tell them to stay hidden in the shadows until I give the signal." The old man's diplomatic mask faded for a moment, and Millicent glimpsed the warrior beneath. "And then we have some sport, old chaps."

The Master stepped out the door and glanced back at Harcourt. "And for Merlin's sake, keep your shaggy head inside the coach."

Lady Yardley followed him out of the carriage without a word, her face as white as a sheet, her lips tight with grim determination.

Millicent could no more keep the disbelief off her face than Claire could wipe the fear from hers. Convince a woman that the man she loved is lying to her? "It would be easier to fight Ghoulston's men," she grumbled.

Sir Harcourt grunted in agreement, although she did not think he actually followed her train of thought.

It became very quiet in the coach. Millicent strained her ears to hear what went on outside, her attention divided between trying to ignore Gareth and her guilty feelings, and Claire's sudden peril. What had Millicent done, all for the sake of revenge?

Apparently Gareth and Harcourt concentrated on listening as well, for they all sat frozen, taking shallow breaths. She heard the jingle of harness as the horses danced in place. No, as Charles and Grayson danced in place. They might be half-human, but their animal natures would still prompt them to nervousness around a pack of predators.

Millicent could not hear or see them, but she could *feel* the rest of the baronets prowling around the two carriages.

Sir Harcourt cocked his head. Millicent heard it too. The sound of footsteps approaching their coach. Light, delicate footsteps. And then the sound of Lady Yardley's voice.

"Men," she sighed. "We must allow for their protective natures, Your Majesty. We will follow along behind your coach for a time, to give them their privacy."

"Hmph," replied Queen Victoria. "You would think my uncle would have allowed for this chat before we left, despite his initial disapproval of my plans."

As one, Millicent, Gareth, and Harcourt slid across their seats to the far side of the carriage.

Claire opened the door, and stepped behind the queen.

And several things happened at once.

The windows of the carriage lit up from a flash of brilliant magic outside, creating a halo behind the queen's petite frame. Growls and snarls erupted from down the road; a crack of gunfire from up ahead.

Claire unceremoniously shoved the queen into the coach. She landed across Sir Harcourt's lap, a mass of silk blue skirts and lace petticoats. The large man flushed beet red, and hastily assisted the queen to a sitting position beside him. Claire scrambled through the door and slammed it behind her.

The carriage vaulted forward, swung crazily about— pitching Millicent into Gareth, and the queen into Harcourt once again—and sped back toward London.

"What is the meaning of this?" demanded Queen Victoria.

Gareth glanced at Millicent. "Even if we had the time, she would not believe us."

"I know."

"Do you remember how Selena…?"

Millicent shuddered. But he was right. It would serve them best to have the queen in love with Gareth instead of Ghoulston.

Harcourt was trying to reason with the queen, who just kept batting her fists against his broad chest. She looked even smaller next to the were-lion, and Millicent felt a flash of pity for her.

"This is kidnapping—treason!" she shouted. "I demand you turn this carriage back around this instant!" Magic sprouted from her hands, and Claire screamed, then slumped forward in a dead faint. Gareth shuddered. Millicent felt nothing, but she could see the struggle it took for Gareth to overcome the pain spell.

Her empathy for the queen faded a bit. The young woman could take care of herself, despite her youth and innocence.

Gareth slowly pulled out his knife, and then sliced open his thumb.

Harcourt, unaffected by the queen's spell as well, glanced at Gareth's bloody finger in confusion, and then his face cleared and he nodded.

"Forgive me, Your Majesty," said the were-lion, and captured her head in his hands. Gareth leaned forward and stuck his thumb in the mouth of the most powerful woman in England.

Seventeen

QUEEN VICTORIA'S BLUE EYES WIDENED IN SHOCK, AND she inadvertently swallowed. Then she twisted her head out of Harcourt's hold and splayed her hands with another burst of magic.

The carriage tilted and Millicent clutched the edge of the seat for support. The conveyance ground to an abrupt stop.

The queen smiled triumphantly.

Harcourt briefly stuck his head out the window, and then turned around with a grin. "She destroyed the harness between coach and horse. She knows we're immune to her magic and has used it indirectly. *Well done*, Your Majesty."

The queen gave him a look that confirmed him as a madman, then raised her hands again.

"Err, your potion better take affect soon Sir Ga—" began Harcourt.

The bolts and glue and nails that held the carriage together suddenly disappeared as well. Harcourt and Gareth raised their hands to prevent the top piece from smashing upon their heads as the bottom collapsed beneath them at the same time, and they all tumbled to the dirt road. As one, the men tossed the roof onto a patch of heather.

Millicent rolled to her feet, looking for Claire while the men gathered up the queen. Her friend lay atop the cushion of the seat, still unconscious, but apparently uninjured.

"Unhand me," snapped the queen, struggling against Harcourt's hold. Then she spun and slammed into Gareth's chest. "You—you... who are *you*?"

Her blue eyes glazed and a besotted smile spread across her face. Millicent scowled. Gareth's blood worked a bit *too* well.

Harcourt suddenly shifted to lion and leaped over the carriage rubble. Millicent turned. They had not gotten far from Ghoulston's men. The Master's magical light still hovered above their carriage—despite it now being in bits and pieces—making them an easy target. She did not know what magical battle waged within the other carriage between Ghoulston and Lord Sussex, but the conveyance rocked on its wheels, shuddered betwixt and between, and spouted great grouts of crimson, indigo, and silver smoke from the windows.

The shape-shifters had already made a good account of themselves. Ghoulston's army now looked as if they outnumbered them only four to one. But Millicent could see the baronets tiring. When several of Ghoulston's minions broke away from the main group and headed in their direction, only a half-dozen shifters followed.

Sir Harcourt turned and pierced Millicent with a

golden gaze. She nodded, shifted to panther, and took position beside him. They would protect the queen with their lives.

Millicent could hear Gareth speaking calming words behind her, the same tone he'd used to tame her beast. "Your Majesty. Stay behind my sword."

"Oh," she replied. "Ghoulston's men won't harm us. Poor creatures. He rescued them from the Underground, don't you know? They cannot help the way they look, but we needn't be frightened of them."

Millicent could only feel amazed at Ghoulston's powers of persuasion.

Wisely, Gareth did not try to argue with the queen. "They will take you away from me, my lady."

Silence.

"In that case, I suggest you step out of my way, my dear knight. I wouldn't want my magic to harm you."

Queen Victoria's attempted spell and Gareth's reply were lost in a roar that shook the road beneath Millicent's paws. Ghoulston's creatures froze, glanced behind them at the coach, which now lay in splinters upon the road. Atop it stood a black dragon, with barbed tail, scales as sharp as daggers, and crimson eyes. It opened an enormous maw and spat liquid fire.

"Impossible!" said the queen. "My uncle would not create... dragon spells are illegal..."

"Not your uncle," replied Gareth. "But Ghoulston. He has become proficient at black magic, Your Majesty."

Millicent glanced over her shoulder. Love potion or no, she could see the queen's mind working through her addled senses. Those large blue eyes narrowed to slits. "I will demand an explanation... later." And

Queen Victoria raised her arms, whispered something beneath her breath, and she changed. Not as a shape-shifter changed, altering swiftly to his or her other half. This appeared to be more unnatural, magic forcing her bones to grow abnormally large, to take the form of...

An odd mixture of unicorn and lion, with a glorious spread of wings.

"Her royal coat of arms," murmured Harcourt. "Half-magnificent... although the addition of the wings is a nice touch."

The enormous creature neighed, tossed its white mane, raked the ground with its powerful claws.

Gareth ducked as she took wing, the backlash of wind from the beat of them tousling his golden hair. He watched with a frown as the queen flew toward the dragon, his gaze turning to Millicent's. "She cannot win."

Millicent shook her head. She wasn't so sure. As Ghoulston's minions turned back around and started toward them once again, she thought the queen had a better chance than they did. The few remaining baronets harried them as they came, but did little to slow their enemies down.

Gareth took up a position on her other side. Harcourt growled a welcome as Timison material-ized out of the shadows and joined them. Hoofbeats pounded behind them. Charles and Grayson returning.

Six against... over two dozen.

Millicent could feel them approaching now. The road vibrating with the pounding of running feet, claws, misshapen limbs. She could smell them. Sweat, sewage, the metal tang of blood. The dirt raised a dark cloud above them, and she could not see the dragon or the queen. She could hear only the roars and screams.

Gareth laid a hand on her head, stroked her fur as he bent to whisper in her ear, "Let me protect you."

Millicent growled. She did not deserve his faithfulness.

"Nothing you do can ever make me stop loving you," he continued. "*Nothing*."

He had forgiven her for betraying him. Of course. He wouldn't even make her ask. She felt even less worthy of his love.

Timison snarled, startling them both, for the tiger stared at the shadowy trees on the side of the road, and not ahead of them at the advancing hoard.

A great bear lumbered into their circle of light.

Gareth took a step forward. "Bran? Wait... no!" He held up his blade as a warning gesture to the spies, who had gathered back on their haunches, preparing to leap at the bear. "Sir Harcourt... Timison. Stop. He is a friend."

Bran shifted to human. Millicent blinked. How... where...?

"Did ye truly think I'd let ye go off and get captured again?" he said to her. "Ye've had a penchant for trouble lately, me gel. I would not send you topside without me own spy."

And then Ambrose swooped forward, spinning about Bran's bushy head. "Yes! I followed you to Lady Yardley's and saw the beasts capture you." The sprite stilled his spinning and hovered a moment, giving Harcourt and Timison a pointed glare.

Millicent recalled the flash of wing she thought she'd spied in Claire's bushes.

Bran glanced from her to the baronets to the advancing horde. "I cannot fathom what has changed… but at the moment, it appears we have a common enemy. Can we give ye a hand, lads?"

Timison and Harcourt exchanged a look.

"That's what I thought," grunted Bran. "Come on out, ye scavengers."

Jackals, hyenas, and wolverines slinked into the light. Millicent had never felt so grateful to see her fellow creatures of the Underground. But she had no time to wonder at Bran coming to her rescue once again, for a club swung down at her and she leaped aside, only to see Gareth stick his sword into the arm of the giant.

Millicent clamped her teeth around the other arm.

They fought the giant as if they could sense each other's actions without words. The creatures that challenged them could not prevail against Gareth and Millicent. And she felt something different. Not just that they moved as one. But something…

Her beast. It did not fully control her. She gave mercy when she could. She mourned the creatures she killed. She felt saddened by the necessary violence. Because of Gareth, the blind killing madness of the cat did not consume her.

As the world erupted into fighting, clawing, steel-flashing fury, she hoped the other baronets would not mistake Bran's army for the enemy. But the spies must have figured out who was fighting whom, for when the last of Ghoulston's creatures fell, the predators did not attack the remaining scavengers. Instead, they stared distrustfully at one another as quiet descended.

Millicent stood next to Gareth, both of them bloody, both of them winded.

And yet, it seemed over too quickly.

Thanks to Bran.

"The queen," muttered Gareth, rising from cleaning his blade on the back of a tattered shirt. But Harcourt and Timison and the remaining spies had already sprinted down the road toward two shapes—one white, one black, locked together in a struggle that flattened the trees around them.

Millicent found the sprite hovering near the wreckage of their carriage. Claire still lay atop the cushions, unconscious of the chaos around her. "Stay with Lady Yardley. Call if you need me."

The little man's chest puffed. "It shall be my honor to protect her. I may be small—but never a coward."

Then Gareth and Millicent sprinted after the predators, Bran and his men right behind them.

"Where is the Master?" huffed Gareth when they caught up with the rest of their force.

Millicent had wondered the same. Surely Lord Sussex would not allow his niece to fight this battle alone. But she could see only the dragon and the unicorn-lion.

They had left the Master's magical light behind them with the coach, but another hazy sort of light with the glow of powerful magic surrounded the area around the carriage. And within it, Millicent could glimpse speckles of blackness swirling in a mass like small tornadoes.

"Do you hear that?" shouted Gareth.

Millicent nodded, the buzzing noise rising in volume.

"Bees." Gareth grinned. "It's a swarm of bees… that's what your Master has conjured to fight the dragon."

Harcourt's face sagged in disappointment. "Insects?"

"Do you think another dragon would defeat Ghoulston without hurting the queen in the process? Your Master is clever."

One of the insects flew past Millicent. It might have appeared tiny in comparison to the dragon, but to her, the bee looked about the size of her fist.

The bees swarmed the dragon's head. The beast snorted, frying some of the insects, which dropped to the ground like a flurry of black snow. But most of them remained, beyond the dragon's maw, covering those red eyes. The dragon loosened his hold on the neck of the unicorn-lion and clawed at his eyes.

Millicent turned and gave Bran a meaningful look. The big man stared at her with his liquid brown eyes, then slowly swung his head from side to side. He understood.

She could not leave until she knew the queen was safe. But neither could she tarry long after. Millicent had no doubt Harcourt would give the relic to the Master and doom Gareth to a life of imprisonment. She did not think the were-lion would allow *her* to walk away, either.

Bran's men could hold their own against the Master's spies. But not against a Royal's magic.

The queen's creature reared away from the dragon, who was now covered in the dark swirling mass of insects. The bees burrowed into places a blade of steel couldn't reach, but the majority of them still attacked the dragon's most sensitive areas… especially the eyes.

The dragon howled and clawed… and began to shrink, to turn back into the odious personage of the Duke of Ghoulston.

"Make it stop," he screamed. "Have mercy—I am blind!"

The dark, swirling, buzzing mass coalesced into the portly form of the Duke of Sussex, who had just proven to Millicent to be shrewd enough to have actually earned the position of the Master of the Hall of Mages. "Oh, do stop whining," he said to Ghoulston before turning to look up at the unicorn-lion. "A combination of your royal coat of arms? Well done, Victoria—but kindly change back now. We have much to discuss."

When Queen Victoria changed back to her normal, diminutive stature, the baronets let out a cheer, followed by another resounding cheer from the underground shifters. She acknowledged their adulation with a wave of her hand, then lifted her skirts and delicately stepped over to her uncle and the duke—who still writhed on the ground in agony.

Millicent felt her lips curl in a grim smile.

It was less than Ghoulston deserved… but her Nell had been avenged.

And yet… she did not feel quite as triumphant as she thought she would.

Millicent turned and glanced up at Gareth, allowing herself to truly look at him. Blood spattered the front of his tunic, obscuring the red dragon embroidered in the thick weave. He'd fought wildly as usual, with little care for his own skin. Moisture curled the hair at his temple and brow into tiny spirals of gold. A cut along one sculpted cheekbone gleamed an angry scarlet, and dirt smudged his broad forehead and angular chin.

He looked… sublimely delicious… heartrendingly beautiful. He had always been an attractive man, but now… now she saw more than his handsome features. She knew his heart and soul, and loved him more than life itself.

Millicent nodded at Bran. He rose a bushy brow, but stepped over to Gareth's side, and wrapped his arms around the taller man, trapping the knight's arms in a bear hug, so he could not get to his sword. She shifted to panther and leaped on Harcourt's back. He went down like a felled tree, flat to the ground, with an oath of surprise. It took a moment for the baronets to react. They were tired and injured. But within that moment, Bran had already signaled to his own men, who now outnumbered the spies, and they guarded the combatants.

Harcourt had no one to come to his defense, but she rather imagined he didn't mind.

He shifted to lion, threw her off his back. Millicent landed, crouched to attack. They circled each other, looking for an opening. The were-lion's eyes glittered gold, oddly delighted as he studied his opponent.

But Millicent had an advantage. Gareth had helped her master her beast. She did not think Harcourt had managed the same feat, for she saw little trace of his humanity at the moment.

They clashed, snarled, striking with fang and claw. Parted. Both a bit bloody.

But Millicent had come away with a clear knowledge

of how Harcourt's beast fought. He did not protect his left side.

When they clashed again, she concentrated on that weakness. She did not want to kill Harcourt, but she knew she had little time before the Master finished scolding his niece and turned his attention to his baronets.

They rolled across the dirt. When they came to a stop, Millicent was on top of Harcourt once again, but this time with his face and belly toward her, his neck in her teeth.

He growled.

She bit down, feeling his hot blood cover her lips, drip down her furry chin.

Please don't make me kill you.

Harcourt tried to throw her off once more. Millicent kept him firmly pinned to the ground. She shook her head, worried at the skin.

She saw Gareth's pointed-toe boots. She should have known Bran would not be able to hold him for long. "Don't do this," he said. "There has been enough bloodshed tonight."

The rest of the men watched quietly.

Gareth sighed. "Verily, my lady. If you will not wear the bracelet, it does not matter. If I cannot have you, I do not want anyone at all."

Millicent slowly closed her jaws.

Harcourt's eyes rolled back into his head and he shifted to human.

She almost sobbed with relief. She released his neck and pulled the bracelet off Harcourt's arm, slipping it onto her own wrist. She rose to her feet, waiting for it to tighten, to claim her once more as Gareth's lover. She stared at the band of silver, the colors within the moonstone swirling and winking.

"What's this?" demanded Lord Sussex, breaking through the circle of men who surrounded them, Queen Victoria hard on his heels.

Millicent lifted her chin, winced at the memory of steel bars surrounding her, but faced the Master of the Hall of Mages with every intention of defying him. "I go wherever Sir Gareth goes."

Lord Sussex raised his white brows, which climbed even higher when his niece ran to Gareth and threw herself in the knight's arms.

"Your powers astound me, lad," he said to Gareth.

Millicent frowned. "The queen is just under another spell. We used Sir Gareth's blood to bind her to him... it seemed... easier, than trying to explain about Ghoulston."

"And what's your excuse?"

"I... I have none. Other than I owe Sir Gareth my life."

"I see." Lord Sussex bent down, patted Harcourt's cheek. The were-lion's eyes flew open and he clutched his neck, tried to speak. "Hush, lad. You'll be fine... unlike many of my other baronets. I lost too many today, and Ghoulston will pay for that." He glanced up at Millicent. "If not for your aid, and that of your underground friends, I would not even be talking about this, my dear. But as I understand it... isn't the relic supposed to choose who wears it?"

Millicent glanced back down at the bracelet. She squeezed the band of silver, but it continued to dangle loosely on her arm. She stifled a cry of dismay. She had willingly given the relic to another. Could the blasted thing have somehow sensed it?

It would never claim her as Gareth's lover again.

No. She would not believe it... and it did not matter! Damn the stupid hunk of metal! Millicent would never forsake him again. She clamped her teeth and shoved the bracelet higher up her arm until it stayed there.

Gareth stared at the relic, his forehead creased in bewilderment. Queen Victoria continued to hug his arm and gaze adoringly up at him.

"Obviously the relic no longer chooses you, Lady Millicent," said the Master. "So you might as well give it to me."

"Never."

Bran shifted to bear, let loose a growl that reverberated louder than the black dragon's. Harcourt responded, shifting to lion, the fur around his neck bloody, but facing off against the bear with a snarl that revealed his wicked long teeth.

"My spells cannot harm them," continued the Master, nodding at the men shifting to beasts all around them, "but I can open a chasm in the earth to swallow them all. Is that what you truly want?"

Millicent glared at the old man. "I cannot let you keep the relic."

"Enough." Gareth stepped forward. "Stop it, all of you!"

Lions, tigers, jackals, hyenas... they all turned to stare at the knight, their growls fading.

Gareth nodded, then turned toward Millicent. "I said no more bloodshed. And I meant it."

"I will not give him the relic!"

"Then give it to me."

She blinked. He could not mean it. But Gareth held out his hand, his glorious blue eyes fixed on her, and she saw the sadness within them, the sorrow that spoke of centuries of living, of seeing too many deaths, too much wickedness. She could not add to his grief.

Millicent squeezed the band of silver one more time. It would not tighten. She could not force it to choose her. She slipped it off her arm, held it within her fingers.

She would be handing him her broken heart. Surely he knew that?

Gareth nodded, his long blond hair swaying in the light breeze.

Millicent placed the relic in the palm of his large hand.

Her breath caught on a sob. Ah, no. She could not cry. But neither could she breathe.

Gareth turned to Bran. "Take her home."

Bran shifted to human. She felt his arms circle her, his gentle tug. "Come away, Millicent. Come away."

She threw Gareth a last silent look of appeal. But he just stared at the relic, his face creased with misery and confusion.

Millicent shifted to panther, and followed Bran into the shadows of the night, back to the dark recesses of the Underground. Where she belonged.

Eighteen

GARETH WATCHED MILLICENT UNTIL HER BLACK FUR blended with the night, until all the Undergrounders disappeared from sight. He did not understand. He knew he loved Millicent with all of his heart. So why had the relic not chosen her again? Why had it tightened before, and not now? Perhaps... perhaps Millicent had been right all along, and he had been a fool to believe in her love... especially after she had betrayed him.

But the proof shook him to the core.

Queen Victoria plucked the bracelet from his hand. "Surely it will work for me." She slipped it over her wrist, frowned when it did not tighten, then shoved it up her arm. "Well, I shall just keep it until it does."

Lord Sussex scowled. "When will your... potion wear off the queen, Sir Gareth?"

"I'm not sure. A few hours, perhaps a few days."

"I suppose there's no harm in letting her keep the relic until then." The Master turned to his baronets. "Now, then, gentlemen. Let's get the wounded back to the Hall. Victoria, will you reassemble your carriage? We can carry most of them—ah, the message sprite."

Lady Yardley strode toward them, her eyes round with wonder at the carnage about her, Ambrose flying near her shoulder.

The Master rattled off a list of demands to Ambrose, sending the sprite back to London for more wagons for the injured. Lady Yardley approached Gareth while the rest of the baronets scurried to do their master's bidding.

"What happened?" she asked. "Where is Millicent?"

Gareth sagged to the ground at the sound of her name. Sorrow had dogged him for so long he thought he had become used to it. But this... this soul-tearing agony threatened to overwhelm him.

"Oh, you are injured," cried Queen Victoria. "Uncle, we must get him into my carriage."

And Gareth suddenly realized his pain wasn't all mental, that most of the blood covering his tunic might be his own. His vision began to fade to black. Well, the relic would soon suck him back in and he would reappear healed and whole like always, the pain just another memory.

But the pain in his heart would still be there, and that hurt far worse.

Gareth had only a jumble of impressions after that. He felt someone lift him, felt the bouncing of the carriage as they traveled back to London. Heard snatches of an argument between the queen and her uncle about where Gareth should be taken.

The queen must have won, for he saw the diamond-studded walls of Buckingham Palace, and not the warded ones of the Hall. He was carried upstairs to a bedroom paneled in strings of diamonds, and laid on a bed of clean linen sheets. Cupids danced above him, carved into a wooden canopy. He heard whispered conversations, felt the calming warmth of healing magic, and was stripped naked and washed by a stern-looking matron.

When would the relic suck him back in and end this nightmare?

"How is he?" whispered Queen Victoria.

"He'll recover," answered Lord Sussex.

Gareth cracked open an eyelid. His entire body still ached, but the sharp pain in his side had faded with the healer's magic.

"He is awake," said the queen, who stood in a beam of sunlight that slanted from a floor-to-ceiling window. "Thank heavens. I am... yes, I am rather fond of him."

Gareth bolted upright in bed, gasped in pain, but refused to collapse back against the linens.

The queen stood in a beam of sunlight.

Sunlight.

"It's about time you quit playing possum," drawled the Master.

"It's morning," replied Gareth in amazement.

"Jolly right. You've been winking in and out of consciousness for hours." The old man studied him with a frown. "Wait... by Jove! Aren't you supposed to be taken by the relic with the dawn?"

"Yes." Gareth swung his legs over the side of the bed. They had dressed him in some kind of gown, but he wouldn't have cared if he had been stark naked.

He stood, his legs a bit shaky, but managed to walk over to that beam of sunshine. Queen Victoria backed up a step, staring at him with wondering eyes. Gareth walked into the golden light, felt the warmth spread over his shoulders and down his arms. He narrowed his eyes against the glare and smiled at the queen. Truly smiled. For the first time in centuries. "Yes! I'm not supposed to be here. I should be in the relic. I should *not* be in pain. But I welcome both. Both!"

"You're babbling, man," said Lord Sussex.

"Babbling? Yes! The enchantment is broken and… and I have not turned to dust! After centuries of darkness, I stand in the light. After eons of immortality, I am finally mortal! Me, Gareth Solimere, once a knight of the Round Table, and once cursed by the great Merlin himself. Do you not understand what this means?" Gareth spread his arms, lifted his face to that glorious sun. "I am free! Finally free to live out a normal life."

"But how?"

The Master's softly spoken words brought Gareth up short, and his arms fell limply to his sides. How, indeed. What had happened to break Merlin's curse? Had the relic finally acknowledged Millicent as his one true love? No, the bracelet had not tightened on her wrist…

Gareth stepped from the glare of that circle of sunlight. He blinked, stared at the haggard face of the Master of the Hall of Mages. They stood in a sumptuous room decorated in diamonds. The walls dripped with strings of them, and any slight movement caused those strings to sway, the stones to sparkle with mirrored light. Magic had crafted tables from enormous stones, including a fireplace surrounded with a mantel of the rock. A curtain of diamonds hung from the corners of the canopied bed, draped the sides of the tall windows. Chandeliers with teardrop-cut diamonds studded the ceiling. In the evening, the room would sparkle in the glow of fire and candlelight. Right now, it flashed with a dizzying array of prismatic color from the refracted sunshine.

He frowned.

Had Merlin's curse truly, finally, been broken?

"That is not an *illusion* of the sun coming through the windows?"

"No, Sir Gareth," replied Queen Victoria. "It is as real as you or I."

"I do not understand."

"That is obvious," said the Master, his white brows creased together in thought. "Surely you had some inkling that the curse had been broken."

"None. I…" Gareth turned to Victoria. "Your Majesty, do you still wear the relic?"

She nodded, brown curls bobbing against her cheeks. She pushed up the sleeve of her gown, the blue poplin cording into folds at her shoulder. The bracelet easily slid down her arm, dangled at her wrist. "It still has not tightened for me. Although, oddly enough, that fact isn't as important as it seemed to be a few hours ago."

"Thank Merlin!" snapped the Master. "I think the spell is finally wearing off. I've had enough of *love* spells to last me a lifetime."

"You know, Uncle," mused Queen Victoria, "I

did not believe you… about Lord Ghoulston… and Sir Gareth." She frowned, a delicate wrinkling of smooth skin. "But I feel as if I am waking from some strange dream…"

"May I see the relic, Your Majesty?" interrupted Gareth, forcing his voice to stay calm.

"Oh, yes. I don't see why not."

Lord Sussex sighed with relief as the queen removed the bracelet and handed it to Gareth. "You wouldn't have given it up a few hours ago," he said to her.

"I rather think you are right, Uncle."

Gareth studied the band of silver, turning it until the moonstone caught the reflection of the sun, something it had not done since the time of Merlin. A crack ran along the middle of the gemstone, something it had not possessed before, either… when had he first noticed it?

"What is it?" asked Lord Sussex, turning his attention away from his niece.

"The gemstone is cracked."

"And it did not have this flaw before… no, apparently it did not. Do you think it has something to do with why you have not been… taken, again?"

"I am not sure." Gareth felt the room sway. Alas, he could not ignore his injuries. They would never be magically erased again. He smiled, although he rather imagined it resembled a grimace, and staggered back to the canopied bed, collapsing onto a puffy blanket.

Why must they always be puffy?

"I first noticed the crack when Lady Yardley gave it to the were-lion in the Hall of Mages. Yes. But I thought it a trick of the light. Nothing happened to cause the break… nothing that I can recall."

"Mayhap it did not happen then," said Lord Sussex, dragging over a silk-cushioned chair sprinkled with diamonds at back and arms, and settling his bulk atop it. "Good heavens, Victoria. Do you realize we are witnessing an historic event?"

"The entire past twenty-four hours have been historic," replied Victoria, who began to pace the room, stepping in and out of that glorious beam of sunshine, her brown hair sparkling every time the light touched her head. She looked beautiful. Almost as beautiful as Millicent.

Gareth squeezed the band of silver.

"Think back," prodded Lord Sussex. "Can you recall anything unusual that happened before then?"

"I…" Gareth flinched. Before they had met with Harcourt, he had woken up in Lady Yardley's bedroom… and he had discovered that Millicent had broken his heart. "Can it be?"

"What, man?" exclaimed Lord Sussex, leaning forward in his chair, his eyes bright with excitement.

"I heard something crack…" But he had thought it was his heart.

"And?"

"And… could Merlin be that vengeful? Yes, of course he could. And after the way I felt when Millicent betrayed me, I cannot blame him."

Lord Sussex let out a huff. "I'm not following you. What, exactly, is the nature of the curse that confined you to the relic? I have only bits and pieces of rumors."

Gareth nodded. Yes, best to start at the beginning, and reason this through. If reason could be found from it. And who better to help him puzzle it out, than the Master of magic? After the battle with Ghoulston, Gareth had every reason to respect the intelligence of this man. "The words have been etched in my mind, for they have echoed to me again and again over the centuries. He said, 'Only true love will break this spell, boy, and I curse you to search until you find it.' And I thought I had."

"With whom?"

"Lady Millicent. The shape-shifter who helped us stop Ghoulston."

"Ah," acknowledged Lord Sussex, "the one who tried to take the relic."

Queen Victoria paused in her pacing, a fleeting look of hurt passing her features. Then she shook her curls and resumed her course, only the slight tilt of her head in their direction indicating that she still listened.

"And so I could not understand why the spell hadn't broken," continued Gareth. "For I knew I loved her truly. So I thought Millicent must love me in return in order to break the spell. I used all my powers of persuasion to make her fall in love with me. And I thought I had succeeded—until Ghoulston's men killed Nell."

"Who is she?"

"A firebird, methinks. But perhaps more." Gareth stretched his back, loosening the bindings around his waist. It hurt. But he had no time for that… or time to puzzle out the origins of Nell. "She is the only person Millicent had ever loved, and when Nell was taken from her, it hardened Millicent's heart once more. She is… Lady Millicent has a strong sense of self-preservation."

"Wise girl," muttered Queen Victoria.

Lord Sussex frowned as he glanced at his niece. "You cannot blame yourself... or doubt your judgment of love because of a potion. It seems to me that Prince Albert had managed to capture your true affections before Ghoulston interfered."

The queen smiled at that, her eyes suddenly glassy. "He *was* extraordinarily charming. And handsome." She blinked at Gareth. "Not as handsome as you, of course—good grief, the drug must still be affecting me." She started to pace again.

Lord Sussex turned back to Gareth, tiny dots of colored light sprinkled across his heavy features. "You must have been wrong about the shape-shifter. Her love must have been strong enough to break the curse—because here you are."

Gareth shook his head. "No. I think I had it all wrong. When I was in Lady Yardley's bedroom—"

Victoria gasped.

"Because Millicent had given her the relic to prove to you the truth of Ghoulston's plans," Gareth hurried to explain, "Or, well... yes, to see if Lady Yardley could break the curse."

"Lady Millicent must love you very much to give the bracelet to another," said the queen. "That is an unselfish act. She cared more for your happiness than her own."

"Or she did not love me enough to keep me." Gareth held up a hand as Queen Victoria opened her mouth to protest. He winced as his bindings pulled with the movement. Anyway, he must become accustomed to pain, and mortality. If he died now, he would never wake again. He grimaced. "At least, that's what I thought at first. That she had betrayed our love, had betrayed *me*. And it broke my heart. And in that moment... my world turned upside down, and I felt as scattered as I often do when the relic releases me. And I thought I heard the breaking of my heart." Gareth glanced down at the moonstone. "But now... I think it was the gemstone, and I believe I was set free at that very moment. Aah... of course! No wonder it did not tighten around Millicent's wrist. The curse had already been broken."

"Betrayal." The Master rubbed his forehead. "What, precisely, did you do to make Merlin curse you into a relic?"

"I seduced his lover. Vivian."

Victoria stumbled. Lord Sussex nodded with wisdom. "Then it makes perfect sense, Sir Gareth. Merlin did not curse you to find your true love. He cursed you until you were betrayed by your one true love. So you felt the same pain he did."

"I believe you are right." Gareth glanced down at the moonstone, ran a finger across the jagged crack in the gem. "Only now do I understand what I did to Merlin, and how deeply my actions hurt him. The old wizard fooled me for centuries. He wanted me to suffer as he had suffered. I had always thought a woman's love would break the spell. Verily, women have betrayed me before, but none have broken my heart because of it. Only my own pain from the betrayal of my one true love could break the spell... *my* love for a woman... not the other way around. It just took this long to find the one woman who could wound me so deeply… And I no longer believe Merlin designed the relic to help me. Indeed, I think it just chose women at random, making it harder for me to find my one true love."

"I find this most distressing," said the queen. "Now you are free, and yet…"

"And yet, I am not sure if Millicent will have me."

Lord Sussex snorted. "I lack your tender sensibilities, my dear Victoria. My concern is for the safety of the Crown. Will you give me the relic, Sir Gareth Solimere?"

"Gladly." Gareth placed the bracelet in the other man's outstretched hand. "And good riddance. Lock it away in the deepest, darkest recesses of the Hall of Mages. I hope never to see it again."

"I rather imagine not." The Master slipped the band of silver over his wrist. "I can still feel the power within it. There may be other uses for it, you know… other than for imprisoning a man."

"I want nothing more to do with relic magic."

"I believe you. And yet… although you now appear to be free of the curse, you still present a threat to me and mine."

"Uncle!" interjected the queen. "Don't be ridiculous."

Gareth frowned. "In what way?"

"Your blood, dear boy. It has already proven a danger to my niece."

"I will hear no more of this," snapped Queen Victoria. She stepped over to the bed, her footsteps stomping indignantly on the floor. Her skirts stirred the air of the room, making the strings of diamonds ripple, causing the sparkles to dance merrily in dizzying motion. She lifted her chin, and looked down her nose at her uncle. Despite her youth, she radiated authority, and looked every bit the ruler of England. "Is this how we reward our subjects for their bravery? If not for Sir Gareth, I would be married—ugh! This very moment! To the odious Duke of Ghoulston. And although I did not appreciate your thumb in my mouth…" She gave Gareth a grimace. "I now understand the necessity."

Lord Sussex crossed his arms over his chest. "That is precisely what I mean. You are still under the influence—"

"I am not. Well, perhaps a little. But my head is ruling at the moment, Uncle, and I will not have one of my subjects treated so unfairly. Sir Gareth has been imprisoned for centuries for one small… error in judgment. He has more than paid for that crime, and I will not see him imprisoned any longer. In fact, it is in my mind to reward him for his services."

"That is not necessary, my lady."

"I do not wish to hear from you either, Sir Gareth. You have no home, no income… I will rectify that matter. There is a small manor in Ipswitch that needs tending. Hobover House. I don't imagine a shape-shifting panther used to living in the Underground would be comfortable in London. She will adjust to our world much better in the country."

Gareth's chest twisted. "You assume she will have me."

"Of course."

"I am not so sure."

The Master of the Hall of Mages rolled his eyes.

Queen Victoria shot her uncle a glare. "Nonsense.

Of course she will have you. You have searched for her for centuries! I refuse to believe you two will not work it out... somehow."

Gareth felt... ah, he felt hope. How could he not? The spell had been broken. He was no longer a prisoner. He could lead a normal, mortal life. At long last.

And he would lead that life with Millicent. There had to be a way...

And perhaps the Master of the Hall of Mages could help. Nell's death had caused Millicent to harden her heart again, but something about Nell had been niggling Gareth for some time, and he had brushed it aside for more immediate concerns. Yet, he had thought of it again just a few moments ago. Perhaps it was time to listen to his instincts.

"My lord. What do you know of firebirds?"

Lord Sussex did not bat an eye at the abrupt change of subject. "I assume you mean the magical kind." He dug a finger beneath his cravat and scratched. "They possess feathers varying in shades from reddish-yellow to crimson. They can ignite those feathers at will, and can breathe fire as lethally as a dragon. But unlike dragons, who became illegal ages ago because of their massive appetites, firebirds are natural creatures of the animal kingdom, and as such are protected by certain laws... I assume you are asking because of this Nell person?"

"Yes."

Queen Victoria frowned. "The lady who died and broke Millicent's heart?"

"Again yes, Your Majesty. I have this wild idea..." Gareth stopped. Surely it was only a foolish hope.

"Magic brings us many evils," said Lord Sussex, "but can bring us great joy, as well. There is no subject within my Hall that is too outlandish for discussion, Sir Gareth."

"Indeed," agreed Victoria. "It is why Lord Sussex continues in his post. He is always open to the most outrageous magical notions. If there is anyone who can educate you on magical creatures, it is my uncle."

Gareth nodded. "I had heard—so long ago that I have forgotten the details—that there is a certain type of firebird that rises from the ashes to be reborn again."

"Hmm, yes." Sparkles danced on the Master's brocade coat as he rocked in his chair. "The phoenix…"

"Yes! That is her name… Millicent said it only once, when she first introduced the shape-shifter to me. Nell Feenix. It must have stayed in my mind— that is what has been nagging at me." Gareth leaned forward, his heart filled with so much hope that he barely acknowledged the sudden sharp stab from his injury. "Is it true? The myth about a phoenix?"

"As far as I know. It has been a long time since I have heard of one. Even firebirds are uncommon. But many myths have turned out to be the truth, as evidenced by this city below London… and Merlin's relics."

Queen Victoria clapped her gloved hands, the sound a soft whisper in the quiet room. "Oh, Sir Gareth! If that is true, this Nell might be able to return to your Millicent."

"And heal her heart," he finished. "I did not know what compelled me to keep the firebird's ashes, only that I could not bear to leave her remains lying on that battlefield near Ghoulston's underground castle."

"You have them, then?" The Master's gray brows rose in surprise.

"They are Underground. With the were-bear who aided us against the dragon. I must get them at once."

Lord Sussex put a restraining hand on Gareth's shoulder as he started to rise. "Slow down, young man. What do you know of the legend of the phoenix?"

"Just that she rises from her ashes to be reborn again."

"That's not quite the entire story. The phoenix will build a funeral pyre of special tree limbs and spices, set it afire, be consumed by the blaze, and then be reborn. How did this Nell die?"

"I think a silver bullet hit her, for she fell to the ground. And burst into a column of flame."

"Then it may be too late."

"Uncle!" interjected the queen once again. "I refuse to believe that. Sir Gareth, do not listen to him. There may still be a chance."

Lord Sussex gave her a wry look. "Well, I am glad to see Ghoulston didn't entirely destroy your romantic notions."

Gareth dropped his face in his hands. He might be clinging to a futile hope. Just because Nell's last name was Feenix—or perhaps Phoenix—did not mean she was one. Many baronets possessed surnames from the genus of their were-shape, like Millicent *Pantere*, the Old French name for panther, but not all. Some baronets purposely changed their names to protect their identity. And even if Nell was a phoenix, she did not have the special boughs or spices when she burst into flame.

It might be too late.

Gareth raised his head. But it might not. He would not know until he tried… and he would do anything to earn Millicent's true love. Anything.

"What branches do I use to build the nest? And what spices?"

Victoria clapped her hands again, mouthing "bravo" to him, while the Master heaved a sigh.

"The spices and boughs are difficult to procure, for they primarily come from the Arabian wilderness, where the phoenix originated. But Britain has a presence in Arabia, so they are not unobtainable. I can make you a list of what you need, and how to go about crafting the nest. But after that…" He raised his hands. "You will have to improvise."

"Based on the legend," mused Queen Victoria, "perhaps you should craft the nest, put the ashes in it, and then set it on fire." She shuddered. "It sounds like a dreadful way to come back to life."

Gareth smiled. "Not for ladybird—ah, that is what I call Nell. She loves fire. I cannot accurately describe to you how beautiful she appeared in her were-shape. Feathers aflame like molten liquid, her tail like the train of a woman's gown, but alive with flickering light."

"If you should succeed in your task, brave knight, I would like to meet this ladybird."

Gareth grinned broader at her words and then rose, a bit stiffly, and bowed as low as he could, stifling a grunt of pain. "My thanks, Your Majesty. For your support, and the gift of this Hobover House." He turned to the old man. "And Lord Sussex… I believe I have already proven my loyalty to you and yours. And

I vow that I will never allow anyone to use my blood for ill… although I rather imagine your spies will be checking up on me now and again, yes?"

"You assume correctly."

"Excellent. Am I free to go?"

"Not until you are fully healed," said Queen Victoria. "No, don't look at me that way, Sir Gareth. You have a legend to fulfill and a woman to reclaim. And you are not used to mortality. A few more days to mend will do you good… and no, I am not sure if it is because I am still under the influence of your blood and require your company a few more days."

Nineteen

GARETH USED LADY ROSEUS'S STAIRWAY TO RETURN to the Swill and Seelie when he finally went back underground. The lady had not seemed to be surprised to find him on her doorstep, or particularly disturbed that he requested the use of her stairway, although she asked that he deliver a note to Bran.

He did not wonder about the contents of the missive. The lady had daubed the pink paper with the same scent she wore.

As Gareth reached the bottom of the last step and made his way through the catacomb of tunnels, the darkness surrounded him like a shroud, only the odd glowing fungus on the walls keeping it at bay. He could still not get used to the idea that he would never live in darkness again, that tomorrow morning, he would see the sun rise once more. He had marveled over it for the last few weeks and had not missed a sunrise or a sunset, even when the sky had been darkened with clouds and rain for a day or two.

He reached out and ran a finger along the green-glowing plant on the tunnel wall. Millicent had not only given him his freedom, but had gifted him with more light in his life than he could ever have imagined. He would do anything for her, including the task of chasing after a legend.

The tunnel abruptly ended and opened onto the massive cavern that sheltered the underground city. The network of streams running through the streets stank as badly as the Thames above. The buildings he passed resembled those of London's East End, except for the lack of solid roofs. The fairylights studding the ceiling high above looked like nothing more than the twinkling stars in the sky. The resemblance to London always astonished him.

But the Underground never saw the sunlight.

Millicent lived in the dark.

He would give her the same gift she had given him. If only she would let him.

Gareth passed over one bridge after another, feeling only a slight twinge from his injury. He'd had the most powerful healer in the country to tend him. Queen Victoria herself. Even though the love potion had worn off, the queen still seemed to retain a fondness for him… although she had enthusiastically set her cap on Prince Albert. But as soon as Gareth could move without wincing, she had taken him to Ipswitch, to see Hobover Manor. Gareth had learned that the house had been named after the hobgoblins that roamed the halls of the stone structure. The creatures were rumored to be mischievous but harmless. And he had seen only one of them, a little fellow with hunched shoulders and a crooked grin. Gareth had managed to hire some staff while he was there, and had set them to putting the manor in order. The queen had pointed out an enormous hearth in the middle of a neglected ballroom as a likely place to build Nell's nest.

Surprisingly, Lord Sussex himself had acquired the branches and spices for the nest and had them delivered to Hobover House with his regards.

Gareth needed only to bring Nell's ashes home.

He opened the door of the Swill and Seelie, the wood creaking on the hinges of the door. Gareth had a home. A real home. Not the inside of an enchanted moonstone. And he wanted nothing more than to live there the rest of his life with Millicent. He glanced at the door that led to her chambers as he waded through the chairs of the common room, careful to avoid jostling the few customers slumped over the tabletops.

He also wanted nothing more than to drag her from this place and take her home with him, but he couldn't be sure she would stay, unless he managed to bring Nell back to life. Such a slim hope to gamble his happiness upon.

Gareth stepped behind the bar, where Ambrose lay snoring atop an abandoned leather glove, and gently tapped on the door of Bran's room.

The were-bear opened it with a growl. "Egads, man, do ye know what time it is?"

"Aye. The sun rose aboveground about an hour ago."

"The sun rose…" The big man shook his head like a bear coming out of a long hibernation. His eyes widened as the implication of Gareth's words seemed to sink in. "Ye saw the sun, lad?"

"For several weeks now."

"How—when? Wait, come inside. We don't want to wake the regulars."

Gareth followed him into the storeroom, and took the same seat he had once before, atop a wooden crate full of bottles. "It's why the bracelet did not tighten around Millicent's wrist," he said without preamble. "The curse had already been broken."

Bran settled his bulk on another crate, the wooden slats bowing under the big man's weight. "That's a relief. The gel has done nothing but sulk. And start fights. Crikey, I hired her to stop them, ye know." He scratched at his chest. "So, Millie's love was strong enough to break yer curse after all?"

"Yes. But I'm not sure it's strong enough to make her marry me."

"Then why are ye here, if not to take the gel off my hands?"

Gareth's gaze swung over to the low shelf Bran had pointed out before. "I came to get Nell's ashes. I have a home now. A place where she can… rest in peace." He couldn't bring himself to tell Bran about his hopes to bring Nell back. It seemed a foolish proposition beneath Bran's steady practicality.

"A home? Ye move fast, lad."

"It's a gift from the queen, in recompense for saving her from an ill-fated marriage. She told me to tell you she would like to reward you, as well."

The were-bear's heavy brows lifted in surprise. "Ye don't say? Well, tell Her Majesty I have everything I need right here. It was an honor to do queen and Country a service, lad. It doesn't come about too often, belowground."

Gareth felt little surprise at Bran's answer. He rose and took the bag of ashes from the shelf, stuffing it into the deep pocket of his new morning coat. Another change he had to become accustomed to. Different clothing. The queen had outfitted him with an entire new wardrobe of trousers, brocade waistcoats, velvet frock coats. He preferred his new boots over the pointy toes of his old ones, but missed his sword. Queen Victoria had deemed it quite out of fashion, but had come to his rescue by outfitting him with a bamboo cane that held a hidden blade inside.

Paper crackled and he pulled out Lady Roseus's note. "I have a message for you."

Bran's face lit up and he quickly rose and splashed water on his face from a washbowl in the corner of the room.

"Aren't you going to read it?"

"Not necessary," replied Bran from behind the cloth he dried his face with. He quickly pulled on a shirt, boots, and a worn leather overcoat. "I can smell the scent on it from here."

Gareth stepped aside as Bran stumbled past him.

"Where are you going?"

"Ain't it obvious, mate? When duty calls, I do not delay in answering. It will be a few hours before the regulars wake." And with that, Bran opened the door and left the pub.

Gareth stood for a moment, only the soft sounds of a little snoring sprite breaking the silence.

He should leave as well. Return to Hobover House with Nell's remains.

But he could feel her. So near.

He had hurt her when he'd demanded she give him the bracelet.

She had been furious when it had not tightened about her wrist.

Now was not the time to explain everything to Millicent. He hoped to have Nell's rebirth as an assurance for his proposal.

Gareth threaded his way through the tables again, stopped at the entrance to the hall that led to her room. He could not be sure if she would welcome him. But he did not have the willpower to be this close... without touching her.

Gareth took a breath, strode to her room, and opened the door.

She lay on her pallet, hidden in her were-form, the glossy fur of her panther blending with the dark night. He knelt next to her, laid his hand on her velvet head, and Millicent shifted to human. Gareth smiled in triumph. If nothing else, he had tamed her beast.

Millicent turned her head, her face haloed within a square of fairylight filtering through the small window next to her bed. Her skin glowed like porcelain, like fresh-fallen snow. Her dark lashes fluttered and her mouth parted on a sigh.

Gareth reacted without thought. He leaned down and pressed his lips against hers.

The scent of windblown moors replaced the sour smell of ale that permeated the rest of the tavern. He gloried in the taste of her. Stronger than wine. Sweeter than honey.

In his time, he would have composed poems about her.

The hell with this modern age. He would do so anyway.

Her lips moved beneath his and he deepened the kiss, until her arms stole around his shoulders and his heart fluttered in joy. In triumph. Millicent might never be sure of her feelings, but her body knew what she wanted.

Gareth shed his overcoat, his coat, his waistcoat. He had not lost the skill of removing his clothing without breaking the kiss, despite no longer being cursed. Millicent's hands fluttered about his shoulders, tugged at the knot of his cravat. She wore a gown of soft cotton, the fabric so thin in places he could feel the heat of her skin beneath. Gareth smoothed his palms over the curve of her breasts, and she purred.

He pulled up her skirts, ran his hands up her muscled leg, along the sweet jut of her hipbone.

Millicent fumbled at the buttons of his shirt, managed to open it enough to smooth her hands along his chest. Her touch set Gareth on fire. Alas, how she managed to heighten his senses, to bring his body to a level of excitement he had never experienced before.

He must have her. He would do anything to win her. Gareth pressed closer, claimed her tongue with his in a dance that mimicked his intent. Millicent clutched his shoulders in a possessive grip. He touched her. Touched her wet heat, her silky folds, and she arched against his hand.

He delved deeper. Deeper, until she squirmed beneath him. Until she growled with need.

In one smooth motion, Gareth slid his body over hers and kissed her entrance with his swollen flesh.

Then gently, slowly, filled her with his need, with his desire. With his love.

Millicent arched back her head, breaking their kiss, exposing the smooth white curve of her throat. Her harsh gasps sounded loud in the tiny room. He ran his tongue over the creamy skin, relishing the salty-sweet taste of her.

Gareth ground his pelvis against hers.

You are mine. Whether you choose to acknowledge it or not, you are mine. But I will have more than your body. I will have your heart. The whole of it. Not just the damaged bits and pieces.

Millicent began to shake. The tremor ran from her center and spread through her limbs as her release overtook her. And Gareth's body responded to her pleasure, but his own release did not spread like a wave. It imploded inside of him, shattering his senses in a burst of ecstasy, making spots of light dance before his eyes.

He stilled, gathered his wits about him, and pulled away from her. Then sat for a moment with his head bowed in his hands.

She mewed. Some soft, sad noise that made him want to return to her. It would be so easy to stay. To tell her she had freed him, that her love had been strong enough after all. She would believe his words with her head… but he could not be sure if she would believe it in her heart. And he had a chance to make Millicent whole. He could tell her about his plans, about his hopes to bring Nell back. But if it did not work… no. He could not risk it. The disappointment might destroy her.

Gareth rose, dressed, and left as quietly as he had entered.

He did not look back at Millicent, nor did she make another sound to try to make him stay.

Perhaps she too understood that words were meaningless between them now.

He ran into the guard Bran had placed at the door during the tavern keeper's absence. The man half shifted to jackal before he recognized Gareth, then moved aside. Gareth strode through the city like a blind man, his hand in his pocket around the bag of Nell's ashes. He got lost several times on his way out of the tunnels, his mind distracted with thoughts of Millicent.

And ran into Bran at the top of Lady Roseus's stairway. They stared at each other in silence for a few moments.

"You should marry her," said Gareth.

Bran grinned. "I plan to… if she'll have me." He shuffled his feet, stuck his hands deep in his pockets. "And what about my Millie?"

"If she'll have me."

"We are a fine pair, old chap."

Gareth grinned back at him. He suddenly felt lighter, as if his task wasn't as impossible as he thought it might be. If a gruff bear could somehow manage to make a timid flamingo fall in love with him…

"Well, then." Bran stepped to the side and they passed each other on the stairway.

Gareth did not see Lady Roseus as he strode through her house. Just the footman, who called for the carriage Gareth had left waiting. It had come with Hobover House. Indeed, he had several conveyances provided with his new estate. This coach had been kept up particularly well, with a coat of fresh varnish and smoothly oiled wheels. He ducked through the door and made himself comfortable, for he had a lengthy journey ahead of him to return to Ipswitch… and only Nell's ashes, and memories of his encounter with Millicent, to keep him company.

Twenty

MILLICENT HAD CLOSED HER EYES FOR WHAT SHE thought had been just a moment, a delicious feeling of lassitude overwhelming her. And then she heard the door to her little room snick shut. She sat up with a start, blinking in the gloom. He had left her. After making love to her until she was so exhausted she'd fallen asleep, he'd just walked out without a word.

She glanced around the room in confusion. Perhaps she had only dreamed of him?

But she now felt fully awake. She could smell sour ale, could feel her hard pallet beneath her. She was still in the Swill and Seelie, where she had wallowed in misery for weeks. Her surroundings were too painfully real.

As real as the gentle ache from Gareth's lovemaking.

Millicent hugged her shoulders. No, it had not been a dream. He had come to her. Had made love to her like a man starved for affection. Yet he had asked her to give him the relic…

She had thought it had been his way of saying good-bye.

For the last few weeks she had resumed her old life once again, determined to forget him. But she couldn't. A head of blond hair would set her heart racing, and then plummeting to earth when she realized it wasn't him. She would dream of him night after night... of his goodness, his courage, his gentle touch.

Millicent eavesdropped on every conversation she could, trying to find out what had happened to him after that fateful day. Talk flowed about the battle between Queen Victoria and the Duke of Ghoulston. The patrons of the pub relished the tales of Ghoulston's blindness and eventual madness. But no one mentioned her enchanted knight.

Millicent dropped her arms. She knew the queen had taken him to Buckingham, but after that, Gareth seemed to have disappeared from aboveground. She feared the Master had taken the relic to the Hall, and trapped Gareth inside it forever.

But her knight had come to her. Somehow. Someway. And he still needed her. She had felt it in his kiss, with his every touch.

And she had promised she would never forsake him again.

Millicent surged to her feet. How dare that piece of metal try to tell her she wasn't good enough for him? That her love wasn't strong enough? So—so she couldn't break the spell... who knew what sort of torture Merlin had intended with his curse? Perhaps he wanted to deny Gareth any happiness at all, and despite their different natures, she knew she could make him happy.

Her anger at having someone—or something—

other than herself determine her fate, did what no persuasion could have. It made Millicent look at herself in a new light.

She had changed since she had first met Gareth. He had tamed her beast, had taught her about the value of charity and honor. She had been raised in the Underground, had learned to be selfish in all her concerns… and yet, she had still loved Nell. Millicent had taken care of her and risked her life for her.

Nell had died to help queen and Country.

And Millicent knew if she could ask Nell, the firebird would answer that she did not regret it.

So, what made a person good or bad? She'd always known the answer, but now embraced it fully within her heart: their actions. Not the cost of the clothing they wore, or the size of their home, or where they lived, whether in the grandest part of West London, or deep within the Underground. Even if they shape-shifted to a beast, their animal natures did not define them.

Millicent yanked open her door, strode into the pub and over to the bar. When she discovered Bran had left his room, she spun and poked a finger at the messenger sprite snoring on the counter. "Where is he?"

One translucent wing fluttered. "Eh, what?"

"Bran. Where did he go?"

Ambrose wobbled upright to a sitting position, screwed up his little pointed face, apparently trying to summon all of his brainpower to answer the question. Bran saved the sprite from further effort by striding into the pub, a self-satisfied grin on his face.

"Where have you been?" snapped Millicent.

"'Tis no concern of yers, little she-cat. What's got ye in such a lather?"

"The dress."

"Wot?"

"The ridiculous dress Lady Roseus loaned me."

Bran scratched his head. "The one ye told me to burn?"

"Yes. Where is it?"

He folded his arms, raised a brow at her. "And what would ye be wanting with it, now? I seem to recall ye sayin' ye'd never go topside again."

Millicent scowled.

Bran laughed. "So ye're gonna go to him, is that it? I think ye might surprise him, gel. Yes, I think it might come as a big surprise."

He looked as if he kept some sort of secret from her, as if he knew more about the situation than he let on.

"You saw him tonight, didn't you?" demanded Millicent.

"He might have popped in to give me his regards."

"Stop teasing, Bran. This is serious. Do you know where I can find him?"

"What did he tell you?"

"What do you mean?"

"I think ye'll be in for some surprises yerself, Millie. And far be it for me to spoil them." Bran strode to his room and returned with the bronze gown. "I meant to return it to Rose, but kept forgetting. I'm sure she wouldn't mind ye borrowing it again. And I'm sure she wouldn't mind offering ye a carriage to find yer knight."

Millicent gathered the gown into her arms. So, Bran knew more than he would tell her, but he didn't know where Gareth might be. She didn't bother pressing Bran for more information; he could be obstinately tight-lipped when he wanted to be. And now that she had made the decision, Millicent could not wait to find her knight. "Does Lady Roseus know where Gareth is?"

He shrugged. "I'm not sure. But I know who might. That friend of yers, Lady Yardley."

❧

London appeared to get more crowded every time Millicent came aboveground. The sun hid behind gray clouds, and it seemed as if every maid and footman scurried to purchase their morning groceries before the clouds belched out their impending rain. Millicent turned her face away from the carriage window and closed her eyes. She really had no interest in the scenery, despite the astounding sight of a maid who carried her purchases on the humped back of a gangly beast and the footman who sported a small dragon curled about his neck. She wanted only to find Gareth.

After an interminable length of time, Lady Roseus's carriage lurched to a stop in front of Claire's peacock mansion in the West End... although the peacocks now appeared to be supplemented with gigantic purplish bluebells, which hung down from foot-wide stalks that surrounded the building. Millicent passed under an array of them as she walked to the front door, and the movement from her passage set them to tinkling as if they each possessed a clapper of crystal.

The butler led her into the elegant home, informing her that Lady Yardley already had a guest. Millicent came to an abrupt stop when she entered the withdrawing room of Sothby Manor, one of the most aristocratic mansions in London, and saw a shape-shifting baronet lounging on the satin cushions. "Sir Harcourt!"

The were-lion rose from his seat next to Claire, where they had been sitting most inappropriately close together. The last time she'd seen him, he had bloody fur around his neck. Blood she had put there.

Harcourt gave her a low bow. "Lady Millicent. What a pleasure to see you again."

She raised a brow in doubt, and turned her attention to Claire. "Your father may have an apoplexy, what with all the animals you choose to befriend."

Claire smiled, her hazel eyes dancing with mischief. "I rather think my engagement may come as something of a shock… but Father has enough mistresses to comfort him from the upset."

Millicent supposed if she had been raised aboveground she would have gasped at that shocking little speech. Instead, she wrinkled her brow. "Engagement? I thought you despised Sir Harcourt."

"Her feelings have changed," rumbled the golden-maned man, laying a possessive hand on Claire's shoulder. "Obviously."

"Do have a seat, Millicent," interjected Claire, nodding at a wingback chair beside her, "and tell me what brings you here in such a state. For you do look rather… intense."

The harp that stood in the corner of the room changed

tune, a fluent string of harmonious notes washing the air. Millicent relaxed her shoulders, unclenched her hands from the handle of the black lace parasol that went with her bronze outfit. She also wore the little beaded hat and light green gloves, and found herself staring at the seams in the fabric covering her hands. She did not want to do this in front of Harcourt. They might be acting civil for Claire's sake, but Millicent could feel the man's resentment vibrating with the harp strings.

Lions did not like to be beaten in a fight… especially not by a female panther.

But Sir Harcourt resumed his seat next to Lady Yardley, and did not look as if he was going anywhere soon, and Millicent had no desire to dawdle. Well, then.

She raised her eyes and chin. "I am looking for Sir Gareth."

"Ha," said Claire. "It's about time." She leaned over and rang a golden bell sitting on a marble table carved in the shape of an upside-down bluebell. "You will join us for dinner, Lady Millicent, for we have much to discuss. You must explain where you have been the last few weeks, and what on earth you have been thinking."

"There is nothing to explain. He is—what? What do you mean, *dinner*?"

Claire frowned, and Harcourt gazed at Millicent with a smirk on his handsome mouth.

Millicent backed up a step, turned, and glanced out the window. Time. "What time is it?" She had assumed it was morning, because she had been with Gareth no less than a few hours ago.

"She has always lived in the Underground," said Harcourt, "and they have an odd sense of time down there."

Lady Yardley shushed her fiancé. "What is it about the hour that disturbs you, Millicent?" She turned her head as a servant responded to her summons and waved the maid away, before placing her gentle gaze on Millicent once again.

Claire was a true friend, to accept Millicent's odd history so readily... but Millicent could not give the thought the appreciation it deserved, for one thing kept bouncing about in her head.

If it was close to dinnertime, then Gareth...

"I saw Gareth but a few hours ago. It cannot be that late in the day."

The were-lion's handsome face altered, becoming gentler somehow, his scar making him appear more sympathetic than dangerous. "She does not know."

"Know what?"

Claire smiled as she answered, "Sir Gareth has been released from his curse."

The world spun. Millicent took a step, and fortunately managed to maneuver a chair beneath her when her legs collapsed. She could not believe it. The spell had been broken. But...

"Who? Who broke the spell?"

Claire shook her head. "It was not I. The bracelet would not tighten on my—"

"Then who?" interrupted Millicent. "I assumed he kept it—who did Gareth give it to the night we fought the dragon?"

"The queen took it," replied Harcourt. His eyes

widened at Millicent's stricken face, and he hurried on to say, "But it would not tighten on her wrist, either, although I imagine she kept it for a time. That taste of Gareth's blood kept her by his side for weeks. She even granted him a manor to go along with his title, ancient though it is—the title, not the manor. Although it *is* a rather old heap of stone—"

"Then who?" demanded Millicent. "Who broke his curse?"

"She sounds like an owl," muttered Harcourt.

Claire gave him an indignant glance and crossed the room to kneel next to Millicent, placing her gloved hands over Millicent's own. "You did, dearest. No, do not look so surprised. I was there when it happened, although I did not realize the significance of the moment until the queen explained it all to me later. The curse lifted when Gareth found out that you had given up the relic to me. I think... I think it broke his heart, to realize you had betrayed your promise."

If Harcourt had not been in the room, Millicent might have felt inclined to cry at Claire's words. But she stiffened her spine, and the tears barely burned her eyes. "I did not fully realize..."

"Hush, he knows." She frowned. "Or at least, he had enough faith in you to hope you still loved him. Afterwards, of course."

"After?"

"After he recovered from his heart being broken. I daresay, I heard it... although the queen says it was the sound of the gemstone in the relic breaking."

Several things suddenly made sense to Millicent.

Her heart felt like a bird trapped in a cage, threatening to break free. "Then the bracelet did not tighten on my wrist because the curse had already been broken."

"Merlin was a crafty old coot," interjected Harcourt. "He didn't damn Gareth to find his true love. In fact, Merlin made it harder for him as the relic had no design for the women it chose. The only thing the relic had been enchanted to sense was Gareth's broken heart. The Master of the Hall of Mages thinks Merlin cared only that Gareth should earn his freedom by feeling betrayed... the same way Merlin had felt when your knight had broken his heart by dallying with his Lady Vivian."

"Gareth has more than paid for that crime," retorted Claire.

Harcourt nodded. "Merlin made sure of it."

Millicent bowed her head, the silly hat tugging at the shaggy coiffure Ambrose had managed to twist up for her. "I must go to him." Had Gareth felt this way, when she had rejected him? She could not bear thinking of him in such pain. She would not shy away from him this time. She would confess her mistake and demand his forgiveness, and if he did not forgive her... if she had broken his heart as badly as hers had once been broken... then she would heal it. As her knight had healed hers

Claire rose. "He is not in London. I heard he left for his estate this morning."

"Where?" Millicent would follow him to the ends of the earth. Her resolve to be with Gareth... to reassure him that she loved him... to take away any pain she had caused him, overrode her feeling of dread at

being alone aboveground. Of traveling beneath the
sun, living a life in light instead of darkness.

She might even come to like it.

She would, for Gareth's sake.

"Are you sure you want to rush off?" asked Claire.
"Perhaps you should give yourself some time to let
this all sink in."

"I have already taken up too much time," growled
Millicent. She felt her beast waking, begin to start
pacing inside her. She wanted her mate. "If I had not
been so afraid of loving him... I never would have
hurt him like this."

"I shall loan you one of my carriages."

"No, Lady Yardley. I will travel much faster on...
paws. I am already several hours behind him."

Claire gaped. "Millicent. You cannot go galloping
through London in your were-shape. It is simply
not done."

Harcourt's belly groaned. "Egads, Claire, let the
woman go. She knows how to keep to the shadows.
My meal has been delayed long enough."

"You are unconscionably practical."

"Which is why you adore me." The were-lion
rose and strode over to a secretary, pulled a sheet of
stationery from the top drawer, and began to draw out
a map with a fountain pen. "Here, Millicent. Take
this road out of London, then take the left branch
here. After that... if you cross country, which I rather
imagine you will, head northeast. Hobover House is
in the district of Ipswitch, right here."

Millicent rose and studied the finished map he
held out to her. She had developed a good sense of

direction, a necessity when living underground. She would find him.

Claire reached out and pulled Millicent into a hug. Millicent had never noticed her friend's short stature before, for Claire's vibrant personality did not allow for it, but her auburn coiffure barely reached Millicent's chin.

"Oh, Millicent. You will be careful, won't you? There are dangers on the road... and through the forest. And our world is so unfamiliar to you."

"It is less dangerous than the Underground. You forget my true nature, dear friend." And Millicent shifted to panther.

Claire stepped back, and Harcourt wrapped one comforting arm about her shoulders, and she leaned into his embrace.

Millicent found the sight of the two of them together most astonishing. Her thought must have reflected in her eyes, for Harcourt smirked at her, but oddly enough, not in an unkind way. She leaped onto the windowsill, and threw her friend one last glance over her shoulder.

"He will forgive you," said Claire.

Millicent turned and vaulted out the window. She wished she could feel as confident as her friend.

Twenty-one

GARETH'S CARRIAGE FINALLY CLEARED THE MILES OF woodland surrounding Hobover House and the enormous edifice came into view. Rounded turrets of reddish stone reached for the sky. A long drive cut through a swath of green ground, broken by enormous yew trees with trunks so large it would take several men with outstretched arms to encompass them. Gareth suspected the branches sheltered more than a few tree nymphs, although he had yet to see one of the shy beings.

The carriage rolled to a stop in front of the arched stone doorway of the house and Gareth alighted from the coach before his man could pull out the steps. The butler managed to yank open the door before Gareth reached it though, and he shot the older servant a grin as he strode past him, straight for the ballroom. He noticed his new staff had been busy, for the marble tiled floors gleamed and the statues lining the hall lacked their previous cobwebs and coating of dust. Gareth had hired as many shape-shifters as he could, hoping their company would make Millicent feel more at home. Apparently they were grateful for the employment, and pleased that their new mistress would be one of their own kind, for they had set about their new tasks with enthusiasm. He had given the housekeeper full rein in setting the house to rights, and noticed vases of fresh flowers upon every table within the drawing rooms.

But he felt the most delight when he entered the old ballroom. The parquet floors of the spacious room had been polished and repaired, restoring the odd pattern of the blocks of wood. Gareth could not quite make it out, but he suspected the floor made up a larger picture… something to do with woodland and deer. The cavernous fireplace had been scrubbed clean, revealing a white sparkling stone beneath the soot, the mantel and sides carved with frolicking creatures that looked suspiciously like the one hobgoblin he had spied on his first visit to the place.

The branches and spices Lord Sussex had sent him had been carefully laid out next to the hearth.

Gareth could not recall instructing the servants to do so, and he had spoken of Nell only once within this house—with the queen, when she had pointed out the fireplace as the perfect place to build the nest.

The pile of branches crackled, releasing a scent similar to the sharp smell of pine, but with a spicy undertone Gareth could not identify. He did not know what sort of foreign tree could make such twisted branches, or create leaves tinged with silver. He could not imagine what sort of creature might have been living within them when they had been harvested…

…and might still be hidden inside them now.

Gareth flicked the lever that released the thin sword from his cane, and drew it silently from the bamboo sleeve. He took a step forward, eyes narrowed at the pile.

A small being emerged from the mass of twisted limbs. Not some foreign creature, but the hobgoblin of the house. Although Gareth had spied him only once, he could not mistake those little hunched shoulders and that crooked grin.

"Did ye bring them?" asked the small being, brushing a silver leaf off his head. He wore odds and ends of what Gareth imagined he had scavenged from the residents of the house: lace sewn to velvet sewn to brocade, tied with ribbon strung with gold buttons and glass beads.

"Bring what?" replied Gareth, surprised into answering.

Bushy red brows lowered over green eyes. A bulbous nose twitched, and a wide mouth frowned. "Why, the firebird's ashes. As ye can see, I have prepared all in readiness for her."

Gareth sheathed his blade. "You eavesdropped on a private conversation with the Queen of England."

"Oy, ye best get used to it now, sir. There's naught a thing that goes in within these walls that I am not aware of." He strode forward, craned his head up to look at Gareth. "Besides, I think ye will be needing me. And I *knows* yer bride will."

Gareth's heart gave a little skip at the word "bride." How he hoped to make it so. He sighed and dropped to one knee. He'd heard enough about hobgoblins to know they could make life miserable for the owner of a house: curdled milk, accidental slips, tangled laces.

Gareth should consider himself lucky that the creature had taken a liking to him.

"Polite of ye to come down to my level," he said as Gareth lowered his face to look the hobgoblin in the eyes. "I knew we would get along. Now then, do ye have them?"

"Why have you taken such an interest?"

"It's been long and long since we've had such a being within the walls of this house. We shall be a grand place once more! Now show me."

Those sharp green eyes lit with excitement as Gareth withdrew the leather pouch from his pocket for a moment, before stowing it safely back in his coat. But that brief glance appeared to satisfy the hobgoblin, for he grinned and nodded and turned back to the pile of branches, pulling out one of the smallest limbs with a grunt of effort.

Gareth blinked. The creature had a tail. A furry tail, with a ball of scraggly fur at the end. It stuck out of the back of his trousers through a narrow slit, and waved jauntily at him. "What is your name?"

"Again, polite. I suppose I should have expected that from a once knight of the Round Table." He looked over his shoulder. "Parsnip. And don't laugh, or I will have to revise my good opinion of ye. Me dad had a sense of humor."

Gareth kept his expression stony only from centuries of practice. He watched Parsnip drag over his branch and place it within the hearth, step back, eye it critically, and then reposition it.

Gareth rose to his feet. "You look like you know what you're doing."

"Methinks the queen knew what she was about when she gave ye Hobover House. We once had a phoenix living here, did ye know?"

"No, I did not. Nor do I think the queen did, either—or surely she would have mentioned it."

"Oy. Well. It was long before her time… and long after yers. Heh. But betimes magic works in mysterious ways, and methinks this is one of them. Hand me that branch in front of ye—no, not the smaller one. That big one there. Now, place it alongside this one, aye, and twine it about until it's tight."

Gareth followed the hobgoblin's instructions, lacking any of his own on how to go about building a firebird's nest. Parsnip eventually took a seat on the parquet, crossing stubby legs in front of him, leaning back on his hands.

"So," asked Gareth as he twisted another branch together, "did you see your phoenix reborn?"

"No. She was still alive when she left to marry a sailor."

"Then how do you know how to build the nest?"

"I told ye. I know everything that goes on within the house."

Gareth glanced over his shoulder. "You overheard a conversation about it."

A mischievous grin flashed across those rounded features. "She told the mistress about it once. Lucky for ye. Now, take the entire mess and curve it around, aye, just like that. Now ye've got a nice circular nest."

Gareth did as instructed, then stepped out of the hearth to admire his construction. The fireplace stood so tall he did not even have to duck to get in and out. "It looks... well, like a nest. What now?"

Parsnip scrambled to his feet, stepped over to the containers of spices, and began to sniff. "This is the tricky part. Ye can add only so much of this, and then so much of that, and the proportions have to be right. Fortunately I have a good memory for nearly everything I overhear."

Gareth filed away that little tidbit of knowledge for future reference.

Parsnip pointed at a yellow container. "That smells like the myrrh. Take two pinches—only two, mind. And toss it in the middle of the nest."

Gareth took the granules, which resembled yellow tears, and did as instructed.

"Now this one," said the hobgoblin, "is frank-incense. Take four handfuls and sprinkle it on the branches. And the last here"—he laid a small, knobby hand on a red container—"is dragon's blood. It is the most important ingredient. Take the whole pot, and spread it in the middle of the nest."

Gareth picked up the pot and removed the lid. Another strong scent, this one. It made his head spin as he poured the reddish powder into the middle of the twined branches, then carefully spread it out. He rose, wiped his hands on his trousers, staining them with crimson.

"Yes, just so," murmured Parsnip approvingly. "Now, then. Place the firebird's ashes in the dragon's blood."

This time, Gareth hesitated. He could not go back from this point on. "I am placing a lot of trust in a conversation you once overheard."

The hobgoblin scowled. "Did this Master of magic have a better idea of how to go about the rebirth?"

"Lord Sussex said I would have to improvise."

"Oy, then consider us improvising."

Gareth removed the bag of Nell's ashes from his pocket, placed it carefully in the center of the branches, atop the dragon's blood. At least Nell would be honored here, even if this did not work... "Come back to us, ladybird," he whispered.

"Now stand aside," warned the hobgoblin.

Gareth stepped back over the hearthstone, watched in surprise as Parsnip raised his stubby arms, the glow of fire lighting his knobby fingers. A slender column of flame snaked from finger to branch, and the nest they had carefully created lit in a blaze of glorious color.

Parsnip curled his fingers into fists and extinguished them, although the fire in the hearth continued to burn. "Do not look so astonished, Sir Gareth. How can a hobgoblin care properly for his home without a wee bit of magic?"

But Gareth had already forgotten Parsnip, his attention focused back on the fireplace, and the nest burning inside. White smoke curled up the chimney, snaking tendrils of scent into the room, a smell so powerful, Gareth thought he could almost see it. Touch it. He grew dizzy once again, his entire being suffused with the combined aroma of the spices. He never would have thought mere scent could have such an effect upon him. But this was more than smell. It held a power beyond that of mere magic.

The fire roiled with a dizzying kaleidoscope of color: blues, greens, lavenders, and reds, darker shades of indigo, crimson, and emerald. The branches of the nest formed a halo around the center where Nell's ashes lay, and for a moment—a breath of time—Gareth thought he glimpsed the shape of a beak, a long elegant tail of feathers.

His heart rose into his throat. He had wanted Nell to return for Millicent, but realized for the first time how much he had missed her as well. Gareth stumbled forward, bracing himself against the heat of the blaze. "Ladybird?"

And then the fire folded in on itself, and his vision blurred.

When he could see once again, the blaze had dwindled to a low flame along the curve of the branches, only a soft glow of white within the nest.

"Ladybird?" he repeated.

The cavernous room stilled, only the soft crackle of burning wood breaking the silence. Gareth waited, staring at the glowing orb in the middle of the nest.

And waited.

And waited.

"It did not work," Gareth finally said, his voice cracking on his last word. He should have known. He had thought the appearance of Parsnip, and his knowledge of how to build the nest, had been a sign from fate that he would succeed in his task. But now he knew it had been a slim hope, just wishful thinking on his part. Ah, how he wished he could have brought Nell back for Millicent. How he wished he could have healed the shape-shifter's heart.

How he wished he could have seen that delicate, wrinkled face once more.

He turned and looked down, but Parsnip had disappeared. He could not ask the hobgoblin what they might do next. What they might have done wrong.

But Gareth supposed it did not matter. He would not be given a second chance.

Twenty-two

MILLICENT STARED THROUGH THE GLASS PANES OF THE enormous mansion, trying to understand what Gareth was doing. At first she thought he might be speaking to himself, but then she spied a small creature standing near him. The little man had a tail, and rounded features, and a mischievous grin. She could not imagine where Gareth had found the thing, or what they could possibly be discussing.

She swished her tail, paced in front of the double doors. Her journey to Ipswitch had been uneventful—save for the herd of cows, and then unicorns, she had spooked once or twice. She had avoided the roads, using them only as guides, and had traveled mostly at night, her dark fur forcing her to stay to the shadows of the woods within the daytime.

The sun had shone for the few days she had traveled, in a bright sky that seemed too far above her to be real. The wide-open spaces of the moors had made her fur prickle with discomfort, and yet… there had been something intoxicating about padding through tall fields of corn, skulking in grass, and stalking dinner in bushes. The were-cat inside her had often prompted her to run through meadows for no reason other than to glory in the joy of it.

While Millicent had glared suspiciously at every hedgerow and woodland, her beast had purred with a quiet contentment, as if some ancient memory of a habitat she had once thrived in had suddenly awoken.

An owl hooted off in the distance, and Millicent lowered to a crouch, staring off into the deepening night. She stood on a large balcony one story above the ground. She had prowled around the stone building for hours, sniffing for a scent of Gareth, but too many other smells had interfered with her search. Clean smells, foreign to her nose. But then a strong, spicy scent had reached her, and she had seen the light above her shining from the double doors of the balcony.

And had spied Gareth within the enormous room.

And now stood dithering outside it.

Millicent took a breath, and shifted to human. She spread her hands, loosened her shoulders, glanced down, and smoothed the folds of the bronze gown. She had not resumed her human shape for days, for it was easier and safer to travel in her were-form.

Millicent had no idea if she looked a fright or not.

She smoothed her hair, adjusted the silly hat on her head. She should be grateful the magic of her transformation kept her clothing on her; otherwise, she would be standing here naked.

Stop, it, Millicent. You are stalling. Now that the time has come, you're afraid to face him, aren't you?

She reached out and tried the door. At first the

handle seemed to be locked, but when she jiggled it a bit, she heard a faint click. Millicent took a breath, gave it a push, and stepped into the room.

And nearly swooned from the smell.

A scent stronger than the underground rivers at low tide, but with a completely opposite aroma. Spicy, heady, sweet, and glorious. What on earth had Gareth been burning inside that fireplace?

He sat on a velvet fainting couch he had dragged from across the room, based on the skid marks on the wooden floor. The small creature with the curious tail had vanished. Gareth stared into the glowing flames of the fireplace, muted now to a soft, pearly light. The light danced on the sharp planes of his face, on his full lips and round eyes. But those eyes held a bleakness Millicent had never seen before, and a tightness about his mouth spoke of a forlornness that tugged at her heart. His golden hair looked unkempt, as if he had run his fingers through it so many times he had worried out the curls. He wore a smart coat, and equally smart trousers, with a brocade waistcoat and a clean white cravat. Every bit the English aristocrat the queen had made him.

Millicent missed his woolen hose and loosely woven tunic.

She took a step toward him, her skirts making a whisper of sound on the floor.

He looked up. Met her eyes.

And held Millicent transfixed for an eternity.

How could she define the bond between them? How could she have known how special this feeling was? She did not chide herself for a fool. It had taken her some time to open her heart, and she had needed that time. But she would not allow anything to stand between them now.

Not her fear. Nor any fey magic. Not even Gareth himself.

Millicent took a deep breath and then asked, "Will you ever forgive me?"

He blinked. "For what?"

"For breaking my promise to you." She took another few steps closer to him. "For taking so long to see the truth between us."

He set aside the cane he had been gripping in his hands and rose, but did not approach her. When he spoke, his voice was low, his words barely crossing the distance between them. "What truth is that, Millicent?"

He said her name like a benediction, like a caress. Millicent took another few steps toward him, as if some magical tether gently pulled her to him without a conscious thought of her own. "That we… you know I am not good with words, Gareth. Not like you. You come from a time where ballads and poetry were recited every day…"

Gareth crossed strong arms over his broad chest, and raised his brows. So, then. He would not allow her to excuse herself from answering.

"We are… one soul. Together." Millicent continued to walk toward him, trying very hard to put her feelings into words. "I did not know I needed anyone. I did not know I needed to be a better person, or that someone could manage even to make it so. I did not know I needed *you*, until you came into my life and changed everything."

He just stood there in silence, staring at her. But the expression in his pale blue eyes… the sadness began to fade.

Millicent tried harder. She owed him that. She owed him everything. If necessary, she would spend her entire life composing ballads to him, if it made up for the pain she had caused. "You make me feel whole. You bring such goodness and light to my life. To my heart. You are the sun to my moon, and the moon to my stars…"

His lips twitched, and he could not suppress a smile. Millicent had the feeling he worked very hard not to burst into laughter.

A growl of annoyance shivered up her throat. "Well, I shall never make it as a poet; that is obvious. But it is the best I can do, Gareth."

She stood near enough to touch him now, right in front of the massive fireplace. The scent of the burning wood made her head spin. Or perhaps it was just his nearness.

"Millicent." He closed the distance between them. "Do you love me with all your heart, dearest? That is all you need to say."

He touched her cheek with his hand, and she closed her eyes and leaned into the embrace. "Yes, Gareth Solimere. I love you with all my heart… a heart that can never be whole without you."

She heard his breath hitch, felt his arms encircle her. "I love you too, dearest she-cat. I think I have from the moment you put Merlin's bracelet on your wrist."

And then his lips met hers, and Millicent's knees went weak, and she leaned into him for support while he kissed her breath away. She would have stayed like that forever, caught up in his embrace, but a sudden flare of light lit her lids, and her eyes flew open.

Gareth turned his head to stare in amazement at the fireplace, and she followed his gaze.

A circle of flame surrounded a white glowing object, roughly egg-shaped and with a pearly iridescence of reds, oranges, and yellows. A crackling sound echoed through the cavernous ballroom, louder than the crackle of the fire, but softer than the snap of a twig.

"What is that?" she asked, suddenly remembering the odd little being and Gareth's intensity for building the fire. As if she had summoned him with her thoughts, the small creature appeared from above the mantel of the fireplace, swinging open a painting that hung there as if it were a door, and jumping nimbly down to the parquet floor.

He wore an odd assortment of expensive fabrics sewn together in a haphazard fashion, and did, indeed, sport a tail through a tear in the back of his trousers. He had hunched shoulders and a wide grin and knobby features.

"New question," Millicent whispered. "What is *that*?"

"A hobgoblin." Gareth frowned. "He came with the house. I'm not sure if that's good or bad."

The orb in the fireplace flared again, making her narrow her eyes. A new crack appeared in the pearly surface.

The little creature jumped up and down, clapping his hands in glee.

"Parsnip," said Gareth. "What's happening?"

Parsnip? mouthed Millicent. But they both ignored her, their eyes intent on the thing in the fire.

"Oh ho. Methinks... yes, methinks she is finally hatching."

Hatching? mouthed Millicent and then clamped her lips shut, refusing to feel like a dunce a third time.

The circle of burning branches surrounding the egg flared into swirling columns, dancing madly about the object as the cracks in its surface began to spread. To grow. Pieces of white shell broke outward and fell onto the burning ash. Something lay inside the egg. Something with a tiny yellow beak and fiery red feathers.

A shiver shook Millicent from head to toe. She glanced from Gareth to the thing in the fireplace.

No, it could not be possible. "Where on earth did you find a firebird's egg? And why are you hatching it, instead of the mother of the creature?" Millicent could only think Gareth had found it somehow. That the mother had been killed and he had rescued the egg and brought it back to Hobover House. Or perhaps, like the hobgoblin, the egg had *come* with the house?

Parsnip turned and raised a knobby finger to his wide mouth. "Hush, now. The wee thing must concentrate on breaking out of her shell, don't ye know?"

No, Millicent didn't know. And she couldn't imagine what Gareth had been thinking to try to foster a firebird. The creatures could spit flame, for heaven's sake. And until they grew old enough to control it, burst into fire at a moment's notice.

And then it struck her. Had Gareth purposely sought out a firebird for Millicent? To somehow replace Nell? She shook her head, wishing he had spoken to her first. No one could replace Nell. She had left a hole in Millicent's heart that even her love for Gareth could not quite fully heal. But Millicent had come to accept that as a part of her. She would not allow the pain to keep her from fully loving Gareth. But perhaps he hadn't known that until now, when she had come to him.

The very small firebird finished pecking its way out of its shell, and tried to stand on its new legs, but managed only to tumble head-over-feathers out of the fireplace, coming to an abrupt landing on the hearthstone. Parsnip jumped out of scorching distance, and began to croon to the baby bird.

"Do you know how hard it is to hatch a firebird in captivity?" murmured Millicent.

"Alas," replied Gareth, giving her shoulders a squeeze. "This is no ordinary firebird."

She glanced at his face. Heavens, he took her breath away. His eyes shone with triumph and joy, and his ordinarily handsome features now glowed with an almost angelic beauty.

Light to dark. He is the light, and I am the dark. But the thought no longer made Millicent sad, or made her feel unworthy. They balanced each other and were better for it.

The flames of the hatchling began to fade to a dull glow, and Parsnip strode over and petted the tiny head, murmuring reassuring words to it.

Millicent touched Gareth's strong chin, made him turn to look at her.

"You did not need to do this. I… I need only you. Besides, you must know that this little creature cannot replace my Nell."

His mouth softened, and his blue eyes danced. "No. I don't imagine any ordinary firebird could take the place of your Nell. But you see, my dearest—"

An abrupt shout from the hobgoblin interrupted them, and they both turned to stare at Parsnip and the little baby... human.

"Eh, well," muttered Parsnip. "Methinks the lady should take over from here."

The infant screwed up her little face and began to squall. Parsnip placed his gnarled hands over his ears and winced.

"A were-firebird?" gasped Millicent. "Where in England did you find—" But she didn't finish her question, because her body responded to the infant's cries, even though she had no experience with children, and had no idea what she was doing... just that it felt right. She tore off the soft apron that accessorized her bronze gown, while her feet took her over to the baby, and then Millicent wrapped the child in the fabric and cradled it to her chest.

The tiny thing immediately quit crying.

A warm feeling washed through Millicent's body. She stared down at the small bundle in her arms. The child had a cap of red fuzz on its head, and the most delicate face Millicent had ever seen. It had put its fist in its mouth and sucked fervently on it. And then it... *she*... opened her eyes.

Lavender eyes.

Millicent began to shake, felt Gareth's warm arms surround her again, helping to support her and the baby. She leaned into his strength, and did not feel the lesser for it.

"How?" she breathed.

"Ah, well," said her love. "I did not know she would come back as a baby, although I rather imagine it makes sense. I foolishly thought she'd be reborn to her old, crotchety self."

"This is Nell? Reborn?"

"Aye. You introduced Nell to me once—what seems like a lifetime ago now—as Nell Feenix. Her surname has nagged at me since, and although it didn't occur to me at the time, I gathered Nell's ashes from the battlefield and kept them safe, for I could not abide the thought of leaving her there. But the Master is the one who told me the legend of the phoenix. And Parsnip knew how to make the nest, since long ago one of those creatures resided in Hobover House. I thought if I could bring her back, I could heal your heart... and then you would love me without reservation."

Millicent's breath hitched.

"But you came to me anyway, didn't you?"

"Yes. You didn't need—but I'm so glad you did."

He placed one finger onto the baby's hand and stroked the tiny palm. "I thought we had failed to bring her back. And then you kissed me." He laughed softly. "Now I *know* there is magic in your kiss, my lady."

Millicent smiled, staring into those lavender eyes. "Nell?" she whispered.

The baby pulled her fist out of her mouth, and grinned.

"Look, she's smiling."

"It's probably just gas," said the hobgoblin, who

had jumped up onto the couch and craned his neck to look at the child.

Gareth scowled at Parsnip.

The little man shrugged. "That's what they always say, methinks." He hopped onto the floor and clambered up the columns on the side of the fireplace, as if he scaled a ladder, and then paused on the mantel. "She'll be a handful, that one. Full of sass and fire. Good thing ye happen to have a hobgoblin in the house to help ye raise her." And then he disappeared behind the painting once again.

Gareth raised a brow. "I'm not too sure about that. For some reason, I am picturing the two of them plotting mischief of one kind or another as soon as she is able to speak."

Millicent smiled, leaned over, and kissed her knight's rough cheek. "I love you."

"I will never tire of hearing you saying that." He blushed. Charming man. "We seem to have put the cart before the horse, my lady. So I think we should marry as soon as possible. Would a quick journey to Gretna Green suit?"

"It would suit me just fine, my lord." Millicent hugged the baby to her, laid her head on her knight's strong shoulder. "Indeed. I think my life will suit me just fine from here on after."

Look for *Enchanting the Beast*, the final installment
in the Relics of Merlin series, coming in April from
Kathryne Kennedy and Sourcebooks Casablanca

London, 1861

Where magic has never died…

LADY PHILOMENA RADCLIFF CLOSED HER EYES AND
called to the spirit of the late Lord Stanhope. She tried
to ignore the excited breaths of the ladies within the
séance circle.

"Lord Stanhope," Phil said, with as much theatrical brilliance as a stage performer. "Your wife
wishes to speak with you one last time. Is your spirit
still in this house?"

The withdrawing room smelled of candle wax and
the clashing perfumes of the assembled ladies: Lady
Stanhope, Lady Montreve, and their two daughters.
And unfortunately, their daughters' silly young friends,
who started to giggle as the silence lengthened.

It appeared that the late Lord Stanhope had chosen
not to linger in the physical world.

Which didn't make one whit of difference to Phil.
Lady Stanhope had paid her for some peace of mind
and she would give it to her regardless. When Phil had

been orphaned at a young age, she'd used her magical gift to support herself, quickly discovering that half of her job consisted of her theatrical ability to convince her audience. If the spirit she called made an appearance, she just considered it a bonus.

Her primary concern was to relieve the suffering of those that tragedy had left behind.

She opened her eyes. "We must combine our efforts. Lady Montreve, will you douse the candles? Thank you. Now, clasp your neighbor's hand and concentrate on the late Lord Stanhope. Use your will to call him to us."

The fire crackled in the hearth, and the wind made a soft keening noise outside the glass windows. Phil lowered her voice to a husky whisper. "Keep concentrating, ladies. I can feel your will rising, calling out to Lord—"

The drawing room door burst open and the shadow of a large man loomed on the threshold. The circle of hands broke. Lady Stanhope gasped, Lady Montreve stifled a scream, and the other girls collapsed into a fit of giggles.

Philomena suppressed her urge to admonish them like a doddering governess and forced a smile instead. "If you don't mind, sir, we were in the middle of—"

"I'm quite aware of what's going on in this room, madam. If you will excuse the interruption, I would like to join you." He closed the door behind him, shutting out the light from the outer room, allowing the soft glow of the fireplace to highlight his features. The giggles abruptly died, and soft sighs of admiration issued from the mouths of several young girls.

Philomena could hardly blame them. She had never seen such a striking young man. Dark hair liberally streaked with blond fell in waves past broad shoulders that strained his old-fashioned evening coat. The firelight reflected glints of gold in his large dark eyes and played across the angular planes of his face, outlining high cheekbones. Even white teeth flashed as he performed a courtly bow.

Phil's stomach flipped and her hands broke out in a sweat inside her gloves. She struggled to hide her reaction before anyone noticed. Heavens, she was old enough to be his... well, older sister perhaps. But still, too old to be making a fool of herself by gawking at the beautiful young man.

Lady Stanhope recovered first. "I don't remember the pleasure of an introduction, sir."

Again, a flash of those even white teeth. Good heavens, were those dimples?

"I'm Sir Nicodemus Wulfson, Baronet of Grimspell castle."

Soft gasps accompanied his words and several of the younger ladies actually looked frightened. All baronets were shifters and immune to all magic. The aristocracy hated that "the animals" could see through the spells crafted to maintain their superior social status.

"I don't think..." Lady Stanhope began, ready to deny the gentleman's request.

Phil quickly stood. "It would be a pleasure for you to join us, Sir Nicodemus."

He turned those large, glittering eyes on her in surprise, his predatory gaze sweeping over her from head to foot. Phil felt heat rise in her cheeks. As usual, she'd dressed in the artistic style, eschewing the corsets and crinolines of her peers. Most of her friends were followers of the Pre-Raphaelite Brotherhood, but few of them had the daring to wear their medieval-style dresses out in public.

He surprised her with a sudden smile of approval. "Thank you, Lady...?"

"Philomena Radcliff."

"The ghost-hunter," he acknowledged. "I've heard a great deal about you. It's a pleasure."

The Adonis stepped forward and took her hand, sweeping his lips across the top of her glove. Thank heavens for that layer of material, for he surely would have burnt her skin with the heat of his mouth. Phil quickly snatched back her hand and resumed her seat at the table, trying to ignore the flutter in her stomach.

The screech of wooden legs over marble made them all turn to watch Sir Nicodemus drag a chair over to the table and squeeze between Philomena and Lady Stanhope. He sat with stealthy grace.

He looked up and flashed that brilliant smile again, taking in the entire circle of women. "I've always wanted to experience one of these table-turnings. It's gracious of you to allow me to join you." Despite his apparent lack of social standing a few of the youngest girls leaned forward and licked their lips.

Philomena pressed her lips together to prevent the same reaction. It was all well and good for young debutantes to react to him, but she had to be at least ten years his senior and it would only make her look like a complete fool. She really should have allowed

Lady Stanhope to reject him, for if she continued in her obvious fascination in him, she was sure to make a complete cake of herself.

But Phil's sense of justice could not allow her to shun him. So when Lady Stanhope hesitated to link her hand with the baronet's, Philomena hid her fear of the way she might react to his touch and slapped her gloved palm over his with forced bravado.

Tiny shivers traveled from his hand through her body. She'd been correct. His touch flustered her more than the caress of his gaze. For a moment Sir Nicodemus stared at their clasped hands, his dark brows raised in surprise. Then he turned and glanced at her, that wolfish grin back on his face.

Phil abruptly blew out the candle and closed her eyes. Heaven help her if he set his mind on exploring that instant chemistry between them. "Now concentrate, ladies… and gentleman. Lord Stanhope, we summon your spirit, please come to us." A soft tapping sounded at the window, most likely a tree branch in the wind, but Phil grasped at it. "Lord Stanhope! Is that you?"

Sir Nicodemus made a small sound of derision, but she could feel the rest of the circle tense with excitement.

Phil opened her eyes, fully prepared to cast an unfocused gaze at the corner of the room where she would pretend Lord Stanhope stood. His wife only wanted to tell him that she loved him. Who was she to deny the lady that satisfaction?

But Philomena caught a movement from the fireplace and her gaze met that of Tup. The young boy sat atop the mantel, his bare feet hanging over the edge, the glow of the fire shining through them. His brown hair was a mess as usual, his face so dirty that his hazel eyes stood out in startling contrast. Really, such a ragtag street urchin! Phil's heart squeezed a bit and warmth flowed through her.

"Tup," she whispered, trying to rise but anchored to her chair by the grip of Lady Stanhope and Sir Nicodemus.

"What's a tup?" murmured one of the girls.

"The ghost-hunter's spirit guide," Lady Montreve snapped.

Phil was vaguely aware of the shock that rippled around the table, including that of Sir Nicodemus. She could feel him watching her, like a predator studies his prey, waiting for the perfect moment to leap. But she ignored them all, intent on seeing Tup's ghost again. He wasn't strong enough to stay long in the material world.

The only thing she'd ever regretted about not marrying was that she would never have her own child. And then Tup had followed her home one day.

"I come to tell ye to stop that," he said, his large eyes blinking with sadness.

"What do you mean?" Phil asked.

"Cor, don't ye fathom that the man passed over into hell? And he *likes* it there."

Oh, dear. That meant that the man was as close to a demon as they came. No wonder using magic to summon a spirit was frowned upon. But since magical power was based on rank, only a royal could do that, or possibly a duke. Granted, ghosts would sometimes answer the call of a loved one… "But then why would he answer Lady Stanhope's call, Tup?"

They couldn't hear Tup, of course, just Philomena's part of the conversation. She told herself to be more careful with her words.

"Not *her* call," the boy answered impatiently. "Hers." And he nodded at Lady Montreve.

Phil turned and stared at the lady, who refused to meet her gaze. But even in the weak glow of the firelight she could see the dark stain of color flooding the pretty woman's cheeks. Is that why Lady Montreve had come this evening? To see her lover one last time? Philomena glanced at Lady Stanhope. Did she know her husband had been having an affair with her friend? Was that the real reason she'd called the séance, to find out the truth of it?

Tup's eyes widened. "Crikey, I'm too late." And he disappeared.

Phil slowly turned her head. Lord Stanhope's specter materialized beside Phil's assistant, Sarah, and floated toward their table.

"Reginald, is that you?" his wife cried.

But Lord Stanhope only had eyes for Lady Montreve. He circled the table until he stood behind the pretty woman. "Did you call me back for one more round, you doxy? Missing me already, eh?" He leaned forward, his face so close to the back of the lady's neck that Phil could see the tiny hairs on her skin move. "Don't think I don't know it's my money you're missing. But I learned some things in hell, my dear. And when I heard your call I decided I shouldn't have to wait to try them on you."

Lady Montreve shuddered. "I shouldn't have come. I didn't think it was possible…"

"Don't break the circle," Philomena warned. "It's her only protection." She felt Sir Nicodemus's grip tighten but the young girl—Phil wished she could remember her name—on the other side of Lady Montreve was trying to twist her hand from the woman's grasp.

Phil saw Lord Stanhope's arm disappear into his lover's skirts. Lady Montreve screamed.

"What's happening?" Lady Stanhope cried.

"Stop it!" Philomena shouted.

Lord Stanhope ignored them all, his black grin twisted into a leer of sadistic pleasure. The young girl pulled her hand free from Lady Montreve's grasp. The circle was broken. Philomena didn't have a choice. "Let go of my hand," she told Sir Nicodemus. Bless him, he didn't ask questions or argue; he just released his grip.

Phil really didn't want to do this—oh, how she didn't want to do this. She took a deep breath and stepped into Lord Stanhope's black shadow and opened her soul to his. For one horrendous moment the man's spirit melded with hers. Shafts of burning cold swept through her veins. His twisted sense of pleasure shook her body with an evil joy that made her squirm with shame.

She tried to send his soul back then, demanding that he return to the other side. He laughed at her. Phil strengthened her will, fighting with everything she had. Convulsions shook her body and then the world went black.

About the Author

Kathryne Kennedy is an award-winning author acclaimed for her world building and known for blending genres to create groundbreaking stories. *Everlasting Enchantment* is the much-anticipated new book in her popular Relics of Merlin series. Her magical series The Elven Lords includes *The Fire Lord's Lover*, *The Lady of the Storm*, and *The Lord of Illusion*. She's lived in Guam, Okinawa, and several states in the United States, and currently lives in Arizona with her wonderful family—which includes two very tiny Chihuahuas. She loves to hear from readers, and welcomes you to visit her website where she has ongoing contests at: www.KathryneKennedy.com.